# THE TRAITOR & THE WRETCH

Written by
**Jasmine Walls**

Illustrated by
**Rowan MacColl**

Cover Art by
**Amy Phillips**

Copy Edited by
**Charlie Knight**

A BONEDUST PRESS NOVEL

Paperback ISBN: 979-8-9993734-0-3
Ebook ISBN: 979-8-9993734-1-0

*For Ariana, who supported this book every step of the way*
*&*
*For anyone who has ever felt sidelined and forgotten*
*Your stories matter*

# A Word of Warning

Some topics that will appear in this book include:
- Murder, committed by just about everyone on page
- Body horror
- Suicidal thoughts
- Mentions of a person being burned alive
- Mentions of cannibalism
- Depictions of being trapped in the dark in a cave system
- Giant bugs
- Animal death
- Some ableist language

# CHAPTER 1

## *Knell*

Glory, in Deathknell's experience, was overrated.

His brethren were mixed about it, he knew. Some cried out, *"Glory in the name of the Risen! The Great One!"* with fervor as they carved sigils into the ground, tearing up grass still wet with dew, while others followed their lead for lack of a better option. They took up the chant with a listless parody of enthusiasm in the hope that it might keep the more faithful from targeting them.

Personally, Knell didn't bother. Glory wasn't meant for the likes of him. What revelry was there to be had in an unremarkable death after a short and miserable life?

Technically on guard duty, he watched the horizon, staring at the first sunrise he'd seen in months. His eyes ached as the sun emerged and light fractured into a million glittering reflections against the spears, shields, and helmets of two armies pouring into the valley of the caldera. No better place to summon a god than above the heart of a long-dead volcano. The sigils covered a wide expanse that stretched up the wall of the caldera, giving the approaching armies a glimpse of what was to come. To show they'd arrived too late.

On one side was the king's army, all polished steel and bright uniforms. On the other were the rebels, which Knell didn't know much about. He'd been living in a cave for a few years now, and acolytes of the Great one, the Chaos Bringer, didn't get a lot of heralds stopping by with news. The rebels looked like a rough and mismatched bunch even from this distance, but there certainly were a lot of them. Could they set aside their grudges, whatever they may be, to stand united against the true threat on the field? It seemed unlikely, but if they could—

A sensation like a fist closing around his skull reminded Knell why it was best not to let his thoughts wander. He stared at the sliver of white-bright sun and emptied his head of anything other than the sight, the searing pain of it, until the crushing pressure eased.

Knell was a chosen acolyte of the Great One, meant to die on this battlefield in service of his master. Not something he was happy about, but it was the hand he'd been dealt, and no one had asked his opinion on the matter anyway. As the converging stream of enemies drew closer, Knell took up his place among his brethren to join in calling forth their legions of spawn. They'd been scouring the valley every night for nearly a week, collecting any bones or horns or bits of fur they could find, while the stronger brethren went hunting for fresher targets. Now, with the Great One so close to the surface of their world, their power was stronger than ever. The Great One's will burned through them, into their gathered foci of knotted hair and bone, to create the twisted beasts. Formed from the melded remains of both ancient and freshly rotting corpses, the homunculi clawed their way out from the earth between the acolytes and their enemies.

The sigils were completed as screams rose above the clash of weapons in the valley. The homunculi were slow and clumsy, but they were also strong and difficult to put down. What made them truly dangerous was how they consumed the dead, absorbing fallen fighters into their own bodies to grow in size. Knell watched it happen, his bones burning and fist closed over his own foci, unable to let it go when the command clawing through his mind wanted the creatures to *feast*.

He managed to tear his eyes away from the chaos of the fighting to look at his brethren, even as his mouth continued chanting and his hand stayed clutched around the foci. Their dark featureless robes and shadowed faces made them difficult to tell apart but Knell knew each by their height, the shape of their hands, the way they carried themselves. To the enemy, they were faceless, soulless targets. That their enemies weren't necessarily wrong did little to soothe him.

Seeping light began to glow from the sigils, the green of it the only color in a world washed out in grey. Knell felt drawn to it, tempted to reach out and touch even as every human part of him cringed away at the sheer malice it radiated. The acolytes were chanting, their voices rising in volume, and his own mouth called out in unison. Sounds that tasted sour and crawled past his ears without comprehension.

Years of work finally came to fruition as the ground boiled beneath the sigils then heaved underfoot before it split and burst open. When the Great One rose at last, Knell missed the initial show, lying stunned on his back where he'd been flung, his foci lost, struggling to catch his breath. What he did see were bursts of green fire carving up great chunks of earth as excess power broke through the edges of the summoning seal. The Great One's presence was unmistakable as it emerged. It overwhelmed everything else and filled his mind with visions of vast and eternal horrors mortals were not meant to witness. Knell was on his feet, with no recollection of standing, and moving though he couldn't feel his limbs.

The Great One stepped and leveled destruction where it pleased, uncaring if it was enemy or ally under the shadow of its gargantuan tread or in the path of its unstoppable power. Their frail bodies and insignificant lives meant nothing to it.

In a brief blink of agonizing clarity, Knell hoped for that shadow to fall over him, full of desperate anticipation for it all to end. There hadn't been room left for any other thoughts, the Great One's presence made his head feel like nothing more than a gourd filled with soup made of nightmares, impossible to grasp, with streaks of howling knowledge scraping at the sides of his skull. Time stopped making sense. He walked with his hands held high. Raw power shrieked along his nerves and lit up the world in a rainbow of colors so bright he couldn't tell what he was looking at. Not that it mattered.

His body moved without input from him, which was probably for the best. Left to his own devices, he would have been nothing more than a gasping heap on the ground, unable to tell the screams in his head from those around him. It was possible he was smelling emotions. He wasn't sure he still had eyes.

Time passed in glimpses of clarity, not enough for Knell to truly grasp what was happening, but enough to see the tide of battle swell out one moment before rushing back like a wave the next. A flash of fiery light cut across his vision—*was* it his vision? It felt like a memory, but not his own—before the noise in his head reached a feverish pitch. And then came pain. Such excruciating pain. He would never have words for it. Nothing he could shape into sound uttered by human mouths could contain the description.

It was death; it had to be. If he had control of his limbs he'd have opened his arms in welcome. The ground fell away beneath his feet as a wave of pure energy hit him in a full body blow. He didn't even have time to be grateful for it when everything finally stopped with a sudden crack of impact followed by darkness.

Then he woke up.

Sound returned first. The soft clack of small stones hitting larger stones, the uneven *plip-plip* of water somewhere in the near distance. It all echoed oddly, though that could very well be Knell's hearing at fault. He felt like he'd been scraped hollow, husk-like in his own flesh, the soft parts that made him a person carried away in the bellies of wolves. His bones rang like he'd hidden inside a tower bell during the midday tolling, his skin felt like it was filled with hot needles, and half his body was damp from the shoulder down with what he hoped was water. Living continued to be a disappointing experience, so he lay there with his eyes closed in case death was just running a little late.

The usual sickening lurch of power through his limbs was gone. The constant whispering of unknown languages had fallen silent, and it was as disconcerting as it was a relief to only find his own thoughts in his head.

A tiny flicker of hope lit up in his chest, which surprised Knell. He thought he'd run dry of that a long time ago. Strangely, it really did seem as though his body was his own again. And now that he was paying attention, he couldn't hear any telltale sounds of battle.

Had the prophecy been fulfilled? Was there truly a hero on the battlefield strong enough to turn back the Great One?

Knell flinched expectantly, but there was no painful backlash for thinking of the prophesized hero, theoretical or not, and that more than anything confirmed it. The acolytes were always punished for thinking too long on the prophecy unless it was to refute it.

The Great One had been banished. Knell wasn't hopeful enough to think it could be killed, but if it had been thrown back into whatever realm it had been summoned it from, then Knell was...*free*.

His heart hammered a little too hard at that, making him feel lightheaded, aches throbbing in all the sore places where he'd slammed into, well, something. The ground seemed like a good enough guess, considering it felt like he'd been thrown off a building with no small amount of enthusiasm.

Curiosity, his worst and most inescapable addiction, was what finally dragged his eyelids open. He panicked briefly, thinking he really had lost his eyes somewhere along the way before his vision began to adjust to the dark. He was lying at the bottom of a trench, a narrow stretch of raw earth that grew wider above, revealing a strip of evening sky between the jagged edges. The stone walls were hot against his back and looked freshly cracked, sighing thick plumes of sulfurous steam upwards. Dark clumps of dirt clotted with grass roots still tumbled down the sides of the trench. It was as if he lay in an open wound on the skin of a mountain.

There was also someone else there with him.

A man, by Knell's guess, was crumpled against the opposite wall of the furrow, and Knell had a brief, wild urge to laugh. The man looked like he was either dead or having a worse day than Knell. He lay prone in the rocky mud, his face turned away, and the one arm Knell could see ended in a raw stump just above the wrist. Blood seeped from the wound and stained a dark circle in the mud that pooled against the man's side. When Knell squinted, he could see the man's back rising and falling in the shallowest of breaths.

It would probably be a mercy to let him die. It wouldn't take any effort at all, really. Knell only needed to keep lying here just as he had been.

*But*, Knell's thoughts nudged at him, and he breathed out a quiet groan that felt like it started in his spine. But what? Now that Knell's eyes had fully adjusted to the dim lighting, it was obvious the man wasn't wearing the black robes of Knell's brethren or the impractical white and gold of the king's army. He was dressed like one of the rebel fighters. Even if Knell could do something, it's not like the man would be grateful. One look at Knell and he'd be out for his blood.

But...

Knell struggled to his feet even as he continued to mentally list every reason it was useless to bother. The man would probably be dead before Knell could even stagger over to him. If anything, he should be using what little energy he had left to find a way out of here before someone spotted him, voice in his head be damned.

But...

He'd seen so much death. Not on the battlefield—he could barely recall existing in the past few hours—but there was no lack of options spanning the last several years of his life. So much death, so few opportunities to do anything but cause more of it.

He nearly brained himself on a rock trying to remember how to walk as he crossed loose rubble hidden under mud, but he managed it in the end. On his knees next to the injured man, Knell looked him over with a detached, analytical eye. He was still breathing despite the odds, and Knell couldn't help but think the man must have an incredibly stubborn spirit. He knows his own would probably escape its mortal coil given half a chance. All the stubbornness in the world wouldn't keep a person from bleeding out, though.

Knell lifted the man's injured arm into his lap to inspect the damage, ignoring the blood-stained mud soaking into his robes. They had been stained by worse and ruined long before this battle had begun. The wound continued to bleed sluggishly, but Knell was surprised to see that it looked partially cauterized. Probably why the man wasn't dead yet. He briefly wondered what sort of weapon had caused the wound, then just as quickly decided he didn't need to know. The effects didn't look familiar, his fellow acolytes generally preferred weapons that caused as much damage as possible—serrated edges, blades slicked with poison, trebuchets that burst with twisted bits of shrapnel on impact. They didn't have much interest in things like cauterizing blades.

Whatever the cause, the man needed a healer or he would die. If not from this wound, then possibly from another, considering Knell couldn't see his front. There could be an arrow in his chest or some other grievous injury. Knell didn't have the strength to roll the man over, and quite frankly, he was the exact opposite of a healer, so he wasn't quite sure what he'd thought he would do once he got this far.

*But… maybe.*

Knell pressed his mouth into a hard line. He was no healer, and this man was more corpse than not, but that might just work in Knell's favor. He did know how to seal wounds, he'd just never tried it on a living person before. If he did it wrong… well, he supposed it wouldn't make much difference, would it? Only now, he was curious if he *could* manage it.

The man's breath rattled, his heartbeat strained, and Knell gave in to his impulse. He clasped a hand around the man's forearm just above the wound, closed his eyes, and reached for a power he wasn't sure he still had. If the Great One truly had been banished, then had all of its magic gone with it to the abyss?

Reaching it was difficult, but there was something there. Knell had to concentrate until all he was aware of was the thump of his own blood in his ears. There wasn't a way to describe the process to anyone who didn't have the Great One's influence swimming through their blood, and those who knew hardly discussed it among themselves. It was a thrum of sorts, a thread of something alien in his own body that kept trying to escape his grasp, but he'd been forced to use it too often to let it slip away when he actually wanted it. Next came the usual sickening lurch, and though it was a weak echo of the one he was used to, he clung to it. He pushed the power outward through his hand clutched around the man's arm and sank into the sensation of knowing someone else's flesh.

Breathing became laborious, but he ignored it and pressed on. He couldn't afford any distractions with such a tenuous grip on this power. The man felt so alive, even as Knell sensed that life draining away, and he was lost in it for a moment before he regained his senses. The man's inner workings lit up like a map of color across Knell's monochrome vision, layers of muscles and bone, veins bright with life. He had taken a knock to the head. Knell could see the warmth of it, a burst of color swimming across his vision along the side of the man's skull, but it didn't seem too serious.

Knell's energy was flagging fast, and he dragged his sluggish mind into motion. He traced a mental finger along those color-mapped lines to the stump where the brightly lit life force of the man's blood seeped out into a murky dark as it left his body and mingled in the mud. A sharp ache bloomed behind his eyes as he stared hard at the edges of cut skin, mouth moving though the chant of unknown words failed to pour from his throat. The skin under his grip shifted, rippled, then grew slack and stretched to close over itself, gone nearly liquid as it swirled like water closing over a drain until it cinched shut completely over the ragged stump. He did the same on a smaller scale with the veins beneath, sealing off the flow of blood to keep what was left of it inside the man where it belonged.

Even as the colors faded from Knell's vision and he let his own body's complaints flood back in, exhaustion like a weight around his neck, he knew it hadn't been enough. The man had lost too much blood. Knell forced the power in his blood back to the surface, swallowing down bile as his stomach rebelled. Pain radiated through his skull all the way down his spine, but damn it all, he'd committed to saving this one life. If it killed him in the process, so be it. Might as well save some king's soldier the trouble.

It was easy enough to keep a hand on the man as he slumped over the prone form, his vision fading around the edges even as colors burst into view once more. He spread it outward this time, reaching as far as he could manage until he felt the world around him more than he saw it. Threads of life that branched through roots and grass and tiny creatures crawling through the dirt. He grasped those threads and stole them, hauled them back toward the epicenter of his body, and shoved them into the man with everything he had.

The man's body convulsed, a riot of color, a maelstrom of life energy not his own. Knell hoped it worked because that was all he had. His vision crowded with dark spots, and he was unconscious before his body finished slumping across the man's back.

When Knell woke up again, he might have been resignedly amused if he hadn't been so annoyed by it. Most days he felt like he was clinging onto life by the most precarious of grips, yet here he was, still kicking after several prime opportunities for death to pluck up whatever tattered remains were left of his soul. He sighed heavily as a hundred aches rallied up and cried for attention, then paused because his body was moving in time with a breath not his own. He was also warmer than expected, and not only because the last thing he remembered was passing out at the bottom of a god-carved ditch.

Right, there was a man. A man Knell was currently slumped over. He doubted he could crush the man if he tried, but it couldn't be comfortable to be compressed between a malnourished acolyte and rock-filled mud. Good to know he hadn't accidentally drowned the man at least, if he was still breathing. Knell sat up suddenly, then tilted sideways as dark and bright spots burst across his vision with the head rush.

*Alive.*

The man was alive!

Sure, he was still lying there like a corpse, but he wasn't actually dead. The unfamiliar sense of relief made him even more lightheaded, this time with giddiness, and Knell tipped backward into the shallow mud with a lackluster splash and the unfamiliar sensation of a smile.

It took some thrashing around to get upright again, but it wasn't as if he had to worry about impressing anyone. His sole audience was face down in the mud and making much less effort to do anything about it. Knell considered the situation, then gave a little mental shrug. What was a little more effort after all he'd already done? So he grabbed the man's far shoulder and braced his feet as he hauled him over onto his back. Once that was accomplished, he straightened out the man's limbs, and having exhausted his limited energy, Knell sat in the least muddy spot he could find. The heat coming off the rock wall at his back was uncomfortably warm, but he leaned into it, relishing the way it chased the chill from his bones. It also happened to be right next to his unconscious companion, where he could easily monitor his breathing, and Knell patted the man's chest with a satisfied air.

Task accomplished, and with nothing to do other than gain back his wheezing breath, Knell eyed the man. It wasn't easy to get the measure of someone when they'd been unconscious for the entirety of their acquaintance, but he could try.

The man was tall, Knell could tell that much, with a sturdy build, broad in the shoulders and chest. Knell guessed he hadn't taken up fighting recently, nor with reluctance. He looked like someone who trained often or at least did heavy work regularly. His leather armor was well-worn and scarred. Under the mud and bruises the man had rough cut features, high wide cheekbones, a sharp jaw, and strong brows. Excellent bone structure.

Scars cut across his face, pale with age against his tanned skin. Knell wondered what the exact color was, but he hadn't been able to see more than shades of grey in years unless he was drawing on the power lurking in his blood. And even then, he might see the mapwork of a person's life force but not the hue of their hair or clothing, their eyes or skin. The largest of the man's scars ran from temple to chin, cutting through a thick eyebrow and bisecting his upper lip so his mouth had a permanent snarl to it even when slack, revealing a hint of teeth and a gap where one was missing. Probably lost in the same blow that caused the wound in the first place. His hair was dark and roughly cropped, short enough to be safe from an enemy grabbing hold of it.

Knell stared at him for a long while and decided he looked kind.

The man continued to sleep, fever hot but breathing easier. Knell could do nothing but tip his head back against the rock and stare up at the underside of the field, eyes tracing the shapes of dry earth and withered grass where there had been rich soil and green plants just hours before. The overhang would keep anyone wandering above from seeing him, and his companion looked mostly dead. So unless the man was important, Knell doubted anyone would climb down when there were plenty of wounded to carry off the field first.

The sky had grown darker where Knell could glimpse it between dense swirls of steam, nearing night. Knell wondered when he'd last had a chance to sit and watch the sun set, even if he could only glimpse the effect of it in stolen slivers. He couldn't remember.

The sky had faded fully into night by the time Knell decided he should take stock of his surroundings before someone took stock of him. And then another few minutes to convince himself to actually move. The dim clamor of voices, armor, and pained groans had faded to near nothing, and Knell hauled himself up the jagged crevice with all the grace of a three-legged spider. His feet scrabbled against the rock until he found a foothold with enough leverage for him to peer over the edge and past the small mountain range of his knuckles.

The battle was over, but the barely recognizable valley was far from empty. Deep, fume-weeping scars had been carved into the land, and the place where he and his brethren had summoned the Great One was a smoking crater in the distance. Bodies—human and homunculi alike—lay scattered, and while the bulk of the armies had retreated, several small groups still roamed the grounds. Some looked for fallen allies, others looked to fill their pockets.

Not far from Knell's position, there was one soldier jabbing a spear into the neck of a groaning acolyte, finishing them off with a vicious twist of the haft. The woman waited until her kill stopped twitching, then looked up and signaled to someone further down.

"Put down any of the miserable cultist bastards still breathing!" she shouted in their direction and received a salute in return.

With a little nod to himself, Knell made his slow, awkward way back down and returned to his seat beside his unconscious trench-mate.

"Probably best to stay down here for a bit longer," he said to himself and hoped no one would be thorough enough to actually climb down to look for survivors. The stones had been hot enough to leave his hands aching despite the hours that had passed and there were still trails of smoke steaming up from the rend, which would hopefully keep anyone from wanting to approach for a while yet.

The dark didn't bother Knell, and his only company was blissfully unaware of the world around him, so Knell did what he'd always done when he found himself in a bad situation. He explored his immediate surroundings and looked for an escape.

A few minutes later, his fellow pit-dweller woke up.

Percy returned to consciousness feeling like twice trampled shit.

He grit his teeth and squinted open his eyes as he tried to orient himself. The side of his head throbbed in a way that explained why he'd been unconscious. He'd have a hell of a lump to look forward to if he didn't already. The next thing he noticed was that he was cold and laid out in mud, the rocks under his back trying their best to reshape his spine. Light was dim as he blinked away the doubles swimming in his vision until he could get a grasp of his surroundings. It didn't really feel worth the effort of forcing himself to his feet once it became clear he was sitting at the bottom of a ditch that smelled like old eggs.

The last thing Percy remembered was battle. His own rage, a monumentally stupid decision, and a brief moment where he thought he'd struck true. Then, a flash of light and a sharp, searing pain.

Fuck.

Unthinkingly, he tried to wipe a hand across his face and ended up knocking the stump of his wrist into his chin. Percy flinched, hissing at the tender ache of it, then froze, staring down at where his right hand used to be. He had the oddest urge to clench a fist that was no longer there. The missing hand wasn't the strangest part, he knew perfectly well how he'd lost it. What he couldn't explain was the scarred-over wound.

Guessing by the light he'd lost several hours, and he felt weak and woozy. But even in the dim of twilight and the shadows of the fucking hole he found himself at the bottom of, there was no mistaking that the wound looked weeks, maybe months old.

He should have bled out in this muddy shithole. After all, he certainly didn't have a damn prophecy to twist fate in his favor. What the fuck had happened?

There was a noise nearby, the sound of shifting gravel and the rustle of cloth, along with an awkward little clearing of the throat. Percy snapped upright and whirled toward the sound, as much as he could while sitting. The world spun sickeningly at the movement and he reached instinctively for the blade at his belt, only to slam the stump of his wrist into his hip where the hilt of his sword should have been. Between the sharp pain and sudden dizziness, he lost his balance, falling shoulder first into the mud in an undignified heap. An undignified heap open to attack.

Quickly, he shoved himself upright and rolled into a crouch, dagger in his left hand held out warningly in front of him, ready for an attack that never came. Still recovering from the frankly embarrassing fumble and as angry as he was lightheaded, Percy had to squint for a moment before he could pinpoint his target.

What had looked like another patch of shadow against the stone innards of the pit was actually a raggedly dressed person cloaked in dark, mud-splattered robes. A thin hand lifted from the half-hidden shape and gave a hesitant little wave. The person sat slumped against the wall of steaming rock, not rushing at him or brandishing any visible weapons, though Percy was wary of weapons that *weren't* visible. He could only see one of their hands, and he doubted the chances of two people in the same pit with the same disadvantage.

He was about to demand their name and allegiance when they turned their head just enough for him to see two eerily inhuman eyes gleaming, reflecting light from within the shadow of their hood. Percy tensed as fear closed in on him like a vice, ready to throw the knife in his hand, to lodge it between those awful fucking eyes and run. The flesh-mage seemed to sense the danger they were in and carefully raised both hands, palms empty and open in a universal '*please don't kill me*' gesture.

"Wait."

That was it, no further pleading, no begging to be spared. The voice was deeper than he'd expected, if rough and a bit thready. Probably a man. Not that it mattered. The flesh-mages were cultists that had long since given up any ties they had to humanity. He could see now that the color of his hands wasn't washed out by the moonlight, they were actually a pale grey. Paired with those unnatural eyes, it was proof that this wretch had helped summon the horrific being that wrought havoc across the battlefield. The dark chaos god so powerful it could only be defeated by a hero of prophecy, guided by the hand of fate.

Flesh-mages couldn't even let the dead rest, forcing bodies to rise again at their command. Percy had seen their work, had taken down plenty of the twisted creatures himself. The worst of them were the nightmare-inducing homunculi, made of bodies melted together like so much wax into horrific monsters, full of nothing but rot and murderous intent. They let out the most tormented screams when they were put down, and though he'd been told there were no souls or spirits left in them, Percy had his doubts.

For all their fearsome abilities, the flesh-mages were always so weak in person. They hid behind their sick creations and had the gall to beg and plead when they were finally dragged into the light to pay for their deeds. Perhaps this one had enough sense to know he'd receive no mercy and had forgone the act. There was no pity to be had from Percy anyway. There was no such thing as an innocent flesh-mage, and anyone who recognized one knew to kill them before they did worse to you.

Percy would have already cut him down if it hadn't been for the damned wooziness that kept his knee pinned to the mud, his vision swimming so much he couldn't be sure he'd hit the target. He held himself upright and bared his teeth in a snarl so as not to give away just how weak he was. Flesh-mages had to lay their hands on your skin or have some stolen piece of a person, such as bone, to use their powers. He wasn't about to let this one get close enough to try it.

In the back of his mind, he wondered if the Chaos Bringer truly had been defeated. The battle had either moved far enough away that the noise of it was muffled by distance, or the fight was over. Since the sky was no longer filled with bloated green nightmare clouds that crackled with red lightning, he made a cautious guess that the Prophesized Hero had indeed saved the kingdom. Best case scenario, the arrogant asshole had sacrificed himself in the process, but Percy's luck had never been that good.

He'd also hoped the act of banishment would have killed the flesh-mages, but here was proof otherwise. The Chaos Bringer's presence flowed through their blood, blackening it to a putrid sludge that turned their skin grey. Their gums, tongues, and nail beds all turned black, but worst of all was their eyes. Inhuman eyes that glowed in shadow and reflected light eerily, the whites bloodshot with black veins. It made them easy to spot, but it was always enough to put a man off his next meal.

"Stay back, you wretch," Percy snarled at the huddled excuse of a person. "I know your tricks. What were you doing lurking near me? Hoping I was a convenient corpse for some foul scheme?"

Those animal eyes shifted in color as the wretch shook his head slowly; unnaturally bright blue-green flickered into the shine of a polished silver coin, then back again. A grey hand moved slowly, fingers curling in until one was aimed at Percy, sending a shiver down his spine. That finger swung downward slightly to point toward Percy's injured arm, and the shiver became a cold lead weight that sat heavily in his gut.

"You did this?" he asked, even as he knew the answer, and received a slow nod in return.

"I healed it." There was a strange lilt to the man's rasping voice, a detached sort of wonder or bafflement as if this was surprising to him as well. Flesh-mages didn't *heal*, they warped dead and dying flesh to their whims. Percy kept his dagger steady as he stared at his other arm.

It should have been obvious, but in his defense, a lot had happened in the past minute or so. It wasn't as if he'd had time to really process any of it. He'd seen his wound was closed, that there were no stitches or raw edges, and had immediately been distracted by an enemy lurking nearby. Now he made himself look at the shape of his new scars, the way they melded together in a swirling pattern, the spaces between them lined with marks of skin stretched too quickly. It was as if his wound had been twisted and sealed shut.

*Like a steamed dumpling*, he thought with a touch of hysteria.

His posture wilted and nausea clawed its way up his throat, his head swimming as he grappled with blood loss and the horror of knowing this wretch's hands had been on him—had *changed* him— and he had no idea if it stopped at his arm, or if his innards had been shifted around on a whim without his knowing.

Percy staggered to his feet, an ungainly struggle that took longer than he liked and was made more difficult without a hand to balance himself with, but he refused to drop the dagger from between himself and the threat just paces away. The flesh-mage didn't move, keeping his hands in sight as if there was any placating Percy now. Luckily for him, Percy didn't want to be anywhere near the creature. Seemingly unconcerned about the knife and Percy's anger, the wretch looked up toward the ragged opening of the pit.

"There were still some scavengers and patrols wandering last time I looked." His head turned back toward Percy, and he'd shifted far enough from the shadows that Percy could see half of his face. Hollow cheeks and sunken eyes set in a gaunt grey face curtained by clumps of stringy hair. "The prophecy has been fulfilled. You could go find your allies, if they've survived."

If it was meant to be some sort of reassurance, the wretch had missed the mark.

"And you'll be content to simply lurk in this pit, will you?" Percy asked, his voice scathing and thick with suspicion.

The wretch watched him for a moment, then pointed to the far end of the pit, where the walls narrowed into nothing more than shadow. At least, that's what Percy had thought. Now that he actually looked at it, he could see the ragged edges of rock and the yawning dark of space beyond it. The mouth of a cave, unearthed by the same power that had blasted open this pit they were standing in.

"I will go that way." The wretch stated it like that was a normal option for anyone with half a lick of sense. Percy supposed no one became a flesh-mage cultist of a chaos god because they were smart or determined to live long. Good riddance.

"You'll stay right where you are until I'm gone, is what you'll do. Try anything, and I'll gut you without a second thought." Percy began to back away slowly, darting glances between the flesh-mage and his own surroundings as he tried to find a promising incline that wasn't too steep for him to climb. He knew he was running on fumes, and if he had to choose between getting away or killing a flesh-mage who thought their best bet was to wander blindly into a cave, he'd rather focus on his own, much more reasonable plan of escape.

To one side, there were large chunks of grassy field that had collapsed into the pit and remained intact enough to roughly resemble a ramp that seemed sturdy enough to try walking on. Percy watched the flesh-mage warily as he carefully stepped his way toward the ramp, but the wretch simply watched him go, hands still raised where he sat half curled in the shadows like an abandoned gargoyle. When his boot hit the base of the ramp, Percy carefully sheathed his knife before making his way out of the pit as quickly as he could while keeping the threat in his view.

He paused at the mouth of the pit to take a cautious look around just in case his former comrades were lurking nearby. Thick plumes of foul yellow steam obscured his view, but he didn't see anyone in the immediate vicinity. Further afield, he could see figures with torches, easy to spot in their personal halos of warm light. There would be more—search parties for the injured, corpse thieves, soldiers taking the chance to cut short their time in the army. But those weren't the people Percy was worried about.

The flesh-mage was either smart or cowardly enough to heed his warning, and Percy shot him one last glare before hauling himself free. He crept along cautiously, which was the best he could manage with the wooziness, but no one else needed to know that. Finding a body with a decent cloak was quick work, and this one was barely stained, considering its owner had taken several arrows to the chest. Percy yanked the cloak free and threw it over his own shoulders. He didn't bother to try and clasp it shut with his off hand, just pulled the hood up to hide his face.

He hadn't made it as far as he'd hoped when he heard the first whisper of voices, one of which sounded familiar even if he couldn't place the name. He'd worked with a lot of people in the past few years and he had a good ear for voices, even if he couldn't be bothered to learn anything more about the people speaking. The wrecked landscape proved helpful as he ducked—collapsed strategically—in the shadow of a nearby rock cluster, both grateful for the growing moonlight that aided his vision and resentful that it might reveal him in turn.

Moments later, a trio of figures appeared. They spread out to peer at corpses, occasionally kicking one onto its back so they could check the face before closing in again to compare notes.

"It was around here somewhere," one of them said, frustration clear in their voice. The others nodded in agreement.

"Haven't heard anyone say they saw him run off, so the bastard probably died. All we need is some proof for the new king." The second voice sounded nasally, as if they had a cold, and Percy nearly groaned.

He remembered them now. The crony trio, always fawning over their leader, desperate for attention and ready to snitch about any sneeze or fart. There was no doubt they were looking for Percy, and if it was for their *new* king, then his luck had well and truly run dry. He'd have no allies on this field. He needed to get away, and quickly, but there were more figures with torches roaming about, closing in from all sides. A few stopped to gather fallen allies, but too many seemed to be looking for a specific face.

Damn it all. There was a good chance he could make it past the groups wandering the battlefield, he was damned sneaky when he needed to be, but there were entire armies camped in the surrounding woods. Probably ensconced all along every path out of the valley to cut off any fleeing cultists. He considered his odds, and they were, quite frankly, shit. Cursing viciously and at length in his head, Percy retraced his steps.

When he made his reluctant return to the bottom of the pit, his brief hope of finding it empty went up in smoke as he spotted the wretch sitting crouched just inside the mouth of the cave, half covered in shadow. Those inhuman eyes looked his way, their polished silver shine reflecting moonlight the way a wolf's did. Percy held back a shudder at the sight and gooseflesh rose along his arms.

No man should have eyes like that, like a beast. Now that he could see more of the flesh-mage, Percy could tell he was underfed, even with the bulky layers of robes. Just skin and bone and looking all the more ghoulish for it. His shoulders seemed molded into a constant hunch, and his hair hung in greasy, knotted strands down to his shoulders.

His looks might garner pity in other circumstances, Percy had seen his fair share of starving poor, himself among them for a while, but those damning eyes left him with nothing but disgust.

"You came back," the wretch said with an air of tired surprise.

He didn't move, tracking Percy from the shadows like a feral creature. Like something parents warned their children about to keep them from wandering out at night. Percy didn't let his unease show and sneered at the man as he stepped closer to the cave entrance. He'd had to keep his dagger sheathed to climb back down, and he deliberately left it there. Percy was a faster draw than most expected. If the wretch so much as breathed wrong, he'd regret it.

"Why did you wait if you didn't think I'd be back?" he asked, curious despite himself and angry that he was. "What would you have done if I'd brought back some friends and told them what you are?"

The wretch craned his neck to peer past Percy, where it was very obviously empty of anyone else, then looked back up at him with those flat eyes.

"I don't know," the wretch said. His voice sounded lost, and Percy could see the edges of a frown on that thin face now that he was closer. "Waiting just felt right."

Horseshit. There was nothing right about this situation.

"I could kill you on my own," Percy stated, and it was true. Whatever the flesh-mage had done to him had closed a wound that should have killed him. He might be without a right hand or his preferred sword and was probably lacking more blood than he wanted to admit, but he still had his other hand and a deep well of spite. This man, this creature, barely looked fit to stand, much less put up a struggle.

Though he did have that cornered animal air to him. With nothing to lose, he might fight more viciously than expected. Even so, Percy outweighed him by at least half, and he suspected it wouldn't take much effort to carve a smile across that scrawny neck.

"You put your filthy, tainted hands on me. You *changed* me." He held out the stump of his right wrist in accusation, the words coming out as a snarl by the end. Anger had begun to strangle out the fear, and Percy welcomed it gladly.

Double-edged sword that it was, courage fueled by anger came at the expense of common sense. Percy had gotten close enough to loom over the wretch, annoyed by the lack of reaction. Infuriatingly, he simply leaned back against the rock and dirt, tilting his head up to hold Percy's glare with a placid stare in return.

Percy was breathing hard, teeth gritted and exhaling through his nose like an irritated bull. Plenty of men had started fights with him only to go yellow once he was close and angry, and this pathetic excuse of a man hardly seemed brave. Stupid, maybe, that was common enough, but not brave.

Up close, the flesh-mage mostly looked resigned, and that was like a damp cloth tossed over the coals of Percy's temper. Not putting it out completely but making the rage hiss and pop with confusion and smoke-clouded uncertainty. It never felt right to fight someone who looked like they'd lose a tooth under your fist and then apologize for the mess. Percy might not have much of a moral code, but he at least had standards. More importantly, Percy felt like he might fall over any second now.

He changed tact. "You owe me."

The wretch squinted up at him. "For saving your life?"

The question seemed genuine rather than challenging, and his eyes tracked the line of Percy's shoulder down to his wrist, where silvery scars swirled to the center of the stump, reminiscent of a flower bud. Percy could almost feel that look on his skin and he hated it. By all counts, he should be in need of a recovery bed—or more likely, a shallow grave—but he was up and moving with only a few dark spots in his vision and a slight stumble to his step for his trouble. Anything more strenuous than walking would be disastrous, but he was otherwise suspiciously spry for a man on the edge of death a few hours ago. He decided never to think about what exactly had happened while he was defenseless and unaware under this wretch's hands.

Percy bared his teeth at him. "For using your foul magic on me."

Thin fingers tapped a restless, tuneless beat against wool-covered knees, until the wretch finally replied, "I don't have any money."

Percy wanted to haul him up and shake him, but his voice was guileless. Either he was a very good liar or disturbingly apathetic.

"I don't want money," Percy hissed out, aware enough not to yell while people were actively searching for him, no matter how tempting it was. "I lost my fucking *hand*."

Another long stare, then a hesitant, "It was... already gone when I found you?"

As if Percy didn't remember how he'd lost his own goddamned hand. "Is this a game to you? Did you stop me from bleeding out just for your own amusement?"

A shake of the head, though Percy wouldn't be fooled by the confused expression. These flesh-mages never did anything out of the good of their withered hearts.

"What the hell do you want from me? You dragged me back into this cesspit of an existence, and not even in one piece."

The wretch perked up at that, and Percy reached reflexively for the hilt of his dagger. He stayed his hand only because if he was going to kill someone, he damn well wanted it to be intentional.

"It's been a few hours, but if you can find the hand, I think I could—"

Percy's remaining hand clamped over the flesh-mage's mouth, cutting off the words and the horrible promise behind them.

"*No*. I don't want you to," he had to swallow back the taste of bile, "to *reattach* my missing hand to my arm!"

While he'd been scouting the field above, he'd glanced around with a morbid sense of curiosity, but he hadn't seen his hand or his sword among the churned up earth and scattered corpses of the fallen. Even if he had, he wouldn't have agreed. He'd seen wounds go bad, and worse, he'd seen what a person could turn into under the influence of the flesh-mages; the rotting shambles, a living plague in human skin. It was a sight worth a lifetime of nightmares. He'd cut off his other hand before he let this wretch play at puppeting his body.

The wretch was staring at him like Percy was the one being unreasonable, though he didn't fight to get away from the grip clamped over his mouth. The feel of cold, clammy skin and damp breath had Percy snatching back his hand. He wiped it against his filthy pants as if it would help rid him of the sensation and the realization that he'd been the one to touch a flesh-mage's skin. It was the stupidest thing a person could do, and he was grateful that he hadn't paid for it immediately.

Good thing this particular flesh-mage seemed dimmer than most. The wretch simply watched him, lifting one hand to touch the skin of his cheek near the corner of his mouth as if savoring the warmth he'd sapped from Percy's hand. Percy scowled at the heat thief.

"You mentioned escaping through the tunnels," he said, redirecting the conversation through sheer single-mindedness and a desperate need to forget the feel of cold skin. "How do you know it will work? I've seen men attempt the same and never come back. Lost under the mountain, or stumbled into some hole in the dark."

He gestured to the yawning mouth of the cave the wretch was sitting beside as a distraction and took a careful step back. The dark of it was so deep it looked solid just a few paces in.

"Is your plan to wander blindly and hope for an escape before we die?"

He regretted using 'we' as soon as that awful gaze fixed on him with startling intensity. The wretch didn't move, but there was something predatory about having his full focus on Percy instead of his earlier absent air. It made something deep down in Percy want to run. Maybe it would be better to get rid of him now while the man was still acting docile. But if he knew something about navigating these caves, if there was a way to escape this battlefield without having to cross it and risk being seen, then he'd take it.

The wretch pointed into the cave, the shadows so deep that his hand was swallowed by the darkness in a horrible parody of Percy's truncated limb.

"I can lead the way. I'm familiar with these sorts of tunnels."

"Next you'll tell me you can see in the dark," Percy said, his voice thick with sarcasm to hide the way it nearly trembled.

"I can."

Of course he fucking could. The literal god damned cultists lived underground like moles, scrabbling through the dirt and shadows as they chanted languages no one knew and smeared bloody ritual marks everywhere. Percy hated that he'd even considered the option because at least certain death at the end of a sword was how he'd expected to meet his end. Certain death in the hungry dark of a cave at the hands of a flesh-mage was not something he would allow to happen.

Just as he was backing away, ready to knife the bastard before he went, Percy heard voices approaching. A glance upward showed the dim glow of torches growing closer.

"Check the pits, you cowards! If you can't be damned to do the work, then you don't deserve any of the fucking reward," a gruff voice from above called out, not nearly as far as Percy had hoped.

He had a split second to choose between two terrible decisions, and he glared at the cultist, who hadn't moved except to edge further into the shadow of the cave, also eyeing the approaching light warily.

Percy swore softly but viciously enough to strip the paint from a sailor's boat as he drew his dagger. He nicked the edge of his stolen cloak and tore a long strip from the bottom, trapping the bulk of the fabric under his arm as he worked with one hand.

It was an ungainly and awkward effort, but he managed, trying hard not to think about the choice he was making. The only other thing he could focus on was what the hell he would do now that his main hand was gone. He'd have to retrain just about everything with his left, writing, eating, fighting. He could handle a dagger with his off hand, he'd fought that way before, but a sword?

It could be done, and it would. He didn't have any other choice. If —*when*—he survived this idiotic plan, he'd make it his top priority.

He looped one end of the fabric around his forearm with a basic knot he had to pull tight with his teeth to keep his dagger in hand and tossed the other end to the flesh-mage.

"Hold tight to that. If I feel it go slack because you let go or try to get close enough to use your magic, I'll knife you, understand?"

The wretch looked down at the end of the fabric in his hand, then along the length of it to Percy, about two paces worth of space between them. Percy might not be able to see in the dark, but he had quick reflexes and he was fairly confident he could land a solid stab in close quarters. Whether he could manage it before the flesh-mage laid hands on him was the question that hung over them both, but he hoped his threat would be enough to make the wretch think twice about making any attempts.

The flesh-mage nodded as if this was all very reasonable and looped his end of the cloth around his palm, closing his hand to keep hold of it. He must have realized the simple trick worked in reverse as well, and if the fabric went slack from behind, he would know Percy was closing in on him. Even men who could see in the dark had blind spots.

The glow of torches was brighter now, and the voices closer. They were out of time. Already second-guessing his choice but committed nonetheless, Percy gestured with his dagger.

"Move, wretch. Before we're both caught."

The flesh-mage looked at the dagger, then at the approaching light, and lastly at Percy's face for a long, horrible moment before he nodded once more and slipped into the cave. The cloth rope in Percy's hand went from slack to taut as he moved further in, vanishing from sight. Percy swallowed, grit his teeth, and followed the wretch into the dark.

# CHAPTER 2

## *Percy*

The caves were a slow, torturous hell. The dark was thick enough to wade through and Percy's eyes ached from straining to adjust, desperate to see anything at all. He began to imagine shapes in odd colors against the solid black, unsure at times if his eyes were open or closed and unable to grasp any sense of the space around him.

Every sound was distorted by odd echoes. Dripping water in the distance, the clatter of small rocks kicked up by their shuffling steps, the way their breathing seemed to boom in the quiet around them. There was something deeply unsettling about hearing the flesh-mage breathe and being unable to see him, the tension in the cloth rope between them the only indication that he was still just a few paces ahead. Something about the shape of the cave or Percy's own mind playing tricks made it feel as if he were breathing down Percy's neck.

He was on high alert, braced to defend himself from an attack, making the minutes drag like hours. Their pace was so agonizingly slow that Percy thought he might see the mouth of the cave if he looked back over his shoulder. He didn't turn to check. Imagining that small bit of light was the only thing that kept him going when he wanted to lock up from the tension. If he looked and it wasn't there, he had no idea what he might do.

Percy wasn't the type to second guess his decisions, but he was self-aware enough to know when he'd done something entirely fucking foolish, and twice in a single day was a new low for him. It was too late to turn back now. He could retrace his steps toward the entrance if he kept his hand on one wall, but he'd also have to let go of the improvised rope, and then there would be a flesh-mage somewhere at his back with no real way to defend himself. Which was why, against every screaming instinct, he pressed on.

Percy's patience was gossamer thin, ready for an excuse to lash out, but the wretch kept his word. He led the way at an even, if excruciatingly slow pace, staying far enough to keep the cloth between them stretched just as he'd been told. He murmured occasional instructions as they went, speaking softly but startling Percy every damned time his raspy voice broke the silence.

Percy was guided around obstacles, told when to duck, where to step. He quickly learned not to dismiss the warnings after knocking his head against a hanging dripstone. At one terrifying point, the flesh-mage navigated them around a pit in the ground. Percy couldn't tell how big it was, but he hadn't enjoyed the sudden lack of floor under the toe of his boot as they side-stepped along the wall of the cave.

He had spent the entire endeavor thinking about how easy it would have been for his guide to simply let him walk over the edge. How easy it would be to do so in the future if the wretch got the idea. From then on, he was careful to slide his feet forward on every cautious step, testing for solid ground before putting down his weight, all too aware of his own vulnerability.

It was there on the brink, when he was desperate for any reason to excise some of the tension coiled in every limb—preferably with violence—that Percy began to hear the skittering.

At first, he thought it might be his hearing playing tricks, filling in the void with conjured shapes and sounds, but Percy had never been a very imaginative man, and his thoughts didn't lean toward skittering, slithering noises.

"There's a cavern ahead."

The flesh-mage's voice cracked through the dark despite being no louder than a whisper, startling Percy from his thoughts. He'd been so focused on the noise that he'd nearly missed the light tug of the cloth wrapped around his forearm, pulling to the left.

"Take two steps to the left and lean down a bit," the voice continued, disembodied in the dark. "The floor dips slightly here."

Percy's jaw ached from clenching his teeth for so long, but he followed the instructions, careful to make sure his footing was secure with each step. He'd never traveled so slowly in his life, but he'd never been without both a hand and his eyesight before, either.

The ground felt different here as Percy felt his way forward, not quite the same slick-rough texture of the caves so far, but not quite smooth either. He was trying to guess what the change might mean when something crawled across the toe of his boot.

Percy kicked it away reflexively, his hair standing on end. Whatever it was had the heft of a large snake and a multitude of tiny legs that had tracked rapidly across the leather. He heard the creature land and went still, frantically hoping that it was far enough not to simply rear up and bite him, whatever the fuck it was.

The flesh-mage had stopped as well, the cloth between them no longer taut but not loose either. In the sudden quiet, the skittering Percy had noticed before rose a chorus all around him, and he turned to look this way and that in a futile effort to see something.

"What the fuck is in here?" he demanded. "Where did you take me?"

The words were a bitten-out snarl between his teeth, and he was sweating in the cool of the cave air, skin crawling with imagined sensations.

"Ah," the wretch responded unhelpfully from the dark with a tone of bland reluctance. "I think the Great One's powers may have had an impact on the local creatures."

Horrible possibilities filled Percy's mind, each more nightmarish than the last. His hand dropped to the knife at his belt.

"Explain. Now."

"Wait, just..." There was a shuffle of fabric, and the cloth between them rocked slightly. As if the man was swaying uncertainly on the other end or shifting from foot to foot. "I'll have to come closer. Please don't stab me."

He said it as if he needed to borrow something and didn't want to be a bother.

Percy gripped the hilt of his dagger, already half out of its sheath, when something heavy and long fell over his shoulder and half down his back. Way too many fucking legs were scrabbling against his clothing, his armor, and the skin of his neck left unprotected by his leathers. Something long and thin brushed against his face, and there was a loud, threatening clicking noise near his ear. Percy shrieked behind clamped teeth and responded on instinct, trying to grab at it with his right hand only to bat at the thing with his stump. Tender skin knocked against sharply edged armor and more goddamned legs.

Then, the creature vanished. Yanked off him just as he remembered he had another hand holding a dagger and now might be a good time to put it to use. He nearly swiped out with the blade before he registered that the cloth line was slack and the creature was gone, but he reigned in the urge. There was a soft grunt close by, frantic clicks and skittering for a moment, and then a loud crunch and wet splatter just to his right. A cracking thump as the creature hit the ground, and then the briefest flash of blue-green far too close before they blinked out of sight again.

Percy jerked back, nearly stumbling, but no hand reached to grab him and warp his flesh. Around him, the endless skittering had only grown louder and more aggressive. He held his dagger at the ready, prepared to strike at whatever tried to touch him next. Hopelessly outmatched as the only one in this fight unable to tell what was happening.

There were more wet crunching noises, some accompanied by stomping, some without, and one brief, inhuman screech that was cut short. Whatever the flesh-mage had done seemed to scare off the rest of the creatures, their clicks and skittering fading with distance. Percy heard a number of them retreat somewhere above his head and shuddered at the ghost sensation of something falling onto him.

He saw those eyes again and swiped his dagger in their direction without hesitation this time, but the wretch was smart enough to stand clear of Percy's reach. It was impossible to read any expression from the two glowing semi-circles, but Percy readied himself for a fight, grateful to have at least some small point of reference. Wisely—annoyingly—the wretch didn't try to come closer, his voice low and level, almost hesitant when he spoke.

"They're gone now. I think we stumbled into a nest. They must have been riled up from the Great One's summoning," the flesh-mage said instead of telling Percy to lower his dagger. "I think it changed them. They're much bigger than I'm used to."

Percy wanted to scream, to demand to know what the hell had crawled on him and how the fuck the summoning of a chaos entity had *changed* them. He wanted to be out of this shit awful cave.

Oblivious to Percy's internal crisis, the flesh-mage trailed off into muttering before he spoke audibly again, the glow of his eyes drifting away from Percy to stare off into the dark. "I wonder how deeply its power has seeped into these mountains."

It wasn't quite a question. The wretch's tone was too flat, neither happy nor particularly concerned. His apathy left Percy feeling nearly as unsettled as the thought of that foul magic settling into the world even after the Chaos Bringer was banished. How much damage had it caused just by existing here briefly?

Those eyes focused back on him, broken rings of eerie aquamarine that pinned him in place. He'd seen a gemstone nearly the same shade once before, cursed and glowing from a ring on a mage's finger. The mage was dead now, and the gem had been smashed into dust, but he'd never forgotten that particular color.

"I dropped the rope you made," he said, catching Percy off guard.

He'd completely forgotten about the cloth lead and now realized it had fallen from his arm at some point.

Percy glared in the direction of those eyes. "You can see in the dark. Pick it up, and we can move on from here."

He hoped the wretch was more of a follower, the kind of man who did what he was told rather than think for himself. Because if he wasn't, then he damn well knew Percy was useless in these caves. All he'd have to do was walk away and leave Percy to die.

Silence stretched, and Percy tensed, ready to lunge if the wretch tried to abandon him, but there was only an awkward clearing of the throat.

"Are you sure you want it back?" came the hesitant question. "It's got a little..."

"Just give the rope to me."

"If you say so. I'll need to come closer so, ah, don't swipe at me."

There was another pause, and Percy watched those eyes as they stayed at a distance until he nodded and lowered his dagger slightly. He heard the wretch shuffle closer, eyes darting toward him and then somewhere along the ground before vanishing as the man presumably knelt to retrieve the cloth. A cold tap of fingertips to his arm startled Percy and he flinched back, blade at the ready, but the hand that touched him had already retreated.

"Here, I can retie it if you want, but really, it's kind of... wet."

Percy strained to see as the wretch fumbled through the sentence, but even this close, he couldn't make out anything beyond the gleam of his eyes. They flashed in and out of view as he blinked or looked elsewhere, the darting movement disorienting with nothing else to focus on. Reluctance was too mild of a word for how Percy felt about letting a flesh-mage touch him, but he also didn't want to risk putting his dagger away. Lowering the dagger just a bit more, he held out his right arm in a demand he assumed the wretch would understand.

Cold fingers touched his arm again, resting lightly against his skin, and Percy forced himself to hold still. Only to snatch his arm back as a rope of something slimy and lukewarm draped over his arm. Those eyes moved away quickly as Percy swung his knife around at the wretch.

"What the *fuck* did you touch me with?"

"The cloth. I tried to tell you," came the hesitant response. "It must have fallen into the remains of the first centipede I crushed. I wasn't sure how much force to use, so it was... a little messy."

Percy remembered—hadn't had a chance to forget, really—the crunch and wet noise of that first, oh gods, fucking massive *centipede.* He was not about to wrap that disgusting cloth back on his arm now. It felt like he'd been draped with intestines, but it was his only tether to the wretch that felt remotely safe.

He suddenly felt foolish. *Safe?* There was no safe here. He was at the mercy of this wretch who, for some reason, hadn't killed him yet. His good sense screamed warnings, and though he did not *trust* this man, a gut instinct told him to accept that he must rely on him until he could escape this foolishness he'd gotten himself into.

"Leave it, I'm not wrapping that shit on my arm."

"How will you follow me?" the flesh-mage asked without a hint of mockery. His apparent sincerity was fucking annoying; it made Percy sound like the unreasonable one.

Percy chewed over his options. They could cut another cloth, but he was operating blindly and one-handed, and he wasn't about to hand his blade to a flesh-mage. Despite all evidence to the contrary, he had more sense than that. What really mattered now was finding out exactly how much the wretch would let him get away with before he was abandoned or killed.

"I could hold your arm?" the wretch offered slowly while Percy ruminated.

"No."

"I didn't think so."

"Let me hold the back of your robes," Percy said after some thought. It seemed like the best of several bad options; he could keep the flesh-mage from running but let him take the lead without skin-to-skin contact. The positioning would also keep the man in front and facing away from Percy. If the wretch was tempted to lure him into a pit, then he'd take the man down with him.

The flesh-mage didn't argue, and there was a brief sound of shifting cloth and shuffling boots before he felt the stiff wool of the man's robe brush against him. Percy sheathed his knife and reached out warily, finding a shoulder, then strands of lank, greasy hair which he quickly shook off, and finally, the loose fabric of the man's monk-like habit. He gathered a fistful of the rough weave and wrinkled his nose at the man's unwashed smell, unavoidable now that they stood so close together.

Percy traveled for weeks on end with men of the woods. He was used to their smell—and his own, for that matter—but they also bathed when the opportunity presented itself. The flesh-mage's stench had to be weeks of sickly sweat overlaid with some kind of decay, old blood and worse wafting up from the fabric crumpled in his hand. Breathing through his mouth only helped a little, but he pushed the unpleasantness aside as best he could. He was far from fresh himself, coated in dry mud layered with the dust and sweat of hard travel and recent fighting.

He wiped the remains of slimy bug innards from his other arm against his already ruined clothing and wished for the luxury of a hot bath. Or a stream to swim in. A cold bucket of water would do—anything to scrape off the layer of filth he was carrying around.

Through the cloth of the flesh-mage's robes, Percy felt sharp shoulder blades and the knobs of the man's spine against his knuckles. Much to his discomfort, he could also feel the rise and fall of his breathing. It was easier when the wretch was just another black-cloaked cultist, barely counting as human, with rumors that they weren't truly alive. But this man breathed like any other, and Percy had seen the flesh-mages bleed, so he assumed their hearts' did beat. He certainly wasn't about to feel around to check.

It changed nothing. Alive or undead, the flesh-mages were vile either way, and Percy just needed to keep this one in check long enough to escape both these caves and the soldiers searching for him.

They traveled for a long stretch in uncomfortable silence, all too aware of how fragile this veil of trust was, how easy it would be for one of them to kill the other. At least, that was occupying a large part of Percy's thoughts. Their new positions made walking slightly easier as long as he kept his steps short and didn't trip up the wretch by outpacing him, but that was the only improvement.

It was still just as dark and horrible as it had been, but now Percy had the additional skin-itching knowledge that something could drop onto him from above at any time. He strained his ears along with his eyes trying to catch the slightest hint of skittering or movement, but aside from the occasional warning or instruction from his unwanted guide, all he heard was their own breathing and their slow, scraping steps echoed within the cave.

A small eternity later, when the wretch had cleared his throat for the third time without saying anything and Percy was close to shaking him out of sheer anxious irritation, the flesh-mage asked, "What is your name?"

Percy wondered if he should lie but couldn't think of a good enough reason to bother. There wasn't anything the wretch could accomplish with his name that couldn't be done far more effectively by simply slithering out of his hold to run off or kill Percy. He'd worry that the flesh-mage might recognize his name, but his face was more widely known and the wretch hadn't shown any recognition. Bards rarely remembered he existed in their ballads, and when they did, they never remembered his name correctly.

"It's Percy."

"Short for Percival?" the wretch asked in a bizarre attempt at small talk, considering their situation.

"No," Percy replied flatly.

The silence dragged on, and Percy let it. He didn't ask for the wretch's name in return, making his disinterest clear. Said wretch either hadn't picked up the hint or had chosen to ignore it entirely because he pushed onward, apparently determined to keep the conversation going.

"My name is Knell. Short for Deathknell."

Percy tried to hold his silence and not encourage this farce, but really. *Deathknell?*

"I'm assuming that's not the name you were born to," he bit out, regret rearing its head as the flesh-mage's voice grew more animated.

"No, no, it was given to me by the other acolytes." There was something odd about his tone that sounded almost wistful. "I don't remember what my name was before then."

Percy had no interest in finding out what sort of cult initiations left a man with no memory of his own name and let the conversation die, thankful that the wretch seemed content to do the same.

Unfortunately, the lack of conversation and the endless trek through darkness did Percy no favors as the rush from the encounter drained away. He'd been holding up well despite the blood loss and battle fatigue, but he could tell he was pushing his luck now. His head swam, and his feet stumbled as much as they slid across the ground in slow steps.

He forced himself to concentrate on his grip of the flesh-mage's robe, a tactile reminder that it was no tame creature he shared this darkness with. The thought helped him stay focused and keep his feet moving one after the other. His guide didn't seem to be in much better shape, drifting as he walked like a man already several cups deep into his wine.

Worried they'd both wander off a short ledge to a long fall, Percy used the grip on his robes to shake the wretch by the scruff, and he jolted like he'd been half asleep.

"Pay attention. We need a place to rest where I can fucking see something before those goddamned bugs come crawling back after us," Percy said. It came out closer to a whisper than he'd wanted, but he was reluctant to raise his voice and risk attracting more problems.

There was a weighted pause, and Percy took a slow, deep breath. "There are bugs in here, aren't there?"

The pause stretched, and Percy felt lank hair brush his wrist as the wretch turned his head far enough for Percy to see the curve of one bright eye glancing back at him.

"Do you really want to know?" he asked, just as quietly.

Percy almost demanded an answer, then thought about it and bit back the words. "No."

The glow of that eye vanished as the flesh-mage looked away again.

"Probably for the best. We're in their territory after all, but I think as long as we don't bother them, we'll be fine."

How very reassuring, Percy thought as his skin crawled, knowing there were things lurking around that he couldn't see or hear.

"There's a change in the light ahead of us." That bony spine straightened the slightest bit under Percy's knuckles.

He squinted and strained his eyes, but everything looked exactly as pitch and impenetrable as before. He'd have to take the wretch's word for it.

"It could mean a place to rest," that raspy voice continued.

Percy had his doubts, but it wasn't long after they'd begun moving again that he did, in fact, notice the tiniest shift from solid black to the darkest of grey. Now that it had been pointed out to him, he began making out general shapes around himself, his shoulders sinking with relief as the first hints of vision returned to him. He could see the outline of the cave they were traveling through—at least one patch of it—where that dim grey light was filtering in from somewhere. The cave was more of a tunnel, the length of it fading back into darkness further along and free of any hanging dripstones.

It occurred to Percy that he hadn't had to duck or step around any jutting spikes of rock for a while now. The observation was forgotten as soon as he saw an opening. There was a patch of lighter grey roughly the shape of a large oval, and he urged the flesh-mage to move faster, using his hold on the man's robe to propel him forward.

When they were close enough to peer in, Percy was able to see a clear silhouette of the wretch. He had one hand out, pressed against the wall as a guide or just to keep himself upright as he wavered more than ever. Percy had to hold him up by the grip on his robes more than once as he stumbled, and he knew they both desperately needed to rest.

Just inside the opening, which turned out to be taller than he was, Percy saw that it was a hollow formed by thick roots. The tree had fallen some time ago, hauling up a chunk of earth with it as it fell, which allowed air to filter in. It smelled like forest, and Percy tilted his head back to breathe it in. Pre-dawn light fought its way through a tangle of roots, grass, and fallen leaves above their heads.

Had he come down from the surface, Percy would have had a hard time seeing. But after traversing the caves, he could rejoice at so much light, dim and grey as it was. He let go of the wretch, giving the man a shove to one end of the space and claiming the opposite as his own.

In his eagerness to get away, Percy caught his boot on a rock hidden under the layer of leaves cushioning the ground. He moved to catch a hanging root for balance and missed because he didn't have a fucking hand, wind-milling his arms embarrassingly until he regained his balance. Unwilling to acknowledge what just happened or who had witnessed it, Percy kicked some leaves into a passable pile and slumped to the floor. He shifted until his back was pressed to the wall of packed dirt and roots, absently brushing away a beetle that had skittered out at all the movement. There were spots in his vision from either wooziness or the sudden ability to see again after all the useless straining, and he felt simultaneously lead-limbed and lightheaded.

Percy eyed the flesh-mage slumped similarly against the opposite side of the hollow, looking like a corpse in rags, and swore to himself that he'd only rest a moment. Just until he could stand without falling over, and then he'd climb free of this fucking nightmare.

Knell couldn't remember the last time he'd had such a pleasant day.

This morning, he was sure he'd be dead before midday. Yet not only had he survived the battle and the Great One's banishment, he'd managed to save a man's life. He'd even proven himself useful in navigating the caves for their escape, which made them *travel companions.*

Said companion was understandably wary of him, but he'd kept his word and hadn't stabbed Knell. Sure, he lashed out if Knell surprised him, but those had been easy enough to avoid. Maybe he just had the good sense not to kill a guide while trapped in the dark and surrounded by more hungry creatures than he had known, but Knell trusted his gut instinct when it came to people and it rarely led him astray. Even now, with enough light to see by and an escape route —though Knell doubted either of them would make it up the short climb to the surface in their current state, much less have the strength to clear away the overgrowth—Percy was willing to share the space with him.

He'd even told Knell his name.

Percy-but-not-Percival was frightened, tired, and injured, but despite how much he snapped and growled, he hadn't hurt Knell at all. His threats were genuine, as far as Knell could tell. Percy wouldn't hesitate to kill him if he thought Knell was more threat than asset, but he'd done no real harm either. *An honest man,* Knell thought, tucking it away beside his first impression that Percy was kind.

He leaned back against the roots and dirt on his side of the hollow, blinking slowly to adjust to the light, glad that it was dim enough not to be painful. His head nodded forward, and the bone-deep tiredness he'd been holding back as best he could made itself known. Exhaustion weighed him down, turning his limbs lead-heavy and difficult to move. He shouldn't have used his power to crush those centipedes and scare the others off, but he'd seen the venom dripping from their mandibles.

Their bites were vicious enough normally, he didn't want to know what they might do after being mutated by the Great One's influence. Some of them had grown to a size that spanned Knell's spread arms with segmented body parts and legs to spare. Their shells had turned jagged with spikes, and a drop of their venom had eaten a divot into Percy's leather armor. The Great One's gifts were varied and often quite useful, but they were never benevolent. Percy had taken a large —and quite frankly, foolish—risk in trusting Knell to lead him through the caves. Knell couldn't bear to break that bond, fragile as it was.

Even if Percy decided Knell had fulfilled his use and slit his throat now, he would die comforted by the fact that he'd had one day free from the control of the Great One. That he'd spent his last hours doing something of use. Throughout their trek, he'd caught himself getting lightheaded any time he thought too long about how he'd done the impossible, had used that chaos-driven power to save a life. The knowledge sat heavy and warm in his chest. What a nice feeling to die with.

Percy made no such move. He eyed Knell warily from where he was sitting, his ever-present scowl joined by a glare now that he could aim it at Knell properly, but he hadn't drawn his dagger. Curled up in his chosen cradle of roots and dirt, Percy looked as tired as Knell felt. They were a mirrored pair against their respective sides of the hollow, watching each other and nodding off as the light above them brightened by the slightest increments.

"Is this a safe place to rest?" Percy asked, delayed as if he'd just now thought to check.

He did look as if he were clinging to wakefulness by sheer stubbornness, his tan skin gone pale and dark circles under his eyes. Knell knew that he himself looked off-putting on the best of days, one of which was today, and told himself that he was unbothered by Percy's description of him as a wretch. It was true.

Knell hadn't caught any signs of danger but lifted his head with great effort to scan the floor, walls, and ceiling of their little hollow carefully. There was plenty of life, small crawling things that had made their home among the dead roots. Nothing that might be a threat to two grown men, weak as they may be. He started to shake his head, then quickly stopped as the ache behind his eyes throbbed in tandem with the pain marching up and down the line of his neck.

"I don't see anything that would do us harm," he managed in a hoarse whisper. Licked his lips with an equally dry tongue before continuing. "I think the more dangerous creatures prefer to avoid the light."

He hoped that was enough of an explanation, he didn't have the energy to stand for a more thorough check. Thankfully, Percy seemed, if not satisfied with his answer, at least also too worn out to fight him on it. They fell back into silence, and without any distractions to occupy himself with, the exertions of the day settled over him like a shroud. All he was left with were his many aches and the hungry, hollow pit of a feeling that using his power caused. He felt like the burned-out stub of a candle, sputtering the tiniest of flames at the bottom of a wick.

The cold of the caves was unaffected by the weak light within the hollow, and his still damp cloak did nothing but sap the meager heat from his body and replace it with a biting chill. Knell crossed his arms tightly, tucked his knees in close, and began to shiver.

He watched through heavy lids as Percy's eyes slid shut and opened slower with every blink, the man's tense posture eventually going slack as he was brought down by his own exhaustion. The life Knell had stolen and shoved into his veins had worked in the short term, but Percy was still suffering from blood loss and his body needed rest to truly adapt to the foreign life force. Knell would have been surprised that Percy managed to make it this far if he hadn't already seen how resilient the man was. But everyone had their limits. It wasn't long before Percy's hand slipped off the hilt of his knife, and his chin dipped to his chest as he fell asleep.

Knell wanted desperately to rest as well, but he kept forcing his eyes open a little longer to stare at the man across from him. It was the best distraction he had from the hunger gnawing away at his gut, the growing ache in his skull, and most bothersome of all, the cold. The inescapable cold.

It was far from the first time he'd gone hungry. He would find something to eat. He'd considered the centipedes, but they were mostly liquid once he'd crushed them open, and he could already tell he'd need something *more* to truly recover. Access to the Great One's power came with many drawbacks, some more common than others. If he or his fellow acolytes pulled too deeply from that well, their hunger grew fierce beyond their control.

Knell was glad that whatever had been left in his blood didn't cause the same depth of consuming, clawing hunger. Or that he hadn't pushed himself far enough to be caught by it, at least. It hadn't been unheard of to come across acolytes who had reached too far and been overwhelmed. They would strike down the weakest of the group and tear them apart for food. Rare, but it happened. Knell had been lucky enough to avoid ever being involved, but he'd stumbled upon the aftermath once. After that, he'd kept a wary eye out for which groups of his brethren and which rituals were best to avoid. Those were the acolytes he suspected were driven just as much by their own personal hungers as they were by the lure of the god's power.

Pain was also an old acquaintance and the easiest of the problems to ignore. Knell was long used to riding waves of agony in something similar to meditation. Those who never learned to adapt, to separate their mind from their bodies, either went mad or died.

For days, Knell's head would ring like he'd taken a blow whenever he received commands from the Great One. Acolytes were forced to comprehend languages human tongues couldn't hold, to see visions from a being that could stare into the heart of stars. It always hurt.

He had learned his own method of coping with it, riding out the pain rather than attempting to hide from it. The idea that he'd never have to suffer through another command ripping through his mind seemed too good to be true, too overwhelming to imagine. Each time he tried, he flinched in anticipation of pain, his heart thundering when nothing happened. Giddy with relief and terrified that it might be short-lived. He'd never enjoyed pain, but he'd learned to survive it.

The cold was something he'd never managed to get used to, no matter that he dealt with it nearly every moment for the past several years. Perhaps a person could only adapt to so much. He and the small group of acolytes he trusted not to kill him in his sleep would huddle together at night in tight clusters of whoever was available. They would trade news and sometimes food with one another, sharing heat when there was nothing else.

The chill of the cave tunnel had sunk its teeth into him, and Knell couldn't stop shivering. Percy was fast asleep, but men like him often slept lightly, hardened by life on the roads or in the wilderness. Knell was used to that as well. Deep sleepers rarely lived long in the stronghold of the brethren, an extensive cave system similar to this one. Not unless they slept in groups that might wake them if trouble came their way. More likely, the heaviest sleeper would be left behind to buy time for the rest. Knell had become quite adept at settling into a pile of jumpy acolytes as silently as possible.

Could he...?

No. He shouldn't. Percy had made it very clear he wanted Knell nowhere near him. He'd likely kill him as soon as he woke.

Knell considered that, his thoughts bleary and sluggish as he shivered under the weak light. Percy could kill him anyway. He might as well die slightly warmer than he was.

Unsteady—but quietly so—Knell struggled to his feet. There, he paused to wait for his vision and his stomach to settle before he slowly crept his way across the confines of the hollow. The morning light was still dim, the sun hadn't risen far enough to breach the trees above them, but he hoped some warmth might trickle in once it did. Percy didn't so much as twitch when Knell cautiously slunk down into the space next to him, tucking all his angles into the nook of roots Percy had claimed for himself.

Once he settled in next to Percy, he paused, glancing between Percy's face and the slow rise and fall of his chest for any sign of waking. He hadn't needed to worry, Percy's sleep was deep and uninterrupted. The man also radiated heat at his side like a fire. *Just as dangerous*, Knell thought as his eyes drifted shut, *but twice as comforting*. He curled in on himself as small as he could, careful not to touch Percy, and finally let sleep drag down into oblivion.


Knell was woken up by a kick to the thigh, and he jolted from his tightly curled fetal position in a flail of limbs, disoriented and hoping to keep any further attacks at bay. Bright sunlight made him flinch and hiss when he opened his eyes. It streaked down in golden beams through the tangle of roots and leaves above their resting place. He was still squinting and trying to remember where he was when Percy's voice, tight with anger, woke him completely.

"What sick games are you playing at, wretch?"

Percy loomed over him, framed by sunlight, which made it hard to look up at him, but Knell tried. He squinted and grimaced, doubtlessly not appealing himself to the man in the slightest. He was pretty sure something had crawled into his hair while he was sleeping, but he'd deal with that later. Percy let out an impatient little snarl, hand reaching for the knife at his belt, and Knell raised his hands in a placating manner.

"Nothing. I was sleeping," Knell said.

"I could see that," Percy snapped, his lip curled up to bare his teeth. "Why were you so close to me?"

Knell stared up at him, unsure what Percy expected him to say. If he'd had some nefarious purpose, Percy would already be dead. He stuck to the truth because it was all he had.

"I was cold."

Percy made an annoyed sound through his teeth. He was good at those, he had a whole variety of them that Knell was being introduced to.

"Next time, suffer," Percy said with finality.

Fair enough. Knell was already getting away more lightly than he'd expected. The last time one of his brethren had slept next to the wrong acolyte, it had cost him his eyes. The man hadn't lasted long after that.

Percy unsheathed his dagger and Knell wondered if he'd been too optimistic, but Percy moved away. Careful not to put his back to Knell, he reached up to begin cutting away at the net of foliage covering the opening to the outside. The thicker tree roots were mostly within the hollow or had been hauled from the earth when the tree fell, leaving mostly grass, leaves, and knotted vines. Percy clearly wasn't used to using his left hand for such tasks, his grip was awkward and his expression was stormy as he sawed away at the plants.

Knell had managed to sit upright and was getting a crick in his neck from watching, but he knew better than to make any sudden movements when a large man with a knife was so clearly on edge. He cleared his throat to get Percy's attention. Dark eyes darted to him as Percy switched his hold to an underhand grip and forcibly dragged the edge of the blade through layers of vines in one vicious movement. Knell spoke quickly.

"I could help?" he offered.

Percy eyed him with an air of critical judgment, which Knell couldn't blame him for. He hadn't seen his reflection in a long time, but he knew he wouldn't be anyone's first choice for physical labor. Looks aside, Knell was stronger than he appeared and more accustomed to operating on very little fuel than he suspected Percy was. He *could* simply wither away the problem by absorbing the life energy from the plants, but he doubted Percy would agree to that if he offered. Instead, he gestured vaguely toward his hip and the layers of robes hiding most of his belt from sight.

"I have my own knife."

Percy went tense at that, which Knell found amusing. Of all the ways he might hurt someone, Knell with a knife would be the least threatening. He was careful to keep his face blank and, though his features were not inclined toward it, as honest as possible.

Percy was obviously reluctant to agree but seemed to be thinking it over when his knife caught on a particularly stubborn tangle of vines. When he yanked down on them, it all gave way at once. The whole mass collapsed in on itself, showering them both in bits of vine, dead leaves, and loose soil.

Knell coughed out a small cloud of unsettled dirt and shook his head, taking the opportunity to brush away whatever had been crawling around his hair at the same time. Percy had been quick enough to cover his face with his arm and shook his head to rid himself of loose detritus. One leaf refused to be dislodged and stuck out from his short hair like a cocked ear. Knell tried not to be distracted by it when Percy glared down at him.

"Don't follow me," he said as he sheathed his knife, raising his right arm as if to point at Knell before he dropped it back to his side.

With one foot braced on a thick root, Percy pushed upward and grabbed at the edge of the opening, moving quickly despite the recent loss of his hand. He was halfway through the hole in no time at all. A moment later, his feet passed the ledge and Knell heard the crunch of footsteps quickly growing distant.

He waited a bit longer just to be sure. Percy didn't seem the type to believe him if Knell happened across him by chance. Once he couldn't hear anything other than the occasional bird call and insects of the woods, Knell made his much slower and clumsier way out as well.

All around him was dense forest, peaceful in the daylight as Knell planted his hands on his thighs and fought to catch his breath after the short climb. It would have been tempting to simply lay down and go back to sleep if hunger hadn't sunk its fangs into his spine. What he needed was food, or water at the very least. He straightened as much as his posture would allow, wincing at the pull on his chest, and spun a slow circle as he considered his options.

Finally, he shrugged and aimed his feet in the direction of the fallen tree. He didn't know shit about forestry, but standing still would get him nowhere.

The day was pleasant, and Knell found himself stopping often just to tip his head back and bask in the warmth and the breeze brushing past him to set off a chorus of rustling leaves. There was so much *life* here, and no constricting walls closing in on him, physically or metaphorically. The light, even dappled through the foliage, was painfully bright, but he opened his eyes wider to it, letting them water as he tried to take everything in at once. It was perhaps because he was so determined to experience every possible sensation that it took him a while to realize what was missing.

Woodlands are never truly quiet. It was all the more obvious after emerging from the ringing silence of caves. They had their own noises, but nothing that compared to the cacophony of the forest. Birds called to each other, leaves whispered a constant susurrus from tree to tree, and small creatures went about their busy lives in the branches and among the groundcover. Distracted by dandelion puffs trailing between his fingers, Knell hadn't noticed how still it was until there was a lull in the breeze, and even the leaves fell hushed. He went still and immediately began mapping out hiding places and escape routes, long acquainted with the inheld breath of fear.

A city man through and through, he had no idea what to look for as signs of danger in a forest. He was primed for back alleys, the press of buildings and people crammed into too-small spaces. The tightening of rope around his neck, the bite of iron shackles, the sound of a key turning in a lock. Later, he learned to spot trouble tucked away in the twists of caverns and in the shadows at his back.

He shifted closer to a tree, if only to escape the instinctual fear of being caught out in the open, and kept his movements as quiet as possible. As he laid a hand against rough bark, the scent of wildflowers he'd been enjoying was briefly overwhelmed by a faint, unmistakable waft of rot.

Knell's gaze darted around, trying to find more clues. Any worries about local wildlife forgotten as he suspected a much more familiar danger lay in wait. All he saw around him was the usual forest scenery, trees and grass and bushes, lots of leafy things he couldn't identify. He didn't know what to look for, but he paced a small area of grass and, feeling only mildly ridiculous, sniffed the air as he went until he caught a stronger whiff of the stench. Repeating this process, he gingerly began to follow the trail of the smell. It took a frustrating amount of time—Knell was many things, but a bloodhound was not one of them—but eventually, he heard the buzzing of insects and followed it cautiously. The smell led him to a cramped clearing with trees huddled around it like there was a meeting to be had.

Near the base of one tree, Knell saw a lump of flesh peppered with flies and half covered in thick brown fur. The grass around the clearing was flattened out unevenly, and when he crouched, he saw it was streaked with blood. More flies flew up from their feast at his disturbance, buzzing in low clouds before returning to their meals. The smell of rot was stronger here, but perhaps his fears were unfounded. Creatures were killed and eaten all the time in the forest. It was how life worked.

That hope lasted until he took a closer look at the lump of flesh, about the length of his forearm and half as wide. With a sour feeling in his chest, he poked at the lump with a nearby stick until he could see the underside. Flies filled the air and crawled across his exposed hands as he stared at the meat. It had gone grey and rancid, but worse, the blood soaked into the grass and leaves beneath it was a thick, sludgy black.

Knell wasn't the only acolyte in these woods.

# CHAPTER 3

## *Percy*

Percy was quick to put distance between himself and the wretch he'd left behind, more grateful than he'd ever been to return to the familiarity of the forest. He quickly oriented himself using the position of the sun and the angles of the ridge line visible above the trees. It seemed the caves had led them along the edge of the mountain from the valley to here, just north of the battlefield they'd escaped.

A decent distance, but not nearly as far as he'd like to be. His pursuers were—to his best guess—about a day's ride from where they'd started, and only because they'd have to cross the small pass that led out of the valley. The caves provided a more direct route, but their slow progress in the dark cost Percy much of his lead.

Despite his worry, he couldn't help but relax slightly the longer he breathed in the forest air, blessedly relieved to be able to see, to feel the light falling across his skin in welcome patches of warmth. Colors seemed brighter than ever and he let himself stop briefly to simply bask in it all.

There was no one around to see him brush a hand gently over the moss on a tree just to feel it or spend a moment too long staring up through the boughs, looking at the way sunlight and shadows painted layers of green when seen from below. He didn't let himself linger too long. Direct route or not, there was still the risk of dispersed fighters from all sides after the battle—and one particular wretch who might try and follow him.

Percy smelled the smoke before he saw it. Thick plumes of black drifted sluggishly, more than a simple campfire should produce. Something was burning. He moved with practiced silence between the cover of trees to investigate, wary that this could be a trap.

There was no sign of movement, and the wildlife was oddly quiet as well. Percy moved faster, hoping it wasn't the case of an amateur traveler kicking off a forest fire. But when he paused with a small campsite in view, crouching to avoid being caught out in turn, Percy saw the smoke billowing up from a pot on the fire.  He snuck closer, glancing around to make sure no one was closing in on him from behind, but he was alone.

As he waited, the only sounds were the sizzle of whatever was turning to charcoal in the cooking pot and the crackle of a slowly dying fire. The smell of it was so burnt and acrid that he couldn't even guess what might have been in the pot. As unappealing as it was, Percy's stomach still growled loudly enough to announce his presence. He winced and readied himself to run, but nothing happened. For the moment, it seemed the camp was empty.

Whatever idiots had left their food over a fire unattended must have been gone a long while for it to burn so badly. No doubt they'd be back sooner than later once they caught sight of the smoke, so Percy couldn't waste any time. He darted through the camp and into the closest tent, rifling through packs and bedrolls as fast as possible. He snatched up one entire pack, pinning it under his right arm, and shoved anything vaguely useful he could get his hand on that would fit, prioritizing the bundles of food and water skins.

Moving more clumsily than he liked, he knocked over several items in his rush and bit back a curse at the noise. Among the scattered mess was a folded paper with the wax seal of the King's Herald. Something about it drew his eye, and with a sense of foreboding, he flattened out the paper under his palm.

*By directive of the newly established King,*
*His Majesty has declared a most generous bounty for the*
*capture and return of the Traitor to the Kingdom,*

*Percival of Valmere.*

Fuck.

He knew they'd be after him, but goddammit, did they have to be so quick about it? And to have it sealed with an official King's Herald mark meant it had all the authority of the Royal Court. The neat, clear hand of the heralds, so that anyone with basic literacy might be able to read it, was just as distinctive to anyone who knew it. He'd heard of decrees being made on the battlefield, but this was his first time seeing one. That little shit wasn't wasting any time throwing around his new power, was he? The crown must've still been warm from the old King's brow.

It stung to know that nothing Percy had said or done, none of the lives he'd saved or sacrifices he'd made before yesterday would matter to anyone now. He shook his head and made a disgusted noise at himself. It was too late for second-guessing and too damn early for maudlin, pointless regrets. He'd done this to himself. There was no one else to blame for his ruined reputation and the bounty on his head.

Firmly reminding himself that he was wasting time while stealing from the bounty hunters who were out here looking for him, Percy dropped the herald's decree and finished shoving anything of use he could fit into the bag. He eased the carrying strap over his shoulder and was eyeing the bedroll when a splintering crack broke the silence.

Percy looked through the flap of the tent and saw the shape of someone in the trees moving toward the camp. Any supplies not in his bag were left scattered beside the bedroll as he ran the opposite way with all the stealth he could muster. He ducked behind the cover of a tree and some clustered bushes just in time to peer between the branches and see a figure enter the camp.

They staggered into view, emerging from the shadowed cover of the far trees with an arrow shaft jutting from their shoulder, one hand clutched over the wound. The pallor of their skin looked unnaturally pale, more so against the black of their clothing. The filthy blond of their hair seemed to hold the only color on them until Percy caught a flash of those awful gleaming eyes, more green than blue and bright as magefire. Percy froze, holding his breath and cursing the fact that he'd managed to escape one flesh-mage just to run into another.

The camp had been set up for two travelers, with none of the usual signs of flesh-mages. The grass in the vicinity was still green and alive, for starters, and the place didn't smell like a rotting corpse. Percy thought about the abandoned food on the fire, and for the sake of these travelers, even if they were hunting him, he hoped they had escaped the flesh-mage's clutches. He wouldn't wish that fate on anyone.

The flesh-mage raised their injured arm without flinching to look at something in their hand, and Percy wondered if cultists lost more than their names in whatever horrible initiation rituals they took part in. His mind flashed back to the blank, distant look that seemed a constant on the wretch he'd traveled with, at least when Percy could see him. The new flesh-mage peered around with a similarly vague, mildly curious expression, turning in a slow half circle with their hand held out in front of them, clutching something Percy couldn't see.

They stopped, their mouth splitting into a horrible grey facsimile of a smile, and their eyes swung right to Percy's hiding place just as a wall of rotting stench rolled over him.

Percy had barely begun to move when something heavy slammed into his back and knocked him into the dirt.

Knell hurried along the flattened, blood-streaked trail, grateful for its lack of subtlety, the hem of his mud-stiff robes clutched in his hands to avoid tripping.

He'd tried running and managed a few dozen strides before he was gasping for air, his heart beating painfully hard and his vision bursting with spots. So he walked and did his best not to linger on slivers of memory, glimpses of years past when he could sprint for blocks, dashing across the city and laughing at the sweaty red-faced guards who couldn't keep up. The memories, the disgust his younger self would feel to see him now, neither of those were helpful here. If there was another acolyte, Knell had to find them—and quickly.

Maybe he could reason with them. They could work together to escape this land for good if it was an ally he could trust not to kill him. If they weren't someone that could be negotiated with, then Percy was somewhere in this forest as well. Either way, Knell had to make sure they didn't cross paths. Percy might have hesitated in killing Knell immediately, but his own brethren wouldn't risk their survival on the unlikely chance of a stranger's mercy.

He hoped Percy was far from here.

The trail led to a newly made clearing where some sort of fight had occurred. Small trees were uprooted or splintered, others scored with claw marks. Knell had to duck beneath the shaft of an arrow lodged in bark. One tree had escaped damage but had a long splatter of red blood streaked up its trunk. The smell of rot hung like a fog in the air, and the blood was slick and tacky. There were small puddles of black ichor in various places, smeared into the churned-up earth and leaves, along with large animal prints. Knell measured them against his own hand and worried at the sheer size.

If one of his brethren still had the power to raise a homunculus and there had been a fight, the odds were bad no matter the outcome. Either the acolyte had won—and most likely added the flesh of their opponents to the creature—or they had lost, and there was an uncontrolled homunculus on the loose.

Knell looked around at the thrashed trees and wondered what he was doing. Why chase after trouble? This fight was recent, but no one knew he was here. What were the chances Percy was even on the same path? And if he was, what did Knell think he could do? He'd be of no help at all.

*But...*

If Percy did run into the same trouble Knell was tracking, he'd be one man armed with a single knife, still adjusting to the loss of his main hand—Knell had seen how many times he'd attempted to react with his right first—against a fear-fueled acolyte with command over a homunculus. With those odds, it didn't matter how good of a fighter Percy was, he would die.

Perhaps it wasn't Knell's business. Death was nothing new to him, but he couldn't shake the nagging impression he'd had, looking at Percy's unguarded face when Knell had found him laid out in the mud. He thought Percy looked kind. And despite the threats, insults, and suspicion, he had yet to prove Knell wrong. Percy deserved to live.

Knell still had no idea how he might be of any help, but as much as he despised fate, it had proven implacable. He should have died on the battlefield yesterday, and he suspected the same of Percy. What were the chances that they'd end up in the same pit, two strangers who should have killed each other but had chosen to survive instead? Or that there would be another acolyte in the same patch of forest where Knell had parted ways with Percy?

It was too much of a coincidence for Knell to let it go, and his instincts were clamoring at him, a companion to his gnawing hunger. He gathered what little resolve he had and pressed on.

He didn't have to go far. The path of wreckage was easy to follow, though it changed along the way, leaving less damage as it continued. Which meant the homunculus was likely learning to control its movements better and that the acolyte was still alive to guide it.

Trails of acrid smoke drifted in his direction as the wind changed, cutting through the corpse stench, though it wasn't much of an improvement. Knell missed the earlier breeze scented with damp leaves and wildflowers he'd abandoned for this lark. He slowed when he spied a large shape lurching between the trees with surprising stealth and grimaced at the size of it. It had to be taller than Knell by half again, and several times as broad.

The small store of newfound determination nearly left him. Knell was tired, hungry, sore, and still so drained. Doubts, never far from the surface of his thoughts, crowded in. He was no hero, and he didn't want to risk running into a less-than-friendly acolyte.

The number of brethren he trusted not to kill him if they were caught alone was small, and chances were that most of them had died on the battlefield. His earlier dreams of running off with a possible ally were exactly that, and dreams had no place among their kind.

Knell had just about convinced himself to turn around when he saw a glimpse of short, dark hair as someone ducked behind a tree, nowhere near far enough from the looming shape weaving its way toward them.

*It could be anyone*, Knell thought, his heart pounding from more than all the running around. *What are the chances it's Percy?*

It was a desperate hope, one quickly snuffed when Knell glimpsed the layered pauldron of Percy's leather armor. He'd stared at the man too long in their time together not to recognize its shape instantly. The lumbering figure was headed right for the unaware Percy—what was he staring at? Of all the times to *not* be on the constant lookout for danger!

Knell dragged his hands down his face despairingly, then gave up all pretense of stealth and began to run. It was blessed good luck that it wasn't far because Knell's health and well-being had not improved in the past hour. Panting and gasping from the effort, he just managed to weave past the homunculus as it swung a heavy, claw-tipped arm toward Percy's unprotected back.

Knell didn't bother to yell, too out of breath to try, and simply threw himself bodily at Percy, knocking the wind out of them both as they slammed into the ground. Foul smelling air whistled above them as the clawed limb missed by a hair and carved gouges into the tree Percy had been crouching behind.

Percy was quick to roll away, his elbow slamming back into Knell's ribs hard enough to knock him off. Knell wheezed as he curled in around the pain.

"You!" Percy yelled as he sprung upright. Knell would be jealous of his nimble ease if he had the time. As it was, he managed to gasp out a single word and hoped Percy would heed it.

"*Run!*"

He didn't get to see if Percy listened. A twisted limb of flesh and fur slammed into the ground next to Knell hard enough that he felt tremors from the impact. Something wet dropped to his cheek, and Knell looked up at the homunculus towering over him. It must have begun as a bear, the thick brown fur, towering height, and finger-length claws bore that much resemblance, but it had since been warped beyond recognition.

The bear's head was gone, though Knell could see sharp teeth and the vague shape of an open jaw ringing the creature's truncated neck. Threaded in long sinew-like strips up its body was pale human skin, sealed together like braids of dough with that of the bear's to give it more mass. The faces of two men stretched with expressions of pain and horror protruded from the body. One near the creature's shoulder, another near its hip, their smaller human limbs reaching out from the center mass, twitching and grasping, with too many joints and no coordination.

The homunculus swayed, barely holding together as viscera bulged from the seams of its stolen flesh, leaking thick black blood and belching out sickly vapors. Knell heard the dull snap of a bone from somewhere inside it.

It was an abomination even for a homunculus. The desperate attempts of an acolyte trying to use power they no longer had any guidance for. Knell was surprised it had made it so far, but it was big and incredibly dangerous. It lifted an arm to swing down at him. Knell watched the limb rise, claws splayed out, ready to tear into him. There was no chance of getting away in time, all he could hope for was a quick death. A crushing blow to the head if he was lucky.

The world lurched, and he was suddenly choking as Percy grabbed his hood and dragged him out of range in one powerful heave just as the homunculus' claw sheared divots into the ground where he had been. Knell kicked up leaves and grasped futilely at the fabric constricting his throat with a strangled *hrk!*

The cloth went slack, and Knell hit the ground with a thump. He coughed, gasping up at his rescuer's furious expression with no small amount of disbelief. Percy's attention darted between Knell's hapless form sprawled on the ground and the shifting mass that turned to lumber unsteadily toward them. A large hand gripped Knell by the arm and hauled him upright with about as much gentleness as the choking drag that had saved him from being mauled.

"Get *up*," Percy snarled, not giving him much of a choice in the matter. Knell found himself forcefully planted on his feet, rescued by the man he'd been trying to save.

They turned to run, only to find that a hooded figure had blocked their path, one raised hand clutching a foci.

"Fools, you'll never escape my—*Knell?*" Their voice rose several octaves and cracked on Knell's name. "Is it really you?"

Knell felt faint with relief as he recognized the voice, though that could easily be from either the recent sprint or the choking he'd just suffered. Whatever the reason, he started toward his fellow acolyte, Percy following close behind. He doubted it was out of concern for Knell's safety, more likely because the new acolyte was less immediately dangerous than the lumbering homunculus.

"Sibling Ness!" Knell called, his hands raised peaceably. "Please, call off your homunculus. We intend no harm."

There was an arrow in Ness' shoulder, but they barely seemed to notice it. Their eyes had a distant dullness to them, though they recognized Knell. Ness—named Darkness by the brethren when they were initiated—looked worn and faded in the sunlight. Worry grew into a cold knot in Knell's gut as he and Percy drew closer.

His fellow acolyte was lost in a way Knell had seen in others before they vanished for good. Ness was the closest person Knell had to a friend among his brethren, their kinship built on helping one another survive. Their eyes had always been sharp, even when horrors and hunger slowly wore them all down into nothing. Knell held his hands up a bit higher, showing his empty palms and recapturing Ness' attention as it began to drift toward Percy.

"Please, Sibling Ness."

To his relief, Ness lowered their own hands, one tucked back into the wide sleeve of their robe while the other clutched at the foci needed to control the homunculus. It was a pale stub of bone, most likely from the bear. Knell saw the creature shudder to a halt from the corner of his vision, radiating pained fury as it dripped black blood from ill-fitted seams and gasped silently through mouths no longer connected to lungs. Still too close for comfort but no longer advancing on them.

Percy was tense as a bowstring beside him when Knell glanced his way. His breathing was heavy, but he looked focused and ready to strike rather than panicked. He'd drawn his knife at some point after hauling Knell upright. There was a grim recognition in his expression, his split lip curled higher in disgust, but not the horrified shock Knell was used to. This wasn't the first homunculus Percy had seen.

"What are you doing with that one, Knell?" Ness asked, fingers twitching as their gaze drifted over Knell and Percy.

Knell could imagine just how badly this would go if Percy was allowed to answer and quickly spoke over him. "Escaping. We crossed paths and just wanted to get away."

Ness' eyes lingered on Percy, and Knell could see their focus slipping away. Whatever damage had been done when the Great One was banished, it had taken too much of his ally with it. There was a frenetic edge to their stare that had never been there before.

"Escape? There is no escape. We were chosen for the glory of opening the doorway for the Great One. This world and everything in it belongs to the Great One. Have you forgotten that, Brother Deathknell?" Ness spoke with a surety and fervor that was entirely new. "We know the summoning can be done, and we will do it again."

All too aware of the danger at his back, Knell took a small step forward, then froze when Ness' fingers closed over the bone fragment in their hand.

"Ness," Knell started, in the calming voice he used when Ness had woken from sleep screaming, unable to orient themself between nightmares and cruel reality. "It's over. The Great One is gone." He felt lighter for saying it, knowing it was true. "We're free."

"No," Ness whispered, eyes darting around like they thought punishment for this blasphemy would come lashing out from between the trees. They shook their head once, then again, harder, as their voice grew louder.

"No! I won't be tricked! The Great One *will* be back, and its fury..." their voice rang with hollow desperation, "Its fury will be felt by all." That frenzied gaze locked on Knell, and he knew Ness was too far gone. "Those who doubt must be eradicated before its return."

Sibling Ness was desperate to prevent a punishment that wasn't coming, and if it were, there would be no avoiding it anyway. The Great One didn't care for any of their efforts beyond being freed. There was no negotiating, no terms, no case to plead. If it wanted to punish, it did so at its own whim. Knell had to try and get through to Ness.

"Ness, please listen. You know me. I've never lied to you before," Knell tried to soothe, taking small, slow steps closer. "I know it is frightening to consider, but what we secretly hoped for years has truly come to pass. The Hero's prophecy was *true*."

Ness was shaking their head, but their eyes stayed locked on Knell in a silent plea, wanting to believe him. Knell was close enough to reach out, though he hesitated, not wanting to break the tenuous moment. He hoped he was blocking Percy from Ness' view. The sight of him might run Ness off course like a startled rabbit.

"We can go somewhere far from here. If the Great One ever does return, may it be long after we've turned to dust."

There was a weighted pause. They both knew that if Knell had thought those words before, much less spoken them aloud, he'd be writhing on the ground in pain if he was lucky. Nothing happened. Ness' eyes went wide, and a flicker of hope crossed their face before it shuttered once more.

"And what then?" they asked bitterly. "Shall we go back to living under rocks like grubs, afraid of the next person who'll drag us out into the open?" They gestured sharply in the space between the two of them, their voice an angry hiss. "Have you forgotten Brother Omen? He had so much hope in the good of men."

They bit the last few words out with venom, and Knell winced at the memory. "Of course I haven't." That was an ache they'd both silently agreed not to prod at, though he couldn't blame Ness for bringing it up now. "But things are different now. I know you can feel it as well!"

"No," Ness said with all the finality of an executioner's axe. Knell realized with grim resignation that he'd been the one tricked, lured closer to his old ally. Near enough to kill.

Knell saw the flash of metal as Ness revealed their own knife, but the motion jerked to a sudden halt. Ness dropped the knife and the bone fragment to reach for their own throat, where the hilt of Percy's dagger protruded, dark blood surging around the base of the blade in heartbeat pulses. Their hand went limp before it made contact and their eyes dimmed as they choked on blood, crumpling slowly to the ground.

Knell spun to look at Percy, whose hand was still outstretched from the throw. Even he looked surprised at the accuracy of the hit. Then Knell's own eyes went wide when he saw the homunculus over Percy's shoulder lurch back into motion, Ness' hold over it broken with their death.

"Watch out!" Knell tried to warn him. But it moved faster than either of them could act. No longer leashed by an acolyte and full of nothing but furious agony, the beast swatted Percy off his feet with a heavy limb.

Knell dropped to his knees, scrabbling through the dirt around Ness' body for the dropped foci. Their blood pooled in a slowly growing circle, turning the soft ground to black mud. He finally closed his hand around the knob of bone by pure feel, half hidden by dark folds of robe and covered in dirt, but it was already too late.

A crushing blow slammed into his side, and the world was a blur as he tumbled weightlessly before his momentum was stopped by a thin tree. It groaned and bent before the trunk gave way with a crack beneath him. He lay there stunned, the splintered remains of the trunk jabbing into the soft flesh of his back and side as he stared up at canopy-framed patches of sky. *Like a hundred small rivers weaving across a leafy map,* he thought, head full of cotton. Why were his ears ringing?

Then he sucked in a huge breath, and reality reasserted itself with a vengeance. He spasmed, coughed hard enough he might've retched if there was anything in his stomach, and struggled to roll off his back. Sharp pain laddered up his side, deep and torn. He knew that the homunculus' claws had caught him even before he felt the wet heat of blood escaping his body. He gasped through it, trying to find something to cling onto so he could regain his senses. The world was spinning, and the roaring in his ears hadn't stopped.

The roar changed in pitch and was joined by a shout, not in his ears at all. Homunculus. Sibling Ness. Percy.

Percy was probably going to die. Knell was definitely going to die, but he could accept that, even if he wasn't necessarily pleased by the details. But Percy's fate was still a maybe. A very slim maybe. Almost impossible, but if Knell could just *find...* there!

His fingers closed over the rough shape of the bone. Somehow, he'd managed to keep hold of it. This might be the last thing he'd ever do, bleeding out on the forest floor just as surely as Ness had, yet he couldn't help but smile at the sky. It felt wrong on his face, crooked and unpracticed, but he could almost laugh. Acolytes really did all their best work closest to death, didn't they?

He grit his teeth and closed his fingers around the bone fragment, pushing away the pain and spreading numbness as best he could. One last look at the bright expanse of the sky, the shapes of the leaves as light from above exposed their delicate veins, the white-bright of the sun that peeked through to burn his eyes. Even in shades of grey, it was beautiful. At least he wouldn't die in the dark.

With the image imprinted on his mind, he let his eyes slip closed and dragged up that reluctant magic from deep in his veins. His powers were slow to respond, blood seeping out of him faster than he could grasp control, but Percy needed him. Knell gripped the bone shard tighter, even as his body was seized with another painful spasm.

Colors appeared to him in thin strands of light, fainter than ever before, but there. He focused on the bone fragment, fighting past the struggle to breathe, the strained effort of his heart—ah, there were his own listless threads of life, draining away—and latched onto the spidersilk thin strand of color within his grasp. He followed the trail, nearly losing it within the endless maze of forest life, but the homunculus was the brightest tangle nearby, and he used it as an anchor to keep himself from drifting.

A second burst of color emerged, and Knell would've been glad to know Percy had managed to hold his own for this long if he had the attention to spare. But he was busy threading the needle of navigating another acolyte's creation with the bare remains of his own power. Finally, he managed to reconnect the foci in his hand to the riotous, knotted colors of the creature. He used everything left in him, stole whatever he could from the forest beneath his back, and—much like he'd done for Percy—*pulled* with all his might.

There was a snapping sensation, and through his mind's eye he saw the web of color that held the homunculus together unravel in a way he'd never witnessed before. The roaring stopped. There was a moment of absolute tranquility as Knell's consciousness floated untethered by the confines of his body, ready to embrace death with this final act.

Then all of the combined magic and trapped life force holding the creature together rushed back along the thread he'd created and hit him like a divine punishment for his hubris.

Knell never had a reason to contemplate what it would be like to be struck by lightning—he had plenty of other morbid thoughts to keep his mind anxiously occupied, and much of his time had been spent underground—but if he had, it still wouldn't compare to this. The world lit up, and Knell couldn't tell if he'd opened his eyes or if it was purely the excess of stolen energy overwhelming his limited senses. It was on par with receiving direct orders from the Great One, the feeling of being an inadequate vessel struggling to contain the power being poured into it. He writhed on the ground but felt none of it, grasping for the edge between himself and the rush of life force he had not been prepared for.

Years of experience under the Great One's command helped, and he managed to resist the first instinct to fight. He let the force rush through him and focused instead on keeping his own shape solid in his mind's eye. Clung to it with everything he had lest he be lost in the rapids.

At last, the roiling cacophony began to settle, though Knell would bet the power barely contained under his skin was strong enough to set any magically attuned objects within a day's ride to humming. He squinted open his eyes, rolled gingerly to his side, and then slowly made it to his feet.

Confused by the lack of pain, he patted himself down, then did it again just to be sure. His wounds were gone. He pulled at the front of his robe to take a look. There were long, jagged tears in the fabric, and the wool was tacky with black blood that came away on his fingers, but the skin peeking through the new ventilation was whole. Not even new scars to mark where he'd been injured, though his old scars remained as they were.

*Interesting.* Knell would have to think more on that when his head didn't feel like it was packed with angry wasps and his legs weren't itching to run straight up the side of the mountain. His exhaustion was gone, replaced by tremors of excess energy, and his heart was beating so fast he was honestly worried it might give out. The poor organ was not built for this much vitality.

He stumbled toward the steaming heap of flesh that used to be the homunculus. Black ichor leaked from it, and flies had already begun to congregate above the mess in buzzing clouds. Knell skirted around the heap as best he could while he looked for Percy.

It took long enough that he was beginning to contemplate the unpleasant possibility of having to dig through the small mountain of rotting flesh by the time he heard a pained groan a short distance away. Relieved, Knell was quick to follow the sound toward a sprawling, knee-deep cluster of ivy curtained across several nearby trees. He stumbled to a halt, struggling to slow his own movement once he started. His body wanted to keep moving, faster and faster, not sparing a care for whatever state he might be left in once that energy burnt itself out.

Percy was braced with his back against a tree trunk, his lower body tangled in the ivy and one leg clearly broken from the angle it was bent at. Knell picked his way through the ivy, hoping it wasn't the kind that led to rashes, and crouched beside Percy. The homunculus' claws had caught Percy across the chest, ripping through his leather armor and leaving it a shredded mess. Thankfully, the armor had served its purpose and Percy's wounds were mostly shallow cuts. Percy groaned and winced as he came around, face scrunched up in obvious discomfort. He tried to push himself up, and Knell quickly dropped the bone shard from his hand to his pocket without looking so he could hold his hands up, not touching Percy just yet.

"It's over, Percy," Knell said. His voice sounded rougher than usual. He wondered if he'd been screaming. "The homunculus is destroyed."

Percy slumped back against the tree and squinted at Knell with a pained scowl. "I saw you get hit. How the hell are you up? Could've sworn that thing nearly tore you in half."

Knell had no idea. Ever since the Great One's banishment, he'd been working on instinct and dumb luck. His best answer was a shrug. "I'm not sure either. I managed to grab the bone fragment Sibling Ness was using to control it, but I've never been able to, ah, *unravel* one like that before."

Percy glared harder at him, though Knell was beginning to suspect that's just what his face did when he was uncomfortable.

"I don't want to know what you mean by that, do I?" he asked.

"Probably not."

Percy shifted—Knell imagined the crushed vines and broken leg didn't make for comfortable sitting—and hissed through his teeth.

"Fuck, my leg."

"I could..." Knell trailed off as Percy glowered at him. There was no mistaking that it was aimed at him this time, but there weren't any other options unless Percy wanted to sit there with a broken leg in the middle of the woods near a dead cultist and an even deader homunculus. "I could fix it."

Percy glared at Knell, then down at his own leg as if hoping it would mend itself through sheer willpower. When he glanced at Knell's hands, Knell could see the bob of his throat as he swallowed nervously and knew what Percy was afraid of. The chance that Knell would do what Ness had done to those other men and that bear, only Percy would be alive to feel it happen.

"I won't do anything other than mend it," was all Knell could say. He doubted any further reassurances would convince the man.

Percy met his eyes again—something he was usually reluctant to do, Knell had noticed—and after a long moment, he nodded tersely.

"Fine."

It filled Knell with a giddy relief that Percy trusted him to do this, even if it was the only real choice he had. Slowly, gently, he laid a hand on Percy's knee, politely ignoring the flinch he felt, and looked over his leg.

"I'll need to set it first."

"Do it," Percy said, like a man at the gallows.

It was over surprisingly fast. Just a count of three, a click of bone sliding into place, and a single harsh gasp of pain from Percy. The hard part was pretending he knew what he was doing when it came to healing. Knell didn't say it aloud, but he suspected the stolen life energy pinging through his body lent more than enough power to make up for his lack of expertise. Which was good, considering Knell hadn't known he could mend living bodies until yesterday.

At the barest suggestion of a thought, power poured from his hands and into Percy with a sensation like pins and needles. Colors danced along the broken bone and torn muscles, racing and diving in swirls of light. In no time at all, the deed was done. Percy's leg looked whole and hale, and when Knell carefully inspected along his shin he felt no break or telltale bump of natural healing. So much life still hummed through Knell, but it felt less overwhelming now that he'd shared some, easier to contain.

Percy pulled his leg from under Knell's hands and slowly stood, shaking off bits of vine that clung to him. A few steps proved the leg held just fine, and Knell realized he was smiling when Percy looked his way, then off into the forest just as fast. Knell knew his smile was unpleasant—the blackened gums certainly didn't help—and quickly pressed his mouth into a line instead.

A surprised grunt made him look up again, and he saw Percy inspecting his ruined armor. He patted at his chest with a frown, then began unbuckling the whole thing. Knell tucked his hands under his arms to keep from offering to help. After Percy had eased himself free of the leather and discarded it on the ground, he patted his chest again.

Just as Knell had seen with his own wounds, within the torn gaps of the shirt, Percy's skin was smooth and whole, dusted with dark hair and hints of older scars but fully healed. Percy saw him watching and crossed his arms with his habitual scowl.

"Not bad, I suppose," he said with obvious reluctance.

Knell found himself smiling again and couldn't make himself stop. Percy didn't seem to mind it, the corner of his own mouth twitching upward for just a moment before he turned back toward the path. Knell followed him, curious, and witnessed Percy stagger to a halt at the sight of what remained of the homunculus. Saw the shudder of his shoulders before Percy clenched his fist and kept moving. It looked like he was searching for something, and Knell wondered what it was. His dagger, perhaps? Had he forgotten it was in Ness' neck?

Knell gave the homunculus remains a wide berth out of sympathy for his own nose and circled back toward Ness's crumpled body. He looked down at his old ally's face with an ache in his chest for a moment, then reached down and tugged the blade free.

"May you find peace in death the way you could not in life," Knell whispered. It was a common phrase among the acolytes, the best one could offer to their fellows under the control of the Great One.

When he turned away, the toe of his boot kicked something. Knell looked down, then went still. It was a knobby bone fragment. The foci Ness had been controlling the homunculus with. But it couldn't be.

Knell reached into his pocket and pulled out the object he'd used to destroy the creature, only to find a dry chunk of a fallen branch. He stared at it for a long time until approaching footsteps cut through the low pitch of noise that had replaced his thoughts.

Percy's scowl was a welcome distraction, as was the unfamiliar pack slung on his back, which looked fit to burst. He was still adjusting the straps when he looked up and stopped. Knell wondered why until he traced Percy's line of sight to his hand, the one holding Percy's dagger, its blade still coated in black blood. Knell had forgotten it was there. He quickly dropped the bit of wood into his pocket to examine later. A brisk wipe of the knife against a clump of nearby grass scraped off most of the blood but exchanged it for a layer of dirt in the process. Giving it up after a few more passes, he stood and offered it back to Percy, handle first.

Having watched the scene in its awkward entirety, Percy reached out and carefully took the knife, cleaning it much more effectively in just a few swipes using a corner of his now rather tattered cloak before sheathing it at his hip. There was a whistle of birdcall in the distance, noticeable only because all the creatures nearby were still silent and wary. Percy's head snapped up at the sound of it and his eyes darted back and forth, scanning the trees beyond the nearby camp.

"We need to go," Percy said. "That was a scout's call. These men weren't the only ones searching this stretch of woods."

Knell was curious what Percy thought the dead men had been searching for, but Percy's tone and expression invited no question.

"They're not far. We need to be gone before they find this place, and that campfire is a fucking beacon," Percy said, turning on his heel only to immediately stagger.

Knell rushed to his side, hands hovering as Percy steadied himself. His pallor had gone ashen, and Knell wondered if the lack of food, water, and blood loss had caught up with Percy once more. He'd be in much worse shape himself if he wasn't currently vibrating with stolen life energy.

"Lean on me," Knell offered.

Percy frowned, ready to refuse, but his whole body listed to the side on his next step. Knell decided Percy would have to just take his help or stab him for the effort. He ducked under Percy's arm and wrapped his own around his reluctant companion's waist. Percy didn't stab him, thankfully, even though he was clearly tempted and had his left hand free. When Knell peeked at his face, Percy was staring grimly forward. Probably trying to convince himself that as long as he didn't look at Knell he could pretend someone else was helping him. That was fine. Considering the situation, Knell couldn't blame him for being reluctant. He looked forward as well, clearing his mind of anything other than the ground and its many trip hazards.

They made it a decent distance before Knell remembered something vital. "I hope you know how to get back to the cave because I have no idea where I'm going."

Percy's answer was a snort, then a huff, and finally, laughter broke through. Rough and low, it built from a chuckle to a harsh bark of a belly laugh. It couldn't have been that funny, Knell chalked it up to lingering battle rush, but he was too busy staring to care.

Percy's whole face changed when he laughed, the permanent scowl evaporating under a sort of startled delight as if he was surprised at his own amusement. His grin was lopsided and charming, and little crinkles appeared at the corners of his eyes. The expression was gone a moment later as Percy regained control of himself, and Knell missed it immediately.

Back to his usual self, Percy glanced around before pointing in a direction further to the left with gruff instructions, as if the break in his demeanor had never occurred, but the sight was burned into Knell's mind as clearly as the glimpse of sky he'd thought would be his last.

He wondered if he could make Percy laugh again.

# CHAPTER 4

## *Percy*

Percy needed to get away from this man.

He couldn't explain why he'd saved Knell from being crushed by the homunculus' first blow, beyond moving on instinct. In those kind of situations there was no time to think, you hauled a comrade out of the way and kept fighting. Any death tipped the odds further out of their favor, and Percy wanted to live.

It didn't explain why Knell chose to save Percy rather than take advantage of a newfound ally. Why had he seemed so set on convincing the other flesh-mage of a life already lost? Even the new wretch had known their freedom couldn't last. With the distinctive features brought on by their god-poisoned blood, they'd be recognized and killed sooner than later.

So why the fuck had Percy saved Knell *again*? He could have let that filthy flesh-mage stab his even filthier one, then killed the newcomer to be rid of them both.

And then he'd have been horribly mauled to death by a raging nightmare made of rotting flesh once its master died. Just one half-dodged blow had nearly done him in. Injuries which his—no, not his, *the* wretch—healed as if it were nothing. After disassembling that same homunculus into a pile of steaming meat. It was fucking terrifying.

*He* was terrifying, and Percy needed to remember that.

A thin hand was curled around his arm, keeping Percy from stumbling or possibly collapsing face first into the ground, and he kept his eyes forward, forcing his fear into check. Why this flesh-mage decided to keep Percy alive was a mystery. He wasn't sure the man himself knew, but he couldn't rely on the whim to last. When he'd gone to look for his pack, he'd seen more than the felled homunculus. There was a swath of dried, ash grey vegetation and dead trees, ten paces across at least, where Knell had been thrown.

What was Percy compared to that kind of power?

They made it back to the fallen tree, and as much as Percy dreaded returning to the awful dark of the tunnels, he also had a general sense of their location. This stretch of forest was flanked on one side by the mountain, which would have been a treacherous climb at peak health, and on the other by wide swathes of former farmland the king—well, *previous* king now—had salted and burned several weeks back in order to stifle the food supply of the growing resistance.

If bounty hunters had made it this far already, it was likely that news had spread faster than Percy had guessed, and there would be enemies both ahead and behind calling for his head. He wouldn't make it up the mountain paths in his state, and the fields offered no cover. With people filtering into the forest, the tunnels were still the safest bet. Damn it.

Unhappy, but settled on his plan, Percy was determined to stack the odds in his favor as much as he could. If the wretch didn't kill him, then he might still get out of this ahead of the rest. First, they needed food. There was no telling when they might find another way out. He refused to linger on the possibility of being trapped under the mountain with the flesh-mage. Just the thought was enough to make him break out into a cold sweat.

When they were close to the felled tree, Percy was quick to pull away from the flesh-mage, bracing himself against the tree instead. The tree had been ancient, even on its side the trunk was taller than he was. The solid sturdiness of it was a small comfort.

Everything ached and buzzed, similar to how he'd felt waking up in the ditch after the wretch had sealed up his arm, but worse. He wanted to run full tilt, but his legs were barely holding him up. Each joint in his body was alight with a dull, throbbing pain to match the one behind his eyes. But it was ebbing slowly—so fucking slowly—and he found it easier to walk on his own now.

"We need food," Percy said, glowering off into the trees.

The wretch shuffled into his line of vision to look off into the direction Percy was staring, then glanced back at him with a sheepish sort of grimace. "I don't think I'll be much help. I'm not familiar with," he rolled his hand in a vague gesture, "forests? Outdoors in general, really."

"Then stay here, out of sight," Percy said to the air above Knell's head, refusing the draw of those strange eyes. "I'll go forage. I'm not going back into those damned caves without some fresh food, and we're already working on borrowed time."

He started moving before he was done speaking, ready to put as much space as he could between them in what small window of time they had. It wasn't the words that made him turn back and actually look the flesh-mage in the face, but how lost his voice sounded.

"Will you come back?" Knell asked. A strange, lonely figure standing out among the lively greenery and sunshine like an unwelcome weed in a flower garden. But weeds had more uses than the average person knew, no matter how unsightly they might seem.

Percy turned away. "We'll see."

It took less than two hours—how nice it was to be able to tell time by the sun!—before Percy trudged back toward the fallen tree that marked their escape route. As he expected, the wretch was waiting, crouched over something in the grass beside the trunk. At least he'd had the sense to tuck himself away from sight behind one massive branch that had lost its leaves but, in the time since, had been overgrown by ivy.

Unnatural blue-green eyes locked on Percy as Knell looked up from a sad array of berries and mushrooms he'd spread out on a wide strip of bark he must have pulled directly from the trunk of the tree.

"You came back."

There was a hint of wonder in the words that made Percy pause. Knell had said something similar when Percy had first returned to that damned ditch they met in, hadn't he? This was the second time he'd left, only to realize the flesh-mage was somehow the better option. He was quick to kick the thought to the back of his mind where it belonged.

There were more important things to focus on, like setting some expectations before they returned to the hell caves. He'd been thinking hard on it while foraging and had returned with his fear firmly locked away, ready to tell the wretch exactly who was in charge here.

Percy's rehearsed demands were forgotten the moment he was close enough to recognize what Knell had piled together on his makeshift plate

"Tell me you haven't eaten any of those," he said, more concerned than he was comfortable with and sounding angry because of it. Just worried that he'd lose his guide, that was all it was.

Knell's eyes widened slightly, darting between Percy's face and the foraged collection. "No, I wasn't sure which of them were safe to eat. I remember someone explained the difference to me, but it was a long time ago."

"Well, either you remembered wrong or they were a shit forager. None of those berries are safe. Or any of the rest, for that matter," Percy said bluntly. He gestured to the whole sad array. "It takes either shit luck or real effort to collect that many poisonous plants."

The entire lot of it was deadly. Percy just had to hope Knell hadn't tasted any of them because he'd either be dead or violently ill in short time if he had, and Percy was uninterested in dealing with either a sick cultist or a corpse.

"Ah," Knell said, carefully setting down a cluster of bright red berries that had been in his hand and eyeing the rest of his collection with faint dismay. "That's good to know."

It was honestly incredible that the wretch hadn't died long before now. Percy took away the plank of bark, ready to toss the contents into the undergrowth, then paused and looked closer at the darkest of the red berries.

"Where did you get these?" he asked, pointing out the little grape-like clusters. Knell looked closely at them, then his gaze drifted off into nothing as he apparently tried to recall the last two hours with some difficulty. This was who Percy was relying on to keep him from dying in the dark.

Fortunately, for Percy's sanity if nothing else, Knell managed to remember, using the fallen tree as a compass to retrace his steps. The bushes he led Percy to weren't far, growing in dense clumps of tangled branches and clinging to the side of a boulder like it was afraid of being seen. The leaves reminded him of holly, dark green with sharp edges and long wicked thorns. The berries were tucked away in distinctive clusters behind their protective branches. Why the hell Knell had decided these looked worth the effort was beyond him, though even Percy had to admit they looked perfectly ripe, if likely to fight back and win.

Once they were near, he held Knell back by putting an arm out to halt him, careful to avoid contact—with either the bush or the flesh-mage. He'd had more than enough of that today. Knell paused, curiosity a strange look on his sunken features.

Percy made sure not to touch with the plant as he crouched low to inspect the leaves. It only took a moment to spot what he was searching for. Right at the base of the leaves, which branched out in equal threes, was a little teardrop shape in a deep red hue, just where the leaf met the stem. He backed away cautiously, practically able to feel Knell's stare burning into him.

"What is it?" Knell asked, whispering like the plant might overhear.

"Magebane. Or witchblood, depending on who you ask," Percy replied at a normal volume, pointing at the blood red coloration at the base of a nearby leaf. "See that mark? It's the easiest way to tell what they are."

Knell looked at the leaf, looked at Percy, then squinted harder at the leaf like he somehow wasn't seeing the same thing. When he replied his voice was hesitant and questioning, the tone of someone braced to be made a fool of. Or yelled at.

"...No? I don't see anything." He was wringing his hands absently.

Percy scowled and gestured again, wondering what the fuck he was looking at since it wasn't like there were any other leaves Percy could be pointing directly at. "Right there, the red spot."

"Ah," Knell said, his voice losing that animated interest Percy hadn't realized was there until it went oddly flat again. "I can't see colors. Not anymore, at least."

Percy stared at him, his mouth pressed to a thin line. "Another side effect of," he gestured at Knell's general self, "all that?"

"It happened gradually," the flesh-mage admitted with a nod. "As my vision improved in the dark, colors seeped away."

He looked like he wanted to add something but was wise enough to hold it back. Percy didn't want to know.

Percy tried to rub a hand over his eyes and ended up dragging his wrist down the side of his face instead. Not bothering to switch, he rubbed the scarred stump against his temple to stave off the encroaching headache. No colors meant the wretch would have a hard time collecting anything safe, no wonder he'd been so shit at it. Sheer, dumb luck should have meant he'd collect at least one edible plant, though.

Percy considered that as he looked at the wretch—with his haggard, filthy figure and wide, worried eyes like he thought Percy's opinion of him mattered in the slightest. Perhaps it was entirely in line with Knell's luck to pick the worst options.

"You didn't get any of the sap on your hands, did you?"

Knell shook his head, then paused to think about it, which made him smarter than most of the men Percy had tried to teach foraging skills to before.

"I don't think so," he said. "I was careful to avoid the thorns and cut the berries away with my knife."

That was good. The stems of the fruit looked dry, ready to drop any moment, while the stems of the leaves were still bright green and flush. Their sap wasn't as bad as the berries, but it'd still leave burning welts behind if left on skin.

He must not have looked convinced because Knell eyed his own hands dubiously. "But I suppose I might have gotten some on myself."

Percy clicked his tongue against his teeth. "Then you need to wash your hands—and quickly."

The wretch looked around as if a river might appear just for him. With a sigh, Percy gestured for them to move away from the magebane. They returned to the fallen tree and Percy dropped the pack he'd stolen to dig through it for one of the waterskins he remembered shoving in.

He gestured to the wretch with a gruff,  "C'mon then. Hold out your hands, and get your filthy sleeves out the way."

When Knell did as he was told, Percy poured a thin, slow stream of water from one of the full skins, trying to waste as little as possible. It immediately turned a greyish brown the moment it hit the wretch's hands.

"Scrub," he said, and at least the instructions were followed gratifyingly quick.

Knell did as he was told. With some effort, his hands were several shades lighter for it. If some of the plant's sap had gotten on him, Percy doubted it would have been able to breach the layer of filth. It was good enough for the wretch to be safe if he'd gotten some small trace on his hands, but instead of corking the water skin, Percy gestured with his chin.

"Nails as well, properly."

Even as clean as Knell could get them without the help of a scrub brush or soap, his nails were a dark grey and in need of trimming. Pale at the overly long tips and near black at the base, just another sign of his god-cursed blood. His skin wasn't as pale as Percy might have expected under the dirt, and he wondered what shade it had been before the wretch had turned against humanity. A warm brown would be his guess.

Percy pushed the moment of curiosity away and finally nodded his reluctant approval, noting that the wretch's hands were now the cleanest part of him. He looked down at his own grimy hand with a scowl.

Grey fingers twitched in a tiny gesture toward the water skin. "I could pour some for you if you want."

Percy bit at the inside of his lip and considered the offer, then passed the water skin over, more eager to be clean than wary of the wretch somehow making off with his goods. They both knew Knell was useless at foraging, he wouldn't get far anyway.

"Pour slowly. Don't go wasting good water."

Knell nodded and carefully tipped the skin over Percy's hand. Percy scrubbed as quickly and efficiently as he could with one hand and one stump, gritting his teeth and trying to ignore the way his throat went tight as he made himself touch the place his hand used to be. It was easy to push aside when there were a hundred more pressing things to worry about, but staring right at it, touching those strange, swirling scars, he knew his life would be undeniably different. The loss suddenly felt very close and nearly overwhelming.

The water stopped, and Percy was pulled from his thoughts, grateful for the reprieve and angry that he felt anything so generous toward the man. He flicked his fingers to knock off the water, then took back the skin once Knell corked it tightly.

"What does the plant do?" Knell asked. Percy blinked at him, then remembered why they were washing off in the first place.

"Its poison is potent," Percy explained, returning the waterskin to the pack and noting to himself to organize it properly soon. "The berries will kill you quick, but it'll be painful. Bleeding from the eyes, and if you've had enough of them, everywhere else as well. The sap from the stems will leave burns and welts on your skin. Worse if you cut yourself on the thorns first. If it gets into your blood, it's nearly as bad as eating the berries."

He frowned in thought as he looked in the direction of the hidden shrub. "It's a rare plant, said to grow in places of strong magic. Some idiot mage's dropped potion or the aftereffect of a spell lingering around. A phoenix might have shit there for all I know."

Percy glanced at the wretch, expecting the boredom his forestry lectures usually garnered, and nearly startled back to see those eyes watching him so intently.

"How can you tell?" Knell asked. His flat tone made it hard to tell if he was plotting something or just curious. Not that it mattered, it would be easier to lead Percy off a ledge than to trick him into eating food he'd never accept from a flesh-mage. And it had been so long since anyone had cared to ask him for *more* information on plants.

"The berries are blood red and have a thin skin. You can see the black seeds if you hold them up to the light," he explained haltingly, pointing with his chin toward the discarded berries still on the bark tray nearby. How would a person identify it without being able to spot their distinctive colors?

"The leaves are sharp-edged, like they've been bitten, and grow clustered in threes with a red mark resembling a drop of blood near the stems. But if you can't see that, you'll know from the shape of the leaves, the long thorns, and the way the berries grow close together like grapes."

It was the most he'd spoken in a long while. Knell was still watching him with unsettling intensity, bright and unblinking, but his expression was almost awed. "And you could tell what it was just from a glimpse at the berries?"

Percy scowled, uncomfortable under the strangely flattering scrutiny. "I wasn't sure. That's why I wanted to see the plant."

The wretch finally looked away, his gaze drifting toward the deadly collection he'd ignorantly foraged. Percy only realized how tense his shoulders had become under that stare when they began to relax again.

"What about the rest? How do you know which ones are safe?" Knell asked, his hands twitching like he wanted to reach for them, but he held himself back by twisting his fingers together instead. "They all looked the same to me."

Percy opened his mouth to answer, then closed it and glanced up when a sharp bird's cry cut through the usual woodland noise. He spotted the bird hopping along a branch nearby, but it reminded him that they weren't alone in the forest. There were scouts in these woods looking for him, and they'd be twice as eager to cut down his temporary guide as soon as they saw what he was.

"If you really want to know, I'll tell you all about mushrooms and other berries later. For now, we need to get back down into the caves." The words felt like ash in his mouth. There were few things he wanted less than returning to that horrible dark, but unfortunately, those few things were exactly what pressed him to do so.

They were still too close to the battlefield and the fighters dispersing from it with his bounty fresh in their minds.

Thankfully, Knell didn't question him. He even looked interested, which meant Percy would actually have to explain mushroom identification techniques, but he found he didn't mind. The wretch was just as terrible at bartering as he was foraging if this was all it took to buy his continued guidance through the caves. Percy had taught basic foraging to a whole crew of men with the attention spans of children with sticks. He could shove some information into the head of one twitchy cultist.

Knell was the first to lower himself back into the hollow that led to the tunnels, careful of his footholds and moving slowly so he wouldn't slip. It wasn't far, but the dizziness brought on by too much activity and not enough sustenance was making him lightheaded.

Once his feet touched the ground and he tucked himself into the cradle of roots off to one side, Percy followed him down, also moving slowly but for different reasons. Percy had to hook his right arm around the thicker roots to hold himself securely as he dragged the loaded pack over the edge and dropped it with a grunt.

The pack landed with a thud and began to tilt. Knell reached out to hold it upright and pushed it aside to give Percy space to descend, curious where it had come from and what else was in it. He thought longingly about the waterskins, feeling more parched than before after Percy had let him wash his hands.

Above him, Percy was pulling vines and groundcover to disguise their entrance. Knell was grateful for the way it thinned out the afternoon sunlight and equally curious about why Percy was so determined not to be followed.

Apparently satisfied with whatever result he was aiming for, Percy glanced down to make sure the way was clear and dropped to the ground with an easy confidence. Followed immediately by a moment of wavering balance where it was clear that he was still recovering from his second round under Knell's hands. In favor of their current truce, they both pretended it hadn't happened.

Percy eyed the cover one last time then nodded to himself, seemingly satisfied. Knell glanced up as well, with no idea what he was looking for, and stopped trying before his neck began to ache in earnest.

"There are scouts in the forest," Percy explained, brushing his hand against his pant leg to knock away the dirt and leaf bits. "We've only made it about a day's travel from the battlefield. These woods'll be crawling with just about everyone and their bastard cousin soon enough. We need to get farther without being seen."

It made sense for Knell, who would be cut down on sight, but his curiosity had only grown in regard to the reason Percy was determined to hide. Who was he that just the thought of being seen was so risky he'd return to the caves he clearly hated? And with Knell, whom he barely seemed to tolerate? His thoughts must have crossed his face because Percy aimed that now familiar scowl in his direction.

"I have food and I might even share it if you can keep your mouth shut."

Knell pressed his lips together tightly and nodded. Who needed curiosity? Not him.

He did have one question but tried to hold it in, glancing between the covered exit and the bag that had begun listing once more. Percy huffed an annoyed breath and leveled him with a flat look.

"Spit it out. The last thing I need is you getting fidgety."

"The scouts in the forest," Knell began, then rushed through when Percy looked ready to take back his offer to share. "Do you think they'll track you here?"

Percy's posture relaxed slightly, and he made a dismissive motion with his right arm, probably an old habit. "They'll be more preoccupied with the scene we left behind. Besides, I know how to move without leaving a trail to follow. I spent most of my life in the forest. And it didn't look like you got more than a few dozen meters before circling back after I left."

He didn't say it like a question, but when he arched an eyebrow, Knell nodded. He'd been too nervous about losing sight of the fallen tree to wander far. How anyone could know where they were when all the trees looked the same was beyond him.

"Then we should be fine. Not much chance they'll stumble upon us considering how far we are from the nearest hunting trail. But if they do, maybe they'll eat some of the berries you left up there." Percy said, looking bitterly amused

At the mention of eating, Knell's stomach let out a growl loud enough that it might give them away to anyone passing by, regardless of Percy's skill. Percy stared at him, then rolled his eyes and grabbed the pack, dragging it closer to himself as he crouched to dig through it.

"Sit down properly. You look ready to keel over. How you kept yourself alive doing whatever the fuck you cultists do—no, I *do not want to know*—is beyond me."

Knell closed his mouth and sat down clumsily, staring intently at Percy's movements while he kept his own hands clenched tightly in his robes. Percy dug through the overstuffed pack, hauling out a blanket and setting it aside to shift things around more easily until he revealed a series of cloth-wrapped bundles with a satisfied noise. Each one was inspected while Knell held himself in check, tapping his fingers restlessly against his knees. The fabric was both stiff and stickily damp from the amount of blood that had soaked into it and partly dried. One side of his robe had been reduced to shreds with gaping rends in the cloth where the homunculus' claws had caught him. The night had been cold before, and now it would be worse. He tried not to think about it.

In short time, Percy had unwrapped a veritable feast and laid it out in front of him in a semi-circle of temptation. Knell clutched his knees hard to keep from reaching out. There was a large wedge of crumbly pale cheese, a fist-sized pouch of nuts and dried fruits of some kind, the remaining half of a dense loaf of bread, and what had to be a half-dozen thick strips of dried meat the length of his hand.

Percy divided the food, breaking the cheese roughly in two, tearing off a chunk of the bread, and setting aside the pouch. What surprised Knell was that Percy handed him all of the meat. Knell cradled the square of cloth his meal was gathered on in his hands, not quite able to believe what he was seeing. It smelled incredible, smoky and rich. Knell's teeth ached, he wanted so desperately to eat, but this felt like a test.

"This is all for me?" he asked, wary of being tricked. Knell wasn't sure what he'd do if Percy tried to take it back.

"I don't like meat," Percy responded, refusing to look at him or elaborate as he sat with his own portion. He had the majority of the bread, half the cheese, and the entire pouch of dried fruit and nuts.

"Why not?" Knell asked.

Percy chewed a bite of bread pointedly, probably hoping Knell would drop the question. But despite the gnawing hunger and the way his hands couldn't help but hover over the food laid out on his lap—the cloth looking startlingly clean laid over his muddy, blood-soaked robes—he was curious to hear Percy's answer.

With obvious reluctance, Percy responded tersely through a mouthful of bread. "Don't like the texture."

It was clear he wasn't going to say more so Knell let the matter drop, his curiosity no longer able to outweigh his need to eat now that he knew the food wouldn't be snatched away. With a rushed mumble of thanks already half buried in a bite of dried venison, he fell upon the meal and forgot about anything else.

When the food was gone, smoothing the sharp edges of his hunger to something manageable, Knell looked up to see Percy watching him with wide eyes and a vaguely horrified expression. He tried to think of something to say as he gathered up the last of the crumbs to eat, but it had been so long since he'd eaten a proper meal that he kept getting distracted.

In the end, it was Percy who broke the strained silence, lifting his chin in a gesture toward Knell's side. "I didn't know flesh-mages could heal themselves like that."

Knell had crossed his legs to lay the food out on his lap and the gaping tears in his robes had sagged open, revealing glimpses of grey skin beneath the fabric—the curve of his sunken stomach and shadowed ribs. He gathered up the torn part of his robe in his hand to hide away the sight, rough fabric still tacky with his blood, and shrugged a shoulder.

"Neither did I."

Percy seemed torn between distrust and relief. "Then how'd you do it?"

Another shrug and Knell frowned, not sure why the question made him uncomfortable except that he genuinely had no idea how it worked. He'd tried healing Percy on a whim and then himself out of panicked desperation. He didn't know how to put it in words either. Why had the Great One's powers lingered in him after being banished? Why hadn't he ended up like Sibling Ness, grasping at the frayed edges of the lost power and killing anyone in his path?

How had he destroyed that homunculus without a foci?

He didn't know. None of them had ever truly grasped how the Great One's powers worked. A puppet couldn't control the hand that moved it. There was no one to ask either.

"I don't know," Knell said softly, then shook his head when Percy looked annoyed by the answer. "*I don't know.* The Great One's power is overwhelming, we were never truly in control when we used it."

Percy crossed his arms, scowling down at his scarred stump of a wrist. "And you just happened to give it a try when you saw me? For no reason?"

His tone was mockingly sarcastic, but all Knell could do was give an awkward sort of shrug-nod. It was true.

"I thought I was going to die. I thought *you* were going to die. And I decided it might be nice to choose for once."

"To choose what?" Percy asked warily.

Knell picked at the corner of the cloth his food had been laid out on, rolling a frayed string between his fingertips.

"To save a life instead of taking it," he admitted, shoulders curled higher than usual. "I wanted to know if I could."

Knell knew what he was, what The Great One had made him do, and at times what he'd done of his own volition, driven by cowardice and fear. He was not a good man. To make such a statement, well, he deserved whatever scorn Percy cared to cut him down with.

But Percy was quiet. When Knell looked at him, Percy's expression was carefully blank apart from a slight frown that seemed to be the natural curve of his mouth. Somehow that made Knell more nervous, and he tugged harder at the bit of string, feeling restless until a sharp click of tongue against teeth caught his attention.

"Stop picking at that before you unravel the damn thing. We've got limited supplies, don't go ruining them," Percy said, eyeing Knell critically, though his tone wasn't as harsh as it could have been.

With effort, Knell stilled his hands, realizing too late that he'd let his torn robe fall open once more. While he was trying to think of an adequate solution to hold things in place, Percy laid his unfinished food out next to his thigh with a low grumble to go digging through the pack once more.

"Where the hell did you lot get those anyway?" Percy asked as he laid out items from the pack, likely realizing it was the easiest method to find something with one hand.

Knell resisted the urge to fidget. "Get what?"

"Those damned robes. They all match, but where the fuck do you get them?" Percy lifted up some half-carved lump of wood that must have been someone's whittling project and squinted at it before tossing it over his shoulder. "Dyed black cloth, enough for near on sixty of you and your creepy friends? Where the hell do flesh-mages order their clothing from?"

He sounded annoyed by the question, like it had been bothering him for some time. Knell opened his mouth to reply, then shut it again, at a complete loss. Where *did* their robes come from? His gap-filled memory was no of help. It was as if he'd always had these clothes, along with every other acolyte, paired with the knowledge that he'd better keep it in good condition because he couldn't recall ever getting a new one.

Percy glanced up to see Knell's baffled expression and shook his head as he returned to his search, knowing he wouldn't get his answer. After some absent-minded cursing, Percy pulled out a small leather roll with a soft noise of triumph and tossed it at Knell.

Still reeling from the question that might just haunt him forever with eternally unsatisfied curiosity, Knell was unprepared to catch anything. The item had already hit him in the chest by the time he'd thought to raise his arms. Percy looked deeply unimpressed, and Knell quickly fumbled the pouch open to reveal a tidy sewing kit. Three sturdy needles were pinned to the inside, along with small patches of cloth that looked to be cut from old clothing and a tidy spool of thread.

"I didn't grab any spare clothes, so I hope you know how to sew."

Percy's tone made it clear that asking him to help wasn't going to be an option. Not that Knell would. It was bad enough that Percy had been able to see as much of his body as he had. Knell had no plans to remove his robe and feel even more exposed. The rough wool wasn't armor or even that good at insulating him against the cold, but when you hated your body, having fabric to hide away in was its own sort of shield.

Thankfully, he did know how to sew and was actually fairly good at it. Knell nodded and cradled the sewing kit like the precious item it was. He had the strangest urge to smile.

"Thank you."

The urge only grew when Percy just clicked his tongue again and pointedly returned to his food in response to Knell's words.

# CHAPTER 5

## *Percy*

Percy refused to think about why he did it. The flesh-mage could heal himself from being gutted by a bear in moments, he could damn well handle a little cold. What did Percy care if his disgusting robes were torn? Good riddance, as far as he was concerned. But something about the way the wretch had hunched even further in on himself, the frail angle of his wrist as he clutched the torn robes shut over his emaciated body had scraped up some semblance of sympathy Percy hadn't known he'd had.

So he'd gone and dug up a sewing kit because he was tired of seeing the man looking even more ragged than usual. There was a limit to what Percy was willing to deal with. And the greasy little rat had the nerve to thank him for it.

Worse was the look of grateful wonder the wretch had worn at being given some half-decent trail rations. He'd taken the crumbling hunk of cheese, old bread, and dried meat with cautious longing, surprised Percy had been willing to share with him. Percy chose to ignore that perhaps, based on the time he'd known him, Knell wasn't undue for that wariness.

Percy had done nothing but snap at him, though Knell seemed oddly unbothered by his surly attitude, even if he was still cautious of Percy's threats. *Which is a good thing,* Percy told himself. *The man is a fucking flesh-mage.* He'd been reminded what horrors they could create and destroy on a whim. If the best Percy could inspire was caution, he'd take it.

But Percy was a man who kept track of debts owed, and this wretch had saved him several times over in the span of two days. It felt wrong to think that some stolen rations—in place of thanks that Percy couldn't bring himself to say—were worthy of such strong emotion. The man was so desperate for a crumb of decency that he'd lick the floor and probably thank Percy for his generosity. It was driving him mad because it made him feel something like pity for a flesh-mage.

Any and all generous feelings toward the wretch were rescinded as he watched Knell tear his way through his meal like a starving dog unleashed. He ripped into the strips of meat like he thought they might still fight back, barely chewing bites before he was back to shredding it with his teeth. The meat was gone in moments, despite usually needing to be softened in a simmering stew for at least an hour. Percy found himself so fascinated by the whole feral display that he'd been staring in stunned silence, his own food still raised halfway to his mouth.

If the wretch made himself sick, that was his own problem, Percy decided. He kept an eye on him as he ate his own portion at a reasonable pace, watching Knell hold himself in a truly ridiculous pose as he began to sew the robes while still wearing them, arms akimbo and all sharp angles.

One of his sleeves slipped past his thin wrist, and Percy spotted a curve of raised skin on his forearm. Percy narrowed his eyes, trying to figure out where he'd seen something similar before.

"What's that scar on your arm?"

Animal eyes pinned him the moment he asked. It should have looked ridiculous since Knell had frozen in his pose, but it was unsettling how still he'd gone. The afternoon light had turned the deep honeyed gold of early evening, heavy with shadows. The flesh-mage's eyes caught the edge of a sunbeam and turned a polished silver, keen as a fox. His gaze always sharpened from its usual dull apathy when Percy showed the slightest bit of interest in him. Percy cursed himself for never learning to keep his mouth shut. Couldn't seem to help himself from stirring up trouble.

Knell dropped the needle and let it hang from the thread, swinging from the half-sewn gash in his robe as he pushed each of his sleeves a bit higher to show Percy his inner wrists. The stretch of skin was delicate enough that he could have traced every dark vein running under it like winter rivers under ice. Just above bony wrists, Percy could see the scars in full and realized why they looked familiar.

They were prison brands, burned onto the skin of criminals when they were proven guilty. It was meant to be an easy way to spot any escapees or reveal an ugly past if they dodged a hanging sentence. Some of his own men had been similarly marked, but they weren't common. A crime worth being branded for was nearly always punished by death.

Knell had two. One on each forearm, a matching set with slightly different circular designs.

"You were in prison." He didn't bother to make it a question since the answer was right there before his eyes.

Knell nodded, tracing a thumb over the edge of one. Percy guessed it was the first. They both looked several years old. "This was for thieving."

"And the other?"

"For breaking out of the first prison," Knell replied with a flash of impish amusement. It was gone so fast, Percy wondered if his mind was playing tricks, but he'd never been a very imaginative man. He certainly wouldn't have conjured up some image of the wretch in front of him looking mischievous, of all things.

He was also surprised. A thief he could easily imagine; Knell had that sort of suspicious air about him. Even if he'd been decently fed and not irreparably changed by some mad god from another realm, a person would take one look at him and immediately check for their coin purse.

"How did you do it?" Percy asked, curious and grudgingly impressed.

A prison large enough to warrant branding their criminals wasn't some straw hut that was easy to escape from. Percy had been dragged into one such foolish venture, which had taken five of his crew and a week of planning. It had still been a near disaster.

Knell perked up as Percy knew he would at the question, and he shook his sleeves down to pick up his sewing once more. "I had a bit more bravado back then, I think."

A soft, dry chuckle came from behind lank strands of hair as he focused on his stitches, his hands more nimble than Percy had expected. "I don't remember much about my old life, but there's enough for me to know I was good at talking myself into trouble. Not so good at talking my way out of it, apparently. But I've always had a knack for opening locks, slipping out of bonds. I think I used to be quite good at knowing who to bribe and who tended to fall asleep on duty."

He glanced at Percy as he finished sewing the largest tear and smiled, small and crooked and wry. "I'd say I'm more than a bit out of practice."

"But you never escaped the cult. Weren't exactly thriving there, were you?" It had been nagging at Percy, the way flesh-mages always pled for mercy once they were caught, but he'd never seen shackles on a cultist, nothing forcing their hands. He'd seen them laugh at the sounds of their victims' screaming, once. He remembered that very clearly. Perhaps fear kept most of them in line, Percy knew how powerful a hold that could have on someone. But surely someone had managed to escape their trapped god's clutches before.

Knell stared down at his hands and chuckled again, but it was devoid of any humor. The needle, trailing clipped thread, was pinched between his fingers.

"There is no escape from the Great One. It lived in our minds. Whatever realm it came from is so vast that no distance we run would ever make a difference. I could sail to the edge of the sea, and if the Great One wanted me dead, I would cut my own throat or throw myself overboard to drown at its command."

Percy held back a shudder. "Surely you could have found a mage or a witch. Someone powerful enough to set you free of its control."

Knell propped his cheek on a fist and stared at Percy, who had to consciously hold steady and unflinching under the intensity of it. The angle of the light had shifted, and Knell's eyes gleamed blue-green once more, too bright to be natural.

"Several tried. I knew an acolyte who planned to plead his case to the witch of a nearby village, one he'd grown up in. He was sure she would help him. She'd known him since he was a boy. He didn't remember his first name, but we called him Brother Omen." Knell spoke without inflection, and Percy felt cold drip down his spine under that unblinking stare.

"Three of us managed to sneak away during daylight hours. Brother Omen promised to speak on our behalf so the village would know to let us enter at his request. He brought gold, jewels, things we had no use for since they cannot be eaten and no one would trade with us."

Percy couldn't look away. The fading light of day cast Knell's features in deep shadow, giving his face the illusion of a skull, with two circles of blue fire where eyes should be. Was this what it felt like to be under the thrall of a fae, unable to move and desperate for it to be over? That flat voice continued, and dread curled through the air in their little hollow, making every lungful heavy.

"He was so sure they'd help him. I think it was his sister who recognized him first. They had similar looks, and she called his name. His forgotten one."

Despite the words, Percy knew this would not—could not—end well.

"They looked at his skin," Knell continued, voice bleak, "at his eyes, and they knew what he was. It was Sibling Ness with me that day, both of us hidden in the trees off the path. We could do nothing but watch as they grabbed Brother Omen. He kept calling out their names, begging them to bring out the witch to help him. She did arrive eventually."

Percy almost told him to stop, but morbidly, he wanted to hear it through. So he stayed silent, and Knell kept speaking, staring through Percy rather than at him.

"The village was small, and the main road cut right through the center. It was easy to see them lock him in the stocks. When the witch arrived, I don't know what she said to him but he looked relieved. Perhaps she promised to fulfill his wish and free him from the Great One's control, just like he wanted. She sprinkled him with something —oils, I suppose—and then she set him on fire."

Knell's voice sank to a pained whisper as he closed his eyes at last, looking so very tired. It might have been a relief if it didn't feel like all the breath had frozen in Percy's chest. He'd heard of it, of course, burning flesh-mages to prevent a second rising after death, but he'd never witnessed one being burned alive. Knell's rasping voice was soft, but it carried well within the small hollow as he finished his story.

"He took a long time to die, screaming all the while. A single arrow would have done the job, but they all stood there and watched."

Right. Well. Fuck if Percy would ever ask another loaded question like that again. He looked down at his food, lacking any sort of response to that horror of a campfire story, and wondered if he could stomach it.

Hunger won out in the end. So he chewed and swallowed and felt strangely guilty that it did not taste like ash in his mouth but simple bread and decent cheese.

Knell knew better than to unlock the door to those memories. Retelling it had pried open old wounds and left cracks in the shell of muffled apathy that had kept him cocooned for years.

Percy's face, even when he tried to hide his emotions, betrayed so much. Unease at Knell's staring, reluctant curiosity, the slow dawning horror. Knell thought of his brash, startled laugh and focused on rethreading his needle, wondering why he'd opened his mouth and ruined all the progress they'd made.

The silence sat heavy between them, Knell sewing up the rest of the gashes in his robes, Percy finishing his food with all the enthusiasm of a man who would rather be anywhere else. He stitched a few extra rows along the ragged seams just for an excuse to look away. The thread ran out before he could begin another, so Knell carefully tucked the needle back into the pouch. Percy had occupied his time by arranging his pilfered supplies around himself, apparently so he could frown at them in stern disappointment.

Without looking up at him, Percy gestured toward one of the waterskins, laid close to Knell's boot. Knell picked it up, some large emotion lurking in his ribcage, behind his eyes, ready to rush over him until he drowned, and he was grateful for the muffled fog holding it back because it was very clear that Percy did not want to discuss it. Instead, Knell took a gulp of clean, cool water, not caring in the slightest that it tasted like leather. He drained half the water, then forced himself to slow with great effort, stoppering the skin before he could drink it all.

He tried to thank Percy but the man glared him into silence before he could get the words out. Still not in the mood to chat, then. That was understandable. He could thank Percy later when things between them felt less fragile. Curious about whatever intense selection process Percy was mentally cataloging the items with, Knell set the waterskin down close by and tucked his hands into his sleeves where they would stay a bit warmer. It also meant he could pick at the inner seams without bothering his companion.

Percy continued to ignore him and began repacking the bag with careful attention, inspecting each item and either adding it to the pack or setting it aside for some other purpose. Not wanting to interrupt, Knell held back his questions and observed quietly. A blanket was folded neatly—if a bit slowly with Percy using one hand and one wrist, needing more time to adapt to the change—and set aside. A curious polished torch handle with a small metal basket where a flame might be lit earned a pleased little hum and was set beside the blanket, tucked up against a knot of roots so it wouldn't be in the way.

Knell stared at the item, wondering what about it had caught his eye, and after a moment, the memory wriggled free from some deep recess of his mind. It was a mage-touched torch. Once a fire was lit inside the basket, it would stay lit without the need for fuel until it was doused. They were expensive but popular with travelers who could afford them. No wonder Percy had been pleased.

A pair of boots that were obviously too small for either of them to wear was set aside with less care. The socks bundled inside of them were held up between pinched fingers with a grimace that pulled at Percy's largest facial scar and showed off the gap of his missing tooth. His nose wrinkled, and he moved as if to toss them in the same direction as the boots. Then he paused, smirked, and threw them over to Knell instead.

The socks were dirty. Old mud had turned the crumpled creases stiff, the knitting had gone all felted, and they stank. They were the best socks Knell had been given as far back as he could remember. Granted, he couldn't remember much in general before the Great One, but that didn't change the fact that he'd been given a gift, no matter what Percy's intentions had been.

His own socks smelled worse anyway. Knell was quick to tug off his boots and peel away his threadbare socks—more hole than fabric—and pulled on the new ones without a moment of hesitation. He wiggled his newly covered toes, delighted at how thick the socks were, and held back a smile at the look of disgust on Percy's face.

It wasn't the look of revulsion at who Knell was, but simply a man displeased now that his prank had backfired. Knell was tempted to toss his own, much worse socks at Percy but didn't want to push his luck. Instead, he tucked them between some roots near his hip before shoving his now warmer feet back into his worn leather boots.

With a noise that managed to match his expression, Percy went back to his sorting. Into the pack went the sewing pouch, a cloth-wrapped bundle of what Knell suspected were more rations, a single spoon, a second bundle that smelled fresh and green when Percy lifted it, the second waterskin, and a battered tinderbox. Knell made a mental list of his own new items; wool socks, a half-full waterskin, and a square of clean cloth that had held his dinner. He folded it small and tucked it away in his sleeve, hoping Percy wouldn't ask for it back.

Afternoon slid quickly to evening, and the light was growing dim. Percy had begun squinting in the dim, and Knell noticed him glancing between the torch and the hidden entrance above them. The risk of being seen stayed his hand. Knell was used to long stretches of stillness and silence, it was one of the best survival methods among the brethren, but Percy was restless. He unpacked and repacked the bag several times over, then used his knife to clear out enough roots to make a space large enough to lay in, his shoulders sagging more and more as night crawled in. Knell was surprised he lasted so long. It seemed Percy possessed as much fortitude as he did stubbornness.

Finally, Percy shoved his things to one side and made to settle down. He shook out the blanket and Knell watched the motion of it, realizing how cold it had become even with two bodies in the small space. He curled in tighter on himself, but he knew he was staring. Percy glanced his way and flinched the slightest bit, startled by Knell's eyes in the dark.

It had unsettled Knell at first as well, seeing the eyes of his brethren gleaming at him from the shadows before his own had adjusted to it. Knowing his eyes would become the same. His eyes had been brown before, hadn't they? They must have been. His memory of colors was muddled, or maybe it was just the memories of himself. He let the thoughts drift back into the muffled, apathetic box of his mind that he kept them tucked away in. Enough reminiscing for one day.

Percy was staring at him, and Knell realized his eyes felt dry, which meant he had forgotten to blink again. He did so, and Percy frowned in thought. Then, much to Knell's surprise, he gestured for Knell to come closer with a jerk of his head.

"C'mon then. We'll sleep back to back."

Despite being the one to offer, Percy sounded reluctant and suspicious, but he didn't rescind the words. "If you snore, it's back to the cold."

The flat tone of his words made it clear that if Knell tried anything to harm him, he could expect to be responded to in kind. Knell had no plans to hurt him and was already moving before Percy finished his sentence. He practically tucked and rolled into position, curled up on the ground with his back to Percy, ready to share that promised warmth.

A pause, and then Percy lay down as well, his back not touching Knell's but close enough to feel his body heat. Even more so when the blanket was tossed over them both. He was tempted to lean a little closer and press their backs together, but he knew it would likely get him thrown out from under the blanket altogether. Behind him, Percy shifted a bit before settling, and Knell waited for his breathing to slow before his curiosity got the better of him.

"Is it just the texture of meat that bothers you?" he asked quietly, though it sounded loud in the hollow.

There was a long pause—Knell suspected Percy was debating if he should pretend to be asleep—then a sigh. "What's it matter to you?"

Knell shrugged one shoulder. "I'm curious. There was one acolyte who said they didn't eat meat for religious reasons, but he didn't survive long enough for me to find out more."

"It makes me ill, alright?" Percy said gruffly. "Anytime I eat meat, I get ill."

He could feel the tension along Percy's back even without touching and wondered what he was bracing for. Did he expect mockery? Knell hadn't realized the question would cause him so much discomfort.

Not sure how else to reassure him, Knell hummed a little noise of affirmation. "I understand."

Percy remained tense, waiting for something else, but it was all Knell had. If plants could kill a person, surely it wasn't so odd for meat to turn a man's stomach? Not sure what else to say, he stayed silent, feeling Percy slowly relax as the satisfaction of a half-filled stomach and more warmth than he was used to lulled him to sleep.

# CHAPTER 6

## *Percy*

Food and rest had done him well. Percy woke up feeling better than he had since starting this nightmare journey, which meant he only felt somewhat awful instead of half-dead. The strange buzzing thrum of energy under his skin had completely faded, and his limbs no longer felt weak. He could tell the wretch was already awake even as he feigned sleep, holding himself too still to be convincing. Percy played along if just to avoid any more unwanted conversation.

What improved his mood more than anything was spotting the torch he'd set aside the night before, his excuse to be rid of the wretch once and for all. No time like the present.

"Get up. And fold the blanket while you're at it."

The flesh-mage had the decency not to embarrass himself with further pretense and simply sat up to do as he was told. Leaves stuck out from his tangled mess of greasy hair, several tumbling free as he moved about. Percy watched a beetle crawl over one of them and was grateful that he'd be on his own again soon.

Breakfast would have to wait. Percy might have been moved by pity and reluctant gratitude to share his dinner, which was more than enough in his opinion. Knell had proven he could kill just about anything, so Percy would damn well keep the rest of his food. There was no telling how long it might be before he made it to another exit from the caves.

Getting the torch lit was a stark lesson in the things he'd have to relearn. Without his main hand, he ended up trapping the fire striker under his knee, right on top of a small pile of kindling, and gripping the flint in his left hand. The first hits felt clumsy, but he managed to land the right angle at last for the kindling to catch. He was quick to scoop the tiny flame into the basket of the torch, not wanting it to spread and catch on the tree roots weaving around them like a trap.

Knell was watching him, expression carefully neutral as Percy instructed him to fit the blanket into the pack before he shrugged it over his own shoulder. Then Percy gestured for the wretch to lead the way, not wanting Knell at his back while his one hand was occupied holding the torch.

Following him into the mouth of the tunnel, Percy was grateful to see that most of the bugs in the cave were their expected sizes and quick to hide from the light. The torch didn't illuminate very far in the dark of the tunnels as they left the hollow behind, but Percy could see a few paces ahead and behind himself, his soon-to-be-irrelevant guide lurking just on the edge of the glow.

The flesh-mage ran his hand lightly along the wall as they walked, wincing a bit whenever he turned to glance back, and Percy wondered if the torch hurt his eyes. If whatever change he'd gone through made bright light harder to handle as his eyes adapted to the dark. No better than the insects crawling around in the shadows, meant to dwell in caves until they died.

He'd seemed unsure about the use of a torch, almost wary of it, but Percy didn't have the ability to see in the dark, now did he? He assumed the wretch was afraid of losing his advantage, and with it, his limited usefulness to Percy. Both were true, and Percy looked forward to being rid of him.

His chance came sooner than he'd expected, arriving in the form of a split in the tunnel. When Knell opened his mouth to speak, Percy cut him off before he could get a word out.

"We part ways here, wretch."

Knell folded in on himself at that, even more so than usual, but nodded. He splayed one thin hand against the wall of the tunnel, yellow torchlight casting the illusion of a more natural brown onto his skin, and spoke in a flat rasp.

"Keep to these tunnels. You can tell by the markings on the wall." He ran his fingers over the odd striations Percy hadn't noticed before, though he remembered feeling them underfoot. They looked like gouges, constant and regular across the whole of the tunnel. Percy wondered if it was man-made, but who would build tunnels with so few exits and no source of light? It certainly didn't seem like a natural occurrence.

The wretch must have noticed his confusion. "They're scale marks. These are ancient wyrm tunnels."

Percy looked closer, intrigued despite himself, and brushed lightly over the markings with his right arm. Feeling the shifting texture of it against the sensitive skin of his stumped wrist. The last of the great wyrms died centuries ago, hunted into extinction, but he'd heard tales of their strange burrows. Tunnels carved under mountain ranges that, for some lucky explorers, could lead to the main lair and supposed legendary hoards of treasure.

Percy thought it more likely that they'd find themselves lost or in a pile of old bones. What use would a great big lizard have for gold and jewels? But the legends had outlasted the wyrms, and he thought every lair had been uncovered by now. No one had found one on this mountain that he'd heard of, and he'd been knee-deep in the local gossip since he was a boy.

"How can you be sure?" he asked.

Knell made a face that looked like a grimace, but Percy suspected it was an attempt at looking friendly because he recognized the way he perked up. "I've spent a long time navigating tunnels like this. There was a large system of them beneath the prison where we—the acolytes, I mean—spent most of our time."

That sounded depressing, in Percy's opinion, but looking at the wretch, he couldn't say it was easy to imagine him living anywhere but some dank underground lair.

"As long as you follow these tunnels, you can avoid being caught in small caverns or dead ends unless there's been a cave-in," Knell continued. "You still have to be careful of pits and drops, but at least there's much less danger of dripstones along the floor and ceiling."

Those animal eyes met Percy's and he felt caught by them, the expression on that gaunt face uncomfortably earnest. "If you stop feeling those marks, you must turn back. There's no safe way to navigate unknown caves alone."

Percy frowned but nodded.

"How do I know I'm not being led into some endless trek in the dark?" Percy asked. He hated to get directions from a flesh-mage, but he knew better than to let pride outweigh good advice that could mean the difference between life and death. *If* Knell truly had the knowledge he claimed. Percy couldn't be sure, but the man certainly knew more than he did and had gotten them this far.

"It is suspected that the deeper caverns the wyrms claimed were for hibernating," the wretch said, his intense stare drifting away, much to Percy's relief. "But even those tunnels will eventually lead back out. Most will remain close to the surface. I think it was so the wyrms could hunt easily. Even acolytes who wandered into the deeps were rarely lost for more than a night if they kept to the tunnels."

"And if they didn't?" Percy asked.

Knell stared past him with an empty look in his eyes and an absent shrug. "Those ones didn't come back at all."

Right. Ask a dumb question, get a horrible answer. Percy couldn't be gone from this wretch's company soon enough. "Fine. Then we each choose a path and be done with it."

"I'm not sure if the torch is a good idea," Knell said, squinting toward the light. "The things living down here..."

"Will know to scurry off back into the shadows," Percy cut in, annoyed. "You'll not talk me out of being able to see, wretch. Your use has run dry."

Those thin, knobby-knuckled hands wrung at each other worriedly, but Knell took one last look at Percy's face and slowly nodded. Good, Percy didn't want him getting any ideas about either comradery or backstabbing. Now that Percy was no longer relying on him or half dead from blood loss and shock, the wretch could leave on his own as agreed or face Percy's blade and rot here, a forgotten corpse.

Percy gestured impatiently for the wretch to choose a path and then watched him eye both tunnels before he shuffled toward the one on the right with wilted posture and obvious reluctance. He paused, half submerged in shadow where Percy's torchlight failed to battle back the weight of the dark, but Percy was already moving toward his own tunnel, uninterested in prolonging their parting.

He felt the wretch's eyes on his back and ignored the soft, "Goodbye, Percy."

It hung in the air behind him and was lost to the shadows soon enough.

With light at hand and able to see—if not far in front of himself, at least where he was stepping—Percy moved at a much faster pace, careful of his footing but no longer crawlingly slow. The cave tunnel still unnerved him, the unending dark of it and the echoing quiet that made every sound larger and more ominous than it had any right to be. His steps thudded against the stone like those of a giant, every breath was too loud, and his heartbeat thundered in his ears. And though he was sure it was his mind playing tricks, he couldn't shake the feeling that he was being watched.

More than once, he'd stopped, held his breath, and looked back the way he'd come. He'd stay like that, scowling and squinting into the dark, but the silence was complete, and nothing shifted in the far edges of his torchlight. So he'd take a steadying breath, sternly remind himself not to get worked up over nothing like a panicky greenhorn, and move on.

He should have remembered to look up.

The faint sound of clicking stopped Percy dead and saved him from being directly below the creature that dropped from the ceiling of the tunnel, but it was close. He startled back, swinging out with the torch on instinct, and the thing skittered away long enough for him to get a look at it.

Percy's first thought was that a mountain was a ridiculous place to find a crab, but he didn't have any other frame of reference to categorize the thing. It had six long segmented legs and a wide, almost flat body, all encased in a thick, thorn-edged shell. A tail curled up over it's back with a grasping claw at the end. There were no eyes he could see, but there was a gap along the seam of its body where the hint of a reflective shine gleamed from within. As it sidestepped warily toward him and the flame, two large claw-like mandibles unfolded from where they'd been tucked close to its face. They looked viciously sharp, with jagged edges perfect for grabbing prey and tearing at soft flesh. The creature was deceptively fast, long legs moving in quick, darting motions.

Percy swung the torch again, but the crablike creature didn't back away quite so far, more interested in possible prey than deterred by the fire. Percy might not like the way it skittered, but it was still just a pest, small enough to crush.

When he lifted his torch on the upswing, he saw movement from above and danced back as more armored legs reached down and another of the creatures pulled itself free. The first followed Percy's retreat, skittering just into the circle of the torch's light. As the light steadied, he saw more of the things closing in on him, hidden until now in the dancing of shadows across the walls.

Percy tossed the torch to the floor, where it clattered to a stop against the wall of the tunnel but still lit the space around him. Hand freed, he drew his dagger and turned a slow, cautious circle to keep as many of the horrible little creatures in view as possible. He glanced up briefly to locate the crack in the ceiling where a few had dropped down, but at least none were clinging to the space directly above him.

Their legs clicked in a quiet chorus, and Percy tried to guess which of them might lead the attack. The one that had arrived first was the largest, its shell a dark blue that looked like an oil slick in the light. The others ranged from blue to green to red, all mottled and dark, some nearly black. They all had thick, dense-looking shells with jagged edges, protected everywhere but that wet gleam tucked into the seam of their armor that were likely their eyes. Around him, their claws opened and closed slowly, readying themselves.

His instinct proved correct when the largest one came at him, even faster than he had guessed it could move. But he was a man who'd been on edge for days now with some violence of his own to let loose. He kicked it hard and heard it crack twice. Once from the force of his boot and again as it slammed into a wall, but he had no time to see if it was dead because the others swarmed, rushing toward him in a wave.

A multitude of sharp feet jabbed against his legs as they began to climb him quicker than he could shake them off. While he managed to fend off another two with swipes of his knife, a third snuck by and he shouted as sharp pain dug into his other arm. One of the creatures had sunk its mandibles into his forearm. Percy snarled and smashed it bodily against the side of the cave, throwing his weight onto it and crushing one that had made it up to his hip as well. The sharp splinters of its shell, now soaked with warm, wet innards, dug into his hip before it fell away. The one on his arm took two more blows to release him and its own mortal coil.

More were crawling up his back and closing their claws on the meat of his legs. Percy managed to jab the blade of his knife into the gap of one of their bodies and the creature immediately went limp.

Finally, a weakness. Too bad it was all the width of a fucking coin stood on its side. A claw closed on his shin hard enough to draw blood and Percy cursed, dropping hard to one knee to crush the beast under his weight. Then regretted it as the rest of them piled on in a frenzy now that he was at their level. It was at that point when he gave up on any coordinated attack, knowing it was foolish but not given any time to *fucking think.*

He swatted and swung at them, stabbed out only to feel his blade glance off their shells more often than it landed, though he managed to slice off a reaching limb or two in his efforts. He gained one more kill by sinking his dagger into the gap of another crab's shell but lost his grip on the handle as it fell away. Despite his efforts, the creatures were quickly overwhelming him, clawing bloody scratches in his legs and arms and the soft flesh of his sides.

One of them hinged open the lower half of its armored body like a cooked clam, and the entirety of the inner shell was a valley of sharp, serrated little teeth. Not wanting that anywhere near him, Percy swung his arm, along with the creature currently clawing at it, and smashed the two together as hard as he could.

It worked, sending them both careening off into the dark, but his knee slipped in the shard studded viscera of the one he'd crushed and he fell off balance. Reaching out to catch himself with a hand he no longer had, Percy landed hard on the stump of his wrist, slamming bone against the stone floor of the tunnel.

He screamed and more of the creatures crawled over him, clawing and biting. They weren't very large, but they were endless, and Percy did not imagine his end would come at the claws of fucking goddamned cave crabs. He would die screaming, eaten by giant fucking *bugs*.

Beyond the noise of clicking and his own shouts, rapid footsteps approached. Grasping claws reaching toward his face never connected because the creature was kicked away with what Percy had to admit was an impressive amount of force.

The wretched flesh-mage himself was suddenly there, kicking and swinging a sizable rock like it was a bludgeon. He was panting like he'd been fighting for hours instead of just arrived, all determination and no skill as he grabbed one that had been reaching its claw toward Percy and flung it spinning off into the dark like a discus before soundly cracking the shell of another with the gore-painted rock in his hand.

Knell let out a wordless yell and bared his teeth, looking all the more nightmarish with his blackened gums in the flickering light. Surprisingly, the scrabbling beasts shrank back slightly, though the ones that had attached themselves to Percy clung on stubbornly, not ready to let go of such a promising dinner.

Percy took advantage of the strange lull and fought wildly, not caring how foolish he looked as he kicked them off. One was flung into the wall, where it fell on top of his torch with a shriek that felt like a knife through his skull. Ignoring it, he threw himself bodily to the ground, crushing the one on his back. He winced as its sharp legs dug into his flesh from the impact but rolled with the motion until he was on his knees, then his feet, only gagging a little as he felt the dead creature slide wetly from his back.

The torch was guttering now, their circle of light wavering and shrinking. Percy reached for it, ready to save the flame before it was extinguished. The injured creature was hauling itself away from the flames on four legs, the others dragging limply behind it.

"Put it out!" Knell snapped, sharper than he'd ever been with Percy before.

"And leave us—leave *myself*—in the dark with these things?" he bit back, breathing hard into the small space of reprieve the flesh-mage's show of aggression had earned them.

"The light is drawing them in," Knell shot back, and Percy looked between the torch and the creatures, dread sinking like a lead weight in his gut.

He swung the torch slowly in a wide arc from one side to the other and the entire swarm seemed to lean in time with the movement. Fucking *fuck*. He really didn't want to put out the light, the one illusion of safety he had, especially not while surrounded by these things.

"You need to put it out. They'll only keep coming," Knell said with urgency. And he was right. Percy could already see more shapes scuttling over each other in the dark, closing in on them. If he snuffed the light now they would be surrounded, and no matter how much bravado the wretch had, they were wildly outnumbered.

But if they were attracted to the light...

He looked Knell in the eyes. "Don't you fucking leave me in here."

Knell nodded, and that would have to be good enough because the creatures had begun closing in once more. Percy drew his arm back and with more regret than he'd felt in a long time—a bold claim considering he'd gotten his hand cut off not more than two days ago, but true—he threw the torch as hard as he could in the direction he'd come from.

It spun, the flame blurring into an orange circle that shrank into the tunnel, carrying the light with it. The last thing he saw was Knell's face as the dark closed its arms around him, and inexplicably, found himself reassured by the sight.

*Knell*

Knell hadn't intended on stalking Percy through the dark. He hadn't gone far down the path he'd chosen, blinking past the spots Percy's torch had left lingering in his vision, before he'd been met with a wall of rocks. At some point there had been a cave-in and near the very top, where small amounts of light peeked in through sliver-thin cracks, a layer of vegetation had begun to grow on their surface. Not recent, then.

Surely, even Percy couldn't find fault with Knell turning around. There wasn't any other option, and since Percy didn't seem much interested in company at the moment, Knell could simply follow at a distance. Far enough back that his eyes wouldn't give him away if Percy looked behind himself—which he'd done more than once. Knell winced and fell back a little further each time, not surprised that Percy's instincts were strong enough to know he was being watched.

The torch worried him. It hurt to look at, too bright in the deep dark of the tunnels. His eyes strained to adjust to both at once, so he did his best not to look directly at it. The creatures here weren't used to light, and it might illuminate Percy's immediate surroundings, but it left him blind to anything beyond. Knell watched many-legged things slither and climb to escape the encroaching unknown, only to creep back out after. Some, worryingly, began to follow after it.

He'd seen similar creatures before, though the shell spiders he knew resided deeper in the tunnels, close to heat vents deep in the mountain, drawn to the warmth. These were larger and twice as thickly armored, but if they were anything like the ones Knell had dealt with before, then light made them aggressive. He picked up his pace.

Ahead of him, Percy noticed the shell spiders just as they were beginning to swarm. Knell dropped all pretense of stealth as Percy was quickly overwhelmed by their numbers. He had no idea how he'd help once he caught up. Knives were near useless, and soft human

110

flesh was no match for shells and sharp-edged claws that could take off a person's fingers or open a belly with ease.

Knell looked around frantically, trying to find something, anything useful and spotted a loose hunk of rock. It took an embarrassing amount of effort to lift, which meant there must be veins of denser mineral in these tunnels. After nearly straining his back trying to pick it up quickly and meeting more resistance than expected, Knell resorted to squatting and heaving the stone from the ground with both hands and the extra lift from his knees. He staggered back a bit, off balance from the momentum and added weight once he managed to lift it up. The stone was a rough oval shape that fit in one hand with his fingers splayed, but he had to use his other hand to brace it.

The shell spiders were too caught up in their swarm toward Percy to pay Knell much mind, and his robes took the brunt of any stray claws pinching at him. He waded in just before Percy went down hard on a knee with a crack that Knell hoped was a shell and not Percy's bone. Not wanting to accidentally hit Percy, Knell simply kicked away one that was close to snapping its claws into Percy without slowing down. He used the rest of his momentum to swing the stone with both hands and knock away another.

Thankfully, the shells were no match for the heavy stone, and all Knell really had to do was heave it upward and let it fall on whichever one was nearest. He stopped thinking after that, swinging the stone as best he could, kicking those who skittered too close—did he just grab one and throw it? No time to think about that.

Still more came, drawn to the heat and the light of the torch's flame. Knell yelled for him to be rid of it and, to his great relief, Percy listened after a moment's hesitation. Knell watched the light arc away, then dropped the stone in his hands onto one persistent shell spider with a satisfying crunch, kicking away others that lingered. Most of them rushed after the thrown torch, crawling over one another in pursuit despite the actual meal standing nearby. Shell spiders were deadly in swarms, but also predictable.

One dead shell spider near his boot had Percy's knife sticking out of it, and Knell had two immediate thoughts. First, that it was an impressive target to hit, barely half a finger's width between the two halves of the creatures shell. Secondly, he recalled that shell spider meat was bland and slimy but filling, and he was still very, very hungry. Percy had been generous the night before, but using and burning through so much magic, not even counting the excess of physical activity Knell was unused to—like all this running and lifting of heavy objects—had left him ravenous still.

He snatched up the creature, larger by far than the stone he'd abandoned but much lighter in comparison despite feeling dense in his hold. His stomach grumbled at him, and Knell tucked the shell spider under his arm. Its legs and tail dangled limply, and the hilt of the knife was wedged uncomfortably into his armpit, but it would have to do.

"I'm going to touch your arm," Knell warned, not interested in being mistaken for a shell spider and struck. Percy jerked at the sound of his voice, panting from the fight, but nodded, and Knell placed a hand on his scarred forearm. "We should go quickly before they catch on and double back."

"Goddamned *fucking* caves," Percy said with fervor, bleeding a bit from scrapes where shell spider claws and mandibles had gotten him.

Knell agreed wholeheartedly with the sentiment as he led the way further into the tunnel, putting as much distance as he could between them and the swarm of shell spiders. One of them must have crawled on top of the fire because he could smell cooked meat. It made his mouth water even as he heard a soft, disgusted huff from Percy.

The light behind them dimmed and went out not long after.


They reached another branch in the tunnel and Knell, only feeling somewhat guilty, kept that knowledge to himself, choosing the path that led at a slightly upward angle. It was likely to stay close to the surface rather than lead toward the heart of the mountain.

They traveled mostly in silence, Percy tense and quiet, brows low and frown severe every time Knell glanced his way, but the man didn't protest Knell's hold on his sleeve. Still, Knell made sure not to touch his skin, he'd rather not be banished from Percy's company twice in one day. He wasn't sure he could find a decent excuse for coming back again so soon and it was becoming clear that Percy tended to attract danger when left alone.

Hours passed, and Knell was still wracking his mind for a topic to break the silence beyond mumbled guidance when he noticed the first soft hints of light. So subtle he nearly missed it, but the further they walked, the brighter it became—to his eyes at least, Percy gave no indication of noticing and continued to stare aimlessly.

"There's some light up ahead," Knell said softly, though Percy still startled slightly at the sound of his voice. He gave no answer beyond a small grunt of acknowledgment.

It didn't take long for the light to grow visible to his companion, and Knell knew the moment Percy noticed. His shoulders straightened and his whole expression became more focused.

"What is it?" Percy asked, his first full sentence since they'd failed to part ways.

Knell shrugged, then realized the motion was useless in the dark.

"I don't know. Possibly another cave entrance?" he replied, uncertainty turning the statement into a question.

The conversation died as quickly as it began. Knell was weighing the odds of genuinely angering Percy if he tried to talk about the weather when the source of the light came into view.

Branching off from the tunnel was a cavern. The entry resembled a fanged mouth where smooth tunnel walls gave way to natural cave formations. A soft glow was emanating from within the cavern, bright enough that Percy was able to take the lead and step in first.

Great pillars of pale mineral reached from ceiling to floor, like massive candles of slowly melting wax. The floor of the cavern was relatively smooth and even, and it all had a thin sheen of moisture, water fed to the cavern from somewhere far above. More noticeably, spread over nearly every bit of wall and floor was a dense layer of mossy growth. The moss radiated a soft glow of light, made stronger by the way it reflected off the pale pillars in the cavern.

It was beautiful.

They both stared around in wonder, and Knell heard Percy's slightly shaky inhale of relief. Knell admired his fortitude, there weren't many people who could stand being trapped in darkness for so long when they were used to relying on sight.

It wasn't merely the lack of vision either. The caves had an oppressive feel to them, one Knell had long grown used to, but he remembered the way it weighed on him in the early days. The slow, crushing dread of them a sign of the Great One's presence, even as brief as it had been. And Percy had faced the caves twice now. Knell thought about what it must have cost him to throw that torch, no matter the danger it had brought. He knew better than to ask.

Knell was distracted by the texture of the moss, running his palm and fingers over its spongy, carpet-like surface, when Percy's simmering frustration boiled over. He threw down his pack near a space of open ground.

"What the hell do you want from me?" Percy asked, his back to Knell, shoulders tight. It felt like a loaded question and Knell floundered, not sure how to respond. Percy didn't give him a chance to answer anyway.

"You've come to my aid multiple times now, knowing that I detest your kind." Knell didn't flinch at this. He did know, and while it hurt it, was no secret. "So *why* do you keep helping me? What sort of debt will I have to repay?"

Knell shifted from foot to foot, feeling unsure. *I don't know why I helped you* wasn't quite right, but he wasn't sure Percy would accept the truth either.

"There is no reason. I just wanted to."

"Everyone has a reason. What will be your price? Money? Favors?" Percy crossed his arms, the lines of his back sharp against his shirt in the low light now that his armor was gone. He let out a humorless chuckle, and Knell wished it was the sound of his real laugh instead. The bright, loud bark of it he'd glimpsed in the forest.

"If you're hoping I can put in a good word to keep you from being executed, you picked the wrong man."

That was curious. Not that Percy would be no help—Knell knew no argument would save his life whenever he was caught—but that he sounded sure that he'd be on the executioner's block as well. The desire to know why he was on the run only grew. Why these tunnels and Knell's company, which he hated so much, were preferable to being captured. But now was hardly the time.

"I don't want any of those things," Knell insisted, twisting his fingers so hard his knuckles popped in rapid succession. "I just don't want to be alone."

There was a time in his old life, though it was distant and hazy, when Knell used to be very convincing. Maybe not charming, but there had been a certain surety to his words, a weight of charisma that he'd long since lost. Now, all his words felt empty no matter how true they were. He sounded like a pleading child, only without the endearment of youth to incite more than disgust.

There was that annoyed click of the tongue, and Percy finally turned to glare at him. "I don't believe—what the *fuck* are you doing with that," he sputtered for a moment, gesturing as he grasped for words. "That *crab thing*?"

Knell had almost forgotten the shell spider under his arm, he'd gotten so used to the weight of it as they walked. Though now that he was paying attention, his arm was a bit sore from the awkward hold and the weight of it.

"The shell spider? It had your knife."

Percy squinted, so the light must not be that good after all, but he gave a curt nod with a grimace, his tightly wound anger thoroughly waylaid. "I can see that, but you didn't need to bring the whole damned thing along."

"The rest is for me. I'm going to eat it."

"We just had to run from the fuckers because they're drawn to fire," Percy said in an aggravated tone, and Knell nodded, pleased that he was so quick to learn.

"Yes, they're drawn to the light and heat, as far as I know."

"So how are you planning to cook it?" Percy asked with a sneer and a little raise to his eyebrows that made it clear he thought he'd won this argument. It was nice to see him so animated again.

Knell pulled the knife out with a wet pop and passed it hilt-first to Percy, who paused for a moment before he took it with a grimace and flicked away the worst of the slime from the blade. Then Knell hefted the shell spider between both hands to weigh it, satisfied at how good of a meal it would make.

"I wasn't going to."

# CHAPTER 7

## *Percy*

Percy cinched his mouth shut against a heaving gag as he watched Knell suck the meat right out of the creature's leg shell with a wet noise that would haunt his nightmares. Nausea wrapped around the hunger in his gut and strangled it, so he set the hunk of cheese he'd pulled out for his own dinner back onto the cloth he'd laid out over his thigh with an unhappy grunt.

He had to scrape his tongue against the roof of his mouth in the hope of avoiding a dry heaving spell when Knell tore open the creature's undercarriage to reveal slick, lumpy white flesh streaked with dark veins. The wretch, truly living up to his moniker, had the nerve to look up at him with a questioning expression.

"You sure you don't want any? Does every kind of meat make you ill?"

This one most certainly fucking would. Percy wondered, briefly, if he'd get more relief slitting the man's throat or his own. Knell was meticulously working around the edges of the slimy flesh, his fingers spidering along, loosening it from the shell to, presumably, haul the entire mass out in a single disgusting lump. Unable to look away, he sternly reminded himself that this was the best resting spot they'd managed to find and he was *not* about to sleep near his own vomit.

"That'll probably give you worms," he bit out instead. "Seen folks eat little beasts like that from the riverbed. Half of them nearly shit their insides out."

A pause. Knell resembled nothing more than a rat in that moment, thin hands clutching at a lump of refuse, ready to feast. Percy was feeling hopeful that his words had gotten through until Knell narrowed his eyes and asked, "What kind of worms?"

"Does it make a difference?" Percy asked, incredulous.

"Of course. I've only really seen them on corpses. I always thought it was a part of the decaying process, but perhaps they'd been there all along."

"Not like maggots." Percy hated everything about this but was somehow drawn far enough into the bewildering conversation that he felt compelled to follow things through. "Long, ugly fuckers. Lurking in your guts and feeding off of you."

"Ah," Knell said, nodding in understanding. "A parasite, transferred through food. Fascinating. Can you tell by looking at the meat itself?"

Percy had no idea, but Knell had already begun pulling at the lump of flesh in his hands, eyes full of detached curiosity. As soon as it began to tear with a wet, horrible noise, Percy snatched it from his hands and threw it as far as he could into the yawning dark of the nearby tunnel. It landed with a distant splat. Wide eyes glanced from empty, slick hands to Percy's snarling face.

"That felt unnecessary," Knell muttered sullenly, sucking his fingers clean.

He was mollified easily enough when Percy shoved the last of the nuts and a portion of the wild peas he'd foraged and saved carefully for his meal at him. If sharing meant he could avoid watching this horror show, he would do so without hesitation.

"That was the most necessary thing I've ever done. Now shut up and eat this instead."

Knell clutched the bundled cloth just like he had the dried meat the previous night, as if it was something far more fragile and precious than some spring greens. Percy wondered if anyone had ever given him food before, then thought about the fact that eating giant cave bugs raw was apparently normal for him, so it was likely no one had. What a fucking depressing thought.

"What is it?"

"Almonds. The rest is wild peas. You're lucky it's a good time of year for them, I found a whole patch back in the forest."

Knell bit a pod in half and began to chew. Percy nearly told him to string them, but the pods were still tender and green. They wouldn't do any harm if eaten whole. Even if they could, it would be nothing compared to what he'd been eating moments ago. A delighted little noise came from Knell and his whole demeanor seemed to ease. It was difficult to see his expression in the light, but his eyes were wide enough that Percy could see the full moon circle of their strange glow.

"It's sweet!"

They were sweet. Percy had made sure to pick a few of the best from each plant, leaving any half-nibbled ones for the bugs to finish. But Knell's simple delight made Percy uncomfortable. He'd seen what happened in places cultists gathered, usually shoddy encampments or tucked into hillside caves. Easy to find once you knew the signs.

They drew the life out of everything nearby, given enough time. A person could tell how long a group of cultists had been in one place by how large the circle of death around it was. Like a barrier or a moat, though it was easy to cross, it was hard to make yourself take that step from natural footing to the dry crunch of dead dirt, scorched grass, and withered plant life. Crops refused to grow in those places, and animals abandoned them. Salted earth couldn't compare. Percy hated to imagine the result if they were close enough to spoil wells.

When was the last time Knell had eaten fresh vegetables?

Knell finished the pod, chewing slowly and clearly enjoying it, then carefully wrapped the rest back into its bundle.

"What are you doing?" Percy demanded, glaring at him. "I gave it to you to eat, not bruise them up uselessly in your pocket."

"I will!" Knell said quickly. He clutched the bundle to his chest like Percy might snatch it away—he might, he'd thought about it—and pointed at the remains of the cave crab's limbs spread haphazardly around him.

"I really do need to finish that, though. Using these powers... It makes me hungry. Meat helps."

"The peas aren't good enough?" Percy knew he was being an ass, but that had rarely stopped him before, and his annoyance easily won out.

"They're better than good. I was going to save them for after." Knell ran his fingertips lightly over the cloth of the bundle as if it wasn't just repurposed rags clean enough for the job. "They taste like springtime and bright things. I wanted to be able to enjoy them."

Then his stomach growled louder than Percy would have expected of a man who seemed used to hunger. Knell hunched further in on himself, chuckling awkwardly even though Percy hadn't said anything. Percy rolled his eyes.

"Fine. As long as you don't fucking pick at it like before."

"I won't," Knell said earnestly, then snatched up a leg the length of his own forearm and cracked it open at the joint.

Percy grimaced and turned to put his back to the scene, making slow progress through his own dinner to the melody of cracking shells and wet chewing. His stomach churned despite his best efforts to tune out the sounds. This time, at least, Knell ate quickly. Percy glanced back over his shoulder when he heard the gentle crunch of pea pods and a soft, satisfied hum of enjoyment.

Knell had eaten the creature with a sort of grim intensity, but he was picking up each pea pod and inspecting it before taking a bite, savoring each one with that strange curiosity he had. Percy refused to feel pleased by it. Nor by the quiet thank you Knell said when he passed back the empty cloth.

Later that night, when they'd both eaten their fill and nearly all the food Percy had foraged was gone, Percy lay on his side and listened to Knell's whistling breaths. They were back to back beneath the blanket once more. The cavern might have light but was just as cold as the rest of the tunnels and damp as well. They'd set their waterskins beneath slowly dripping rivulets that streaked down the wall to fill while they slept, which eased one of his worries, but the chill of the place was enough to make his bones ache. Percy couldn't even complain about it now that he knew the cold was keeping those awful fucking cave crabs away.

There was just enough scant warmth between them for sleep to begin lulling Percy mercifully from wakefulness. At the sound of a slow, deliberate inhale, he glared at the shadow-carved wall of rock in front of him before Knell even spoke.

"If I did have some sort of large parasitic worm," he started, and Percy dearly wished he'd killed him earlier, "could I consider it a companion of sorts?"

"Go the fuck to sleep, you foul witch of a man," Percy snarled back, not bothering to turn.

He was surprised when Knell actually listened, falling quiet. It lasted a minute or so before he heard a rustle of cloth and the scrape of clumsy movement. Knell's thin back pressed against his and Percy let him settle close without a word. The cave was cold, after all, and the wretch was all skin and bone. He had no interest in waking up next to a dead guide. They still had a ways to go, and Percy couldn't fucking see in the dark.

Shared warmth slowly gathered now that they were closer and Percy could feel the knobs of Knell's spine through the layers of fabric, pressing against him with every breath. It was almost peaceful, and the heat was nice if he ignored the strength of their combined stench.

He'd nearly drifted off when he heard Knell's soft whisper of, "Perhaps I could name it. Like a familiar."

"I'll kick you into the next hole we find," he said, voice heavy with sleep but not relaxed enough to let that sort of nonsense go. Knell's shoulders trembled against his back, his breath gone all high and wheezy in ugly, muffled laughter. Percy ignored the noise along with the upward pull at the corners of his own mouth.

The next day passed in much the same manner as the previous one, aside from the swarm of what Knell insisted were called shell spiders—a name Percy refused to use because somehow, referring to them as cave crabs made the fact that Knell had eaten one raw marginally less disgusting. In short, it was damp, cold, and fucking dark as ever.

Once they left the moss cavern and its welcome glow, the tunnels were wide enough that Knell walked beside him rather than in front, murmuring his usual instructions with one cold and clammy hand closed lightly around Percy's scarred forearm. Percy did his best not to think about the contact and how easily it could be used against him.

No matter how hapless or grateful Knell acted, he was a flesh-mage, and something about the press of these tunnels kept Percy pointedly aware of the fact. The dark didn't change, except for the occasional thin patch of dimly glowing moss that Percy was always grateful to see, but those failed to light up much other than themselves.

Eventually, he noticed the air growing warmer and more humid, his shirt sticking along his spine and against his ribs. Not long after, he saw the faintest shifting light against what he assumed was a tunnel wall, though it looked like more solid darkness, just with some texture where the light hit it. He blinked and glanced away, then back again to be sure it wasn't his eyes playing their usual tricks in the dark.

"What is that?" he asked, hoping Knell would answer about the obvious shifting light and not announce some other horrible, many-legged creature had crawled out of the walls or ceiling without him noticing.

A thoughtful little noise of interest came from the darkness to his right. "We must be farther in than I thought. It looks like there might be an underground spring here, maybe even heated by a vent from the heart of the mountain."

Knell's voice was flat as ever but had a lilt to it that was different than usual. Excitement? Eagerness? Percy couldn't fucking tell. His own response was a wary but desperate longing. He'd never wanted a bath so badly in his life. If there was some horrible demon eel or cave sirens or some other bullshit, he wouldn't hesitate to fight them just for the chance at hot water.

There was no one to fight, as it turned out. Just a large cavern with a low ceiling and a large stretch of water that Percy only recognized in the dark because soft light was reflecting off the water's surface. Where the light came from, he couldn't tell. There was no obvious source, and the colors were constantly changing like seeing candles through a chandelier.

The answer revealed itself when Knell carefully led him closer to the water and Percy's eyes adjusted. Within the spring were tiny pinpricks of light, darting in shifting waves of endless colors. Percy knelt carefully near the edge of the spring, and darkness spread in a wide arc near his boot as the lights scattered.

They were fish. Thousands upon thousands of tiny fish with strange flashing stripes of glowing color down their small bodies. Of all the nightmarish things he'd braced himself for, this was an unexpected delight. Still, it never hurt to be cautious. He looked up at Knell who lurked at his side, the color of his eyes shifting from blue-green to silver as the light from the fish changed with their movements.

"You don't see anything else in here, do you?" Percy asked, pulling Knell's attention from the underwater display.

This close to the water, with fish slowly returning to the edge of the spring, he was able to see Knell glance around for any lurking dangers.

"I don't see anything big enough to be worried about," he said in a tone that he clearly thought was reassuring.

Percy chose not to comment or think about whatever Knell might have seen. More bugs, he decided firmly. Perfectly normal, tiny, harmless bugs. Steam rose from the surface and the whole cavern had a sulfurous smell, but it was more hot water than Percy had seen in an age, and he was not about to waste this opportunity.

The water was blissfully hot and the tiny, glowing fish darted around in schools that looked like small clouds full of lightning, enough of them to reveal the uneven rocks beneath the surface. A few dozen paces in, the water went dark and deep, and Percy was more than happy to stay close to the edge. The bottom of the spring looked as unwelcoming as the cave roof, jagged with loose rocks in some places, slick and sharp where stake-like pillars of mineral reached upward toward twin dripstones hanging low from the ceiling.

As glad as Percy was to be able to see, he was careful not to look up too often. The few times he tried, he was reminded that they were small, weak creatures crawling around like insects under the weight of a mountain, its teeth poised above their heads. The immensity of it made him want to run, made his skin crawl with panic, and he had to look away and try to calm his breathing each time.

But the hot water was nice.

It had felt near boiling when he'd first tested it. Even in the warm damp of the cave the difference was stark, but it only took a minute or so to adjust. It hadn't cooked off his skin, and the tiny fish had cleared a wide circle as soon as his hand breached the surface. Knell watched with curious eyes until Percy demonstrated the water wasn't too hot or some horrid form of clear acid, then dipped his own hand in with a noise of delight. He looked up at Percy with a crooked smile, those ever-shifting eyes glowing through locks of lank hair.

Percy focused on the buckles of his leather armor.

"We're bathing. I don't care if it smells like old eggs, we smell worse," he said, stripping as quickly as he could when he kept forgetting he only had one hand. Or, more accurately, his body moved through motions he'd done all his life and every fumble was a reminder of the loss.

For once, he let the irritation of it sweep past him, too eager for the chance at a hot bath. He didn't have any soap, but he pulled out one of the extra scraps of fabric he had tucked away for a washing cloth. As far as he knew, Knell didn't have anything of his own beyond the clothes on his back and the small knife at his belt that Percy had only glimpsed. If they had to share a washing cloth, he was going to use it first.

The shallow edge of the spring seemed safe enough—and unlikely to suck him into some hellish pit in the world—with a few larger rocks that had settled along the bottom, providing a slightly more comfortable place to sit that didn't consist entirely of gravel or spikes. The water reached his hips when he stood and up to his ribs when Percy eased down onto his chosen seat to scrub himself with determination.

He glanced up when he heard Knell step into the water with a splash, arms flailing as he slipped almost immediately, catching his balance just in time to avoid going down completely. By the time he was done splashing about, his section of the spring was nearly dark as the fish fled from the chaos. Only to return a moment later with all the sense a creature with a brain the size of a pinhead was capable of.

Percy snorted, amused and ready to mock the man when the words dried up in his throat, forgotten before they'd formed. Knell's sickly gray skin was bared to the air, all thin limbs and knobby knees. A thin trail of dark hair over his stomach led down to his groin, where the water protected any modesty he might have. His ribs were shadowed hills and valleys, and his hunched posture was ever-present, but what Percy stared at were the scars. He'd seen the brands near Knell's wrists, thick ridges of shiny circular scarring on the soft skin of his inner arms, but he hadn't known there were more.

Knell had told him, hadn't he? A brand for each prison. Prisons he had broken out of. Percy hadn't asked if there were more, hadn't thought about what that meant, how many times Knell must have been strapped down and pressed with hot iron. But there they were, marching up his arms to the elbow in a matching set of four, with one extra standing out on the inner part of a bicep. Smaller scars were littered across his skin, ones Percy could easily recognize as mementos of street scraps, knife fights, and other badges of survival, but the worst of them all was at the center of his chest.

The more fish that returned to weave between Knell's legs, the more clearly Percy could see it. The scar looked like someone had done their best to carve out Knell's heart and then set him on fire out of spite when it didn't work. A large, uneven white line right along the center of his breastbone, with mottled burns spreading outward from it in a starburst pattern that reached from his sternum to his collarbones, carving off half of one nipple. The damaged skin looked tight, and Percy could see the way it pulled every time he shifted. No wonder Knell hunched constantly, the scarring made it impossible to hold himself entirely upright.

A soft huff of breath knocked him from his thoughts, and Percy knew he'd been caught staring. Not that he'd been subtle about it, gawking wide-eyed, his cloth forgotten in hand when he should have been washing himself. Knell's expression had a wry edge of self-deprecation as he touched the fingertips of one hand to the mass of scarring at his chest. His eyes had taken on that flat, dead look they got sometimes, the one that always sent a chill up Percy's spine.

"A delightful little reminder of my initiation."

"You let them do that to you?" Percy asked, disturbed.

Knell waded carefully to sit on another rock nearby, sunk at just enough of an angle that he had to lean slightly to stay upright. It would be funny if Percy wasn't distracted by the battlefield of his body.

"No," Knell said. "They collected the most troublesome prisoners and used the Great One's power to, well, make us easier to handle."

The information brought Percy up short and he shook his head, recalling what he knew about the first rising of the cult. "That can't be right. The prisoners used the ritual to escape. All the guards were killed."

He hadn't seen the site himself. The flesh-mages had turned the former prison into their stronghold, and the place was crawling with undead monstrosities. But there were few people in the kingdom who didn't know the story. The blast had shaken the nearby hills, and wildlife in the area had never been the same again. Troops had been sent by the king, but each campaign ended in such crushing defeat that he'd had to stop before soldiers began to openly rebel.

Knell leveled him with a wry look, not quite amused and deeply tired. "They did die, that much is true. But they were the original cultists, tapping into a force they only thought they understood. They would sacrifice troublesome prisoners in order to gain the power they needed to control the rest of us."

Knell leaned forward to scrub at his arms with his hands, avoiding Percy's eyes as he continued. "It kept everyone in line, easy as a little chant, and we were nothing more than puppets. Hard labor with no complaints. No escape attempts. They'd found the perfect solution, and it was all approved by His Majesty, the king himself." His voice was steady but had grown bitter by the end.

Percy took that in, weighing the implications of what Knell was telling him. He finally resumed scrubbing harshly at his own skin, wanting to feel clean again and not sure he'd ever accomplish it.

"You're saying none of you wanted to be under the god's thrall?"

"No, there were some who thrived. They embraced the power it gave them and lured in more who shared their mindset. There are always people hungry for power, hungry to hurt others, and it would be a lie to pretend every prisoner there was secretly kind." Knell's mouth twisted in a sad attempt at a humorless smile. "But no one there *asked* for it. I had no idea how they'd been controlling us until it was my turn on the altar."

His voice faltered there, and Percy's own morbid curiosity made him ask, "What did they do to you?"

Knell still avoided his eyes, though he gave up the half-hearted attempt at washing and seemed to be simply soaking up the heat of the water instead. Percy made a mental note to insist he scrub properly before they got out. Then Knell's words made him forget anything else.

"I was trying to break out. I'd planned it for weeks, learning the guards' schedules, keeping track of who went where, noting which prisoners were taken and never came back. I thought it would be just like every other prison. There had to be something to exploit.

"The troublemakers would be taken further into the prison, to one of the levels between the cells and the mines we were forced to work. I knew that if they were killing them, there had to be somewhere to dispose of the bodies, and I'd never seen a large enough chimney for cremation. I assumed they were being dumped into the quarry surrounding the prison. Beasts roamed there and would take care of any remains, or they might be lost into the earth. If there was a chute leading out, I figured I could scale the sides and avoid the biggest danger. I'd done something similar on my third escape."

Knell tapped at a brand halfway up his forearm with a brittle smile and a brief glance in Percy's direction. Percy was struggling to imagine Knell scaling a wall, but then, he figured the man had been a bit less ragged at the time.

He was also feeling deeply grateful that his own prison break experience hadn't involved any corpse disposal chutes or chimneys as escape routes. When you had plenty of rowdy bandits at hand, it was easy enough to storm a small jail.

"The biggest risk was letting them drag me there," Knell continued. "I had no idea what their process was, but I had assumed they, like most guards, liked to take a little time to burn off some steam before killing. Not exactly a pleasant thought, but a risk I was willing to take if it meant escaping. I'd been trapped there for weeks, my days spent in a haze I couldn't shake, doing hard labor and unable to step out of line or even ask for water."

His fists clenched and unclenched just under the surface of the water, scaring off curious little fish, then welcoming them back to dart between thin fingers, careful not to crush any by accident. Percy could do nothing but watch, caught up in the story. Knell's flat, thready voice, laced with old pain.

"If only I'd known what I was getting into, I might have been content to," he paused there, brow furrowing, and then met Percy's eyes briefly. A real smile, slanted and small as it was, broke through for just a moment. "No. I wouldn't have been able to stay. That place was terrible. But I might have thought of a better plan."

The flash of humor faded, and his shoulders curled further in on himself as he continued. "It's funny, I don't mind these tunnels even though I spent my worst years in similar ones. But to be forced into another cell, with four walls trapping me in like a tomb? I can't stand the thought of it."

Percy could see the shiver go up Knell's body, the truth of his words in the tremble of his hands. Knell paused, needing to gather himself before he could go on.

A better man might have told him to stop, not to relive this painful memory, but Percy had never claimed to be a good man, had proven beyond doubt he'd never be a better one. He wanted to know how a person could get scars like Knell had and live. So he sat, quiet and cruelly patient, for Knell to continue.

It wasn't a pleasant memory by any stretch of the imagination, and recalling the details was like grasping fistfuls of sand, but he'd shied away from it for so long that it was almost a relief to speak it aloud. Knell wasn't sure he'd ever done it before. The other acolytes had either been there with him or had joined later of their own accord, and those were not the sort Knell ever attempted to spend more time than strictly necessary with.

But Percy was curious. Hadn't interrupted him at all, and Knell *wanted* to tell him. Wanted to try and recapture all the details his fog-shrouded mind could gather so there might be one person in the world who understood the truth of it all. Whether Percy believed him or not didn't matter. He could think Knell invented the whole story, that every word was a lie, and Knell wouldn't care because at least Percy had let him speak it and *listened.*

This man, who knew Knell was a wretched creature and had no qualms about saying so bluntly to his face, was willing to hear him out. Knell doubted Percy knew how much that meant and fought to find the words so he could spill it all out before Percy changed his mind.

His own mind fought him as it always did, unable to recall any particular faces, but the smell of the place, the exact shape of the rust-colored stain on the floor in his cell, those he remembered with clarity. How had he gotten himself dragged away? It came back to him slowly, like liquid seeping into cloth.

"I made myself into an annoyance. Pushed boundaries, asked for water, stepped out of line too often. The first few times just got me knocked around a bit, yelled at, but there was one guard in particular who really loved looking down at us. You know the type. Always droning on about respect for our betters and knowing our place, scum of the kingdom, the same old speech."

Percy wasn't looking at him, he'd moved on to scrubbing industriously at his legs and feet with a scowl. Did Percy think Knell was making some sort of comparison? Perhaps there were some similarities, but while Percy also thought he was scum of the earth and told him so, at least now it was true. And Percy had yet to beat him, despite all his threats, so really, they weren't the same at all.

Apparently, he'd paused too long while sorting those thoughts out because Percy surprised him by urging him on with a gruff, "Perfect target?"

"The perfect target," Knell confirmed with a sense of smug satisfaction he'd forgotten about until it suddenly rushed back along with the memory. He felt a grin pulling at the sides of his mouth and let it, just to experience the ill-fitting memory of simple mischief. He could almost recall the guard's face.

"I timed it perfectly. Along with our daily meal of gruel, I'd managed to convince someone to give me a second cup of water and shoveled it all down just before we were lined up. He was easy to piss off and liked to go for soft targets."

Percy looked up at him, clearly fighting down a grin of his own. "You were willing to risk a kick between the legs?"

Knell huffed a laugh, short and crackling where it fought up through his chest, but it was a delightful feeling. He wasn't sure the last time he'd had a proper laugh that wasn't the result of nerves or misdirection. More than an attempt to break rising tension or just to hear a sound that wasn't ringing silence.

"It was a calculated risk. He normally went for the groin after someone was already on the ground. I'm not sure what I said to him, but it must've been good because I remember how his face went all splotchy and purple." He couldn't recall the man's hair or eyes, but the color his face had turned in indignant fury was clear in his memory, even if his vision would never capture it again.

"Sure enough, he got me in the gut, hard as he could."

"Just like you'd hoped, huh?"

Knell smiled a little wider. It felt wrong on his face, and he looked down at the water so Percy wouldn't have to see the black of his gums. "I'd put a royal fountain to shame. It was worth getting hit to ruin his uniform."

Percy let out an amused hum, and Knell counted it as another win. He cleared his throat, which felt scratchy and rough after speaking so much, though the damp air helped a bit. The rest of the memory wasn't so amusing, and the smile faded along with his humor. Percy had finished scrubbing and was looking at Knell meaningfully.

Knell stole a few extra moments by easing himself to the floor of the spring, careful of the mineral deposits rising like stakes. Most weren't too sharp, but that didn't mean they would be pleasant to slip and fall onto. He rubbed at his limbs, feeling filthier than ever but too listless to really try and scrub. He wasn't sure he wanted to find out if the feeling would stay once the grime was scraped from his skin.

"That's all it took, really. My memory's a bit foggy after that, but I'm sure there was a beating in there I don't mind forgetting." He watched as fish darted under the arch of his bent knees.

"I thought it would be, not *simple* exactly, but an act. Believe it or not, I've played a convincing corpse a time or two," he tried to joke. Percy huffed, but there was little humor in it, his dark eyes too intent, seeing too much of Knell, so he looked back at his knees, at the grey skin he'd been trapped in, and not for the first time, wanted to claw it all off.

He scooped up a palmful of water and drank, ignoring Percy's noise of disgust. The water was warm and soothing along his throat, with a strong mineral taste to it. Not exactly pleasant, but hardly the worst.

"I remember being dragged into a large chamber, the floor between floors, and realizing I'd made a grave mistake. There was no chute, no exit. There were more cells, and the people inside..." His voice had gone rough again and Knell swallowed, wishing his

memories of those prisoners would fade like the rest, but they were clear.

The bodies, gaunt and moving in ways they shouldn't, too fast and too slow all at once and entirely wrong-feeling despite being unable to see them clearly, like crawling shadows with glowing eyes.

Maybe that's what he looked like to Percy.

*Wretched.* That's what they had been. What he was now.

"There was an altar," he said just as Percy had begun to speak, cutting him off. Now that he'd started telling the story, he couldn't bear to leave it unfinished. "Just a big stone block, but something about it set off my instincts. I wanted to run. The moment I saw it, something in me knew what would happen."

He gripped his knees and dug in his nails, the sharp pain of it anchoring him. "I didn't get away. Obviously."

"Hey." Percy said it hesitantly, the softest his voice had ever been towards Knell, but he wasn't listening.

"It's a bit muddled up here," Knell said, tapping at his temple with a chuckle that felt too sharp around the edges. "I remember them tying me down. And the knife. Not a big one. I remember thinking it looked like something you'd use to cut fruit. It was very sharp."

He dug his nails in harder. "I think I was screaming. I could swear they were going to reach in and take my heart. I had to die, right? There was so much blood. And then it started to burn."

There were little black crescents in his skin when he let go of his knee to press a palm hard to his chest, trying to push the sensation back inside. "There was this... this *light* coming from inside me. As if something was trying to crawl out. Some part of the ritual must have gone wrong. They couldn't seem to make it stop when they wanted. It just kept burning, and it wouldn't let me *die,* and it never seemed to end."

Knell looked up when a large hand covered his, prying his fingers from his other knee where thin trails of black blood were slowly dripping toward the water. Percy was close now. When had he moved?

"Later, one of the older acolytes told me the guards had gotten careless, spoke some of the words wrong or something. I don't know. I don't remember any of that, wouldn't know how to recognize it if I did. Not much need for a ritual when it's always in your head. By the time I woke up, everything was rubble. The acolytes were all unscathed by the blast, though. We thought the power had protected us, had given us a gift. We were fools, and we learned the truth quickly after that."

Percy was staring at him with wide eyes, but Knell was done, the story complete, and he felt empty of words. So he just stared back, feeling far from his body, except where Percy was gripping his hand. Making sure he didn't hurt himself.

His fingers twitched at the thought and Percy quickly dropped his hand. Knell let it fall into the water with a splash that sent the fish darting away in a wide circle and missed the touch immediately.

After some time—maybe a moment, maybe long minutes, Knell was still too far gone from his body to tell—Percy shook him by the shoulder until Knell managed to look him in the eyes and resettle in his own skin enough to understand the words he was saying.

"It's done. They're gone." It sounded as if he'd repeated it a few times, and Knell nodded. Not because he agreed—they might be dead, but they weren't gone, they were right there in Knell's mind, in the changes they wrought in his body—but so Percy knew he understood.

Percy made a small, relieved noise in the back of his throat. His voice was gruff, but his eyes were worried. "Alright then, enough of all that. Maybe just relax a bit. Enjoy the water and stop sharing such depressing fucking stories."

That startled a snort out of Knell, closer to a laugh than he expected, and Percy's mouth crooked up at the corner for a flicker of a moment. "That's it. Now sit right there and let me enjoy the peace for a bit, yeah?"

Much to his surprise, Knell did feel better. Percy didn't offer any pity or platitudes, and somehow, it made Knell think he understood in some way. Knew they wouldn't help, but a distraction would. So he did as Percy told him to and clambered back onto the rock. He still felt too displaced to sit upright, but that was fine. When he lay down on it, the water cradled him up to his shoulders in soothing warmth. He let his mind drift as he stared at the ceiling of the cavern, where its countless fangs hung over him, and felt oddly at peace.

# CHAPTER 8

## *Percy*

Percy wasn't sure what to believe. He'd known this man all of three, perhaps four days now, but if his words were true, it changed everything he knew about the origin of the Chaos Bringer's cult. Perhaps it didn't make a real difference in the end. The god had to be banished, and the flesh-mages it commanded needed to be stopped, that was simple fact. But the same could be said for many people without a trace of magic, chaos-tainted or not. Percy knew better than most that plenty of people killed and wrought havoc just fine on their own.

The story seemed true enough, or at least Knell's view of it. In the short time he'd known him, Knell had proven to be a shit actor, and the haunted look in his eyes was not easily imitated.

Not even the beloved Prophesized Hero had questioned the stories they'd all been fed. It was so easy to believe that prisoners would turn out evil, whispering occult secrets beyond their comprehension until the day they rose up to slay all of their guards and claim the prison fortress in the name of their new god.

He thought about the King, the *former* king now, hopefully cut down by his unwanted successor if the golden boy had any sense. The former king had been endlessly hungry for power, always scheming up some complicated new bullshit Percy and his crew would inevitably have to unravel. It wouldn't surprise him in the slightest if it had been the King's hand stirring this particular pot of horrors. Experimenting on prisoners knowing that no one would care, least of all the guards given total control over their well-being.

It was no secret that Percy wasn't a man who readily changed his opinions. He could out-stubborn a mule—had gotten quite good at it, considering how often he was left to handle the packing of their camp supplies for their journeys. Basil had been an ornery old mule with a mean kick, bless her cranky soul. Percy got into a good number of fights thanks to someone telling him what to do or think, as if he were too stupid to understand facts himself. He'd spent most of his life among liars, thieves, and grifters. Had done it all himself at one point or another. It took a lot more than some charm and smooth words to change his mind once it was set. But it could be done.

He'd gone from mocking some nobody farm boy to believing in his destiny with bone-deep conviction, even if he'd never stopped disliking the fool. The golden boy himself had been a waste of perfectly good air, but his cause—the one they'd all been fighting for, freedom from tyranny and the looming threat of a god-wrought apocalypse—was one he still believed in.

Knell didn't have a grain of charm in his whole body, and that was part of why Percy couldn't dismiss his words. The wretch was painfully, hauntingly earnest. That lost look in his eyes, the way he'd sunk his ragged nail into his own skin as if he wanted to claw it off. Percy had moved to stop him before he'd realized what he was doing. He couldn't deny the relief he felt when Knell regained some level of awareness, looking at Percy rather than through him to something better left in the past.

Actually, the wretch in question had been awfully quiet for a while now. After his newest shit-awful stroll down memory lane, Knell laid himself out across his chosen stone like a rag, leaving just his head above the water to soak in as much of the spring's heat as he could and hadn't so much as twitched since. Percy had turned away and given himself a second scrubbing just for the pleasure of feeling scoured clean and gotten lost in his thoughts. Usually, Knell would have made some grating attempt at a conversation by now, but maybe he'd been too wrung out by telling his story.

"Hey," Percy began, not bothering to turn. Not sure why he was breaking the silence at all.

No answer.

"You. Wretch." There was still no answer.

Percy frowned and took a breath, expanding his chest to take the steamy air deep into his lungs. Despite everything, the water had him thoroughly relaxed. Even his usual irritation was hard to grasp, so he let it go. The man hadn't talked his ear off in a while, Percy could play nice for a bit.

"Knell?" he tried.

Still nothing. Percy frowned harder. He had never done well with being ignored. He opened his eyes with a grunt of annoyance and looked toward the other man, then leapt to his feet with a curse as Knell, skin flushed fever dark and face slack, slipped off his rock and under the water.

Nearby fish fled at the motion and left Percy splashing around in the dark. He stubbed his toe on some unseen pillar and knocked the stump of his arm painfully against the slab of rock before his other hand closed around a thin limb. He gripped hard and hauled Knell up from the water, nearly losing his own balance, and quickly wrapped his free arm around the man's waist, grateful to find that he'd grabbed a wrist and Knell was mostly upright, if alarmingly limp.

It was too risky to try and stumble his way to the edge of the pool in the dark, even if it was just a few paces away. There were loose rocks and goddamned floor knives all around. He was still figuring out his own balance with one hand missing; Knell might not have much mass to him, but he was still a full grown man gone completely deadweight in his arms. If Percy went down, with his luck they'd both end up impaled and bleeding out in this fucking cave.

So he waited impatiently for the fish to return, then mapped out a safe looking footpath and slowly made his way to shore with what he hoped was an unconscious travel companion rather than a dead one.

Knell was hot to the touch when Percy got him laid out on a flat stretch of ground, his skin flushed a dark grey. His chest wasn't moving, so Percy rolled him over onto his side and thumped his back hard—once, twice, and the third knocked a cough loose.

Knell coughed hard, then heaved, spitting up water. He couldn't have swallowed too much, Percy thought, but Knell kept heaving like it was lodged in his throat or lungs. Percy cursed, trying to get a decent grip when he was missing a fucking hand and they were both slippery. He thumped Knell's back a bit harder, and the man nearly slammed into the stone floor, barely catching himself on his hands as his back arched on a particularly painful looking heave. Then, with a wet retch, a thick black sludge poured from Knell's mouth. The smell of it was pungent and foul, sickly sweet with rot strong enough that Percy gagged.

Knell gasped in a deep breath, and Percy was honestly surprised that he could breathe in with the smell right under him. Black liquid spread to pool around his hands, mingled with water dripping from the sopping mess of his hair. Knell tilted, his brief return to consciousness over and about to fall face first into the sludge he'd hacked up. Percy hauled him upright just in time for Knell to fall back against his chest in an uncomfortable tangle of limbs and wet nakedness.

Percy stared down at the man sprawled across him, limp as anyone made entirely of angles could be, streaked with stinking black filth he'd coughed up, and still too warm to the touch. He hissed out an impatient sigh and gathered Knell's limbs into some semblance of order. Dragged him bodily over to lay him out on a cleaner patch of cool stone within the visible glow of the spring, far from the stinking puddle of liquid black *whatever* that was.

Finally settled, Percy let the man cool off for a few minutes while he spent longer than he'd like to admit fumbling around in the near dark of the place to locate a decently sized dip in the ground for his purposes. After a quick check to make sure Knell wasn't as dead as he looked, Percy busied himself with soaking up the washing cloth and wringing it out to fill the dip with water.

He didn't know what the hell that black fluid was, but he wasn't about to poison the spring with it. The fish might be brainless little things, but they had provided light when he needed it and he wouldn't return that favor with unnecessary cruelty.

Once he had enough water collected—he hoped, he really couldn't see for shit outside of the spring and was going by feel more than anything—he began scrubbing the wretch clean with firm efficiency. He found himself pausing over the thickly scarred skin of his arms and chest before shaking away the distraction and continuing on, though perhaps he took a little extra care to wash the scars with a gentler touch.

Thankfully, the foul black liquid washed away easily. By the time he was done, Knell was just as painfully underfed but had at least lost the layer of greasy filth he'd worn like a second skin. The biggest improvement of all was the smell. Beyond the lingering sulfur from the spring, there was no more of that hair-curling, unwashed stench clouding around the man. He was still unconscious but breathing easily, and his skin no longer felt overheated.

Percy dropped the now grimy cloth into the puddle of remaining water and thought about what to do next. He considered washing his clothing as well, but between the damp air of the springs and the chill of the tunnels they'd never dry, and he'd likely end up sick. He eyed the man laid out like a corpse next to him and found himself staring at the ragged spill of his lanky hair.

It had been bothering him every time they had enough light to see by. How unkempt it was, stringy with grease and who knows what else. Percy kept his own hair cropped close to his scalp for plenty of reasons, but if he'd bothered growing it out, he'd at least try to keep it clean. Some of the men in his former company had been almost as bad, and Percy was always put off by their lack of basic hygiene.

Well, he thought to himself as he prepared to make a few more arduous trips to the spring for clean water, if the wretch didn't want it washed, he should have woken up sooner.

Awareness came at Knell with a bludgeon and a grudge. He woke suddenly and was immediately confused. There was an arm around his head holding him in place, and his cheek was squashed into a firm, warm chest as a hand massaged his scalp. If this was an attack, it was a wildly ineffective one.

His limbs felt like uncooked dough, boneless and slow to respond, so he simply didn't move, bewildered and curious. He recognized that this must be Percy, for lack of other plausible options, bizarre as this one was. As far as he could tell, Percy had him clamped in a headlock and was... washing? His hair?

Knell must have twitched or changed his breathing because Percy went abruptly tense and still. In a moment of pure instinct, Knell decided to pretend he was still unconscious. He kept his eyes closed and evened out his breathing as he let his body go limp. After a moment, Percy went back to his task. Knell lay there, his mind racing and blank all at once as he filed away details.

They were both damp and naked, and it had been a very, very long time since Knell had been near anyone in that state. But Percy was warm and not hurting him beyond the general confusion of the situation. He didn't feel injured or sore anywhere, and the strong, steady heartbeat under his ear was soothing. As was the unintentional massage Percy was giving him as he worked to clean Knell's hair, grumbling so low that Knell felt it more than heard.

Percy *tsk*ed softly in annoyance each time he encountered yet more tangles and knots, but his fingers were gentle as he eased them loose and washed each section thoroughly with what felt like a damp cloth.

Unexpectedly, Knell felt a hot, prickling sensation behind his eyes and had to work harder to keep his breathing steady. In a rare stroke of luck, Percy was preoccupied with an especially troublesome patch of hair and Knell was able to get himself under control, though the hot ache in his eyes stayed.

Knell lay there, too caught up in the drum beat of Percy's heart, the warmth of a body so close to his own, and the gentle hand working fastidiously through his hair to care about anything else. How strange this whole situation was; Percy's uninvited but not unwelcome decision to wash Knell's hair when Knell himself might have been tempted to just hack it off to save the trouble. Not to mention his own decision to playact at sleeping just to feel it for a little longer.

The thoughts slid away, and he let himself float on the sensation of a touch that didn't hurt.

After a small, blissful eternity and nowhere near long enough—though his backside had gone numb—Knell realized Percy had finished. The sensation and soothing rasp of cloth scrubbing section by section had stopped, and now Percy seemed to be checking for any last tangles by running his fingers through Knell's hair.

Knell braced himself for it to be over, but Percy kept at it, almost like he was petting him. The heartbeat under his ear was slow and steady, and just beneath it was the faintest hum of contentment.

Then Percy's fingers caught on damp curls near the nape of Knell's neck just hard enough to make Knell flinch with a little hiss, and Percy jerked as if he'd forgotten he was holding a whole person. Knell was released quickly but not unkindly and he blinked up at Percy, disoriented from the sudden lack of touch and warmth.

Percy stared down at him, looking caught out and as confused about it as Knell was.

"Hi," Knell said, at a loss of what else might be appropriate for this sort of situation.

Percy seemed just as lost and refused to meet Knell's eye, scowling fiercely at his forehead instead. "You passed out from the heat. I cleaned you off and washed your hair because it was fucking disgusting and I was tired of looking at it."

Not sure what to say, Knell sat up slowly, lightheaded, and looked down at his body, doing his best to ignore the immediate urge to hide it all away. Not out of modesty—he didn't have much of that anymore, if he ever did—but the idea of Percy's gentle touch on this body he hated, all knobs and angles, grey and wretched, made his eyes feel hot again.

He pushed the thought aside to marvel at the fact that he was *clean*. His skin no longer looked grubby or felt coated in filth. He lifted an arm to sniff under, which made Percy snort beside him, and while he hardly smelled *nice*, the stench he usually carried was all but gone.

Lastly, he inspected his hair, and his chest ached at seeing it fall in front of his eyes in damp curls instead of greasy, knotted lanks. His fingers trembled as he tugged lightly on a loose curl and he had to swallow hard when it felt soft to the touch.

He dropped his hand, afraid of the rising tide of emotions welling up. Some deeply seeded instinct told him that if he let them close in, he'd be lost to it, but it was harder than he remembered to gather himself and push them back.

Percy cleared his throat, his expression awkward and tense. Knell was relieved to have something outside of his head to focus on and knotted his fingers together to keep from reaching out to touch Percy's arm.

"Thank you."

His voice felt as creaky as it sounded, and Percy gave him a searching look, then grunted in acknowledgment. Percy stood, stumbling slightly with what were probably numb legs, and headed carefully in the direction of their piled clothing. While the fish provided some light, it probably wasn't strong enough for Percy to move confidently in, especially this far from the water. Percy must have carried him here.

There were flashes of memory. Being hauled from the water, rough stone under his palms and knees, the awful taste in the back of his throat from heaving up... something. The last of the Great One's influence, he suspected. After long rituals in their attempts to perfect the summoning spell, many acolytes had expunged similar black sludge, even if they'd eaten nothing that day. Knell had always felt slightly more clear-headed after, until the familiar muffling fog crept in again.

What that meant now, he wasn't sure. He'd never known why their bodies occasionally purged them of the substance. It wasn't as if the Great One had ever explained the effects it had on them, if it even could. Maybe it would kill him. But it might not, and he suspected the real consequence was the looming wall of unchecked emotions lurking in the back of his mind. That had the potential to go very badly.

They needed to get out of here.

Percy was saying something to him about their clothes and having to wear them filthy. Knell couldn't find it in him to care as he forced himself to stand on wobbly legs. He skirted around the puddle of black bile and pulled on his clothing while Percy did the same.

Individual words washed over him, but he nodded and did his best to hum a response in the right places until they were ready to go. Percy eventually fell silent, and if Knell had been allowing himself to acknowledge any emotions at all, he might have felt a twinge of loss at that, but he needed to get them moving. The spring had been a lucky find, but eventually something would come along to drink or bathe and Knell didn't have the energy to handle whatever it may be.

They needed to find a place to rest, somewhere Percy didn't have to depend on him because Knell had a very bad feeling that the moment he let his guard down, he'd be useless. And there were too many dangers lurking in the tunnels to leave Percy alone in the dark.

# CHAPTER 9

## *Percy*

The rest of the day's journey was spent in unsettled quiet. Not silence, as Knell still had to guide Percy through the dark, but the flesh-mage was more subdued and on edge than usual.

The warm spring waters had rejuvenated Percy, but they'd also relaxed him. Even the variety of horrible dangers that might be lurking around them couldn't keep his eyes from drifting shut. Exhaustion dragged his steps and made it difficult to tell how long it took them to find the next cave opening. The hours of trudging felt like days.

Their camp for the night wasn't a proper exit for anything larger than a rabbit, but when Percy peered up through the hand-sized hole in the roof above him, he could see tiny points of stars winking their farewells as the faintest hints of dawn began to seep over the sky. It was such a relief to see that he stood there and stared until his legs began to waver.

Knell had tucked himself into the far side of their small space, more of an alcove than a proper hollow, but Percy wasn't willing to abandon this window to the surface to see what he was up to. They'd eaten sparingly as they walked, finishing their rations, and Percy hoped they'd find a proper exit soon, or they might starve in this damn tunnel. What did surprise him once he managed to look away from the circle of sky was that Knell wasn't sharing the view. He had drawn into himself like a dying spider, limbs curled in tight to his body.

Percy sighed, possibly out loud, and set up their bedding, as pitiful as it was. When that failed to entice Knell from his spot, Percy moved to sit closer. If he had to get this man to talk in order to get some decent rest, then so be it. The cave was too damn cold to sleep without the little weasel at his back.

"You ready to explain what's made you so miserable?" Percy asked. He wondered briefly if his uninvited washing had done this. He winced and conceded that may be the case. He'd have been furious if anyone had taken the same liberties with him. "Listen, I shouldn't have—"

"It's gone," Knell interrupted, breaking his long silence and looking up to meet Percy's gaze with that lost look in his eyes.

Not the same vacant stare he'd occasionally take on before, but the way people look when they've seen too much battle and haven't quite grasped that it was over.

"The last of the Great One's hold over me. It's been lifted."

Percy eyed him. Knell didn't seem particularly happy about it. Stunned maybe. "That black shit you coughed up back at the spring?"

Knell looked at him, brow furrowed, like he'd forgotten he was talking to someone, then slowly nodded.

"Yes. I think so."

"You're telling me it still had control over you this whole time?" Percy asked, but it came out more weary than alarmed. Every bit of him was begging for sleep despite all the bullshittery happening. He couldn't quite work up his ire.

Knell frowned deeply in thought, his head shaking in a single slow negation.

"Not controlling me. I think it's too far gone now for that, but its influence was still in me, part of my blood." Percy watched the muscle in Knell's jaw tense a few times as he struggled to explain.

"It kept everything," he motioned toward his head with a vague hand gesture, "muffled. Emotions, sensations, they were all so *dulled*."

He said it with the kind of awe a person feels when they realize stags are much larger up close than they were expecting. The opposite of the soft wonder he showed at all the small pleasures of the world. Percy preferred the latter, it was less discomfiting.

"And now it's all... unmuffled?" Percy asked, not quite keeping up. "Why would dulling your senses be useful?"

"Apparently, the first few trials of sacrifices went badly."

Percy wasn't sure he wanted to know what qualified as bad if Knell's experiences were a product of the successful trials, but he kept his opinion to himself. Knell looked like he was having a hard enough time saying this once, and Percy knew that feeling all too well. If Knell was anything like him, then he may never attempt it again, and this seemed like something that would fester.

"They kept killing themselves or simply dying from the strain," Knell explained.

Fucking lovely. Percy's appetite soured in his gut, which was for the best since they were out of food. He didn't want to ask, but that good old morbid curiosity got the better of him, as it always seemed to.

"Why?"

"When the Great One made demands of us, there was no translating it. It's not words or even a language." Knell scrubbed a hand over his face in frustration, and Percy waited him out.

"It's all sensation and colors that shouldn't exist. Something like *agony,* so big a body can't hold it. We didn't get orders so much as a," he gestured again, rolling his wrist as he tried to put it into words, more animated than Percy had seen him before. "A concept of what needed to be done was hammered into our minds."

Knell huffed out a humorless laugh as he dropped his hands into his lap like their strings had been cut, his expression bleak.

"Minds are so easy to break. And the things we were made to do..." His voice went ragged, those strange eyes glossy as they welled up.

Percy had no idea how to respond, panic rising in him at the sight of tears. He was bad at comforting people at the best of times, and he sure as fuck didn't know how to react to *this.* There was nothing comforting to be said, and a pat on the shoulder would be condescending at best, even if Percy had wanted to initiate contact with a flesh-mage so clearly struggling to control his emotions.

Not knowing what else to do, Percy looked away toward the wall of their little alcove, hoping to give the wretch—to give *Knell*—some privacy to pull himself together.

From the soft sounds of wet, hitched breathing, it wasn't going well. Fuck. What the hell was he supposed to do with a crying cultist? The man had probably seen horrors Percy's nightmares couldn't compare to. He struggled to think of something to say, wincing at each useless platitude. The minutes stretched out painfully while Knell tried and failed to cry quietly.

In the end, Knell spoke up before Percy could put his foot in his mouth with his usual tactlessness.

"Could I..." Knell started, his voice a watery croak.

Percy looked his way, eyebrows raised in question when Knell trailed off. "Can you..?"

Knell mumbled something, then fell silent, picking at his nail beds so roughly Percy wanted to slap at his hands before he began to bleed.

"Spit it out," he groused, like the charitable and comforting person he was.

Knell took a breath, sniffled thickly, and looked anywhere but at Percy, but he spoke clearly this time.

"Could I hold your hand? Just for a little while?"

*No* should have been his immediate answer, and Percy nearly voiced it, but Knell's shoulders had already hunkered in even further than usual, his expression resigned to an answer he knew was coming, and suddenly Percy was angry. This wretch barely knew Percy but already thought the worst of him. And maybe Percy hadn't given him a single reason to think otherwise, but damn if it didn't piss him off that Knell assumed he'd be too afraid to offer the simplest of comforts while the man fell to pieces.

Percy grit his teeth and made himself stare down the truth of it. Knell had not accused him, in word or deed, of being a coward. Percy had acted the part all on his own. If Knell wanted him dead or to toy with him in some hideous way, he had dozens of opportunities by now.

Percy was angry, but it was at himself. He'd never been a coward, and he wasn't about to get into the habit now.

His internal argument had gone on for too long, and Knell was roughly scrubbing at his eyes. Uselessly, because they refused to stop leaking, and his thin frame was shaking with repressed sobs.

"Sorry," he said in that pathetic, creaky voice. That was the last straw.

Percy clicked his tongue in annoyance, and when Knell still hid behind his knuckles, he bit back an annoyed sigh.

"Hey."

Knell finally looked at him, frozen in a half flinch like he was bracing for a blow, then dark-ringed eyes went wide as he stared at Percy's outstretched hand. And kept staring, even as tears continued to track down his hollow cheeks. The bags under his eyes were swollen, his thin mouth twisted up and trembling, and his nose was running. It was not a pleasant picture. Percy was tempted to rescind his offer but instead gestured with an impatient crook of his fingers.

"Hold it, or I'm taking it back," he said, and thin hands darted out to latch on quicker than Percy expected.

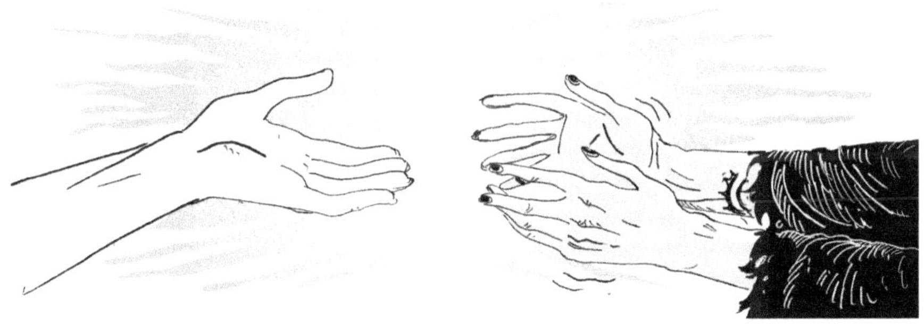

Percy let Knell pull his hand closer, cradling it like something precious before clasping both of his own hands around Percy's. All spidery thin with knobby knuckles against Percy's blunt fingers and rough calluses.

To his dismay, Knell stared down at the hand in his like he'd been gifted a chunk of pure gold, then turned his wet eyes toward Percy with all the intensity they were capable of—how had it somehow become *even more*? Unable to hold that gaze, he turned his head and scowled at a patch of moss, ignoring Knell's soft, warbled thanks.

Knell's fingers were cold despite the heat from the springs earlier, so Percy closed his hand over them in an attempt to trap some of his own heat before the leech stole it all. Knell clung to Percy's hand like it was the only firm hold in a flood that would sweep him away. A sympathetic burn started up behind his own eyes as Knell's breathing hitched on broken sobs, but Percy ignored it. He'd always hated that his eyes watered anytime someone else cried. The last few days had been a lot, that was all.

He planted his elbow on his knee and rested his chin on his wrist. Narrowed his focus to the rough brush of unshaven bristle against the newly-scarred skin of his stump as he stared hard at the wall, waiting for the storm to pass. If he had to wipe his own face once or twice, it's not like Knell would notice, preoccupied as he was.

Knell curled around Percy's hand and let himself shatter.

Emotions crowded in on him like they'd been waiting for the opportunity to collect on their various debts. They rolled over each other, ever-shifting and each so strong he struggled and failed more often than not just trying to tell them apart as they dragged him into their undertow. Despair, familiar but sharper than ever without the leash of the Great One's power, hooked his ribs and hauled him down while a small, white-hot ball of joy burned painfully in his chest.

Fear and something bottomless that the word sadness couldn't even begin to encapsulate was filled with newer, tiny bubbles of hope fizzing to the surface. He was drowning, falling from a great height, weighed down yet floating, and unable to catch his breath either way, so he cried.

Being so vastly overwhelmed was not a new sensation, but it was the first time he'd experienced it without the rush of dreaded power. This was all his own, and there was no magic in it at all. He sobbed and then cracked out a half-hysterical laugh before the next one.

It was gone. Truly gone. His head was a mess of knotted memories and emotions he might never be able to untangle, but he'd outlasted a god, no matter who had finally banished it. He'd spent that last few years—how long had it been? What year was it now? He could ask Percy. *He could ask*—expecting to die. Even looked forward to it at times. Yet here he was, against all odds.

Alive.

He clutched Percy's sturdy, warm hand in his and cried, purging it all. The good, the bad—there was so much bad, but the good was so new and so bright.

Percy's fingers curled around his own, rough and gentle, an anchor stronger than stone, than iron. More real in this moment than the very mountain they were sitting under the ancient weight of.

When the worst of the maelstrom passed, Knell felt wrung out. Thoughts were sluggish and his head felt hollow behind the ache of his still-damp eyes. His body was strangely light, a dandelion puff that might float away at the slightest breeze.

He was curled around Percy's hand, all but folded in half with that warm anchor clasped between his own, his forehead pressed to the cushion of palm at the base of Percy's thumb. He stayed there for a moment longer, absent of any thoughts other than a vague desire for Percy to card fingers through his hair again.

Instead, he forced himself slowly upright, wincing at the ache across his chest and the rapid series of loud cracks from his spine after so long in his cramped position. He scrubbed his face with his sleeve and felt grimier for it, which was a new sensation. He was usually too filthy to notice a little extra.

"You done? Because I don't exactly have hands to spare."

Percy's voice startled him, cutting through the fog, but it wasn't nearly as gruff as the words implied, and he could have easily taken his hand back if he'd wanted. Knell was holding it clasped in one hand, but there was no denying that Percy could escape with little effort. It was his choice to let Knell take comfort for as long as he needed. Knell didn't have the words to express how grateful he was for that.

The appearance of Percy's rare dry humor was a good sign as well and the easiest thing for Knell to latch on to.

"I'd be happy to loan you one of mine," he teased weakly, his voice ragged to his own ears.

Percy looked away from the wall to stare at him in surprise, then a sort of amused disgust. "You'd better not mean that in a literal sense."

Knell snorted out a startled laugh. The wordplay hadn't occurred to him. "I hadn't, but now that you mention it..."

"Shut your fucking mouth," Percy sneered, but his eyes were bright with humor, and Knell realized he was smiling in return, his cheeks aching with it.

And still, Percy hadn't pulled away. Knell gave his hand one last squeeze between his own and let go. He was surprised that Percy didn't immediately try to wipe it clean of Knell's touch but simply shook it and flexed his fingers as if to get the blood flowing properly again.

"You could get revenge if you wanted," Percy said, his good humor gone, eyes serious.

Knell stared at him, head still half empty and slow to keep up with the shift in conversation. "What do you mean?"

"The original experiments were approved by the old king, that's what you said. Well, he's likely gone now, what with a new king and all, but it's not like he actually ran the kingdom on his own. All sorts of royalty and the rest of the court have their greedy hooks in these schemes too. Put your mind to it and I'm sure you could leave a few less of 'em in the world."

Knell tucked his hands into his sleeves, hoping to retain some of the warmth left by Percy's hand while he considered the words. Was this some sort of test? From the start, Percy had considered himself Knell's enemy. By that logic, was he trying to see if Knell wanted to take out some of his pain on him?

Was he hoping Knell might agree and leave on some harebrained vengeance rampage that would lead him right into the hands of those hunting him?

None of the theories fit quite right.

Maybe Percy was just curious.

*Could* he find and kill the nobles who had a hand in the experiments that led to his fate? Now that he thought about it, he probably could. It would be difficult, but it was possible. Finding them, at least. Killing was horribly, nightmarishly easy.

But...

"I don't want revenge," Knell replied at last with a shrug in response to Percy's dubious expression. "It won't return what I lost, and I'm so tired of killing. If I started, where would it end?"

Percy's frown deepened, but Knell suspected he knew exactly what Knell meant. He gestured at himself and at the greater world beyond the little alcove they were sitting in. "I will never be the same person as before, and we both know I'll never be able to blend into a normal life. Not with the way I look. Everywhere I go, people will take one glance and know that my death will only improve the world."

He clutched at his elbows within his sleeves and tilted his head to watch Percy's reaction closely. "Does that mean I should kill them too? Wipe out villages who would happily see me dead?"

Percy swallowed hard but held his gaze, not offering an answer.

Knell looked away and shook his head. "No. I don't want that. If all I have left is a bit of time to walk alongside—" he nearly said *a friend,* but Percy had been clear that they were to be temporary allies at best, "—a companion before my inevitable death, then I want to enjoy it as long as I can."

Percy's whole posture had gone slack with surprise, his brow pinched in confusion as he listened intently.

Face suddenly warm, Knell confessed the secret hope he'd been holding onto so tightly he'd barely admitted it to himself. "And maybe, somewhere on the other side of these mountains... there might be a place where the Great One's influence never reached. Where I might make a home, even looking the way I do."

His voice trailed off into a whisper, as if saying the words too loudly might snuff that tiny flame of possibility. His vision wavered as more tears welled up and he stared down at his lap, unable to look at whatever Percy's expression might be. "Silly, isn't it?"

Beside him, he heard the shift of fabric as Percy crossed his arms and leaned back with a huff. "Of all the goddamned flesh-mage cultists, I had to end up with the one optimist of the lot."

Knell peeked in his direction, surprised to hear Percy's gruff voice sound almost fond. It might have been his watery vision, but he could swear he saw the slightest upward curve at the edge of Percy's mouth.

Somehow, that was enough.

# CHAPTER 10

## *Percy*

Percy wasn't sure what he'd expected after the emotional outburst the previous night, but a cheerful Knell hadn't been it.

Cheerful for Knell, at least. The man had a sort of kicked dog air about him at any given time, but he was certainly more expressive than before. More animated while speaking and more restless than ever, always touching things, picking at his robe, running fingers along the walls of the alcove, poking curiously through the pack of supplies. Now that Percy had allowed him to hold his hand—which apparently erased a boundary he certainly hadn't meant to—he kept touching Percy as well.

Little darting touches, like he was too nervous to linger but couldn't help himself. Fingertips catching at Percy's shirt to get his attention, thin hands curled over his scarred arm to lead him through the dark, little pats to his upper arms, shoulders, even his chest or back as if Knell was worried he'd disappear like some fucking wizard.

If he'd been able to simply vanish, he'd have done so long before now, but he was disgruntled to note that the touches didn't actually bother him all that much. As long as they weren't a surprise.

That morning, he'd slapped Knell's hand away and told him off the first time he'd been startled by a sudden touch to his back in the dark. Knell, surprisingly, had listened and stuck to holding his arm when they were traversing the deep dark of the tunnels. Though it seemed like he made up for the lack once they found the occasional patch of moss-carpeted tunnel where Percy could see.

Percy was self-aware enough to recognize himself as a man who was annoyed by anyone existing in his personal space and had been known to snap at any unwanted touch. Yet he found himself less annoyed than he expected to be by Knell's... everything. Clearly, he'd spent too long with the man and adapted to his oddities.

Knell talked so much *more* now. His raspy voice gained confidence as he chattered on endlessly, his free hand gesturing as he spoke. Though Knell was careful to never drop the loose guiding clasp he had on Percy's arm, he more than made up for the lack of motion in one hand by doubling his efforts with the other. Even without light, Percy could feel the displaced air and knew he was doing it.

The thought amused Percy enough that the side of his mouth tilted up in a smile, which he forced into a scowl when he heard Knell briefly stumble over his words. Best to remember that the man could see him perfectly fine.

If pressed, Percy might admit that the chatter helped pass the time in those long, dark stretches, though he had complaints about the fact that most of Knell's stories were morbid, horrific, and depressing as hell. The occasional few from his life of petty crime before his final imprisonment were entertaining.

Escapades in escaping previous prisons or outwitting pursuers as he made off with their goods, only to lose them twice as fast. Percy suspected that many of the details were either embellished or made up entirely, but he was glad for the distraction. Knell's memory had more than a few gaps, but he claimed it was clearer than it had been in years. Whatever the case, it was obvious that Knell's luck had been shit all his life.

Percy wondered if he remembered his real name. He didn't ask, and Knell never brought it up.

When Knell managed to drag Percy into a conversation, as unevenly balanced as it might be, he listened attentively. Almost too intensely—bright eyes surrounded by nothing watched Percy from the dark—but he remembered the things Percy said. Asked questions sometimes, thoughtful ones. It had been a long while since Percy had anyone to talk to who cared—genuinely cared—about his opinions.

Half the day passed that way, Percy adjusting to this new, just as strange but slightly less absent and downtrodden version of Knell, when they came across an opening to the forest.

The jagged crack of an opening was just large enough for someone Percy's size to fit through, if they were determined enough. He was grateful for the streaks of pale light that carved holes in the darkness after hours of solid pitch. Even more so when they got close enough for him to see that the opening was around shoulder height, and he wouldn't have to find a way to climb up to the ceiling of the tunnel. Again.

He and Knell peered out, shoulder to shoulder and squinting into the sudden daylight. As his eyes adjusted, the first thing Percy noticed was the difference in the trees. Less of the gnarled and knotted thick-barked trees of the deeper valley, most of these were knife-straight with a mix of black and white or red bark. Newer trees were as thin as his smallest finger, while others were big enough to hug and only reach halfway round. He knew there were places higher on the mountain where towering ancients blocked out chunks of the landscape, their trunks wide around as five men linking arms and tall enough to part clouds.

It was enough to orient himself in a general sense, and he was glad to know they were still aimed to the north. They'd made decent progress as well. The road that led back toward the deeper valley they'd come from was easier to walk but also far more winding. Even those who knew the forests well would be at least a day behind them.

And for good reason, the trees here grew plentiful, but the ground was near barren of vines or grass. It was an uneven stretch of steep mountainside, sheets of pale grey stone layered up the slope like scales. The rocks were fragile and broke off in thin sheets, sharp as flint, that dropped onto anything below with the weight and finality of an executioner's axe.

They would need to be very careful from the moment they stepped foot out of the caves. He told as much to Knell, who watched him from under the fall of distractingly soft-looking curls. It was infuriating that hair so neglected and foul had ended up so soft and lush after a single, if thorough, wash. His hand twitched at the memory of how those curls felt between his fingers back at the spring, like fine silk. It was a damn good thing Knell had been unconscious. Percy would be mortified if he'd been caught, lost in the act of petting a flesh-mage's hair, of all things.

"If you fall, I'm not climbing down to get you, so watch your step," he concluded firmly.

Knell nodded, opened his mouth, closed it, cleared his throat, and repeated the cycle. When Percy glared at him, he grimaced—or tried to smile, Percy wasn't sure.

"You aren't planning to part ways here?" he asked. It looked like it pained him to get the words out.

Percy couldn't deny that the thought had occurred to him, but he also couldn't deny how foolish it would be. While the patch of land around this entrance looked to have decent footing, he knew most of the pass was much more treacherous. Not even the wild mountain goats, creatures built from concentrated hubris and seen casually wandering sheer cliff faces, dared graze here. Abandoning the tunnels would get him nowhere but to an early grave.

"Not this time," he admitted, refusing to acknowledge the definite smile that caused. "But this spot looks solid enough to risk exploring. Might even find some food if we're lucky."

They were lucky, as far as luck could go in this scenario. The trees were clustered densely enough that as long as he didn't look down at the steep angle of the ground, Percy could avoid the worst of his vertigo. Early spring rains had lured out stubborn patches of greenery between cracks in the rock, and he was almost tempted to give a prayer of thanks for the gift, but he knew better than to draw the attention of a god—any god—when he was in so precarious a spot.

Tender mustard greens and piles of chickweed dressed the base of the trees like skirts, sharing what small amount of soil there was. Nearby, some tenacious burdock had staked its claim on a fissure in the rock and clawed its way outward with plenty of young leaves.

There were small mushrooms as well, but none that he recognized, so when Knell pointed at one with a look of askance, Percy shook his head.

"This isn't a place I usually harvest and I'm not familiar with those. Best not to risk it." He said it with some regret, but hungry as he was, he hadn't lost his reason.

"What about this?" Knell asked as he carefully navigated over to where Percy was harvesting all the chickweed he could reach. Hairy stems or not, it would get eaten.

When he looked up to see what had been brought, Percy squinted at the small spotted mushrooms, their color garish against the pale grey of Knell's palm, squinted up at Knell, and then sighed deeply.

"How do you only manage to find the most poisonous things possible?" He watched Knell's whole figure droop even more and rolled his eyes. "Go wash your hands, and don't touch your fucking eyes. I'll explain once you're clean."

Their luck had been twofold, which made Percy suspicious, but he knew better than to waste any good fortune that he found himself in possession of. Thin trickles of water flowed in small streams that more closely resembled waterfalls at their angle. They ran clear, tasted clean, and none of it mattered because they needed water too much to be picky about it.

Waterskins refilled, hands carefully washed, and all the food they could fit into their pack gathered, there was just enough daylight left to sit and bask in it. He found a spot near the cave entrance wide enough to sit and lean back against the wall of rock, his feet braced against a decently sized tree and arms crossed as he relished the warmth.

Beside him, Knell sat as well, and Percy counted the seconds of blissful silence until Knell couldn't contain himself any longer. "I thought you didn't know the mushrooms here."

Percy snorted and pointed without uncrossing his arms or opening his eyes. He knew exactly where the mystery mushrooms were. "I don't know *those* mushrooms. Some things grow in isolation.

But I know all the other plants, they're pretty common along this side of the mountain."

"What about the other side?"

"Never been, but I suspect they've got plenty of 'em over there too."

Knell went quiet, but Percy knew he wanted to ask more, could tell by the rhythm of fingers rubbing fretfully against fabric. He always rubbed at his sleeves like that when he wanted to talk. Percy ignored him. They had another long stretch of who the hell knew how long in the dark to chat, Knell would figure himself out sooner or later.

"And the second mushroom? I've eaten those before, and they were harmless."

Percy looked at him, ready to refute the claim, then paused. Took in Knell's storm-cloud skin and bright irises with their unnatural hue, the whites of his eyes a veined grey. Remembered the way he ate a raw mutated cave crab without hesitation. A resistance to poison seemed less far-fetched than it first sounded.

"If that's true—hush, you're the one who told me you can't see colors, plenty of mushrooms have spots—*if* that's true, then you've got a stronger stomach than the average person. One of those would put me out of commission for a week, if not worse."

Knell's gaze drifted toward the small patch of spotted red and white mushrooms he'd picked from earlier with an interested look. "Yes, you're right about that. Perhaps I could—"

"You will *not* mix your poison mushrooms with my food," Percy said with a tone he'd developed commanding misfits and ruffians with more pride than sense. Knell settled back down.

"Ah. Yes, that could be bad."

With one last narrow-eyed stare to make sure Knell wasn't about to get any funny ideas, Percy closed his eyes once more. He listened to the rasp of cloth under fingertips and counted the seconds until—

"It could be useful, if you ever needed it. To poison someone else." His voice wavered, like he knew it was a terrible suggestion but couldn't help but point it out.

Percy's lip curled up on one side in an automatic sneer, pulling at his scar, and he nearly spit out his usual response. But stopped before it could leave his mouth because his usual response was *I don't need anything more than my sword or my two hands to end a fight.*

Well.

It sounded a lot less impressive now that he'd lost his sword along with his main hand. So he went with his second best response.

"Poison is a coward's weapon," Percy said. "There's no honor in that sort of killing." The argument was rote, the sort of thing said because everyone could agree.

"Is there much honor in any killing?" Knell asked instead of nodding in agreement like people usually did.

He didn't ask it slyly, as if he wanted to trap Percy with his own words, simply with the same detached interest he seemed to take in every detail of the world with. He was more interested than detached now but still had the air of not being bothered either way by the answer, just curious to know it.

"People kill in all sorts of ways, some by accident, some slow and cruel. Every time I've done it, it's always just felt sort of terrible."

That brought Percy up short for a moment, stumbling in the comfort of his well-worn argument. He rarely felt guilty for killing. It was usually a very brief flash of violence and a choice between them or himself. He had yet to meet a person trying to kill him that he hadn't wanted to outlive.

Unluckily for all who had tried before—prophesied heroes aside— he was damn good at winning fights. But, if he was honest, that was little more than the lizard part of his mind screaming for him to duck, to strike, to end things. All he felt at the end of it was tired, angry, and depending on who it was, a little satisfied at outliving them.

He'd killed friends before, comrades who had turned on him or been lured to the other side of whatever political bullshit they'd found themselves neck deep in. He could kill Knell if needed and lose far less sleep over it if he had to. And yet, he was reluctant to linger over the idea of it. In the last few days, Knell had shown more comradery to Percy than some mercenaries he'd walked beside for years. The man had risked himself more than once for Percy's safety, and whether it was some misplaced idea of friendship or sheer foolishness, Percy couldn't disregard that truth.

Yes, Percy would kill him if needed, but perhaps he could admit to himself that he didn't particularly *want* to anymore. There would be no honor in it because there never was.

He wasn't about to agree with Knell out loud though, so he merely grunted in return, refusing to answer the question. Soon enough, Knell moved on, nattering about something or other as they both watched the sun dip low on the horizon.

The night passed without incident, the two of them crammed against the wall of the tunnel, shivering from the cold winds. Percy had refused to move away from the entrance, determined to soak up all the moonlight and view of stars he could before the next day's return to the mountain depths.

The greens filled their bellies, but he knew they'd need something more substantial soon. He could afford to lose weight and still keep pace, but Knell was already skin and bone. If he lost any more, he'd be swept off the side of the mountain at the slightest breeze.

Thus, it was with yet more good luck—and Percy was now deeply wary of future calamities—that they arrived at another opening in less than a day's travel through the dark. An opening barely wide enough for Percy's shoulders and covered in a thick netting of vines and brambles. It took the both of them, dagger edges probably blunted for the effort, to cut their way out.

That first deep breath of loamy forest after the stagnant tunnel air was worth all the swearing and thorn scratches. He stood to take in a few deep lungfuls before he got tired of the hopeless scrambling he could hear behind him and turned to haul Knell bodily out of the dark. Knell looked like a rat dragged from its den, ragged robes more dust and dirt than black wool, hands held close to his chest like little claws, and squinting blearily around as his eyes adjusted to the late afternoon light.

*Horrible man*, Percy thought, though the voice in his head sounded discordantly fond. He blamed it on the lack of sleep.

They'd made it beyond the rocky shale of the pass and back to more lush forest. Percy had already spotted some promising looking berry patches along a steep incline. It must have recently rained because the ground was damp, muddy where leaves didn't cover, and he didn't relish the idea of having to keep Knell from taking a tumble. The man's bones had to be fragile as a bird's if he'd spent the last few years surviving on scavenged cave creatures. And frankly, Percy needed some time to himself.

"Stay here and gather some food. *Only* the plants you recognize as safe," Percy instructed, shouldering his pack and handing Knell the squares of cloth they'd designated for foraging. Knell took them and squinted up at Percy, one eye clamped shut against the glare of the sun.

"You'll be back?" he asked.

Percy, already busy navigating the dense springtime overgrowth, waved him off absently with a hand he no longer had. "Get to it, only so much daylight left."

Stomach full of sweet, tart berries and twice as many tucked carefully into his pack along with plenty of other greens and roots, Percy began his much less eager trek back toward the tunnels. The sun was dipping low, and he didn't want to risk the muddy path back in the dark. He'd stopped several times to take in the quiet murmur of the forest, the welcoming smell, the plant life all around, and been tempted to keep walking without turning back.

But those same familiarities meant they were near the base of the mountain once more, too close to the kingdom's major trade roads. He might not have seen anyone today, but he knew mercenaries were roving. Which meant the caves were still their best bet. The pass would have slowed down most, but he had a man out for his head that now had wizards at his beck and call. Teleportation spells were the highest magic, expensive as hell and twice as rare. Something only royalty had access to.

No one would deny the request of a king who had just saved the world from ending.

Percy was focused on hunting down a few more berries in an effort to avoid lingering on his all but inevitable capture when he looked up to track the approaching storm clouds on the horizon. A break in the trees opened up a view into the forest beyond, and Percy realized that he recognized the valley below. He abandoned his search and waded carefully through the grasping undergrowth, wary of loose rocks and anything that might be slinking within the knee-deep ground cover, until he had a better angle to see into the bowl of the valley.

Yes, he knew that far rock face. Had seen it nearly every day for years and regularly on his returns between raids, then later, quests. He hadn't realized they'd gotten so close to his old mainstay village because he normally arrived from the eastern pass on the far side of the valley. Tracking down the location of the cult's summoning ground and the place of the final battle had led them southwest, toward the main holdings of the kingdom. A direction Percy had generally avoided traveling before.

The village was too far to be visible from here, but he had a decent vantage of the road leading into the valley from the south. While there was a thin flow of traffic, he didn't spot any royal banners or tabards among the tiny figures traveling below and something like hope settled warily in his chest.

A little further would place Percy and Knell firmly in the woods he knew best. They could hole up in one of the caches Percy had dotted around the area to stash away goods or to avoid the law on the rare occasion it reached this far north. It meant a respite from the damned tunnels, and a chance to plan out a way to resupply in the village without being seen.

He eyed the far side of the valley, mentally considering and discarding the most obvious options. Several could be known by his—*former*—men, but he'd always been a paranoid bastard, so there were one or two that might still be around if time and weather hadn't taken too much of a toll.

Relieved to have a plan of action that relied on his own skill and involved moving through territory he knew well—territory he could fucking see in—Percy made his way back down the incline. Best to find his wayward cultist before Knell managed to eat something deadly or fall into a ditch trying to be helpful. Sure, he'd been getting better about asking Percy before eating things, but the man couldn't seem to keep from touching everything like a child who was rarely let outside.

Percy winced and considered that it might be exactly the reason why, but damn it, unlike a child, Knell was old enough to know better than to poke at things in the forest. Especially things with distinctive markings that indicated they were dangerous, no matter what Knell said about being able to digest them. He'd had to slap the man's hand away from several rash-inducing plants, a gut-rotting mushroom, and a cluster of beetles that would have released a nauseous cloud of stench if they'd been startled.

Thankfully, he found Knell not far from where he'd left him, carefully navigating a large patch of berries, which had sprawled out into a dense knee-high carpet between the trees. Knell reached in to pluck berries from between tangles of thorny vines with all the fierce concentration of an archer aiming to take down a sparrow mid-flight. His mouth was stained from berry juice, though he'd at least collected enough to weigh down the cloth he was holding by the corners to use as a pouch. Percy generously waited until Knell had pulled his arm free, two large berries held delicately in his fingers, before he spoke.

"Those'll kill you, you know."

Knell froze, eyes wide and staring at Percy in alarm before they narrowed. He eyed the plant carefully, then pointed at a nearby vine with confidence that was almost convincing. "These are dewberries... or maybe blackberries? They both have white flowers and look sort of nubby, but you told me it's too early for those, so probably dewberries."

He leaned far enough toward the thicket that Percy wondered if he'd fall in, but to his disappointment, Knell managed to keep his balance. "The thorns are small, and it hasn't grown very high either."

When Percy stayed silent, Knell looked up at him again, his expression hesitant. "You said the nubby-looking berries were all safe. Right?"

He was right. On all counts, he'd remembered the identifiers Percy had told him, and not just the vague recollection most people held onto after Percy explained how to tell plants apart. They only bothered to remember enough to keep them from eating anything immediately deadly and quickly forgot the rest. Knell had been paying attention, actually memorizing the things Percy had been telling him just to fill the silence with something that was at least useful. He hadn't expected Knell to actually take it all to heart.

Knell was looking more nervous now, fingers twitching against the bundle of collected berries, and Percy shook off his surprise to keep the man from pulping the fruit before they could eat it.

"No, that's... that's right. I'm surprised you remembered."

The backhanded compliment earned him a crooked smile and Percy couldn't have that. Knell would start thinking he liked having him around.

"Now stop fidgeting before you bruise up all the fruit. It's time to move."

"It needs some work, and quickly if we want to avoid the worst of the storm, but it'll do. It'll fucking have to since it's the best option I have." Percy had his hand and wrist on his hips as he glared at Knell in a way that made it clear he wanted neither comments nor suggestions.

Knell considered the half-collapsed excuse of an entrance to Percy's hideaway. It resembled a root cellar in that it was a hollow space dug out of the hill, hidden by what used to be a decently sized cover made of branches and leaves meant to mimic the ground around it.

"Were there other options?"

"I've got others that are probably in about the same shape, but this is the only one with enough space for two people to fit," Percy said absently, kicking away broken branches from around the shelter and looking around with an assessing gaze.

"What?" he snapped when he noticed Knell staring.

He didn't seem angry, more like he was nervous. Did he really care what Knell thought of the hideaway? That wasn't why he'd been staring, Knell could sleep anywhere. The fact that this had a roof and something resembling a door was the height of luxury. What had caught his attention was Percy's words.

"You picked the one big enough for both of us," Knell said with a cautious flicker of hope, delighted when Percy's expression went slack with surprised realization right before his brows drew sharply down in denial.

Knell thought that Percy would surely have abandoned him this time, yet here he was, making plans for the both of them. But maybe he should have kept the observation to himself because Percy was wearing the stubborn expression of a man ready to deny any and all evidence, no matter how damning. Knell braced to shrug off the rejection. It was enough that Percy had gone through the effort to find a place to share.

Percy clicked his tongue against his teeth in annoyance. "Would you rather find your own? Maybe I just wanted the extra space for myself."

It wasn't an outright denial, which surprised Knell. They were making progress after all.

Knell took in every detail of Percy's expression and posture, not sure if the question was rhetorical, but Percy seemed mostly at ease. It was a good thing he was such a terrible liar, Knell's social skills couldn't fill a mouse's spoon halfway, but he could read body language just fine. He let out a little huff and felt his mouth crook up in a lopsided little grin, rusty as an old hinge.

"No, you found it for *us,*" he said, rocking on his heels as warmth lit up his chest. "You were being kind."

Percy cringed away from the words as if they were an accusation. He sneered at Knell, whose grin only widened and an old, long-buried spark of mischief flared briefly. This was teasing. He was *teasing* Percy—like they were friends!

Percy pointed at him, eyes narrowed, and Knell's smile fell away, too unpracticed to keep it in place. But that spark hadn't faded, and by the way Percy glared at him suspiciously, it showed on his face somehow.

"Don't insult me or I'll abandon you here to fend for yourself. Just you wait and see. I know these woods, I could vanish off to another cache."

Knell held up his hands in surrender, all out of clever comebacks and not eager to push his luck anyway. Percy glared at him for a moment longer, then ordered Knell to gather some sturdy branches and *do not, for fuck's sake, wander off and get lost*, or Percy would leave him to the elements and the wildlife.

He had begun to suspect Percy said it so often to convince himself as much as Knell.

It was hard work to prepare the space before the storm closed in, but Percy was efficient in his instructions and managed three times as much on his own. In short order, they had enough sturdy branches to satisfy Percy, a decent length of rope, and plenty of braided long grass to make up for the rest.

Percy had set to the tedious task of tying them all together with one hand, which required sitting on a fallen tree and clamping branches together between his knees as he threaded the rope into sturdy knots. Knell offered to help but had been sent away with an impatient gesture, which was for the best. Knell might have two hands, but lacked the knowledge, and they didn't have time for him to be guided through the process. Instead, Knell mostly hovered anxiously as he looked over Percy's shoulder until Percy's patience ran thin. He set Knell to the task of sifting through the remains of what had been stashed inside the hideaway.

Most of it was unusable. Rags that used to be clothes, long since ruined by wet and mold. Some unidentifiable burlap sacks of food, chewed up by scavengers or long since rotted to so much mulch. A pair of boots in the same state—a shame because they looked about the right size to fit Knell just before they'd fallen apart at the slightest touch.

But judging by Percy's reactions, the real loss was the cooking pan Knell pulled from its half-buried place in the dirt. A sturdy iron thing that had been so irreparably rusted that Percy took a single look at it and sighed mournfully.

"Damn, but I'd have liked to actually cook some food for once."

"You can cook?" Knell asked, setting the pan aside with the rest of the ruined goods.

Percy glared at him, but Knell was starting to decode them and this one was barely annoyed. "You think I do nothing but eat berries and leaves? They've held us over, but that's not going to work for long. We need real supplies we can supplement with foraging, not the other way around."

Knell nodded, warmth flaring up in his chest again at Percy's use of *we*. He tried to keep his face impassive, but Percy's scowl deepened, so he must not have done a very good job of it.

Percy jerked his chin toward the supply pack. "Spade's in the side, you can dig the shit pit."

Knell decided the wisest path would be to do as he was told.

In the end, the little hideaway managed to meet Percy's standards—barely—just as rain began to drizzle down. Branches were lined up and tied tightly together, layered with a mixture of mud and grass, topped with broad, glossy leaves to help keep out the wind and rain. He was still muttering to himself about temporary measures and severity of the rain, but Knell's attention had lost any sense of focus. Percy noticed and shooed Knell away from anything important with gruff orders to wash his hands and eat before he keeled over.

Knell was grateful to crawl into the cleared space and eat his portion of dinner, a chance to rest his eyes as well as his overworked body. Inside the hideaway, it smelled of freshly turned soil and crushed grass, so different from the air of the caves. The scent was comforting in its newness, and Knell fell asleep before Percy could finish whatever he was fussing over outside.

Thunder woke him several times as it rumbled overhead, but exhaustion pulled him back down just as swiftly. Until it didn't, and Knell found himself wide awake, unable to get back to sleep again. Percy was nearby, warming the space as surely as a bonfire, his breath slow and steady with slumber. While the air felt humid, no water had leaked into their little den, and Knell had to hold himself back from patting Percy's arm proudly.

He wasn't willing to abandon this pocket of warmth, even if he felt restless, so Knell curled deeper into his robes and closed his eyes. The storm had lightened to a steady rain, and all sorts of nocturnal creatures were calling out into the night. The low hoot of an owl, toads croaked back and forth, the endless chirping of crickets. There was so much life happening, it was a wonder he'd managed to get as much sleep as he had.

Underscoring it all was the patter of rain, and Knell was struck by an epiphany; the reason he couldn't sleep. The sound of it was *almost* soothing. The longer he focused on it, the more clearly he remembered rain falling on city streets, the smell of it, the way it acted as his lullaby. Yet at the same time, it felt completely detached from himself, a childhood friend whose name he couldn't remember. Memories that felt like a passage he'd read in a book. The thought left him too unsettled to appreciate the sound but compelled enough to keep prodding at it like a sore tooth.

The rain eventually moved on, but Knell's restlessness didn't, so he carefully navigated himself away from the siren's call of Percy's warmth with great reluctance and eased past the lean-to that made up their doorway. It had worked well to keep them dry, though a good portion of the mud and leaves had been washed away by the rain. He'd make sure to compliment Percy on his ingenuity, both because he suspected Percy didn't hear that sort of thing very often and also because he made the most amusing faces.

Knell looked up at the sky, expecting clouds, but was surprised to see a blanket of stars stretched out overhead. They were brighter than he remembered, and he knew, in some distant part of his mind he couldn't be bothered to pay much attention to, that they didn't used to be so colorful. Nor would the occasional star chase one another in bright swirls and bursts and streaks, comets at play.

How long had it been since he'd seen colors without having to tap into his unwanted power, never mind hues so bright? His patchwork memories of the night sky seemed dreary in comparison.

Enchanted by the sight—like a theater show with an endless cast of characters laid out above him on an impossibly large stage—he fumbled his way toward the fallen tree nearby and fell as much as sat down in front of it. He leaned back against the rough bark to keep watching the sky without the risk of hurting his neck or getting dizzy enough to fall over. And then he just watched.

Time had lost all meaning. Knell was still caught up in the dance of starlight when Percy's head and shoulders suddenly blocked his view of the sky. A deep frown cut across his face, and his brows were drawn low.

"How long have you been sitting out here?" Percy asked. Memory issues or not, Knell was sure he'd never known anyone else who could fit a scowl into their voice like Percy could.

He also noticed that he was damp with all the moisture meant for morning dewdrops and chilled enough to be shivering. His eyes ached and felt dry when he blinked up at Percy, afterimages of the stars lingering in his vision. It had to be a lingering effect of the Great One's change in him, seeing things most other humans couldn't. Either hallucinations or actually peering between the stars, he didn't know. Since it hadn't done any real harm, he didn't much care either. It was rare, in his experience, to be left with something that didn't hurt. With something so surprisingly beautiful.

"I couldn't sleep," Knell said instead of answering, because he'd lost hours without even noticing and Percy wouldn't like to hear that.

Percy glared harder, unconvinced by the weak misdirection, but eventually looked away with a familiar click of his tongue. Knell might not have regained his old charm, but he could still outstare Percy, at least. It was nice to be able to push back in little ways and not be punished for it. Percy might huff or snarl, but he had yet to do worse than smacking Knell's hand to keep him from hurting himself in some way or other.

"Don't blame me if you're exhausted today. What the hell were you staring at?"

"The stars. I haven't had the chance to just... sit and enjoy them in years. Not sure I ever tried, really. There are so many beautiful colors up there." Knell gestured toward the sky, where the dancing colors had faded back into monochrome shades of grey with the approaching dawn.

Percy shot him a strange look at the last part, then dropped to a crouch next to Knell, who sat up but didn't bother to do more than rub his arms in a futile attempt to warm up. "Let me see your eyes."

Percy didn't wait for Knell to respond before his hand was gripping Knell's chin in a firm but gentle hold so he could get a good look. Knell's face went warm at having Percy so close. Dark eyes darted back and forth to inspect Knell's, his perpetual frown settled in place.

"What did you eat?" Percy asked bluntly.

Knell stared at him, lost. "Eat?"

"Yes. Your pupils are huge, so don't try lying to me. If it was something dangerous, better to know while you're still lucid." Percy eyed him critically. "Mostly lucid."

Knell couldn't help but snort a little laugh, which wouldn't help his defense, but he was too amused to hold it back. "Nothing. I didn't touch or eat anything, I swear."

The look on Percy's face made it clear he didn't believe him but was reminding himself that Knell wasn't his responsibility. Something he said often, yet every action he took revealed the opposite.

"Fine, but if you die or get the runs, it's your own damn fault. I've got things to do," Percy said as he stood. But he held out his hand to help Knell up as he scowled toward the trees.

# <u>*CHAPTER 11*</u>

## *Knell*

They were tucked away up in the slope of the valley after a morning's travel. Close enough to town to hear the faded clamor of noise—and if Knell peered through the foliage at the right angle, he could see a bit of the road leading into the village—but far enough that Percy was relatively sure no one would stumble across them. According to him, this wasn't an area frequented often, long since overgrown with poison ivy that was rumored to be the result of a spell gone wrong.

Percy said that he hadn't seen any such evidence, and Knell agreed. There was no lingering feel of magic, no familiar coppery bite at the back of his throat or swirls of color in his vision. He didn't say any of that out loud. It had taken hours for Percy to stop eyeing him suspiciously for side effects of whatever he imagined Knell had imbibed, no need to get him started again.

"Stay here and watch for trouble," Percy instructed, narrowing his eyes at Knell who raised his hands in surrender.

He had no interest in walking into a town as he was. Knell may have a hood to hide his face, but it was the hood of a very distinctive acolyte's robe, and it would catch as much notice as his grey skin. When Percy failed to look convinced, Knell sat on a nearby stump and did his best to look innocent.

"What should I watch for?" Knell asked before Percy could voice his disbelief.

"People, for starters," Percy said with a pointed look at Knell's general being, which was fair enough and easy to do. Knell was always on alert for people in general. "Keep an eye on the road. Watch for kingsmen or any of those poncy fucking banners they like to carry around. I'd bet there's a bounty for cultists, dead or alive."

There was something nervous about Percy, in the small ways he shifted his weight while he spoke rather than planting his feet as he usually did. Like he couldn't decide between avoiding Knell's eyes and staring right at him as if daring him to argue. He'd suspected for a while that Percy was not simply a man on the run but someone who needed to avoid the new King's attention in particular. Knell kept the thoughts to himself and simply nodded.

"And if I do see them?" he asked.

"Run. Hide. I don't know, what the hell do you usually do to avoid getting caught?"

"But how do I warn you?" Knell clarified.

Percy's face was set in the frown that meant he was more confused than angry. "You don't. If they're that close, either I'll notice and make my own escape or I'm shit out of luck. Nothing to do with you. And to be honest, I doubt being seen with you would help me much at all."

True enough, even if it made Knell nervous. He frowned right back at Percy but didn't attempt to get up. "You'll come back, though?"

Percy clicked his tongue dismissively, eyeing the stretch of forest between them and the village and adjusting the pack on his shoulders. He'd left about half of their dwindling supplies, along with the blanket to bundle them all in, with Knell to make room for any purchases he was hoping to buy or barter for. He also carefully settled his ragged cloak over his shoulder to keep his missing hand hidden.

"Haven't got much choice. I hate those damned caves, but they're probably the only route out of this fuckoff kingdom that won't be crawling with the royal guard and every bounty hunter this side of the mountain."

"And you'll come back here?" Knell persisted, just to be sure.

There were few things that frightened him anymore, but the thought of having to return to solitude without knowing if Percy was safe was one of them. Percy was surly and rude and bluntly mean, but he was also generous and smart. He was an anchor in the times when nothing else seemed to make sense. When the world felt too big and Knell too small to ever truly exist in it. His sharp practicality cut through the noise in Knell's head and kept him grounded. He was a warm comfort at night when Knell could lay still and listen to him breathe, and if he was very careful, he could press his back to Percy's and feel the faintest thump of his heart beating.

In truth, Knell didn't want to be alone again. Certainly not at the cost of Percy's company.

Percy shot him an annoyed look. "Just wait here."

And with that, he left, weaving quietly between trunks with the effortless grace that came to him whenever he was surrounded by trees. In moments, it looked as if he had never been there at all.


Knell managed to sit for exactly the length of time it took to watch a beetle clamber over the toe of his boot and wander off beneath a leaf before he decided it wouldn't hurt to get a *little* closer. Just to get a better view of the road and the people moving along the edge of the village.

Careful to stick close to the camouflage of dense trees and tall bushes with their deep shadows, Knell crept in the direction of the road. He couldn't manage to move as quietly as Percy, not used to the way his boots slid against the damp leaves and soft soil underfoot, but he was good enough not to go crashing through it all. When the general clamor of the village broke up into distinguishable sounds of daily life and voices, he stopped, not daring to go further just yet. Tucked into a low crouch between branches of a sprawling bush, he absently brushed away clinging spider webs as he peered out from the shield of foliage to watch.

It was a large village, one that might even qualify as a small town. But while there was activity, people moving about on their daily errands, it didn't seem heavily populated. There was a smithy on the edge of the village, the extended roof that ran along the open half of the shop just barely visible from his angle. Knell could smell hot metal in the smoke pouring up from a wide chimney, layered over the general scent of a gathered population recognizable anywhere; horses, people, hearth smoke, and meals cooking.

Knell closed his eyes and let it wash over him. The smells, the sounds, the knowledge that there were people living normal lives a stone's throw away—if Percy were throwing the stone, that is. His chest ached at the thought, sharp-edged envy cutting deep long after he thought it had gone dull.

He opened his eyes again to take in the glow of sunlight through leaves, making it easier to look at. He needed to focus on his task. Watching for trouble. From here, he had a good view of the road that, as far as he could tell, carried on straight through the village.

He couldn't see the center of it, though it was easy enough to imagine. Probably a well. Merchant stalls if it was a market day. Perhaps just food sellers if not. Stocks, if the town dealt with criminals.

It was hard not to think of fire and Brother Omen's screams. The weather had been nice then too.

He went still at the sound of voices nearby. Very close by, as if they were right below him.

"Rushed all the way here just to watch a bunch of backwater farmers haul their wares," one voice said, clearly in a bit of a snit.

"The King's orders. If he said that we need to be here, then I'm sure he's right," another voice answered with all the confidence of a true lackey.

Knell craned his neck to get a better angle on the slope below him that led to the road. It was steeper than he'd assumed and sure enough, right at the bottom where they'd been hidden from his sight by the dense bushes, were two figures. He couldn't see much more than the back of their helmets and their shoulders, clad in leather armor and draped in the bright white tabard of the kingsmen.

That certainly explained why they hadn't seen them on the road, Knell thought with a rising sense of panic. The kingsmen were *already in the village.*

The village Percy had just walked into.

Knell contained himself until a large cart rolled by, rattling loudly enough to cover his escape from the leafy hiding place. He hurried through the forest, circling the town to find a less conspicuous way in. Thankfully, the village didn't have much in the way of walls to make things more difficult, apart from the occasional livestock fence. It wasn't long before Knell spied a line of clothing hung out to dry. Now this, he knew how to do. Or he hoped he still did.

Much to his surprise and a little pinprick of something that might have been delight, it apparently took more than a moth-chewed memory to dull his thieving skills. In no time at all—and without being spotted—he'd snatched up enough for an outfit that was neither too distinctive nor overly large on his frame. His robes were bundled up and shoved into the hollow space of a log, abandoned with one last vindictive kick that felt more satisfying than he'd expected.

Then he stared hard at the gap between two buildings, willing himself to walk through them and unable to make his feet obey. He was wearing clothes to help him blend in and he was decently clean. Especially now that Percy had thoroughly, if somewhat aggressively, scrubbed his hair. It might be tangled and messy, but no more than most workers by the end of a long day. The larger issue was that he now lacked a hood, and as loose as the pilfered shirt was, his hands could be seen, along with his neck and face.

He stared down at his grey hands and blackened nails, all too aware that it was one of the few things his monochrome vision saw correctly. The fact of it made him more frustrated than sad.

No, it made him *angry*. Percy was in danger and Knell needed to find a way into the village to warn him without getting himself—or worse, the both of them—condemned to death. He paced back and forth in stilted steps, knowing if he lingered too long he'd attract attention anyway as a stranger lurking on the edge of town.

Just as he'd bitten his nail down far enough to taste the copper tang of blood, he spotted the scarecrow. A ragged thing planted in someone's vegetable garden and already listing precariously to the side on its stick. But more importantly, it had a hat.

Percy circled widely around the village, knowing exactly where he needed to go. There was a chance word had already made it this far, especially if the new king had sent out single horsemen directly to deliver the news. If that was the case, then there was only one person who might still help him.

It was risky, heading to a bustling inn when trying to lie low, but he didn't have a lot of options. They—*he,* damn it—needed supplies. While early summer was a good time for foraging, it wasn't enough to keep a man well fed while on the move. The constant state of alertness and tension from navigating the cave tunnels left him high-strung and exhausted much too quickly.

What he needed was food that was hearty and able to last. Trail bread, cheese, nuts, dried fruit, and maybe, the thought crept in quietly as if hesitant to take up space in his head, some dried meat for the wretch. Knell really did look a sad state, the man needed a few weeks' worth of decent meals at minimum. Not that it was Percy's concern. Even better would be if he had some cooking supplies, like basic spices and a fucking pan. A flat rock he could lay over a fire would do. He was tired of uncooked leaves and roots and berries, no matter how lucky they were to have them.

As he arrived at his destination, he eyed the back entrance to the inn. It wasn't like a house, where the back door was often left mostly unattended apart from servants. There was a regular, if slow, back and forth of kitchen staff, stable boys, maids, and clientele going about doing chores and tending to their horses at the small three-stall stable. The fenced in space beside it protected the hen house where a dozen or so plump chickens were scratching at the dirt. The second story window was another option. He'd made the climb a dozen times before easily, but he'd had two hands at the time.

The glowing coal of slow-burning rage that had been smoldering within him was a dense mixture of fury and frustration that sat heavy in his chest. As it had since he'd woken up with one hand and nothing to his name but a long list of failures. Truthfully, that fury had begun burning long before then. It had just been easier to ignore. But this wasn't the time. Not for his failures, or losses. The years spent training his sword arm now wasted, the constant reminder that he'd screwed up so thoroughly that it cost him everything. The fucking itch on his thumb that couldn't really be there because his fucking hand was gone.

No. Best to deal with those thoughts later. Maybe when the idea of confronting them felt less like standing on the edge of a cliff and staring down at the dizzying height of it.

He was here for the inn. Or rather, the innkeeper. No wall-scaling, no windows. He glanced toward the sun, checking the time, and nearly snorted in memory of seeing Knell staring up at the sky that morning, eyes wide and mouth hanging open like he'd never seen it before. It was a wonder that man was alive and still had more limbs than Percy.

Above him, the sun was high, which meant Percy's timing was just right. The inn's back door swung open with a solid kick and a woman walked out to the yard with a bucket in hand. She was average height, stout and sturdy with plain features apart from thick dark brows and sleek black hair braided back tightly. He recognized the dress she was wearing, or at least the pattern of it. He'd stolen that fabric a couple of years ago, and she'd been quick to take it as her cut.

Ruth was also the only other person he knew with the same mixed parentage he had. Her mother was of the kingdom, but her father was a foreign merchant whose cart had broken down near the village, where he'd decided to stick around rather than move on. Percy's mother had been from the same country, if not the same region, up past the Tempest Sea in the north.

Merchants from his mother's homeland rarely traveled within the kingdom. Their trade routes often led far west, where there were rumored to be long stretches of desert and strangely shaped not-quite-horses. Percy had only met travelers from there once or twice, but it occurred to him that Knell's profile shared a vague sort of similarity.

Percy had learned later in life that the kingdom not only taxed merchant ships heavily, but the main passage through the northern mountains had been cut off by a landslide. It was a strange sort of comfort to see hints of familiarity in Ruth—the wide cheekbones, sleek black hair, and deep brown color of her eyes—that few others shared. He suspected it was part of the reason she'd begun dealing with him years ago. Her parents had even used the same naming tradition his mother had. It was one of the few things he carried from childhood with pride but kept close to his chest because it led to nothing but the same circling questions he didn't care to answer.

Before the last few years of constant and costly quests, before the Prophesized Hero, Percy had led a crew of men with particular skills. The kingdom called them bandits while Percy preferred to say they were value equalizers. Doing the necessary work of making sure no guard for hire was left without a job on these nearby roads.

They'd been good at it too, not taking so much that the upper crust cared to send more than the occasional middling bounty hunter, which was a relief because half of them worked for Percy anyway. It was enough to keep the crew happy, or at least content in their food, drink, and whatever other pleasures they wanted to waste their ill-gotten goods on. This inn had been a key factor; a mostly safe harbor free of snitches and always with a room or two available in return for a cut of the goods. An agreement that had paid off on the occasions when more serious law enforcement came sniffing around.

Percy waited to make sure she was alone, no pesky staff coming to ask questions or confirm orders. This was the one task she refused to assign anyone else, menial as it was. Every day, mid-morning, she came out to feed her chickens like they were her own children and not being fattened up for dinner. She scattered some seeds and he saw her shoulders relax as the chickens rushed to her, clucking brainlessly.

Then she tensed and her head snapped up, eyes scanning over the edge of the forest with a frown.

"Best come out now before I get angry. Nobody lurks in the dark without the manners to announce themself except peeping toms," she stated, clear and calm, eyes still searching.

She'd come close to spotting him. Percy stepped from the trees to meet her eye and moved quickly to stand behind the stable where he'd be hidden from view of anyone in the inn.

"Ruth," he said in greeting.

Ruth was a hard woman to surprise, but she nearly dropped her bucket, her eyes gone wide. She caught it before it could hit the ground and cause a racket, letting out a little hissed breath of annoyance as she glared viciously at Percy.

"You *idiot*! What the hell are you thinking, coming here?" How she managed to speak so fiercely yet keep her voice from carrying to unwelcome ears was a trick Percy had coveted for years and never quite mastered. He'd also never seen her this genuinely angry at him before, and the sense of unease he'd been carrying for days sank its fangs deeper.

"Word's already made it here, then?"

Ruth threw down a fistful of seed, sending the chickens into a frenzy. "A *prophecy* came to pass! We all saw that horrid red storm growing in the sky. And we knew what it meant when it vanished just as quickly."

She eyed him sharply. "Did you see the King die? The official message just says that he fought and lost against the Chaos Bringer. I bet that arrogant old stuffed bird thought that he was a hero of prophecy."

Ruth looked grimly satisfied at the thought of his demise. Her sister had shown signs of magic and been carted off like all potential mages were, with promises of great fortune and maybe even a placement within the courts. Ruth never heard from her again.

Percy shook his head, though he did wish he'd seen it. The former king had been a charismatic man with a regal demeanor that masked his true nature; he was a greedy, vile waste of air. Journeying on endless quests with the actual Prophesized Hero had revealed just how many evils in the kingdom could be traced back to the King's varied plots.

And there was Knell's story back at the spring, how the King had likely approved of the experiments on prisoners. Only for things to explosively escape his control and lead to the rise of the flesh mage cultists, along with the Chaos Bringer himself. Percy couldn't help but feel a little vindicated that the bastard had very likely brought about his own demise.

"I didn't see it, but I did hear that we have a new king to sing praises for." Bitterness seeped into his voice despite his attempt to keep the comment light, and he knew Ruth had heard it.

"Is it true, what they say you did?" she asked in a softer tone.

The question he'd been both waiting for and hoping to avoid.

She was looking to where his ragged cloak hid his right arm from sight. He clenched his jaw, then nodded and lifted his arm just far enough to show her the scarred stump of his wrist. "After everything, how could I trust it to be true? How could I trust *him*?"

She glanced between his wrist and his face, her expression pained. "And you found your answers?"

His short laugh was edged in despair. "Yeah, cleared things up right quick."

He tried to hide his arm under the cloak once more, but Ruth's hand shot out and caught him by the forearm. She stared down at the scarred limb, her brow furrowed.

"How is it so far healed? Magic?"

Healing magic was in short supply, especially any strong enough to have closed a wound like his. The previous king had been particularly covetous of it, and as war loomed, the kingdom had hunted down any healers of notable skill to work among the soldiers and to tend to royalty as personal doctors. Percy wondered if the new king had kept his word about changing that or if he'd found things to his liking once he'd sat upon the throne.

"Something like that," Percy replied. Nothing about the truth would reassure her.

He could see that she wanted to ask why he'd done it, her eyes flicking from his arm to his face, her mouth pressed so tightly that her lips had gone pale. But to his surprise, she let go of his arm with a bone-weary sigh.

"You'll get the usual supplies, just like any other run. To even out the books from your last visit. The goods sold well."

Relief hit him so hard he nearly swayed, and she leveled him with a hard look. "But you can't come back, Percy. I never saw you, and for both our sakes, I'd better not ever lay eyes on you again. It's not just the King who wants you dragged in. Everyone and their cousins have reason to want your head on a pike. Bad for business, having those uptight boys skulking around my inn. They're worse than your old lot."

Percy swallowed, surprised at how much of a loss it felt to hear the words, even though he'd known it would happen. He nodded, thankful that she was as blunt and uninterested in emotional goodbyes as himself.

"Thank you," he said simply, and she nodded tersely in return.

The rest of the chickenfeed was scattered without her usual care, and she turned to head back inside, speaking without looking back. "I'll have to inspect your old room, make sure there's no clues for those useless guards taking up my tables. But I'm a bit clumsy, so watch your head in case anything falls from the window."

She'd never been clumsy a day in the years he'd known her. It was a kindness he didn't deserve and he couldn't think of words to voice his thanks, not that she'd want to hear them anyway.

"Goodbye, Ruthless."

She snorted at the use of her full name and made a rude gesture over her shoulder, halfway to the door. "Try living up to your own name, yeah? And good luck, you'll fucking need it."

Then she was gone, shouldering her way through the back door and already calling out instructions to her staff as if the conversation hadn't happened. He knew it was the last he'd hear from her.

Under the shadow of the stable, Percy leaned into the corner of space where the stable met the back of the inn, along the shared wall of the large kitchen hearth to help keep the horses warm in winter. There was a single window above, and a room that was almost always available, thanks to the ever-present smell of horses and their shit. It was the one Percy, along with a few of his old crew, would often use when laying low after a decent raid. The price of the smell was worth it for the easy escape route if someone needed to get out without using the door. A short drop from the window to the top of the stables, then to the ground, and the forest would welcome him back as always.

The window shutters eased open soundlessly, and out swung a large cloth tied bundle held by a stocky arm. Ruth didn't bother to look for him, and Percy was quick to position himself as the bundle dropped. He caught it in his arms with a grunt, heavier than expected. The shutters swung shut and Percy dropped into a crouch to shove the entire thing into his pack, not wasting time to check the contents—what would he do, go in and complain if she hadn't packed his favorites?

The straps had just been secured when Percy heard the back door of the inn swing open with a bang and the drunken stumble of several people. Worse, he thought as he peeked between the thick slats of the stable's back wall and caught glimpses of leather, chain mail, and the flash of white cloth gone brown with road dust. There were three of them, and while he was hidden, the kingsmen would spot him easily if he tried for the woods. It'd look even more suspicious if he stayed huddled here half-hidden in the shadows until one of them came around for a piss, which was likely their plan.

Cursing his luck and more viciously cursing the guards, Percy pulled his hood low over his face, made sure his right arm was hidden, and quickly ducked into the alley alongside the inn. His only other option was to make his way deeper into the village and take another route back toward the forest. He thanked the stars that it wasn't a market day. As long as he could avoid being seen, he'd be out of here in no time.

# CHAPTER 12

## *Percy*

His hopes were not only dashed, they were crushed under heel and spat on as he reached the far end of the alley and stopped short of entering the main square. What looked like most of the village was crowded into the space, though Percy didn't see any stalls beyond the usual skewer and pie sellers. He did spy a flat cart near the center of the square, and as people jostled in clusters, murmuring among themselves about whatever proceedings were going on, Percy saw a man in a gaudy outfit step up onto the makeshift platform. The man held up his hands and spoke in a clear, carrying voice.

"Hear me, good people of Valmere, hear me! I bring news from the palace!"

Excitement rolled through the gathered crowd in a wave of noise, though they quieted down as the herald raised his hands again, a scroll held in one fist. Fuck. Fucking fuckity fuck. Percy could hear the kingsmen behind him loudly ribbing each other at the far end of the alley, and an entire crowd in front of him was packed from one end of the market square to the other. There was nowhere to easily make his exit, so he tucked his chin low to keep his face shadowed by his hood and leaned against the wall as if he was just another gawker in the crowd while he waited for an opportunity to escape.

"I bring news both wondrous and bitter," the herald went on, his voice carrying with practiced ease. "A great prophecy has come to pass!"

The noise of the crowd erupted, gasps and shouts from all corners. A reminder that not everyone had spent the last half decade knee deep in the muck of said prophecy if this was all news to them.

"I'm sure you've seen the strange weather, the green clouds and red lightning that threatened our skies." The herald was good, Percy had to admit, managing to cut through the noise and recapture attention. Must be used to bigger audiences than this village crowd.

"Just as the prophecy predicted, a hero rose on the battlefield with sword aflame and struck down the Chaos Bringer before its foul presence could fully take hold." He looked around the crowd, and Percy made sure he was tucked far enough against the wall of the building that those eyes wouldn't linger on him. To his relief, they passed him by for more gullible, enraptured faces.

"Every person here still lives, still wakes to a world they know with their loved ones safe at hand, thanks to him. And as those legends foretold, that hero touched by the hand of Fate has ascended to become your new King!"

Normally, news of royalty was of passing interest, but no great excitement this far from the palace and capital cities. It wasn't as if they'd ever meet them, and beyond possible increased taxes, it made no difference to their daily lives. Local lords were another matter, they rode in for their little visits and either did a decent job or were set upon by a mob. Simple and efficient. But this announcement led to cheers, and looking around, Percy hadn't realized how many of the townsfolk looked more than a little touched by hunger. Cheeks were sharper, circles under their eyes darker, clothes a bit more worn and mended over than he'd noticed before.

Fear of flesh-mages and a tightened grip by the old king had left trade floundering and strained outside of the capital cities, and this village was hit harder than most. Percy had noticed it the last time he'd been here in an absent sort of way, but he hadn't thought much of it since, too busy trying to stay alive. Looks like things had only gotten worse.

"Celebrations will commence on the coronation of the new King, to be held in three days' time. His first act of generosity is five hundred wagons of provisions sent out to the towns and villages hit hardest by these recent years of strife, Valmere included," the herald announced as proudly as if he'd made the decision himself.

Another ripple of excitement as the crowd pressed in closer, eager to hear every word. Percy clenched his fist and cursed silently. He began eyeing possible routes along the edge of the crowd, but people were turning to grasp arms and chat excitedly with anyone nearby. He was too well known here, he'd be recognized in no time.

"Yes, rejoice, for our new King is a generous one!" The herald let the crowd's excitement grow before lifting his hands once more, his face turning somber. Percy rolled his eyes at the theatrics. "The wondrous news has been spread, but now we must speak of the bitter. One of the King's closest advisors was revealed to be a traitor."

There it was. Fuck, he had to get out of here. People were entranced, gathering into tight clusters to whisper frantically among themselves. Percy almost had a clear trajectory to a second alley he knew led straight toward a forest path that he could navigate in his sleep.

"The traitor is a man you might know well. A man you may have called neighbor, or even friend. He drew his blade on our new King! On the hero that saved us all from doom at the hands of incomprehensible evil! Yes, he intended to strike down our shining beacon of hope, but he was no match for a man chosen by prophecy!" The herald must have spent time training on stage for the level of theatrics he was injecting into his speech. Percy wanted to kick him off the platform.

"Our King struck true and with mercy, despite this betrayal."

Percy scowled. The story was horse shit, that asshole had tried to get in a killing blow. Percy might not be a Fate-touched hero shitting golden light, but he was a damn good fighter. Not his fault the cheat had a magic sword that had chosen right then to light up, swathed in fucking flames. The herald kept on with his dramatic retelling, oblivious to Percy's ire and basking in the awe of his rapt audience.

"The traitor lost his hand and forfeited his life when he chose to let jealousy rot him through." The whispers, conversations, and outright shouts were beginning to overpower the man's voice. Everyone wanted to know who it was, though plenty of them had likely made a decent guess. The herald looked around at the upturned faces and nodded gravely.

"I can see many of you already suspect who this traitor may be. Not only to our hero, our King, but to all you good people of this kingdom!" Townsfolk began to look around as if the person next to them might turn out to be this heartless traitor. Percy would have found it funny if he wasn't right there and at risk of being spotted.

"The King wishes for this traitor to face fair judgment, as is just! The bounty on his head will bring the person responsible for his capture not only riches beyond their imagining, but a large parcel of land and a seat at the King's table as an advisor."

Percy's heart plummeted. Money he could understand, but to be vaulted to the top of the goddamned food chain of the royal court? Anyone here—anyone across the kingdom, starved and desperate as they were—would tear him apart for pieces and carry them rotting to the new king for that kind of reward. Clamor rose so high that the herald had to actually shout for his voice to be heard, but he was clearly stoking them up, urging them to demand the name of their prey.

"Yes, I suspect most of you recognize the name *Percival of Valmere*! The very traitor himself, a man who can no longer be called a neighbor, or worse, a friend." There was a fervent gleam in the herald's eye at the declaration and the answering roar of the crowd.

For *fucks* sake. Percy was ready to walk back down the alley and take his chances with the trio of drunken kingsmen instead of risking the crowd now calling for his gruesome death in lurid detail.

"I thought your name wasn't Percival," a voice piped up right next to him, and Percy reacted without thinking. He threw his back against the wall to avoid any more surprises while he swiped his dagger between himself and the threat that had managed to get so close without him noticing.

Knell stared back at him from just out of reach, his strange eyes bright in the shadow of the alley, peering out from under the brim of a ridiculous straw hat. Percy's brain took a moment to register what he was seeing, so used to the flesh-mage's filthy black robes that despite being his unmistakable self—grey skin, mage-bright eyes, and gaunt features—he looked nearly unrecognizable. The robes had been replaced with simple brown pants with a patch at the knee and a plain linen shirt that might have fit Percy snugly but hung like a sheet on a line over Knell's thin, hunched shoulders. The supplies he'd left with Knell were rolled into the blanket and slung across his back, tied in a thick knot diagonally over his chest.

"What the fuck are you doing here?" Percy hissed, furious. He put away his dagger despite the urge to stab his annoyance of a companion. "I told you to wait."

"I saw some guards along the road. I came to warn you that they've got—"

"Men in town," Percy cut him off. "I'm aware. They're not exactly subtle."

In fact, he could still spy the men at the other end of the alley, if not hear them. The crowd had grown so rowdy that the herald had to shout above it all. Some officious decree detailing how horrible Percy was and how much richer anyone would be for capturing him.

"They certainly aren't, but it does make for a great distraction. No one looked twice at me," Knell said with one of his crooked little smiles. He held up a hand, which Percy noticed now had a thin silver ring on it, and showed Percy the two small pies he was holding. "They're putting up posters of your face. They got the likeness surprisingly well. Would you like a pie? It's spinach and cheese."

"I don't want a fucking pie," Percy bit out, though it was a lie. He was hungry and they smelled really good. "I need to get out of here. *We* need to get out of here before we get spotted."

Knell nodded in agreement as he took a bite from one of the pies, his eyes closing for a moment as he savored it. "Oh, definitely. Things will be very bad for us if we get caught. Did you have a plan to get out?"

"Did you?" Percy shot back.

"Vaguely," Knell said, taking another bite of the pie and looking far too at ease with it all. But there was something calculating about his eyes, the way they darted around points in the crowd, like he was considering and discarding a dozen ideas at once, that belied his casual tone.

Then Knell glanced back down the alley and tensed. "Ah, that's not good."

It was an understatement. The trio of kingsmen, who had sobered up just enough to walk upright and realize they should probably be doing their jobs, were now headed their way. Percy needed to move, but the three looked ready to pull whatever small bit of rank they had on anyone passing by them and his other option was a crowd that seemed to be circulating a truly ridiculous amount of wanted notices with his own sneering face inked on them in bold.

He reached for his dagger once more, ready to take his chances against the guards when Knell startled the thoughts right out of him by pressing himself all along Percy's front.

"Hold my hat in place," Knell whispered hurriedly.

"What are y—" Percy started, but Knell cut him off.

"Hold my hat!" He hissed at Percy from a hairsbreadth away, as uncompromising as Percy had ever heard him, eyes flashing like silver coins. Percy shut up and did as he was told.

He held the top of Knell's hat in place, effectively cupping the back of his head, and realized exactly what Knell was doing when he tried to catch sight of the approaching kingsmen and saw nothing but frayed straw brim. With Knell all but molded to him from knee to chest, the two of them nose to nose and Knell's head tilted back to make up for his perpetually curled shoulders, their faces were hidden between the fall of Percy's hood and the brim of Knell's hat. For all that it was an uncomfortable crush of limbs between them, it would look like a lover's embrace to anyone else.

Percy's right arm was trapped against his side as Knell's weight pinned his cloak against him. Knell's arms were tucked up between their chests, the pies in his hand leaving traces of grease and crumbs against Percy's cheek. They did smell very good, and despite the danger, his stomach rumbled loudly enough for Knell to feel, if not hear.

Knell let out a nervous little chuckle and Percy heard the passing footsteps falter. Damn it, they'd been so close to going unnoticed.

"Hey. You two," came a gruff voice.

Percy could see the scuffed leather of an approaching boot and the hem of a dusty white tabard. In a flash of desperation, he took a large bite of the pie hovering close to his mouth and chewed as loudly as he could. The pie tasted fantastic, despite Percy's recollection that the pie stall had been mediocre as long as he'd known it. Maybe it was the rush of danger, or it had just been far too long since he'd eaten anything seasoned. Whatever the case, the filling was perfectly moist and sounded like the most off-putting wet, sucking, smacking he could have hoped for.

The boots quickly retreated and Percy had to hold back his own laugh at the emphatic "*Eugh!*" from the kingsman.

Percy took a couple more bites while Knell finished his own pie, tilting his head a bit to peer past the brim of Knell's hat to be sure the alley had cleared out. That it gave him the perfect excuse not to look at Knell's eyes so close, flashing blue-green and bright with mischief, was irrelevant. Once the kingsmen were lost to the crowd, each struggling to look professional while listing slightly to the side, Percy dropped his hand from the back of Knell's head.

"Let's go, and *quickly,*" he said, snatching up the other half of his pie as Knell stepped back. He shoved the rest into his mouth, chewing fast so he'd have his hand free, and moved toward the opposite end of the alley once more.

They had just reached the stables when a girl came rushing around the corner from the inn's yard.

"Sirs! You forgot—*oh*!"

Her arms were full of papers that erupted like feathers from a hen house with a fox in it as she collided with Knell. Knell reached out automatically to steady her by the arm as she stared down at the pile of papers in dismay. Percy couldn't be bothered to care what her face was doing, too busy staring down at his own visage in ink, looking up at him in multitudes. Wanted posters with a truly massive bounty listed—he wasn't sure if he was more horrified or flattered he was worth so much. Time seemed to slow as the girl spotted his boots and looked up at him, her whole body freezing as she recognized his face. His scars made it too damn easy.

"Y-you're..." she stuttered, then glanced at Knell, who quickly let go of her arm. Too late, he was still close enough for her to get a full look at his face, with all that his grey skin and strange eyes implied. He tried to smile at her and she screamed.

It was impressive how fast the mob formed.

Not at all what Knell had hoped for, but impressive nonetheless. It wasn't often a village managed to form rank so quickly rather than fall into chaos, but it seemed that they shared Percy's sense of straightforward practicality. They also had a surprising amount of pitchforks for the center of town, he hadn't seen nearly enough horses to justify the number. Did they do this often?

As it was, he was too occupied trying to keep up with Percy's loping run. Knell gasped for breath as vines clung to his legs and branches whipped at his arms and face. There was a vicious stitch in his side, slowing him further despite his best efforts, and fear clawed its way up his throat. Percy glanced back and turned sharply with a snarl when he saw Knell flagging. He caught Knell's arm in an iron grip and hauled him along, all but dragging him when his boots caught on undergrowth.

Knell had no idea where they were. The forest crowded in around them, but the shouts and crashing of the mob in their wake sounded far too close. Planning anything beyond his next step was impossible, he was taking in too much information and unable to do anything with it. His only real option at the moment was to keep running, so Knell concentrated on staying upright and in motion. Percy, meanwhile, was scanning the forest, looking for something and cursing lowly, the exact words lost in the rush of Knell's breath and the blood pounding in his ears.

"There it is, thank *fuck*," Percy said with fervor, which Knell assumed meant he'd found what he'd been searching for, though he didn't see anything that stood out. Just another patch of forest among many. All dense shrubbery and trees and leaf-covered ground.

He was hauled closer to one particularly thorny bush before Percy released his arm, which tingled as blood rushed back through the limb. They'd gained a bit of a lead, probably from Percy's circuitous and weaving route to get here, but it was a slim one, and the shouting was already drawing closer. Knell looked back at Percy anxiously, only to find him kneeling in the leaves, running his hand and wrist over them in wide sweeping motions like he'd dropped something in the dark and couldn't find it.

"Percy?" Knell wheezed out, his hands braced on his knees.

Percy ignored him, teeth bared in frustration as he kept searching. The gap between themselves and the mob at their backs was rapidly shrinking, which didn't help the tremor in his hands or the grip of chill along his spine. He wasn't afraid of death, but that didn't mean he wanted to die painfully or to watch the same happen to Percy. He was about to ask again, his instincts screaming at him to run, to hide, when Percy hissed out a soft cry of success. His fingers were curled under a section of leaves, as if he could pull up the forest floor like a carpet.

He did, in a sense. Percy heaved up a camouflaged cover to reveal a shadowed hollow beneath it. He'd barely turned to snarl a command at Knell, who caught on immediately and was already throwing himself into the newly revealed hideaway. It wasn't very large, and Knell was grateful that nothing was nesting here, though the smell of some animal's musk lingered. He hit the ground shoulder first and tucked his limbs in tight, rolling until he hit the far side of the bowl-like space. No sooner had his back met the far wall of it than Percy dropped in after him, flattening Knell against the curve of the hollow. The supplies bundled against his back dug into his spine, while roots that had broken through the dirt over time tangled in his hair and snagged his boots.

The cache was clearly made to stash away goods, not hold two fully grown men, but Percy had just enough space to pull the cover shut, the barest filter of light peeking through. Now that he was on the underside of it, Knell could appreciate such a clever contraption. Rough canvas stretched over a sturdy frame of branches with thick twine stitched across the surface, frayed with age and weather. Percy must have sewn the first layer of camouflaging leaves and then let the forest do the rest of the work for him. His curiosity was dampened by the current fraught situation, but he made a mental note to ask more about Percy's many and varied hideaways once it was safe to do so.

They waited, holding still and quiet, listening for their pursuers. Knell forced his breathing to calm as best he could, given how little air he was able to get into his chest between the recent sprint and the way Percy was crushing him into the dirt. The pressure, though not comfortable, was oddly comforting and did more to help calm his breath than anything else. He was sure there would be sizable bruises from the rocks and roots, his chest ached from the pull on his scars, and his arm was trapped under Percy's substantial weight. But he could also feel Percy's heart thudding away where his broad back was pressed to Knell's chest. And he was warm as a hearth fire, more so than usual, thanks to their run. Knell couldn't see anything but the stretch of canvas directly above him from his place behind Percy, so he focused on each soothing detail he could and tried not to breathe too loudly in Percy's ear.

Percy, already on high alert, went tense as a bowstring at the sound of approaching footsteps and voices. Their pursuers were no longer yelling and stomping around, but they were hardly moving silently. They came close to the cover but didn't seem interested in digging through the thorny bush above. After a short hesitation that felt like an eternity, they moved on, calling out to others as they continued their search. Knell let out a shaky sigh of relief and very deliberately did not think about how he'd briefly seen threads of color. Or that he'd begun to consider how quickly he might reach his power through those threads to the villagers like he had with the homunculus. That he'd weighed the cost of keeping himself and Percy alive and found the price acceptable.

No, best not to think about that. It would have been too risky anyway with Percy so close. Knell's powers were destructive at best, reined in by nothing more than instinct and guesswork. He'd just as likely kill Percy as their pursuers while he was so close, and that had been enough to startle him right out of it.

They waited for the voices to fade to nothing before Percy pushed the cover open carefully to make sure they were in the clear. Once he was sure, he climbed out, reaching back in to haul Knell free as well. Knell squinted against the sunlight his eyes had finally adjusted to. He'd have to start the process all over again after the short reprieve of the dark.

"We need to get back to the caves before they bring out the hounds," Percy said, frowning as he watched the spaces between the trees carefully.

"Hounds won't come near me," Knell said, keeping his voice low. It was a fact that gave him mixed feelings. He'd always loved dogs, as far as he could recall. Now they avoided getting anywhere near him. If they'd already been worked up into a lather on a hunt, they might even turn on their handlers or each other to avoid following the scent of anyone tainted by the Great One's touch.

Percy nodded, glancing briefly at him before looking back toward the forest. Whether he was watching out for more pursuers or planning their next route, Knell had no idea. He couldn't tell if they were closer or further than they'd started, had no way to gather his bearings. When caught up in the rush of danger, he tended to pick out details of his surroundings that might be useful, which was handy in a city or a cave—finding little spaces he might fit in or half-hidden tunnels he could vanish into—but it was useless here.

"A scent trail hounds won't follow can be just as damning as one that leads them right to us," Percy said grimly.  "Best to put as much distance as we can and hope it's enough to lose them."

They took a winding route, moving as fast as they could while trying to stay hidden, darting from shadow to shadow as they went. More than once, they had to pause at the sound of others somewhere nearby, ducking behind cover and hoping they wouldn't be seen.

Sooner than he'd hoped, Knell heard the distant barking and baying of hunting dogs set on their trail. Percy bit out a curse between panting breaths. Knell mostly just tried his best not to pass out, feeling unsteady and lightheaded. Pain bloomed behind his eyes, scorched its way up his legs, and it felt like a knife had been slipped between his ribs. During one brief pause, while Knell was embracing a tree to keep from falling over, he could have sworn his shadow moved. It stretched farther than it should, inching up the bark of a tree as Knell remained motionless.

It had to be the fear, the rising panic as his energy flagged sharply. Without the Great One's muffling influence to keep the emotions contained, they threatened to overwhelm him. Now his powers had begun to leak out as well, seeping from the edges of his frayed control. Percy hadn't noticed yet—he was a little preoccupied navigating himself and a wheezing shamble through the forest with a bloodthirsty mob in pursuit—but unless Knell got a grip it would only be a matter of time.

It was early evening by the time they made it back to the cave entrance, in no small part due to Percy allowing Knell as much rest as they could get away with, which hadn't been nearly enough. Knell had no idea what direction they'd been traveling in or how they'd ended up here, likely would have walked right past it if Percy hadn't stopped him. He was grateful just to recognize the thorny bramble he'd been picking berries from the day before. Over the course of the afternoon the baying of hounds had faded with distance, much to his relief. Unfortunately, the constant running might just finish Knell off before their pursuers had the chance. Percy looked barely winded, which Knell found unfair, but he'd been nice enough to slow down for Knell's sake even if he'd looked tempted to throw Knell over his shoulder like a sack of flour.

Knell wished he had. He wouldn't have complained. Percy could banish whatever illusions of pride he thought Knell suffered from because he would have happily taken a break from his own numb-legged stumble. But Percy hadn't offered, and Knell didn't have enough breath to ask. While Knell struggled to stay upright with about ten stitches in his sides, pocketing more berries to distract himself, Percy took one last assessing glance over the surrounding trees before he eased himself down into the cave opening.

When his hand poked back out, gesturing impatiently, Knell staggered over and dropped in with all the grace of an animal that needed to be put out of its misery. His feet met the ground, followed quickly by the rest of him as his legs simply refused to do their job any longer. Percy, the absolute gem, was quick to lift him upright, and Knell mostly just hung from the grip on his arm like a rag doll until his feet were firmly under him once more.

It was cool inside, the dark quiet and welcoming. Knell's shoulders relaxed in the familiarity of it, and even Percy seemed a fraction less tense. They wordlessly retreated away from the arc of light spilling across the tunnel floor, cloaking themselves in shadows as they caught their breath. Knell was flagging hard and shakily tugged the knot of the blanket free to let it fall to the floor. He leaned back against the wall of the tunnel, the cold stone welcome for once against his overheated skin. Percy's pack hit the ground with a louder thump before he leaned next to Knell with a half-laughed breath of relief. His arm was warm and a bit sweaty under Knell's hand—when had he put that there? Percy didn't flinch away from the touch, and they traded half-wild grins.

Knell patted his arm, adrenaline-bright laughter bubbling up in him. "Percy, I can't believe we made—"

A lit torch hit the ground and rolled until the flame was close enough to heat the toe of Knell's boot. Percy bared his teeth in a silent snarl and reached for Knell's arm, which surely had a hand shaped bruise by now, but it was already too late. By the time Knell's tired mind registered what was happening, three men had dropped into the cave.

The trio of kingsmen from the alley, much more intimidating now that they were sober and wearing unfriendly expressions. Their tabards looked worse for wear with grass stains and ragged holes from catching on thorns, muddy up to the knee. The space was too small for swords, but one of them had theirs drawn anyway. The two in the lead had opted for the more sensible daggers, which didn't bode well for Knell and Percy.

Knell didn't bother reaching for his own knife. His skill with it was limited to things already dead, not for fighting. Percy's dagger was already in his hand, drawn with his usual speed, and Knell couldn't help but notice that he'd been getting better at reacting with his left hand rather than the phantom of his right.

"It wasn't enough to betray the man who saved us all, but you'd stoop so low as to keep the company of a *flesh-mage*?" the nearest soldier sneered. He shifted so his knife was between Knell and himself, even as the others kept their blades trained on Percy. His eyes flicked to Percy's right arm, to the scarred wrist where his hand used to be, and his face twisted like he might be ill.

"So that's how you survived. Sick is what you are, crawling away from battle and letting their kind lay hands on you." The kingsman spat the words, and the two men at his back agreed, though the one in the rear looked ready to piss himself.

Light glanced off the blade of his sword, betraying the tremble in his hands. He had that fresh-faced look about him, in over his head but too far to turn back. The kingsman standing beside him was the oldest of the three, and to Knell he looked like the biggest threat. He had the same hard gaze Percy did, a focused intensity honed on the battlefield.

Percy didn't bother to respond. He was sizing up the trio as they cautiously spread to cut off any escape through the tunnels and adjusted his own stance in preparation for a fight. It was possible Percy might win, but he was down his main hand and up against three men who'd had a chance to rest and eat, which was more than could be said for themselves. Knell wasn't much help physically, especially now with his limbs aching and barely responsive. And he doubted they'd let him get close enough to touch them. They obviously knew what it meant, and their expressions made it clear they'd have him dead the moment they had the chance.

The presumed leader who had spoken glared in Percy's direction, but his eyes flicked toward Knell, keeping him in sight. Despite the confidence he held himself with, he couldn't quite meet Knell's eyes.

It hadn't bothered him before—not even fellow acolytes liked to look at one another, to see the changes wrought upon their fellows and know it was a reflection of themselves—but it caused a spark of annoyance in him now. Percy had shown similar disgust and promise of violence when they met, but Percy at least had the willpower to look him in the eyes when he threatened him. He hadn't been cowed, even when he'd woken up alone with a stranger he feared, fresh from the loss of a limb. In comparison, these soldiers were a disappointment. Still incredibly deadly, Knell had no illusions about that, but a disappointment all the same.

Was this it then? He'd known their time on this little escapist adventure would be limited. Knell waited for the expected apathy to sink in, but it never came. He'd grown attached to the idea of living. To making sure Percy made it further than he did, that much he was certain of. The torch near his foot crackled and Knell glanced at it before looking away, wincing at the brightness of it so close. The shade of the wood, dried and pale, reminded him of the knotted branch he'd mistaken for a bear bone, and he wondered.

"Did you follow us all this way just to stare?" Percy said, voice calm and posture coiled like a spring, a man well-versed in violence and ready to share the knowledge by example. "Or are you too scared to make the first move after all that bravado?"

Things moved quickly after that. Flickering torchlight turned every motion into painted stills as Knell's eyes failed to properly adjust. He was slammed against the wall of the tunnel and braced for the cut of a blade, but it was Percy who'd shoved him. The sound of air being sliced just past his nose told him that Percy's quick reaction had saved him from a serious wound, if not worse.

Then Percy let out a pained grunt, his familiar shape doubled over as light flashed against raised steel. The empty part of Knell that was normally filled with apathy had been replaced by a sudden and overwhelming fear, caught in the jaws of fury.

His struggling sight no longer mattered, not when everything lit up in a map of riotous color. There was no plan, no thought that could be put into words, just a white-hot surety. The kingsman's sword never made it to the downswing. Awkward as it was to attack with, he'd been slowed by the constraints of the tunnel, then stopped completely as Knell followed the line of pulsing orange to his heart and *yanked*. The thread snapped and went dark, simple as anything. Metal clattered against stone as the man stumbled and slumped against the bright, familiar tangle of color that made Percy.

The other two leapt back with alarmed shouts, though Knell couldn't process the words. Sound meant nothing, inconsequential as the pain radiating down his body, as the breath his lungs were straining for. All that mattered were those colors, and the threat they represented. The flicker of the torch dimmed, he noted somewhere in the back of his mind, and the shouts turned to screams. But that meant nothing to him. It was so easy, even as his physical body nearly buckled from the effort, to reach out again. To grasp at another bright heartline, and snuff it out. To drag what life remained into himself to keep his own body from collapsing.

He turned to the last thread too slowly. It was already moving in the distance, growing thin. Knell tried to reach for it, but grey crept into the edges of his vision, closing in like a fist. Something touched him, and Knell spun—or tried to. The world dipped sharply, but something kept him from hitting the ground.

Bright. Such bright colors. Knell reached for them. Danger needed to be snuffed out. But the moment his power tried to slide up the first branch of sunlight yellow and verdant green, his mind shied away like he'd been burnt.

*Not this one.* Some small voice shrieked from deep, deep inside, just loud enough to make him pause. In that moment of hesitation, the colors vanished, and Knell heaved in air hard enough to choke on it. His eyes rolled, searching for something to focus on until he saw a hand fisted in his shirt. He coughed and blinked hard to clear the tears from his eyes as he tried to reorient himself. His bones were made of lead, his limbs weak, like he was treading water on dry land.

Where was he? There had been danger.

Kingsmen. A mob.

*Percy.*

Percy was holding him upright, his eyes worried, and that wouldn't do. Knell tried to pat Percy's arm, but something shadowy slid at the edge of his vision where his hand should have been and Percy didn't look reassured at all. He curled his lip into more of a snarl than usual and gave Knell a firm shake.

"Enough of that dark magic shit, Knell. Snap out of it!" Percy commanded. Knell did his best to comply as his teeth were rattled.

This time, when he raised his hands, they looked perfectly normal, or as normal as they could be, fingers splayed open in a gesture of surrender.

"I'm alright." Knell had to say it twice, which was probably not very convincing, but Percy's scowl was an assessing one, and he nodded.

"Stay here," he said. For the briefest moment, it looked like he wanted to say more, but he turned and hauled himself out of the entrance with surprising speed.

Knell stared after him, wondering why he'd left in such a rush until his muddled mind slotted together the chaotic mess of the past few minutes. The last man had gotten away, and Percy was chasing after him.

On the ground lay the two other kingsmen, the young one with the sword right at Knell's feet and the other not two paces away. Knell had nearly missed the second man. The pale shade of his hair marked the body as the leader of the trio, though his tabard was the only other recognizable thing about him. The corpse looked a decade old, withered skin clinging tight to bone that looked too fragile to touch. Knell had the feeling that if he lay a finger on him, the body would crumble into dust.

Right.

Of course.

He'd done that.

There wasn't much to throw up, but he heaved until there was nothing left to lose. His heavy limbs buzzed with the sensation of stolen life energy, enough to keep him standing and more than his tired body could handle. He'd done that, and Percy had seen him.

Percy had gone after the last kingsman.

Percy had watched Knell kill a man without touching him. Without a foci.

Percy was coming back. Wasn't he?

Percy had seen him.

He hadn't said he'd be back.

That last one bounced off Knell's thoughts like a pebble against glass, leaving behind a spiderweb of cracks. One more toss might just shatter something. He carefully emptied his mind, an old habit he'd learned to protect himself from the Great One's punishing focus. He breathed in and out, again and again, and thought of nothing but the whistle of air filling his lungs until it felt easy.

Knell wiped his mouth, spitting once to try and get the lingering taste of bile from behind his teeth. His legs were unsteady and he kept one hand pressed to the wall not only to hold himself upright, but to ground himself. The wavering torchlight swam in his vision wildly enough to make him doubt which way was up, and the floor tilted alarmingly beneath him though his feet hadn't moved.

As he waited out the worst of the vertigo, Knell kept his eyes fixed on his boots and, by proximity, the dead kingsman sprawled beside them. It drifted through his mind that the soldier's jawline looked similar to Percy's. He squinted, taking in the details despite the throbbing pain behind his eyes and bursts of black across his vision. They were of a height as well by Knell's estimation, though the kingsman wasn't quite as broad in the shoulders and chest. His hair was similarly dark, and so were his eyes.

With a different nose, a little change to the droop of his eyes, and a distinctive trio of facial scars, it might be easy to mistake one dead man for another. Especially with the gleam of potential riches shading everyone's perception.

Percy *would* come back, and when he did, they would need a way to stall the mob's hunt.

Feeling numb, Knell reached for his knife.

# CHAPTER 13

## Percy

Percy returned as quickly as he could. Blood was tacky on his hand and streaked across his shirt, but he'd taken care of the third kingsman. All that armor, even if it was leather, slowed a man down. His blade would need better cleaning than the quick swipe it had gotten against the dead man's clothes, but that was something he'd worry about later. More concerning was the unstable flesh-mage he'd left behind.

The way Knell had been cloaked in strange shadows that rose from his skin like steam, eyes unaware and staring through Percy... Unsettling wasn't a strong enough word for it. Percy still couldn't figure out how Knell had managed to land a touch on the first kingsman, but the fight had been a chaotic mess and Knell was a sly creature. He'd managed to snuff the life from one kingsman and wither another into a husk of a corpse, all in a matter of moments.

If Percy hadn't already known how dangerous Knell was, his doubts would have vanished after that display. And yet, despite being half wild with dark power, Knell hadn't harmed him. Even when Percy grasped a fistful of his shirt and shook him like a ragdoll—which he admitted was not his wisest decision, but he'd been a little panicked at the time—the shadows had simply rolled over him harmlessly. His skin prickled at the remembered sensation, like oily smoke. Had he glimpsed a wailing expression in one of the plumes? A grasping hand? He really fucking hoped it was just the torchlight playing tricks.

When he eased his way back into the tunnel, already despairing the trail practically laid out for any other pursuers after all the coming and going, he was more relieved than he expected to find Knell still there. He was braced against the wall of the tunnel just on the edge of the torch's light, looking his usual state of pitiful rather than hollow-eyed and leaking horrid little smoke ghouls, much to Percy's relief.

Percy grimaced as he glanced over the bodies. Knell's magic was an ugly method, but he couldn't argue that it hadn't been effective. At the very least, it had been quick. The desiccated corpse was nightmarish enough on its own, but something about the other body laid out near Knell's feet made him pause. He couldn't see the man's face, but he could have sworn his hair had been longer. He brushed the thought aside as Knell wavered, ready to fall over.

In the fading glow of firelight Knell looked ghastly pale, as bad as he'd been when Percy first met him. It hadn't occurred to him that Knell had begun looking better until now. He was still as grey and gaunt as ever, his eyes still gleamed out from the shadows eerily, and he still lurked in every nearby shadow. But to Percy's great surprise, the revulsion was gone. That bone deep hatred of everything Knell represented had been chipped down to almost nothing while Percy hadn't been paying attention.

He still hated what the Chaos Bringer had done, what horrible things its flesh-mage cultists were capable of, but that was no longer aimed at Knell himself. The truth of it hit Percy like a bludgeon, so sudden he nearly staggered as he adjusted to this new fact. It wasn't often that his own emotions surprised him, he was a predictable sort, not one to change his mind once it had been set.

Knell watched him in turn with a drawn expression. Mistaking Percy's rare moment of introspection as hesitation, his shoulders curled even further in on himself than usual. Without his old robes to hide away in, Knell's posture was more like a kicked dog than a lurking danger—still cornered and capable of biting, but hoping he wouldn't have to. He also looked ready to collapse if he tried to take a step, a sad painting of a destitute farmer in inkwash. Percy snorted at the thought, which had the added effect of startling Knell out of his cowering.

"Can you walk?" Percy asked. "You look ready to fall over."

Knell nodded and Percy reached down to pick up his hat from the floor. It looked more ragged than before, his touch adding a smudge of bloody fingerprints that didn't help as Percy shoved it in Knell's direction.

"C'mon, then. If these fools found us, then more will follow soon enough."

When Knell reached for the hat, Percy spotted dark strands of hair clinging to his sleeve and frowned at him when Knell shoved the hat back onto his head.

"Did you cut a dead man's hair?"

Knell froze, eyes darting damningly to the body Percy had noted on his return before he looked back toward Percy. His hands twitched fretfully, crumpling the frayed straw brim, and his voice was a rough croak.

"I wanted to help."

Percy wondered what the fuck this man could have done to make him look so nervous about Percy's reaction now, of all times. More so than he'd looked after using his powers to seal up Percy's arm or when he'd eaten raw cave creatures. Had he taken the hair as a way to control the corpse? Revulsion soured his stomach. Maybe he had a little left for Knell after all.

But there was something suspicious in the way Knell kept glancing at the body and then back to Percy that made him suspect there was more to it. Percy braced himself for the worst as he rolled the body over with his boot. The worst didn't prepare him for seeing his own face on the dead man, eyes glassy and vacant.

Disquiet fear rose the hair along his arms and neck as he took in his own features. He'd seen something similar before; strange Hill Folk creatures who could steal faces and impersonate their victims. He'd only crossed them briefly, but it wasn't something easily forgotten. Perhaps two years ago now, he and several of his crew were lured into a fairy ring, a clever one made too large to spot easily, and it had taken longer than Percy liked to admit before he'd caught on. The situation had become clear by the third time they'd stumbled back into the same glade, no matter which direction they tried to escape it from.

His men had begun to vanish, one by one. Replaced by Hill Folk wearing their false faces, luring more away to their death with tricks and lies. By the end, Percy and two others, Nathaniel and One-Eyed Marcy, were the only ones left. They'd been the most experienced of the lot and recognized the trap, if much too late. Small bells of silver and speaking in coded memories had kept them alive until, of course, the Hero arrived.

Percy, Nate, and Marcy had made it out, but they'd found the three who hadn't, all dead in gruesome ways. The Prophesized-fucking-Hero had the nerve to claim those men might have lived if they'd been a little wiser, a little more aware. He never did know when to shut his fool mouth, always with a quip, never met a silence he could let lie in peace.

As if the self-important shitheel had a thimble of forestry knowledge between his ears. As if he'd have been any more aware of the danger if Percy's crew hadn't been unfortunate enough to spring the trap for him to see. As if he were better than them.

Maybe he was. He'd been chosen by Fate, touched by the hand of a god to lead a kingdom. Had emerged more powerful after every trial and challenge sent his way, even if it was at the cost of people like Percy and his crew. Or the villagers they met, or any other unworthy soul that perished or was left wrecked in the wake of a Chosen One. A Golden Boy of Prophecy. A *Hero*.

Compared to him, they were nothing but fodder.

Knell's lot was the same—no, it had to be worse—under the hanging blade of inevitability. Percy had known him for mere days, and everything he learned made it seem as if the man's life were a list of varied miseries. Both of them should be dead. Dead as these soldiers at their feet. Men Percy didn't know and felt sorry for, but not sorry enough to put their survival above his own.

By the natural way of things, Knell should have tried to attack him. He'd had ample opportunities, and quite frankly, Percy hadn't given him much reason not to. Yet he stayed his hand. In turn, Percy should have killed Knell on sight.

Fate either had a sense of humor or hadn't spotted them yet, because here they were, still alive and halfway through a mountain range with the whole damned kingdom ready to tear them both apart. Knell knew the price on Percy's head and hadn't even considered using it as a bargaining chip. It would have failed, but he'd seen more foolhardy attempts made over less. In Knell's own warped and grisly way, he'd come up with the perfect solution. Anyone who followed them would think Percy had been killed here and have no reason to search further. Even if the girl from the inn recognized what Knell was —which she surely had—and if people believed her story, not even the most loyal of kingsmen or the most desperate bounty hunter would attempt to track a cultist through a cave.

"It's an uncanny likeness," Percy said rather than voice any of the thoughts rushing through his mind. And it was. Apparently, all of the intense staring Knell did resulted in a near mirror image. Even the scars and missing tooth were exact. He looked at the man's right arm, and sure enough, it ended at a scarred stump of a wrist. Percy considered asking what Knell had done with the hand and just as quickly decided he could live the rest of his life just fine without ever knowing.

He eyed the knife sheathed at Knell's hip, one that hadn't been there, or at least not visible, earlier. It explained the scarring. Knell watched him closely, saw him reach each conclusion, and might have managed a decently flat expression if he hadn't been wringing his hands so tightly. If Percy couldn't see the grey all around his bright eyes. For once, Knell didn't seem to have any words and stared at Percy with tense wariness.

Percy stood, brushed his blood-tacky hand against his pants with a flash of regret that he hadn't thought to steal some cleaner clothes, and shouldered his dropped pack.

"Let's get moving, then."

Knell held himself very still. "Together?"

"I haven't developed the ability to see in the dark yet, so yes. Together." He eyed Knell, who really did appear one wrong step from death. "You look like shit. Drink some water and move slowly. I'm not carrying you."

He might have been able to manage it with two hands, but he didn't want to lose the supplies they'd finally gotten, so Knell would have to drag his own weight. He waited until Knell had laboriously retied his own supplies onto his back before he silently offered his right arm because that awful, yawning pitch black was waiting just past the shrinking torchlight. If that meant Knell had a firm hold to catch himself with when he staggered, it was simply a result of their circumstances.

Though the temptation to bring it was strong, Percy left the torch to sputter out behind them as they headed further into the tunnels. As much as he wanted the comfort of light, the memory of being nearly eaten alive by those cave crabs stayed his hand.

To his cautious relief, there was no sign that the cave entrance had been spotted yet as they made slow progress deeper into the mountain. There were no echoing yells or sounds of pursuit, and Percy was grateful for the reprieve. Running around with a full pack and keeping a stringy cultist from collapsing on the way, all while fueled only by a single pie, no matter how filling, simply wasn't sustainable. As the rush of adrenaline faded, Percy was left with heavy limbs, aches, and the knowledge that he had no safe havens left in the kingdom to run to. Getting to the border would be their best chance at survival. If Knell's theories about the tunnels were correct then the fastest way would be through the heart of the mountain.

Keeping time hadn't become any easier, but if he measured by the state of his aching feet, several hours had passed before they found a place to rest. Knell led them to a small, damply cool cavern bristling with dripstones, a small circle of moonlit sky peeking in from high above. One tiny patch of mossy green had fought its way to survive below it, and the rest of the floor was lumpy, slick rock with small towers of mineral deposits here and there. Percy guessed by the crisp scent of the air and the slow incline they'd been traveling that they were higher up the side of the mountain than he'd first suspected. As he stepped inside, Percy was pleased to see there were several more openings where pale light filtered through in translucent beams. Just enough to illuminate several more caverns that ran alongside the wyrm tunnel, creating what looked like a hall lined with strangely shaped rooms. He investigated one sky-framed opening that was about shoulder height and large enough for him to fit through to forage in the morning. He'd have to collect as much as he could if they were to pass through the mountains, even with the extra supplies.

Knell's bundle of supplies hit the ground with a thump and he slid down to join them in what might generously be described as sitting. He more closely resembled a crumpled heap of old laundry. The day's walking had not been easy on Knell, and they'd had to stop several times so he could catch his breath and rest long enough to keep going. Percy hesitated to admit he was concerned, but Knell had been too quiet ever since the ambush. It was like their first day together, all quiet instructions and stretches of silence in between. Strange how quickly Percy had grown used to the chatter.

There wasn't much to be done about it though. What could Percy say? *Sorry you had to use your horrible necromancy powers to keep us both alive?* Percy had never been in the habit of apologizing for things he wasn't actually sorry for, and he was rarely sorry for anything that kept him alive. The deed was done, and no amount of maudlin regret would bring back stolen lives. He was shit at being comforting, so he didn't bother, but Knell had to be hungry. He'd said using his powers meant he needed to eat more, and thanks to Ruth's generous gift, Percy could at least feed him.

"Is it safe to build a fire, or am I going to lure out some hoard of beasts ready to eat me alive again?" Percy asked.

Knell lifted his head to look around, bright eyes darting all over the cavern before he nodded. His voice was ragged when he spoke. "Should be safe here."

"Good. I'll gather up some wood and figure out dinner," Percy said. He'd spotted branches above them, so there had to be some decent kindling not too far. Knell nodded and slumped back down. Percy hesitated, not sure why he felt the impulse to do something strange and useless, like pat Knell's head. His hat was askew and more of his curls had tumbled free, hiding his face. Percy shook off the urge and quickly walked away before he was caught staring.

Peering out cautiously from the opening he'd noted earlier, Percy saw his guess had been correct. They were much higher on the mountainside, with tall needle-leaf trees all around. The ground was thick with old needles, cones, and fallen branches. Percy gathered as many as he could without having to clamber out and eased back into the cavern with a sense of satisfaction. It wasn't enough to burn for the whole night, not that he'd risk a smoke trail for that long, but it would be plenty to cook with.

He knelt and dropped the wood into a pile, then set down his pack, eager to finally sort through and inventory what he'd gotten. No matter what Ruth claimed, she'd been generous. The supplies were nearly twice as heavy as usual.

The moon peeking in from above was full and bright, but the light it cast was thin, so Percy squinted at the tightly packaged items, then smelled each in order to identify them. Flour, dried fruit, slices of dried squash that were hard and brittle from months in storage but would do well in soups, dried split peas, a decently sized block of rendered fat wrapped in waxed cloth, a small portion of almonds and hazelnuts, several onions and a half dozen apples only a touch wrinkled from long storage. She'd also included a dense brick of tea, an extra water skin, a tined spoon, and much to Percy's delight, several small packets of dried herbs and spices for cooking.

He breathed in the scent of rosemary and let it linger in the back of his throat. That was easier to focus on than the ache that settled in his chest with this last act of kindness he hadn't deserved. Ruth was the last true friend he had, and he'd never get a chance to thank her again. But what he could do was use her gift to make a damn good meal.

*Shit*, he thought as he paused and looked at his bounty, noting a key item was missing. What he really needed was—

"Would this help?" Knell asked. He'd sat up at some point to dig through his own supplies and was holding a cooking pan out toward Percy like it was a sacrificial gift to appease his anger. Or whatever he thought Percy was feeling. It was a little insulting since Percy hadn't so much as raised his voice at Knell since they entered the tunnels.

He took the pan with a nod of thanks. "Yes, that's exactly what I needed. Where did you even get this?"

Knell perked up at that, just as Percy hoped he would.

"I noticed it looked a lot like the one we found all rusted." He paused, then blurted out, "I stole it."

"No shit," Percy said, looking the pan over. It was in good condition and well-seasoned, which would save him a lot of time and trouble. "The whole village was ready to kill us, I'd be annoyed if you wasted coin on them."

Knell was staring at him with an expression that was hard to read, some mix of hesitation and confusion. He opened his mouth as if to speak, then closed it again without a word. Percy left him to figure his shit out and focused on repacking the extra food, setting aside what he needed to make them dinner.

Flour, fat, and water, along with the mushrooms, spring onions, and leafy greens he'd collected earlier that morning. As he repacked the herbs he didn't need, he noted the lack of salt and sighed. No fault of Ruth's, salt was hard to come by, especially with most of the merchants strong-armed into supplying the military rather than small border towns. He'd make due.

Knell, who'd finished sorting through his things and had been staring at Percy since, coughed in an awkward bid for attention despite the fact that they were alone.

"I stole a few other things."

"Like that ring?" Percy said, contemplating exact measurements in his head as he began striking his flint to start the fire, hunched close to see what he was doing in the dim. There was a telling silence from Knell's direction. Percy rolled his eyes as he worked to get the fire from ember to flame.

"I was a bandit half my life, I don't give a shit what you stole. I just want to know if any of it is useful."

"Oh," Knell said, his voice finally losing the timid edge that had been grating on Percy's nerves. "It was actually three rings, a necklace, the pan, some sausages, and that herald's fancy little horn."

Percy barked out a surprised laugh and looked up at him. "Why the hell did you steal that?"

In the growing glow of the fire, Percy saw Knell shrug with that crooked little smile. "He was announcing himself well enough without it. I'm sure the men he travels with will be glad to see it gone."

Percy snorted, shaking his head and amused despite himself. "I would be. Did you eat the sausages already?"

Knell's hands twitched and his stomach growled audibly. "Only one. I wasn't sure if you..."

"You said you needed to eat meat after using your powers," Percy cut in, annoyed at being treated like some swooning court snob. "Don't use me as an excuse when you should be taking care of yourself. If it's dried, eat it while I finish. If it needs cooking, then for fuck's sake, don't make me watch you eat it raw. I'll cook it once the rest is done."

Knell fell quiet at that, and Percy watched his restless hands wander from the corner of his eye. Probably lost without all the fabric of that damned robe to hide in and clutch at. Now all they could do was pluck at the hem of his stolen shirt.

"Stop picking at that before you pull all the threads out," Percy said without thinking, then cursed himself for being such a mother hen. Knell's hands stilled and he looked at Percy curiously, then down at the shirt hem.

"There's embroidery along the cuffs, I think it might be flowers. It's nice that someone took the time to make it," Knell said, smoothing a hand over the stitches that were presumably there. It was too dim beyond the firelight for Percy to tell, especially since the embroidery had been done in the same color as the linen of the shirt. No money for dye.

"And?" Percy replied, more distracted by setting up his ingredients than listening, but he'd gotten the feeling that Knell was holding something back. There was a rustle of fabric, and then a small pouch was held out to him.

"I also took this. The kingsmen traveling with the herald had their own supply," Knell said, his expression oddly hopeful. Inside the pouch was salt—one walnut-sized chunk, the rest crushed into fine grains.

"I could kiss you right now, you little weasel. This is exactly what I needed!" Percy said with a grin, too happy to care that he was aiming it at the same man he'd only thought of as a wretch until very recently. That wretch had gotten him a pan and three month's salary worth of salt. As far as Percy was concerned, he'd earned any meal Percy made with them.

Not willing to waste one more moment, he got to work. The rest of the world faded away as Percy let himself get caught up in the motions of making dinner.

*I could kiss you right now.* Percy's words had all but branded themselves onto the front of Knell's brain. He, in the truest sense of the phrase, could not remember the last time he'd been kissed. Before that final prison, he was sure. His cellmate had been a loud and threatening man always looking for a fight, and Knell couldn't recall feeling any attraction toward him, much less any time they'd been closer than absolutely necessary. He didn't remember the man's face well, but his eyes had been cruel.

Percy had a harsh manner at times, that was undeniable, but there was so much more to him beneath that prickly armor. And it was hardly a chore to look at him, he was a fine man. This wasn't new to Knell. He'd noted it in a distant sort of way from the very start, along with all the other facts about Percy—lying in a ditch, missing a hand, good looking—all filed away objectively. More had been added over their time together, each new piece fitting neatly into place. Percy was bluntly honest, extremely guarded, and no stranger to violence. He was also keenly observant, deeply knowledgeable about forestry, and more thoughtful than he'd ever admit. Despite the threats and distrust, Percy had shown Knell more kindness in these past days than he'd seen in years. Even before he'd been forcibly inducted as an acolyte of the Great One.

*Kissing*, though. It had been a long time since Knell had even entertained the idea, so long it was nearly foreign in his mind, though certainly not unwelcome. His face grew steadily warmer as he lingered on the notion. His own body felt so divorced from any good or pleasing sensations that he had to focus on what it had been like Before rather than After. But as best as he could remember, he'd liked it quite a bit.

To be kissed by Percy? His face felt hot enough to cook their meal, nevermind the fire. He had half a mind to walk back to the town and steal every measure of seasoning they had if it made Percy say such things, his likelihood of a terrible death at the hands of an angry mob be damned.

This cave had been chilly, hadn't it? It felt quite warm where he was sitting despite the hint of a breeze drifting in from the openings above. He really needed to think about something—*anything*—else. The only things nearby were flames, which hurt to look at, or Percy, who didn't hurt at all to look at, and that was more dangerous by far.

Percy had managed to get the fire lit by trapping the striker under his right forearm and on top of the kindling, then striking the flint against it. Knell would have offered to try, but from the focused look on his face, he didn't think Percy would appreciate being interrupted. Or the implication—intended or not—that he was incapable of doing the task himself.

Knell watched, intrigued, as Percy used the pan as a mixing bowl to begin cooking. He set it in the cradle of his crossed legs and measured out two handfuls of flour, a generous spoonful of what Knell guessed was some sort of animal fat that had been refined and set into a soft pale yellow block, and a measure poured from his water skin that Percy seemed to know by instinct. Lastly, a pinch of salt. The sight of it brought Percy's words rushing back, making Knell's face go hot once more.

Percy stirred the mixture, adding a few drops of water now and then until he was satisfied with the consistency of the dough. Knell wondered at what it could be, he'd never heard of bread made without yeast. Perhaps Percy would make the thin salty biscuits that crunched satisfyingly if made right or threatened to break a tooth if made wrong? Knell had never concerned himself much with baking, or cooking for that matter, so his guesses were limited. He was tempted to ask, but it felt wrong to break Percy's focus, which had turned his perpetual frown into an expression of easy contentment Knell didn't want to chase away. So he remained quiet, prepared to hand Percy anything he needed.

Once the dough had been kneaded enough to hold together and form a smooth ball, Percy laid a clean square of cloth over it. He looked between his hand and his scarred wrist, frowning deeply, then looked at Knell—no, looked at Knell's hands in contemplation.

"Scrub your hands clean, *properly,* and you can help me with this."

Pleased at the opportunity, Knell was quick to comply, washing his hands carefully without wasting too much water before settling eagerly next to Percy. Percy lifted the cloth and gestured toward the dough with his chin.

"Hold it for a moment. Carefully."

Knell did as he was told, cupping the warm dough in his hands and resisting the urge to sink his fingertips into its soft surface. Percy quickly used the cloth to wipe away the floury residue inside the pan and set it over the fire, then draped the cloth over Knell's thighs.

"Set the dough on there, and don't let it roll off." Percy made a pinching motion with the side of his thumb against his hand. "Pinch off a bit of dough—a little bigger, yes, that's good—and roll it into a ball between your hands."

That was easy enough, the dough was soft and pliable, rolling into shape without much effort. Percy nodded, and Knell was prouder than he probably should have been at accomplishing such a simple task. Next, Percy made a little pushing motion with the heel of his palm, and if he'd had two hands, he would have gestured with them together. As it was, he simply raised his right wrist in an automatic motion anyway.

"Flatten it out between your palms. Slowly, don't tear it to shreds. See how it cracks along the edges? You're going too fast. Make as wide a circle as you can without the dough falling apart."

It took a few tries, but Knell eventually managed to make a flat disc about the size of his hand with his fingers splayed out, and Percy nodded. "Good enough."

Percy tapped his fingers against the pan in a quick motion to test the heat before snatching his hand back with an approving hum. He took the flat circle of dough onto his own palm carefully, or as carefully as could be, considering the easiest way to hand it over was for Knell to sort of gently slap it into his hand, and he couldn't help but snicker a bit at how silly it felt. Even Percy looked a little amused by it before he draped the dough across the bottom of the pan with a soft sizzle on contact.

It smelled better than Knell had expected from so few ingredients and his mouth began to water as the scent wafted up from the pan. Percy shot him a pointed look, and Knell pinched off another piece of dough to start shaping it the way he'd been told. By his second try, Percy had pinched the edge of the strange, flat bread and flipped it in a practiced motion, revealing browned spots on the other side. To Knell's surprise, the whole thing began to puff up, starting as small bubbles, then slowly, the entire bread ballooned until it was nearly round before steam escaped and it sank back into a flat disc.

For lack of a plate, Percy laid out the cloth he'd eaten berries from over a mostly smooth rock near the fire and pinched the edge of the bread again, lifting it from the pan and dropping it to the cloth in one quick move. Then he looked at Knell, who quickly remembered his own task and finished shaping the dough to hand to Percy. So it went, Knell pinching and shaping, Percy making him redo the work until he was satisfied and then cooking each one. Not all of them puffed up, but when they did, Percy looked satisfied and Knell all but swelled with pride. The stack of cooked breads stood a half dozen tall when they were done, and Knell's stomach was growling as he brushed the remains of dough from his hands.

Next in the pan went a small pinch of the pale fat, which sizzled and melted into oil while Percy dropped in a handful of mushrooms, then half the supply of greens he'd gathered. It barely seemed to fit, but the pile quickly shrank as they cooked. While they did, Percy sprinkled in some salt and a few pinches of other herbs. None that Knell could identify, but it smelled delicious.

With the spoon, Percy carefully nudged the food to one side of the pan in a dense heap, fat pooling temptingly along the bottom, and looked at Knell. "You can add the sausages, the grease doesn't bother me much."

Knell wanted to ask if he was sure, but his hands were already reaching out to drop the sausage into the open space without permission from his brain to do so. There were two links left on the string he'd stolen, and the moment they hit the pan, their smell rose up to join the chorus of aromas. He had to swallow hard to keep from openly drooling.

Percy's lip curled up a bit in a grimace, but he didn't say anything. Knell wasn't sure if it was the smell that bothered him or the fact that they were clearly raw and Knell had admitted to already eating one. He regretted not stealing more pies, but the woman at the stall had been eagle-eyed, he'd barely been able to snatch the two on the edge of her counter. Everything else had been easy in comparison, even a ring slipped right off someone's finger would go unnoticed if the thief was skilled and the owner of the ring was confident it was safe. Confident enough not to pay attention to every slight touch in a crowded space.

"Raw. Of course it was," Percy said.

Well, question answered then. Knell just shrugged in response because it was true. Food was a survival method, and whatever changes had been wrought on his body, it was either luck or cruel irony that the acolytes had become immune to most diseases. Whatever humours they had were either balanced perfectly or, more likely, so ruined that mere mortal ailments couldn't compare. He'd eaten plenty of dubious things, but at least he'd never fallen so low as to partake in the worst of the some other acolytes' appetites.

He didn't think Percy would find that very reassuring.

The food didn't take much longer, but Knell's stomach had grown embarrassingly noisy and was threatening to go after his spine. Percy instructed Knell to take one of the thin breads and heap the cooked greens mixture and sausage on top. It was an ingenious method, like an edible plate. Knell lost himself a bit in eating and only came up for air once half the stack of bread was gone, along with a good portion of the greens and all the sausages.

The food tasted even better than it smelled, and he hoped Percy wasn't insulted by Knell all but inhaling it rather than savoring each bite. He glanced at Percy and found him staring back in silence, half a bread heaped with greens forgotten in his hand. His face was flush from sitting so near the fire to cook, and his eyes were fixed on Knell. Oddly, his expression lacked the disgust from the last time Knell had needed to sate his hunger so urgently.

Then again, last time he'd been eating raw shell spiders. Cooked sausage and greens had to be an improvement, even if Knell's table manners were still nonexistent. The food had been the best thing he could remember eating, and he politely refrained from asking for Percy's share as well by licking the remaining grease from his fingers. Beside him, Percy made the faintest strangled noise in the back of his throat. Knell felt a little bit bad about eating like a, well, like a man who'd been dwelling in caves for several years, but he wasn't about to waste any of it.

The blanket of contentment that had settled over Percy as he cooked lasted until Knell began eating with his usual post-magic frenzied energy. The eating itself wasn't the issue—it was just as alarming as the first time, but Percy had known to expect it. The real problem began with the noises. Knell, without realizing it, had let out the softest, most indecent moan Percy had ever heard outside of a brothel at the first bite. Percy should have been amused by it, he knew how to land a filthy joke with the best of them.

To his horror, his actual response had been a little spark of warmth low in his belly that certainly wasn't hunger. At least not for food.

Percy was neither a prude nor a virgin, though he'd discovered that his libido was slower to stoke than most of the people he'd known. Lust for another was built over time, not something that struck out of the blue when he saw a stranger. Usually, it was a trusted friend from his old crew, a warm body and a friendly face satisfying needs with no strings attached. Romance rarely played a part, but he'd grown adept at making sure he and his bed partners parted ways well satisfied.

To think that Knell might set off such a reaction, even a minor one, was a surprise to say the fucking least. Percy forced himself to eat as he sat with the revelation, his face hot. Distantly, he was pleased to note that the food had turned out well.

He recalled saying something about kissing Knell out of gratitude for the salt and had to quickly stomp out the mental images that tried to rise. The only good thing about it all—aside from his cooking, which was excellent—was that Knell ate with the speed of a starved feral dog, saving Percy from prolonged agony. That relief was short-lived as Knell began running his black tongue up his wrist, then sucked the grease from his fingers with obvious enjoyment.

Percy wondered if this was his true punishment for a lifetime of bad choices. A lost hand and a baffling attraction to this creature of a man sitting across from him. He tore his eyes away from the scene and finished his own food at a more sedate pace, staring fixedly at the small patch of visible sky and wondering what the fuck his body thought it was doing.

# CHAPTER 14

## *Knell*

The next morning, Knell woke feeling heavy and still exhausted, hunger's teeth still sunk into his innards after expending so much energy the day before. But it wasn't nearly as awful as it could have been, thanks to Percy's insistence on feeding him. Knell's mouth was sleep-sour now, but he ran his tongue along the back of his teeth in memory of how good the meal had been, despite Percy's insistence that it was simple fare. He felt a little burst of pride for providing the cooking pan that Percy was so pleased with. His eyes had creased at the corners, it always gave him away when he tried to scowl his way out of a smile.

Knell sat up and shrugged off the blanket, still adjusting to seeing himself in clothes that weren't black robes. He turned to make a comment about it to Percy—maybe he could get a little huff of amusement out of him to start the day off right—when he realized he was alone.

"Percy?"

The cavern was empty, but that was fine. Percy often woke early and went to forage if Knell overslept. Sure, he'd gotten into the habit of telling Knell he was going and a rough estimate of when to expect him back in case anything went wrong, but after the way Knell had pushed his powers the day before, it was no surprise that Knell slept harder than usual.

Percy's pack was gone.

That was fine. It was *fine.* Percy had taken the pack foraging before. Though he usually emptied out all the excess supplies before leaving. And Knell couldn't help but notice he hadn't left much behind. In fact, beyond some shared items, most of what was left belonged to Knell. His heart was beating too fast and his breath was getting short. There must be a good reason. Percy wouldn't have just—

He would.

The thought cleaved through the noise in his head with sharp-edged clarity. Percy said it himself at every opportunity, that they would part ways as soon as their alliance was no longer necessary.

Or when Knell proved too monstrous to be around.

Percy had watched Knell steal the life and vitality out of two men with ease just yesterday, even if he might not have realized that Knell had also accomplished it without a foci. Not even Knell could find a way to twist that truth into something more optimistic. Percy must have been desperate to escape his company without putting himself at risk. Had the dinner just been a way to appease Knell's hunger before Percy made his escape?

His knuckles popped loudly as he twisted his fingers together, everything falling into place as he looked back on the day before. It didn't matter how quiet he was or if he'd tried his best to be a better person. He hadn't done a very good job of it, had he? Using his powers on Percy without a care to what Percy wanted, just to prove to himself that he could. Crying all over Percy at the thought of being free from the Great One's hold, only to use those same powers to kill at the first opportunity.

It didn't matter that Percy had killed as well because Percy had never pretended otherwise, and he could take a life but he couldn't steal a person's very essence. Knell bemoaned the things he'd been forced to do and then fell right back into those same habits without hesitation. Slow, rotting revulsion spread roots within him. He'd mutilated a corpse and hoped Percy might be *grateful*. What could he be other than a monster? Why wouldn't Percy leave at the first opportunity?

Sound went funny. There was a ringing in Knell's ears, and his footing didn't feel quite right, like the world was ever-so-slowly tipping.

"Percy?" he tried to call, knowing there would be no answer, but the air wheezed out of him near soundlessly, his chest tight as a clenched fist. Percy was gone, and Knell couldn't fault him for it. Knell would part ways with himself if he could.

Stumbling, he knocked his hand hard against the wall of the cavern, rough stone streaked with smooth veins where water had once run down it. Observations drifted in and out of his head with a distant absence he recognized all too well. He felt like he was floating out of his body, barely noting the jarring ache as he slid to the floor.

Despite his claims, Percy could manage to navigate the tunnels on his own if he was careful, and he was more than knowledgeable enough to escape along the surface. He'd shared a final meal and had taught Knell enough to forage his own food without poisoning himself —as long as he paid close attention. More than Knell deserved, but at the moment he wasn't sure he cared all that much about living. About anything at all. He couldn't feel his fingertips, and every movement felt sluggish.

Percy must have been stealthy to keep from waking Knell when he left. They'd slept back to back in the way that had become their habit. Knell wondered if Percy had hated it, sharing warmth with a wretch like him. If he'd hesitated before leaving, dagger in hand, and contemplated ridding himself and the world of Knell for good. Knell almost wished he'd done it.

And there was the crux of it. *Almost.* Knell hadn't felt the will to live so strongly in years, but he'd gladly welcome the slide of a knife across his throat if it meant Percy would come back to deliver it.

A suitable punishment, he thought. To know the warmth of companionship and then, through his own actions, be left cold and alone in the dark. Unable to deal with endless shades of cold grey, Knell tilted his head back toward the small patch of early morning sky and reached for any colors he could grasp.

Percy returned to a shitshow.

Knell was stuck in some sort of awful trance, sitting curled up with his arms clutched around his knees and his head tipped back at a sharp angle as if some invisible hand had grabbed his hair and yanked. His eyes were halfway rolled back into his head, and his face was a mask of agony as he rocked side to side. Shadows crawled across his form, rising up like vapors and sighing out mournful little whispers of noise that Percy hoped he'd forget as soon as possible. He didn't need to understand whatever they were saying to know it was some sort of jeering accusation. The air itself had a dark, judgmental weight to it.

Was one normal fucking day too much to ask for? Percy dropped the bundled food he'd spent the morning foraging onto a dry patch of ground and moved carefully toward whatever the hell was happening. Was this some sort of delayed reaction to Knell tapping into a power fueled by a god no longer in this realm? Percy didn't know a damn thing about magic except to avoid it, much less how to handle the chaotic shit-storm swimming through Knell's blood.

As he drew closer, he saw the shadows weren't the only thing moving. The floor around Knell was shifting, and Percy paused on the edge of solid ground to avoid stepping on it. There was enough morning light pouring in to see that it wasn't the stone moving, but the writhing of insect carcasses. Small things that had died here, rattling their tiny husks as they surged up through cracks in the ground, only to skitter around mindlessly before they scrambled out of sight once more in an endless cycle.

Percy shuddered, but at least it was just bugs. No dead hand reached up to grab for his boots. No twisted flesh homunculus was forming. Just a lonely, tortured figure caught in the throes of something Percy couldn't comprehend.

He reached out but left his hand hovering over Knell, unsure if his touch would make things better or worse and angry that he didn't know the answer. There was also the small matter of touching a flesh-mage with his bare skin. He knew Knell didn't want to hurt him, but right now it was obvious Knell wasn't aware of his surroundings. Percy wasn't sure if he was even conscious. He had no desire to test Knell's control in this state—or his own luck—so he cast around for something that might be helpful.

Knell's blanket lay in a heap nearby, and Percy snatched it up, shaking it free of crawling bug corpses with a sharp snap of his wrist. He managed to hold it open by grasping one corner with his hand while pinning another to his side with his wrist, and with a bit of regret at the indignity of it, he tossed the whole thing over Knell. The man didn't so much as twitch in reaction, and Percy grimaced at the thought of climbing into that circle of writhing insects. Dead or not, it was fucking unsettling.

He spotted a decently sized rock nearby, maybe not the most comfortable perch, but unlikely to have many tiny carcasses to summon in comparison to the moss-spotted ground. With a deep breath to brace himself for any number of horrific skin-crawling possibilities, Percy kicked away the bugs trying to crawl up his boots and wedged himself far enough behind Knell's body to hook him under the arms and haul him up.

Knell wasn't a short man, if he could stand upright, he'd be close to Percy's height, but he was still all skin and bone so he wasn't very heavy. His body didn't relax, and Percy hefted him into his arms in a miserable, rigid curl of knees and elbows, muscles tense under his grip. The weird vapor-like shadows had lessened, thank fuck, but a few clung to Knell stubbornly, wisping around Percy's arms and into his face in ways shadows never should. Damned things should stick to solid surfaces where they belonged.

Irritated and trying not to send them both crashing to the ground, he shook his head and blew out a few harsh breaths like he was trying to put out a candle. It worked, surprisingly, and the shadows clouding his vision broke apart with one last haunting whisper. Percy hoped Knell didn't have to deal with these all the time, they were annoying little fucks. Without the ghostly nonsense taking up Percy's attention, he could hear Knell muttering something in such a low voice he'd missed it before.

Once they made it to the rock without any injuries, Percy sat back on it with one arm clamped around Knell and the other supporting his own balance. He edged backward in a thoroughly awkward scooting motion he was glad no one was there to witness until he could rest his back against the wall of the cave. Settled, he realized Knell had relaxed a little in his hold, thin fingers curled around his forearm from behind the barrier of the blanket. His flesh hadn't begun trying to separate itself from the rest of him, so Percy called it a success.

Any hope that Knell had come back to himself faded as the man began rocking in his hold, shadows leaking up through the blanket once more. Percy heaved a sigh and figured he might as well get comfortable, there was no telling how long this might take. He considered leaving Knell here until this whole unsettling song and dance was over, but it didn't sit right with him.

The only requests Knell asked of him were for the simple warmth of human contact, someone at his back, a hand to hold as he broke down. It clearly comforted him, and gods knew the man didn't have enough meat on his bones to generate any heat of his own. If that was the only help Percy could provide as Knell endured whatever he was going through, then so be it. He'd suffered through more trying tasks in worse company. And something about the way Knell's hands held him—like he was something too precious to lose, but Knell was afraid to grip tightly lest he pull away—made Percy want to stay exactly where he was.

He shifted to get as comfortable as he could under the circumstances, dragging Knell to sit between his legs and lean that bony spine back against his chest. Not wanting to suffocate Knell after the effort he'd put in, Percy adjusted the blanket until it was draped over Knell's head like a hood but freed his face. It was quite the image, Knell swaddled up like the biggest, most angular baby, but it kept Percy safe from any direct skin contact. If Knell had a problem with it, he could damn well wake up. Without the barrier of cloth in the way it was easier to hear Knell's mumbling and Percy expected it to be more nonsense. The ramblings of someone caught in a dream or even some language humans were never meant to know, but instead, it was a plea. Percy tipped his head forward, his cheek practically pressed to Knell's blanket covered ear to listen.

"Please," Knell whispered, voice thin and thready but so painfully desperate. "Please don't leave me alone."

Oh. Well, fuck if that didn't make Percy's chest feel a little tight.

"I'm right here," Percy said, at a loss for what other answer he could give. But Knell was too far gone to hear, whispering the phrase between low keening wails. As if he were both desperate for anyone to hear, and terrified that someone would.

Percy curled his hand into a fist and pressed his knuckles into the rock until they ached because he couldn't fix this. He was a blunt instrument, meant for nothing more than looming behind people more clever and important than he was and for knocking heads together. He couldn't fight this battle for Knell.

Though the man was sickly and malnourished as an orphaned lamb in winter, he'd waded into multiple fights on Percy's behalf. Came crashing through, good sense be damned, with nothing more than a rock in hand and more courage than Percy had seen in an age. Prophesized Heroes could take notes. Percy would admire it if it weren't for the absolute lack of survival instincts. Knell had an alarming tendency to accept the worst possible options and resign himself to them.

Percy had never understood that. He'd found himself at rock bottom multiple times in his life, but even when it was tempting to lie there, he'd always forced himself back up, biting and clawing and stepping on any neck he could get under his boot to do so. Knell would have been among that number not so long ago. How many bodies would he walk on to drag Knell up with him now? A voice in the back of his mind wagered that Percy would be willing to rack up a number few others had warranted.

Knell was still a creepy—if slightly less greasy—weasel of a man, but he wasn't the coward Percy had thought. Wretched, yes, but he was more human than many of the people Percy had met who hid behind masks of propriety. Knives tucked in their sleeves, ready for the soft flesh of an unguarded back. He imagined Knell trapped in the dark, surrounded by comrades he couldn't trust, and beyond that, a world ready to kill him as soon as they saw what he was. Puppeted by a mad god and spending every moment trying to survive, alone in all the ways that mattered.

The thought made him angry, and he had to yank his hand away from the rough rock when he pressed hard enough to split the skin of a couple knuckles. He shook his hand with a hiss and checked for blood, but they were shallow scratches. Peeved that he'd let himself sink into self-pondering nonsense, Percy wrapped both arms around the trembling man in his lap and held on perhaps a little too tightly.

As soon as Knell was all but crushed in his hold, his coiled muscles began to relax. The keening tapered off into a warbling, confused noise for a moment before he went back to his whispered pleas the moment Percy loosed his grip. Curious, Percy tightened his arms slowly like a snake constricting its dinner. Displaying that intrinsic lack of survival instinct, Knell's tense form softened up like butter on a warm day to practically melt against Percy.

Of course. Words couldn't reach him, but touch did. The man was always so damned handsy, tapping his fingers nervously, his absent little pats like he thought Percy might have vanished if he wasn't within arm's reach, the way he slept more deeply with Percy at his back. This made things much easier.

With a solution finally at hand, Percy tucked his knees in as well, trapping Knell in a full body hold that would have been a threat to anyone else. Knell's head fell back against Percy's shoulder and his breathing relaxed into a relieved exhale halfway through another plea. The shadows had stopped seeping out of him as well, which was more of a relief than Percy wanted to admit. He hoped whatever comfort he was providing helped lessen the nightmare Knell was trapped in.

He had just resigned himself to a long, cramped morning and a hell of a crick in his back and neck when Knell's fingers twitched, kneading at his arm through the blanket like a contented cat, and he heard a murmured sigh of, "Percy..."

Knell hadn't woken up, a quick glance showed his eyes were still tiny bright slivers rolled up under his lids. Somehow, through whatever had snared his mind, he either recognized Percy or equated this strange, comforting hold with him.

Percy wasn't sure what to do with that, so in tried and true fashion, he ignored it and settled in to wait.

# CHAPTER 15

## *Knell*

The line between dreams and wakefulness had blurred, and Knell wasn't sure which side he'd landed on. Awareness returned in increments, his thoughts swimming lazily to the surface of his mind. It must be a dream. He'd never been this comfortable in recent memory. Wrapped completely in a reassuring hold, warm through and relaxed from head to toe, if this was a dream, he'd happily sleep forever.

The dream world jostled beneath him with a grumbled string of soft swearing near his ear. Confused, he opened his eyes and glanced blearily around. Or he tried to. He was effectively, if comfortably, trapped in a cocoon of blankets with just enough freedom to shift his head a bit. Two arms were wrapped around his chest, one hand grasping a scarred wrist, and thighs more muscular than Knell's had ever been clamped his own legs in place. Definitely a dream, and a nice one, if somewhat odd.

"You awake for real this time, or am I going to inhale one of those fucking shadow ghosts again? Because if I end up possessed, then you deserve whatever happens afterward." Percy's very real voice groused from behind him.

Knell would have startled if he had anywhere to move, but Percy's hold on him tightened and he went limp again, the tension melting away in an instant. So he lay there, trying to grasp a single thought or memory that would make sense of the situation, and came up empty.

"Percy?" he asked. More rasped out, like he'd strained his voice.

"Care to explain what the hell happened while I was gone?" Percy asked in an accusatory tone that Knell felt was unwarranted. Between the two of them, surely Percy had a bit more active engagement in how they ended up here. This was the second time Knell had woken up in Percy's arms, and while he wasn't used to it, the possibility that it might become a habit wasn't something he minded at all.

Then the second half of Percy's question echoed in his head. Percy *had* been gone. The morning's events were coming back to him in brief snatches of awareness. Knell had woken up and realized Percy was gone, having taken all his belongings with him. This time, he fought back the urge to settle bonelessly in Percy's arms and struggled weakly until Percy released him. A bit more struggle freed him from his blanket confines, then he turned to stare at Percy, who was watching him with an expectant look and raised eyebrows.

"You were gone!" Knell said, matching Percy's accusation with his own. How Knell went from feeling hopelessly abandoned to crushed in Percy's full-body hug was a mystery he was determined to solve, but first things first.

Percy frowned at him as if Knell was the one being unreasonable here. "I woke early and went to forage. We'll need as much as we can that'll last, and it would've been more dangerous to wait until daylight."

"You took your things," Knell said, beginning to feel foolish.

"I wasn't about to go out there empty-handed," Percy argued with an annoyed click of his tongue. "I like to be prepared for anything, and that includes hiding out for a while if the people hunting me get a little too close. Doesn't seem like they've made it this far up, though." He crossed his legs to sit in a more comfortable position now that Knell was kneeling beside him and narrowed his eyes. "What are you upset about? I left you with everything you might need until I came back."

Knell looked away and picked at the loose threads along the edge of the blanket. "I thought you'd left for good."

"I didn't."

Percy said it like his return should have been the obvious conclusion, but they both knew it wasn't. Knell tugged harder at a stubborn bit of thread and didn't answer. Percy sighed.

"Next time, I'll let you know I'm leaving, alright?"

Knell abandoned the bit of string to look him in the eye. "And when you're coming back?"

His expression must have been more intense than he'd intended because Percy suddenly looked less confident, crossing his arms and fixing his gaze past Knell's shoulder. "Fine. I'll let you know when I'll be back."

The fact that Percy had said *when* rather than *if* warmed him more than it should have. "Alright."

"Settled then?" Percy asked, levering himself to his feet with a wince and knuckling at his lower back. "No more summoning up freaky little whispering shadows and making bug corpses fucking dance because I went out to get breakfast?"

Oh dear, is that what happened when he panicked now? It could be worse, but it probably hadn't been pleasant to witness. "You're making breakfast?"

"Not the fucking point, Knell."

Knell nearly toppled off the squat boulder, legs still tangled in the blanket, and had to hurriedly catch himself before Percy saw him flailing. He hadn't expected to hear his name come from Percy's mouth, much less in a tone that, while irritated, didn't carry even a hint of disgust.

"Right, sorry." It came out a little more breathless than he'd meant it to. Percy shot him an odd look but carried on brushing himself off. Knell shuffled closer to him, trying his hardest to act casual, but judging by the suspicious look Percy shot him, clasping his hands behind his back and attempting—badly—to hum a tune hadn't done the job.

"Now that we've established the cause of my little, ah, panic session," Knell started, and Percy caught on quickly. He turned sharply in the direction of his abandoned pack with Knell right at his heels. "I think it's fair to ask why I woke up in your arms?"

Percy spun back toward him with a fierce scowl, but his ears had gone a shade darker, and Knell bit back a smile as he raised his hands in surrender.

"Don't make it sound indecent." Percy was probably trying to be intimidating, but Knell would swear his expression was closer to a pout. "I was moving you somewhere with less goddamn bug corpses to cover yourself with, but you only calmed down when I practically crushed you."

If Percy hadn't been so clearly at the limit of his patience, Knell would have offered to test the results again while he was fully aware. Survival instincts kept him from voicing the thought, and he grasped at his own elbows in a facsimile of a hold instead.

"Thank you. I know you don't like to see..." Knell gestured in the general direction of himself rather than say it. Percy could have just waited it out or left for good without Knell being any wiser. That Percy chose to help him instead was doing something strange to his chest and made his eyes burn a little, but it was also dangerous. "Weren't you worried? About my powers?"

Leafy greens had fallen loose from their bundled cloth and Percy was carefully gathering and resorting them. He made a vague waving motion with his right arm. "I made sure there wasn't any skin contact, I know that much."

"Ah, about that," Knell said with a wince. He clasped his hands together so tightly he felt a knuckle pop when Percy lifted his head slowly. "There's something I should tell you."

"What," Percy said the word with such a flat tone it wasn't a question so much as a demand.

"Do you recall the homunculus from the forest?"

"It rings a bell," Percy replied tersely.

Were his palms always this sweaty? Knell scrubbed his hands against the rough fabric of his trousers.

"When it struck me, I didn't have much time to think. I just had to stop it," *from killing you*, he didn't say. "I thought I grabbed the foci to control it and siphoned its life force that way, but when I went to Sibling Ness' body, the bone fragment was still there."

The lack of color in Knell's vision meant Percy—and everyone else—always looked some shade of ash grey, but his complexion went alarmingly pale as the words sank in.

"You did all of *that*," Percy asked with the careful steadiness of someone facing down a feral animal, "without touching any part of the creature?"

Knell shrugged one shoulder, feeling stiff and awkward in his own skin, not sure what else to do with himself. His heart was pounding and his skin felt clammy, but at least he hadn't started leaking shadows again.

"Yes," he said because Percy deserved honesty.

"The kingsmen, too." It wasn't a question, Percy was just adding up the facts. Knell nodded anyway.

He raised a finger to make a point, already wincing because even to his muddled moral compass, it sounded terrible. "It takes effort and focus, and it's very draining. I did have to touch the one man to, well, change his features."

Percy had his face in his hand and was taking long, controlled breaths, so Knell waited for him to finish. The air up in these mountains was quite thin, wasn't it? Maybe he should be taking more measured breaths too.

At least this time, he might get a chance to say goodbye when Percy left. Or killed him. Knell had just admitted to being far more dangerous than the average flesh-mage. Knowing he could use his powers at a distance without a foci must be Percy's worst nightmare. It should worry Knell more that dying seemed like a better option than abandonment.

With one last deep inhale, Percy dropped his hand to stare hard at Knell, who began sweating again in earnest. Percy rose to his feet in one smooth movement and stalked close enough to grab the front of Knell's tunic in his fist.

"We've gotten too damned far in this for you to scare me off. We're getting through these fucking mountains, and I will lie, steal, and kill to make sure that happens. I'm not some fainthearted green soldier who'll run at the first sign of danger." Percy was looming again, much like he had when they first met, but this time he was putting himself intentionally in Knell's space. Proving to himself he wasn't afraid.

A terrible tactic with anyone who actually wanted to hurt him, but Knell wasn't about to complain. The knuckle of Percy's thumb was pressed to the skin of his collarbone in a single point of warmth that Knell didn't want to lose. Percy was still talking, but Knell had lost the thread a bit. Whatever point Percy was trying to make, it meant he wasn't leaving. So when he glared pointedly, Knell just nodded rapidly in agreement.

Percy let him go and purposefully turned his back to return to sorting his foraged goods. "Then it's settled."

Unsure what just happened but feeling at ease now that he wasn't being left behind or killed, Knell smoothed out the wrinkles from his tunic and couldn't help but smile, a soft sort of warmth spreading through his chest.

He wasn't going to fucking think about it.

Percy returned to his bags and finished sorting them a bit more roughly than he'd intended, but fastidiously enough to keep his mind focused. Lunch was made perfunctorily, consisting of grains and greens, salt and herbs. It tasted fine, though Percy had no recollection of measuring any of it. The whole while, Knell hovered at a distance, folding and refolding his blanket, retrieving his half of the supplies and presumably packing them away. Percy wouldn't know because he wasn't thinking about it.

Gods above, below, and in-between, if flesh-mage powers weren't confined by touch, the havoc they'd wreak would be limitless. If they'd known it was possible, entire swathes of the kingdom would have been wiped out before anyone could even begin shoring up a defense. Which begged the question, was it an ability any flesh-mage was capable of, or was there something about Knell in particular?

Not that Percy was thinking about it. Because if he thought about it then he broke out into a cold sweat, and that did nothing to help his situation. So they ate their lunch, and he carefully didn't think about it. He focused on the food—decent, might have been nice with some mustard greens, but the salt lifted the whole dish—the weather—pleasantly sunny outside, same fucking damp cold in the caves—and stared at Knell.

He didn't look too badly affected by his time half-aware and conjuring up shadow ghosts from his skin. A little tired and as messily ravenous as usual with his meal, but it was almost endearing now. Lamp bright eyes darted around curiously as always, and a crooked little tilt of a smile appeared every time they landed on Percy. This was the man capable of killing him with nothing more than a thought.

And as much as he *wasn't thinking about it*, Percy found himself the tiniest bit curious. How the hell did it work?

He didn't want to know. He *didn't*.

Except maybe he did, just a little bit. And he'd be the only person with access to answers who might live long enough to remember them. Generally, Percy was only ever as curious as he needed to be—anything more only invited trouble. But Knell was right here, and damn it, he did want to know.

Percy passed off the pan for Knell to wipe down once they'd finished eating and gave in. "How the hell does this magic shit work, exactly?"

Knell, who had been either considerate or smart enough to give Percy the space and silence he needed, lit up like a fucking beacon at being asked a question. He quickly tried to tamp down his excitement as he caught Percy's unimpressed look, clearing his throat and rifling around in the pack to make room for the pan. He mostly looked like an opportunistic weasel. "What would you like to know?"

"What makes you so different? How are you able to do what none of the other cultists could?"

Knell thought it over as he tied the pack shut, and Percy couldn't find any fault in his neatness, which only made him grumpier. "I don't know," Knell said. "I wasn't very powerful among my brethren or very talented with the rites. I don't think I'm particularly special at all."

Percy squinted at him, eyeing him from tangled hair to dusty boots, but he didn't get even a mild sense of the man being Fate-touched. No subtle draw of charisma or tug of sincerity and belief. Percy had gotten to know those too damn well when traveling beside the Prophesized Hero, and it made him itch every time. But there was none of that, just Knell in all his awkward, earnest glory.

Satisfied, Percy nodded and slapped Knell on the shoulder before hauling up his pack to carry. "Then you'd better get to explaining how the fuck you can turn a man into a dried-up husk or a bear monster into a pile of meat without whatever it is you flesh-mages use to control things."

Knell scrambled to his feet, gathering up his own bundled supplies like he thought Percy might start sprinting off without him.

"I'm still not sure exactly how I've managed to do it," he said as he struggled to get himself sorted. Percy watched it happen without offering to help because he deserved some small amusement before they wandered the halls of Knell's depressing, horror-laced memories.

"Then start from the beginning and lay it out simply for me," Percy said as he reached out to tug the knot of Knell's blanket bundle into place. He ignored the grateful look he got in return and gestured for Knell to start leading the way.

"That might take a while," Knell said slowly, giving Percy a chance to back out. As if that had ever done anything other than make Percy double down.

"Good thing we've got nothing but fucking time, isn't it?"

They stayed in the caves as long as they could hold out, traveling as quickly as possible without getting trapped in smaller tunnels or dead ends. It was impossible to tell the time of day in the caves, no matter how strong one's gut sense for it usually was. The oppressive dark fooled every sense, so they simply walked until they were too worn out to continue, then rested in short shifts for just a few hours before pressing on. Knell's long, winding explanation of his powers occupied them for the first day of the trip, and if it weren't for the exhaustion, Percy might not have slept afterward. But much to his relief, the efforts of the day dragged his eyes shut as soon as they'd settled down for rest.

They slept under thin cracks in the ceiling of the cave, with sun or moonlight filtering in to create the barest of havens in the dark, balancing on a thread of safety between the creatures lurking in the dense shadow and the danger of men hunting them in the forests above. Percy had been dreading Knell's usual pre-sleep questions, but he'd grown quiet and distant after laying out how effective he was at killing.

The dark of the caves was always worse when they traveled in silence. Percy prompted him with a question here and there, but the answers were short and listless. He had no interest in spending the next few days stuck with a dour companion. One was enough, and he had already claimed the role, thank you very fucking much. Percy was tired, his eyes shut, ready to sleep, but the tense line of Knell's back against his kept him awake. He could feel every small twitch of restlessness, and it was souring his already rotten mood.

"Go to sleep," he grumbled. Knell went still but didn't relax at all.

"Sorry," came the whispered reply, and Percy breathed out a long sigh. God damned sad gutter-rat of a man and his miserable raspy voice. Percy was tempted to suffocate him in another crushing grip if it meant they could both get some sleep. Then he paused and really considered it.

Curious to see if it would work again—but mostly desperate for a few hours of uninterrupted rest—Percy gave a mental shrug and rolled over. "I have an idea."

One bright eye peered back at him from over Knell's shoulder. "What are you doing?"

"If I hold you, will you calm the hell down so we can sleep?" Percy asked bluntly.

Knell let out a sound that was more wheeze than words, but he didn't move away or shake his head, so Percy curled himself against Knell's back and wrapped his arms around him. "Don't turn me into a husk or a meat pile."

Knell let out another strangled noise, but it had an edge of laughter so Percy figured it was as good a reassurance as he was going to get. He tightened his arms slowly until Knell relaxed all at once with a half-formed noise of contentment that Percy felt more than heard.

*Well then*, Percy thought to himself once he was sure he wasn't about to die immediately, *this could be useful.* He nearly teased Knell for it, but a soft snore brought him up short. Incredulous, he squinted through the dim light at the limp man in his arms, vaguely worried he'd passed out from lack of air, but Knell snored again, breathing just fine. Face gone slack and relaxed like he was laying on the finest bed instead of being crushed in Percy's grip.

Unable to help himself, Percy snickered. A bit of shifting and Knell was pinned down so Percy didn't have to keep his arms tensed. He tucked Knell's head under his chin so he wasn't stuck breathing in the smell of sweat, cave, and grease. Nowhere near as bad as it was before the spring, but not exactly pleasant. Knell's hair was still as surprisingly soft as Percy remembered, falling in loose curls instead of matted lanks. It was more attention than Percy usually spared for anyone's hair, but he was asleep before he could find something else to focus on.

During their second night of rest, Percy rolled in his sleep and woke up squashing Knell underneath his full weight. He'd sat up quickly, wondering if he'd smothered the man, but his companion simply let out another contented snore. Knell's expression shifted from the slack drooling of deep sleep to something vaguely annoyed, brow furrowed and mouth tensed into a frown. Was the weight so helpful to his sleep? How could it possibly be comfortable? Percy shoved away the fact that he felt better rested than usual himself, and nudged Knell roughly awake with his elbow so they could move on.

Later, they found themselves in a cavern with a shallow pool on one side, fed by a trickle of a stream sleeking down the wall from above. Pockets of light filtered through greenery from long, jagged divides in the rock that led to the forest floor above them. Underfoot, moss and lichen carpeted nearly every surface in lush green hues. The watery, early dawn sunlight beamed down in slanted pillars, tinted gold and red from layers of leaf litter, and the air had a weight of quiet reverence only felt in long abandoned temples.

"It's beautiful," Knell said, voice soft with awe, like he was afraid to shatter the calm. When he passed a hand through a patch of sunlight with an absent little smile, the glow of it painted his skin a warm brown.

Percy looked away and took in the whole scene again. "Yeah, it is." Even he couldn't be bothered to try and downplay it. The cavern looked like a place that belonged in a tale, not something to be ruined clumsily by a couple of grubby men. He spotted tiny mushrooms and flowers dotted across the carpet of moss and felt an old urge to investigate them. "Walk where you can see stone, and don't go trampling on everything," he ordered gruffly.

Knell looked at him, those strange eyes darting over his face before glancing across the span of green laid out in front of them. Percy expected him to ask why and had a ready answer; if anyone did follow them this far or stumbled upon the place, it would be best not to leave obvious evidence they'd been here and where they were going. But Knell simply looked back at him with that now-familiar little crooked smile and a nod. "It would be a shame to mess it up, wouldn't it?"

Percy was quiet after that, following Knell's lead when he pointed out a decent place to set up camp, and wondered how long it'd been since anyone had understood him so quickly.

# *CHAPTER 16*

## *Percy*

When Percy cautiously led the way up into the forest above their camp, he found abundant foraging grounds. There were several promising locations that he planned to return to after briefly scouting the area. He'd spotted more spring peas, entire swathes of sorrel, and even a glimpse or two of early strawberries ripening in sprawling patches.

They would eat well and get to bathe in the small spring, which felt like the height of luxury. He didn't care if the water was cold as ice, he was desperate to feel clean. Something about the cave air made his skin feel coated twice over compared to a week spent roaming the woods. It was like the dark and damp of the place settled on his skin as surely as sweat and dust.

After he gave the all clear, he and Knell each went their own way, spreading out to gather as much as they could in the last of the early morning hours. With the risk of bounty hunters chasing them, it was best to move quickly with pre-dawn light and retreat to camp before full day. It meant being on high alert for possible Hill Folk—they did love their times of transition—but Percy knew these mountains, and as populated as they were, stories of fae were few and far between. Not enough to let his guard down, but enough to feel confident in spotting the signs.

The sun had risen well above the horizon, and Percy was feeling damn good about his foraging haul when he heard the distant sound of raised voices coming from the west in the direction Knell had gone.

"Damn it all to hell and back," Percy hissed to himself as he shoved his sack of harvested greens through the small cave opening and let it drop into the space below. Unburdened, he adjusted his gait to a stealthy lope and headed toward the noise.

In short time, he spotted movement between the trees and slowed, letting old hunting habits take over as he ducked silently behind trees and brush until he found a good vantage. As soon as he caught sight of the full scene, Percy bit back a curse. Knell was on his knees, hands raised in surrender, and his own patchwork foraging bag discarded without care. The food he'd collected was scattered around him in untidy piles of greens and pulped berries. Even his hat had been taken and tossed aside, stomped into a ragged mess.

Knell looked sickly under the dappled sunlight. His skin undeniably grey in the bright of full morning, his hair tangled and on its way to being greasy once more. The fabric of his tunic was light enough to cast the thin shape of his figure into a blurred silhouette, like a cruel puppet theater display. Those distinctive robes might be gone, but the clothes he'd stolen did nothing to hide the damning truth of his skin or eyes. A swelling bruise darkened his cheek as he looked warily between his captors, and if nothing else had been proof enough, there was a cut above his brow dripping black blood.

Four men surrounded him, their expressions a mixture of fear and disgust. While it was a relief that they weren't dressed in kingsmen's tabards, they were all well-built and dangerous enough. Each had a sword drawn, and their leathers were worn but well cared for. These weren't peasants taking up arms, they were career fighters or guards, likely working for the local lordship.

Damn it. They must have managed to pass each other by sheer chance when Percy had scouted and arrived after he'd given Knell the all-clear. The man Percy assumed was the leader, given his air of casual arrogance and control—something Percy knew all too well— had his sword pointed directly at Knell.

One of the others kicked at Knell's bag. "Can't even hunt, this one's collecting weeds to eat. No wonder he looks half corpse."

"Nah, that's the dark magic they taint themselves with," another said with a sneer. He was wearing thick leather gauntlets and flexed the fingers of his free hand. Knell pressed his lips into a tight line at the motion, and Percy suspected he knew who had given him that bruised cheek. "I hear every one of these sick fucks has that look to 'em. Like they've come crawling out of their graves."

Knell swallowed but wisely stayed silent as the group kicked through his gathered food, trampling it in search of weapons or hidden threats. One was brave enough to pat him down and take his knife. There was a weighted pause when they found the blade. Knell went still as stone, eyes fixed on the blade held in front of his face. Percy tensed as well, wondering if the man would simply slide the knife into some soft part of Knell, but after a long look that made it clear he was tempted to, the man withdrew, slipping the knife into his own belt.

The relief was short-lived. Anyone with a lick of sense knew to either avoid or kill flesh-mages on sight. While Percy was grateful Knell hadn't been put down as soon as these men had captured him, he didn't like the looks on their faces. People were capable of terrible things when there was no one around to judge, especially when they had a captive no one cared about. Percy clutched at the hilt of his own dagger until his hand ached and then forced himself to relax. He was confident he could take out a couple of decent fighters with one hand if he didn't forget himself, but four? He'd be dead in short order, and for what? A brief moment of distraction?

"I don't trust that thing not to try its dark magic on us," the fourth man said, clearly unnerved by the sight of Knell. Percy hated that he understood the emotion, it had been his first reaction to seeing a flesh-mage up close as well. Their strange pallor, the way their black-veined eyes flashed between an unnatural glow and the flat shine of reflected light, the glimpse of blackened gums and tongue when they spoke, it would unsettle anyone.

But at that moment, all Percy saw was Knell, who stole spinach pies and salt for him. Who kept insisting Percy was kind when he'd been anything but, and was braver than anyone would guess. Now forced to kneel, meek and subdued with no more protection than his careworn tunic and trousers, while men with swords and armor looked ready to cut him down at the slightest flinch. Percy knew Knell could probably kill them all if he tried, and they wouldn't be able to stop him. But he also knew as sure as the sun rose and set that Knell hated his powers more than he feared these men.

"I think we should just kill him and bring back the body. That should be good enough for his lordship."

"No," their leader finally spoke. He glanced briefly at his men but kept his focus on Knell, staring down the length of his sword at him. "There's double pay for bringing them in alive, and I'm not losing out on good coin because you're afraid, Aeril. They can't use their magic unless they're touching you. Wrap his hands and tie them."

Aeril, who Percy grudgingly admitted had the most sense of the group, chose to stay far away from their captive as his knife-happy companion bundled and tied Knell's hands, leaving a long length of rope that would act as a guide leash. The familiarity of it was discomfiting. Knell barely winced at the rough treatment.

"We could always cut off his hands," the man with leather gauntlets suggested casually. He was watching Knell with a malicious gleam in his eyes. Percy wanted to remove them from his head.

The leader finally sheathed his sword when Knell had been fully subdued. He nodded at the man who had confiscated Knell's bag before looking at the gauntleted one with a smirk that said he wasn't so different from them at all.

"Perhaps if he tries anything you'll get the chance, but we can't risk the beast bleeding out so soon after we've caught him. I'm not wasting that reward."

Just as the sack Knell had sewn for foraging was being lowered over his head, his gaze landed on Percy, surprising him. He knew he was well hidden, but Knell's eyes fixed on him unmistakably. Knell didn't cry out or try to negotiate Percy's value with his captors in exchange for his own life, not even to beg for help from Percy himself. Nothing more than a look of resignation as the cloth covered his face.

Another length of rope secured the bag around Knell's neck, tighter than it should have been, before he was urged to stand with encouragement from the men's boots. Knell struggled to his feet, wavering without his hands or sight for balance, but managed not to fall. The man with the gauntlets gave him a shove, and Knell scuffed his feet along the leaf-littered ground as he tried to navigate without tripping, heckled by the men around him. Percy remained in place, letting his eyes go heavy-lidded so they wouldn't gleam in the light as the leader scanned the area one last time, passing over Percy's hiding place without pause. The leader turned at last and followed his men back the way they came, presumably toward the town that housed this lordship they'd mentioned.

It occurred to Percy that he could simply walk away. Even if Knell spilled everything and admitted that they'd been traveling together, he was only a few days travel from the border. Percy could make it to the next town through the familiar territory of the forest, maybe even stock up on supplies if he kept a low profile. By the time anyone tried to follow him, he'd be long gone. Far from the godawful caves he'd suffered through and even farther from anyone who might know his face.

If he really wanted to play it safe, he could go toward the northern coast and catch a boat. With his mother's looks, he wouldn't stand out much up north, as long as he kept his mouth shut and his southern lilt under wraps. He could move a lot faster on foot across the lower peaks and valleys at the base of the mountain range without Knell slowing him down. Half the supplies and none of those awful freakish powers to worry about. Percy let the idea settle into him with a bone-deep surety as he watched the group shrink into the distance.

When there was no trace of them beyond some scattered, crushed greens, Percy stood and went in the opposite direction.

The walk wasn't long compared to the days of trekking through tunnels, but it was hardly easy. An undercurrent of violence threaded between his captors' goading words, ready for any excuse to lash out. Every time he slipped or stumbled, he wondered if the edge of a blade would greet him for the trouble. He felt his way along the ground as best he could to avoid tripping often, but the men urged him none too gently to keep up with their pace.

Had it felt like this for Percy? Trying to find solid footing without a moment of reprieve from the disadvantage of his situation, forced to rely on someone he couldn't trust to lead him along? He understood better than ever why Percy had taken a while to warm up to him. The experience was not a comfortable one.

Funnily enough, it was thanks to Percy's kindness—the meals he'd prepared and shared between them, his patience with Knell's need for frequent rests as he slowly built up his endurance—that he was able to keep up with these men now. Though less than a fortnight of walking could only bring so much improvement. He was wheezing and sweating from the effort by the time they arrived at their destination.

One of the men had wrapped a cord of rope around his neck to hold the sack covering his head in place, secured too tightly for comfort. Knell couldn't catch a glimpse of where they'd ended up. What he could tell was that his voice had gone hoarse, each breath whistling in and out with effort. But there were still clues to be gathered with his other senses. Over the course of their march, the ground had changed. From the sliding, cushioned footing of leaf-covered forest floor threaded with gnarled tree roots, to the unevenly packed dirt of a well-traveled road, then to the lumpy but relative flatness of cobbled stones he now stood on.

He couldn't smell much beyond his own morning-sour breath and the lingering scent of spring greens now gone to waste, but he could hear the distant sound of people bustling along their everyday lives. Not loud enough for a proper town, but likely the edge of a village property. Chickens clucked from somewhere nearby, joined by the occasional snort of a horse. Or perhaps goat or sheep?

A sharp jab between his shoulder blades cut the investigation short. There must be a bruise by now, he thought distantly, his mind already drifting, readying itself for the pain sure to come. The man behind him had been using the tip of his sheathed sword to jab at Knell's back, and the ache had settled in a while ago.

Memories of another village crowded in on him. The smell of burning flesh, the grim satisfaction that had swept through the villagers watching their former neighbor scream through the flames. Knell's heart hammered against his ribs, and he fought to steady his breathing. Fear tightened his throat even further until shadows began creeping in at the edges of his vision. He didn't want to kill again, didn't want to use the power lurking in his blood to steal the life from the men around him, awful as they may be.

But he would. If they planned to torture him. If they meant to burn him alive. He would do it if it meant living a little longer. If it meant sweet spring peas and sleeping warmly through the night. If it meant he might see Percy again. Might get to hear him laugh one more time. He was greedy for life in ways he'd never anticipated.

When the noise and warmth went muted, the floor underfoot now smooth squares of stone, Knell knew they had moved inside. A room with a high ceiling? The men's sneering jibes reverberated oddly in here. He went in the direction he was herded, annoyance beginning to outweigh the fear with every shove. Then his stomach dropped along with the rest of him as his foot found air where there should have been floor.

A startled shout escaped him as his heel slipped against the edge of a stair, and he fell hard into a heavily muscled figure who'd been descending in front of him. They threw Knell off and followed up with a punch that Knell took to the nose with a crack of pain and a burst of stars behind his eyes. He hit the wall hard with a grunt and landed sprawled on the stairway. Blood pooled thick at the back of his throat, making him cough and adding to the dark stain already spreading across the cloth covering his head. It clung to his skin and made breathing even harder. He managed to wedge his heel against the wall and flung his arms out to keep from sliding further down the stairs, then froze as he felt a blade against the side of his neck.

"Think you can take me by surprise, you god-forsaken worm?" the man growled. Knell stayed silent, swallowed down the blood, and tried to reorient himself rather than respond. There was no answer that would be good here.

The man behind Knell let out a mean laugh. He recognized the voice as the one who'd offered to cut off his hands. "Settle down. The idiot missed the steps. You cut his throat, and the boss'll have the lost coin coming out of your portion for the next year if you're lucky."

The sword blade lay heavy against Knell's collar before it was withdrawn.

Strangely, Knell found that his earlier panic had subsided. In its place, he felt something like disdain at the threat, much like his disappointment in the kingsmen that had cornered them in the caves outside of Valmere. When Percy called him a wretch that first night on the battlefield, it had been a word steeped in hatred. Percy had recognized exactly the kind of danger Knell was. This man's threats were genuine but lacked the same level of knowing terror. Knell suspected he'd never met an acolyte of the Great One in the flesh before. He doubted any of his captors had.

Percy's hatred had been born of fear, and rightfully so. These men were relying on rumors and still had the confidence of the upper hand. Which was for the best, Knell's plans often depended on being underestimated, but the thought lingered. How good it would feel to show these men exactly what they should be afraid of.

Instead, he held still until that ungentle nudge jabbed him again, this time in the juncture between his shoulder and neck. The man behind him laughed again at Knell's flinch, but he was given enough room to stand and carefully descended the stairs at their prodding. It was a dozen or so steps until he was on flat ground again, the air stale and cold like a cellar.

Or a prison. Knell heard the creak of metal hinges, a sound he knew so well even his spotty memory couldn't erase it. The scabbard jabbed him hard enough to send him stumbling forward before he hit the ground. His knee cracked against the stone floor and he crumpled to a heap under his own momentum. The door of the cell slammed shut behind him, knocking against his boot, and he heard the sound of a key in the lock.

The men left with parting jeers and a few phlegmy streaks of spit aimed his way, but they did leave. Knell lay where he'd fallen for a bit, catching his breath and trying to ride the pain radiating from his knee, shoulder, and face as he considered his situation.

Captured, with his knife taken away, his hands wrapped in cloth and tied behind his back, a cloth sack over his head, and a rope around his neck, in what was clearly some kind of cell. He didn't hear any movement or breathing, so there was a good chance he was alone in here, awaiting the arrival of some lordship his captors were working for. His fate was to be brought back to the palace where he would be executed, presumably in some horrible, painful, and public way.

Honestly, things could have been much worse.

It took some work, but Knell managed to free his hands, though they were left chafed by the effort. He then untied the rope from around his neck and yanked the sack from his head with a deep breath of relief. The last he was almost tempted to put back on as soon as he saw the stone walls boxing him in. They felt too close, shrinking in on him the longer he stared.

He closed his eyes and forced himself to breathe through it, using the various aches as a distraction. Pressed his fingertips against his knee and was relieved to find it was merely bruised and not more deeply injured. With a small tug of power, a sharply painful pinch of his nose, and the strangeness of navigating his own map of muddled colors, the worst of his injuries were taken care of. Without any life energy to pull from but his own, that small bit of healing left him feeling twice as ragged and wrung out as the forced march had.

Once he was finished—and could open his eyes without falling prey to his particular aversion to prison cells—Knell carefully inspected his accommodation. It wasn't large, three paces at the longest and two from the cell door to the back wall. The door was made of iron bars rather than wood, so he could see the small standing area beyond, just a few paces of more empty space and the stairs leading up. They hadn't left him a torch, which was fine with Knell. He was glad not to deal with the headache of a bright fire constantly at the corner of his eyes when the gloom was easier to see in. There was a single thin window near the ceiling on the other side of the bars that looked to be on level with the ground above, grass crowding in around the opening and stifling the light it let in.

Within his prison, there were no furnishings. Just some old straw piled along the back wall with a moldering smell to it and metal loops hammered firmly into the stone where chains could be secured.

At a loss for anything else to do, Knell kicked the straw into a pile and eased himself down to sit and wait.

# *Chapter 17*

## *Percy*

A calm had settled over Percy by the time he stood before the lord's outpost. Nothing more than a sparse collection of buildings scattered around the base of a short tower parading as a manor. It had taken some time, but he'd managed to pinpoint the location. It used to belong to a mage a few generations back, and while most people had the good sense to leave a place like that well enough alone, there were always some who thought they were safe from danger if they denounced it loudly enough. Over time, it had become a small pocket of a village full of people too stubborn to leave once they'd settled in. Their huts kneeling at a wary distance from the architectural equivalent of a festering boil squatting at the tree line.

He considered all the various ways a person might get into the building without being caught before he simply walked up the steps to the front door. It was made from sturdy wood with ornate metal fittings that had begun to rust along the edges. The snarling face of a beast forged from the same metal was mounted on the door like a warning. Percy ignored it and knocked.

It was near dark now, dusk shifting to the night and deepening shadows in every nook and cranny. A woman opened the door, sturdy as the structure she worked in, and eyed Percy warily. He smiled back at her, insincere and with teeth on display.

"Evening, miss. I'm here to see the master of the house. I'm an old friend, you see."

Her mouth pressed to a thin line but she held the door open, allowing him into the short hall. She led him up a set of stairs to a sitting room which was just a touch over-warm from the fire, but would become pleasant as the night air cooled. She gestured toward a chair, one of two near the fireplace, each with a small table beside it over a well made—if noticeably worn—carpet.

The chair was plush luxury after days on end with nothing but rocks to rest on. Percy sank into the cushions, lounging with all the ease of an alley cat that had found its way in and decided it owned the place now. The woman was quick to leave without having said a word the entire time. He couldn't fault her for it, he was a dangerous-looking man coming in at odd hours and making demands of the staff.

Percy hoped she'd be kind enough to bring up a bottle of wine, he'd hate to have to go hunting for it himself.

It wasn't long before she returned, trailing behind the lord of the outpost. A tall man with dark blond hair and an amiable face beneath his neatly trimmed beard. Percy had heard him arriving, his voice a touch irritated as he questioned his head housekeeper.

"A strange man visiting at this hour? Did he look official?"

Percy was careful to keep his expression neutral as the man stumbled to a halt at the sight of his guest. Jacob Carpenterson looked like he was doing well in his recently titled status. *Lord* Carpenterson now, Percy supposed. Though he'd bet that good ol' Jake, always desperate for respect from the higher classes, had taken on a name with less peasantry associated with it. His step up to titled status had been a short one, considering the cost. Percy wondered if Jake knew it was a snub to be granted lordship over a struggling excuse of a half-forgotten mountain village in return for his betrayals, but he could already tell the man was clinging to it with everything he had. His clothes were finer than before, and he'd kept himself well fed the last several months, without the hollowed cheeks common among anyone living out this far.

Was he hoping this place, at the edge of the kingdom's map, would be far enough to avoid the wrath of the new king? To save him from the man he'd sold out to the former monarch not even a year ago?

Percy knew better. No one held grudges like a man who could have whatever he wanted. The adoration of the kingdom wouldn't be enough, every possible enemy with knowledge of the King's fallibility would be scrubbed out. It was why Percy was being hunted so thoroughly despite posing very little threat to the Prophesized Hero-turned-King.

No, Jake's fate had been sealed when he chose greed over loyalty to his own. It was almost funny that Percy had discovered this place belonged to Jake of all people, but he knew how to recognize the meddling hand of Fate. For once, he was grateful for it. Jake had taken such pains to hide himself away after secreting off information about a critical ambush to the former King's spies. The price of his lordly title had been the lives of Percy's old crew.

The last of Percy's closest comrades, left alone to face down ten times the opposition they'd expected while Percy had been stuck playing bodyguard to a lovesick man-child determined to catch a glimpse of the princess. The fool had seen her once and declared she was his soulmate, delaying missions without a care just so he could pass on a love note. When they got news of the catastrophic disaster, something in Percy had broken irreparably. A sharp-edged wound that festered into loathing, bitter and unforgiving.

"You're supposed to be dead," Jake said, and Percy almost admired how quickly he managed to rally. "I received word that they found your body."

That was better news than Percy had expected. He'd wondered if Knell's ploy would be discovered in time to work. Clever man. Affection bloomed in his chest and for once, Percy let it, just for a moment before focusing on the problem at hand. For Jake's own sake, Percy hoped he hadn't done any harm to Knell. Percy knew so many ways to hurt a person slowly, and the current lever of his morality was locked in this man's basement.

The truth he'd been avoiding for days now had cut through him like a perfectly aimed arrow when Knell was taken. He couldn't say what exact moment Knell had become irreplaceable, when distrust had morphed into such deep affection. But once he'd seen it, he couldn't look away. Knell, in all his strange, generous, awkward, caring, terrifying glory, had carved himself a place in Percy's heart that no one else had managed, and Percy would be damned if he let anyone take that away from him.

"Is that how you greet your guests, Jake?" Percy asked. "I come all this way to say hello and that's all I get?"

"It's Lord Johnston Mistmyre now," Jake said, drawing indignity around him like it might keep him safe.

Percy laughed, cutting and mean. "How long did it take you to come up with that one? Staring out the window for hours and thinking yourself clever."

"Why are you here?" Lord Mistmyre—what a fucking joke, he'd forever be Jake as far as Percy was concerned—cut in. His annoyance began to outweigh his fear, exactly as Percy had hoped. It would've been doubly suspicious if Percy had arrived, metaphorical hat in hand, inquiring politely to be let in.

"I need a place to lie low. I've run short on supplies and it was my good luck to happen across this little haven you've built for yourself, *m'lord,*" Percy drawled out the title mockingly, thickening his own country accent.

That finally eased some of the tension in the room. Jake nodded to the housekeeper, his lordly air regathered now that it was clear he could look down his nose at Percy. Nothing more than a brute playacting at power to cover up the fact that he was at a disadvantage. Jake could practically smell it, like blood in the water. Or bait on a hook.

"Fetch us some wine, Gladys."

She dipped her head and turned after one last nervous glance at Percy, who watched her leave with keen eyes.

"You'll not harass my staff, Percival." Jake tsked at him disapprovingly, as if he hadn't been making unwanted advances on every woman who caught his eye as long as Percy had known him.

Percy narrowed his eyes at the man, running his tongue along his teeth as something darker than anger settled into his bones. "Not my style, Jake. And that's not my fucking name."

But Jake was settling into the comfort of having the upper hand as easily as he settled into the plush chair opposite Percy, smart enough to stay out of easy reach. "As endearing as ever, I see. But I'll play along. Entertain me by providing a single reason why I should offer you safe haven."

"You could turn me out, but it wouldn't be very difficult to get a message to our newly crowned king. One that might confirm a certain turncoat's whereabouts. All I need is a night of decent sleep, some basic supplies, and then you'll never have to see me again."

The housekeeper returned with a bottle of aged red wine, its corked sealed in thick wax, and presented it to her lordship who barely glanced at it before gesturing dismissively at her. He regarded Percy with a suspicious gaze while she worked, efficiently opening the bottle and pouring two glasses. Percy noticed she was very neat about it, careful not to spill a drop against her own fingers. When the cups were handed to both men, Jake dismissed her with a lazy gesture. She took her leave, silent as ever.

"I'm not convinced," Jake said when her footsteps had faded, leaning back in his chair and lifting his cup to breathe in the scent of the wine. Both cups had been filled high, probably in the hopes that she wouldn't be called back to top them off. Percy raised his in a toast and they both drank, the ever-paranoid Jake waiting until Percy's cup tipped back to take a pull from his own.

Jake sighed at the taste, which Percy found a bit too dry for his liking, and kept to a small sip. "There's something you're hiding, and you've always been a terrible actor."

True enough, Percy rarely bothered to put on a song and dance when he could approach situations in a much more straightforward manner. "Your men dragged in a cultist today."

Jake lowered his cup from a second sip, frowning in confusion. "That beastly flesh-mage lurking in my basement? I'm glad they had the sense to lock it up, but it'll be on the first cart headed toward the palace. Good riddance too. I'll take the bounty, but I'll be happier just to have that creature gone from here. I'm sure there's a pig cage or something to keep it locked up in." He eyed Percy over the rim of his cup. "But what business is it of yours?"

"He's with me, and I'm going to need him back," Percy said, his grip on the cup tightening. It didn't matter that he'd thought much the same when he'd first met Knell. He'd been wrong, and nearly a fortnight traveling together had proven it beyond a doubt.

Jake, the fucking spy rat that he was, didn't deserve to speak of anyone's worth. At least when Percy stabbed someone in the back, he did it himself.

"I understand," Jake said, not understanding shit-all. "You were hoping to plead your case using the flesh-mage as some sort of peace offering?" He looked smug and delighted at his guess, gleeful at the thought of Percy's folly.

"No, but I'll need him back anyway." Percy eyed the wine absently, noting that the cup wasn't gold or silver, but a finely crafted pewter with delicate engravings. It would fetch a decent amount of coin.

Jake's mouth curled with distaste. "Whatever for?"

"I've grown fond of him," Percy said simply. It felt good to say it aloud.

Jake looked stunned, and then his expression cracked as he began to laugh. A slow, disbelieving chuckle that grew when Percy made no attempt to take back or lessen his words. He laughed so hard he spilled some of his half-finished drink over his hand and slapped at his thigh. Percy watched him and knew without a doubt that he wouldn't regret killing this man.

When Jake regained his composure, he regarded Percy with a mix of amusement and derision. "I knew you were a sick man, Percy, but to have affection for some filthy corpse-puppeting worshiper of the Chaos Bringer? I never would have guessed you were that desperate."

Percy didn't bother trying to defend himself, or Knell for that matter. Jake's opinion wasn't worth the effort, and he wouldn't believe it anyway. So he waited.

Finally, after it was clear Percy had no more to say, Jake sighed, his expression falsely sympathetic and truly patronizing. "You can't actually expect that I'd agree to this. Especially after that sort of admission. You'd be better off leaving now. I can forget all about this little visit and you can cut ties with that thing locked up downstairs.

"Though," Jake added after a thoughtful pause as greed sunk its hooks in, "the bounty on your head is no easy thing to forget. After you came in here, making a nuisance of yourself and threatening to reveal my location, it would be quite ironic if your head was what put me back in the King's good graces."

"You said it yourself, they've already found my body," Percy said, relaxing further into the chair. It wasn't as comfortable as it looked now that he'd been sitting for a while, but he was making it work. "Not that you'll be alive long enough to test your theory even if they hadn't."

Jake made as if to sit up, probably remembering that Percy did not, in fact, limit himself to fighting with words. He paused when Percy leaned forward in a smooth, sudden movement, pointing a finger at him around the cup. His scarred wrist was braced on the arm of the chair. "Don't bother getting up, m'lord. I'm sure we can keep this civilized."

"My men," Jake started.

"Are dead," Percy finished for him.

"Impossible," Jake refuted with that learned superior tone. "They may be louts, but they follow orders. Even you couldn't take down all of them. In fact, I heard them carousing on my way here."

Percy swirled the wine in his cup, rubbing his thumb along the swoop of a bird's wing etched into the curve of it. "I'm sure you heard them crashing about, maybe heaving up if they were loud enough. Thought they got into the drink again, didn't you?"

Jake was looking a little pale. He took a long pull from his own cup as if he was hoping to draw strength from the liquid. "It happens sometimes, as you know all too well. They're quick to respond if I call for them."

Percy shook his head, not taking his eyes from Jake's face. Noted the way his pulse jumped just below his jaw, quick with fear. "Not this time. Do you remember the lessons I tried to knock into everyone's heads when they joined my crew?"

"Is this some play at loyalty?" Jake asked with a sneer. "I don't think you've got much of a leg to stand on there." His eyes drifted toward Percy's wrist and Percy could tell he'd barely held back a jab about his hand. So the man wasn't a complete idiot.

"No." Percy's patience was wearing thin. "I meant the lessons in forestry."

"Telling leaves and berries apart so we didn't wipe our asses with poison ivy? What the hell has that got to do with anything?" Jake always did get riled easily, the facade of having the cool-headed upper hand cracking already.

The small amount of wine began to sour in Percy's stomach and he'd long since grown tired of this man. "The valley here is an impressive ecosystem. Pines, firs, cedar, all needle-leaf trees, but the ground is saturated like a bog thanks to snow runoff. I bet crops rot in the ground half the time. Great for mushrooms, though. Tiny orange-capped things popping up like weeds, but the locals won't touch them. Do you know why?"

"They're poisonous," Jake said, the whites showing around his eyes.

Percy lifted his cup toward him in acknowledgment. It was always important to reward a correct answer. "Indeed they are. Just one will ruin your night, two will leave you bedridden for a month, if not worse, and four will kill a grown man in hours. Considering I added as many as I could carry into their dinner pot, I expect your men won't be answering any calls from now on."

Jake was so pale Percy could spot his faded freckles. He glanced from Percy's cold smile to the cup in his hand, clearly doing the calculations.

"Don't worry, there aren't any mushrooms in the wine," Percy assured him, and Jake swallowed, his shoulders sinking with relief.

Percy watched him with a cold sort of enjoyment. Despite his dislike of playacting, he always did enjoy a decent bit of dramatic timing. "Magebane berries blend in much better with a vintage red like this."

Jake tried to set his cup down, hands visibly shaking. It clattered to the floor, wine spilling like blood. "You're bluffing."

But he said it with an edge of desperation. By now, he must have realized his chills and sweating, probably joined by intensifying cramps, were not a result of Percy's presence alone. "You drank from the same bottle."

Percy set his own cup down, still nearly full. "I did, and it may yet kill me. But it *will* kill you, Jacob Carpenterson, and that brings me more joy than you know."

Jake was slumped weakly back in his chair, his breath gone thin and strained, the white of his eyes now a vein-streaked pink. When Percy stood, ignoring the first hints of cramping in his guts, he could see dark red wetness along the edges of Jake's nostrils. There was blood between his teeth as he bared them at Percy when he passed. One pale hand managed enough strength to grab at his arm.

"All this," Jake had to pause and pant between every few words, spraying a fine mist of bloody spittle when he spoke. "For a damned flesh-mage?"

Percy tugged his arm free, watching a trail of blood leak from the corner of Jake's mouth dispassionately, and wondered how long he had before the same happened to him. He'd wasted enough time here.

"I don't give a shit about flesh-mages." It was true, any other and he'd likely still kill them rather than risk the danger they presented. "I would have slit your throat anyway for what you did to my crew."

Percy wiped Jake's bloody spittle from his hand onto the man's finely tailored jacket. "But for *him*? I'd do much worse."

Jake's wet gasps and the heavy thud of a chair falling over followed Percy as he left the room. At the bottom of the stairs the head housekeeper was waiting, her hands folded neatly at her waist. Her expression was shrewd and wary, and there was a travel bag set at her feet.

"It's done then, I expect?" she asked once Percy was level with her. She didn't step back from him, but she'd made sure to position herself close enough to the door that she might escape faster than he could reach her. Would've made a fine bandit. Might still, considering what she'd just helped him do.

He nodded. "It'll be a mess up there. Worse where the guards were eating. Did you set up a horse like I asked?"

She sniffed as if the thought of her failing at the task was much more distasteful than murdering her employer and a good number of his men. "I think you'll find it adequate enough."

Percy smiled, amused at how much she reminded him of Ruth. A spine of iron, this one had. The only difference was that Ruth would have cursed him up and down for implying her work might be subpar. But he had more pressing things to worry about, so he dipped his chin in thanks. "Much appreciated. And a word of advice?"

She waited, watching him through narrowed eyes, likely readying herself for some unwanted advance. Percy didn't blame her.

"Take everything you and yours can carry. Blame it on me if you like, but might as well get something for your years of service."

The head housekeeper had a good face for cards, but the way her eyebrow lifted just the tiniest bit made it clear that she'd already made plans of her own and Percy's estimation of her grew higher.

He turned to head further into the tower when she asked, in a tone that sounded like she'd wanted to hold her tongue but was too curious to manage it, "How did you keep the wax seal in place?"

"Cut a neat line around the cork and pull it free, then restopper it, and you can use a little heat to melt the wax back together. If he'd bothered to open his own bottles, he might have noticed it."

She nodded, satisfied. "The key is on the hook at the top of the stairs. Far as I know, none of the men went back down there before they had supper."

"Thanks."

She brushed off her skirts, though Percy didn't see a speck of dust or flour on her, and picked up her bag. "Second stall in the stables. She's a good horse, so don't treat her badly." With that, she pulled open the door and stepped out into the night.

Percy continued down the short hall, passed Jake's overly flattering portrait hung in the main hall for everyone who entered to see, and turned down a much smaller corridor tucked away near the servant's door. One dim lantern stood guard at the entrance to a dark stairwell leading downward. Just beneath the lantern was a large iron ring with a single key dangling from a hook, just as the housekeeper had promised. He latched the ring to his belt so he could take the lantern and descended the stairs.

The basement of the tower was cramped, barren and cold, divided by iron bars caging in a cell. He lifted the lantern higher, then rushed down the last few steps when he saw a figure lying limp on a pile of straw. There was no doubt it was Knell, his clothes streaked with dirt and the sack still tied over his face stained black with blood. The skin around his hands and neck looked bruised, still bound too tightly with rope.

He wasn't moving, and it was too dim to see if he was breathing in the wavering lamplight.

"Knell?" Percy's worry eased when Knell's limp form sat up.

"Percy?"

"You alright? I'll get you out as soon as I can," Percy replied, relieved to hear Knell sounded no worse for wear, aside from the stuffiness of a bloody nose. Percy would check him over once he got him out of the cell, just in case. He set down the lantern and was reaching for the stolen key at his belt when Knell did some kind of liquid motion with his hands that made the cloth and rope binding them simply fall away. Then he pulled the sack from his head and dropped that rope as well. Percy couldn't see much detail in the dim light, but it looked like Knell was smiling. It should have been horrifying, pale teeth gleaming through the black blood smeared across half his face, eyes glowing from the shadows with reflected lamplight. But all Percy really cared about was the endearingly crooked tilt of his mouth.

"You came back for me?" Knell asked, and that was definitely a smile in his hoarse voice. The same soft awe that appeared whenever Percy did anything vaguely decent. He decided to be offended that Knell thought he wouldn't come for him.

Percy had plenty more reason to be pissed when Knell casually pushed open the cell door to meet him.

Then the memory struck, and how had Percy forgotten? Of all the fucking things.

Five prisons. Knell's criminal specialty was *breaking out of god-damned prisons*.

Percy came back for him. He looked angry about it, but he had come to free Knell, and he almost always looked angry, so Knell knew to let his actions speak. Even Percy's furious snarl couldn't cut through his joy.

"Why the fuck didn't you escape earlier?" Percy demanded.

Knell grinned at him, then tried to smooth his expression into something more somber in the face of Percy's scowl, but he could feel the edges of his mouth curling back up without permission. It had been a long time since he'd had to put effort into *not* smiling and he was out of practice.

"I was planning to break out in the middle of the night. Easier for me to sneak off when most people are asleep, and I don't need a torch. The edge of the forest isn't far, just a bit of sneaking and a quick dash to get there." Knell made a helpful little running gesture with his fingers that had no effect on his rescuer's stony expression.

Percy drew in a breath as if to berate him, then winced slightly and turned abruptly toward the stairs instead. "Let's go."

He made no attempt at stealth, walking up the steps like he owned the manor while Knell followed behind with more caution. But there was no shouting, no alarm raised, not even the scuttling of frightened servants. It was as if the entire place had been vacated.

"What happened to the guards? Or the lord they worked for? And where are all the servants?" Knell asked as he peered around, following in Percy's shadow.

"Servants are gone. The rest are dead," Percy stated with all the gravitas of discussing mild weather. Knell nearly tripped, staggering to a halt to stare at Percy, who paused and glanced back at him with an impatient look.

"You fought all of them?" Knell knew Percy was a decent fighter, but against four guards? While still adjusting to the loss of his main hand? Knell had seen the way he reached for things as if he still had it, or tried to scratch an itch that couldn't exist. Percy's expression would turn pained and complicated before smoothing over just as quickly.

Percy frowned. "I'm good, but I'm not that good. Or that stupid. I filled their dinner pot with death-shroud mushrooms and told the servants they could get in my way and die or take their leave. They chose the latter."

"And the lord of the manor?" Knell hadn't met very many lords. The closest he normally got was stealing from their homes and slipping away before he was caught, but he knew they didn't tend to eat the same fare as the people in their employ.

Percy's lip curled up into more of a sneer than usual, showing the gap of his missing tooth. "I added crushed magebane berries to his wine."

The same berries Percy had warned him never to touch, even avoiding the leaves and stems.

"Why?" Knell asked, stunned at the lengths Percy had gone to.

Percy looked annoyed by the question. "Because they took you." He paused, then added, "And I had some debts to repay, but that was more of a happy accident."

Knell's chest felt tight, this time with a warm brightness rather than the pressing fear of the cell or the ever-present ache of his scars. He smiled so wide his cheeks ached. Percy stared at his face for a moment, then let out a little sigh through his teeth and gestured with a jerk of his head.

"Let's get moving before we get caught. I'm not putting all this effort to waste."

As they moved through the kitchen, Knell pocketed several apples, a head of garlic, and a string of dried sausage in passing. On their way out the door, a round, flat disc of stone caught his eye and he snatched it up without a pause, tucking it under his arm as he juggled his newly pilfered wares. Ahead of him, Percy was headed toward the stables.

"There's a horse prepared with new supplies. We'll take it back to the caves and set it loose rather than risk being seen along any trails."

This was no impulsive, panicked rescue. It had been planned as meticulously as a person could in a single day, and Percy had done it for *him*. Knell was still trying to grasp that fact and found it to be a more slippery thought than expected, even as he witnessed it in action.

The reality of it finally began to sink in when they made it to the stables unbothered, and there was indeed a horse neatly burdened with supplies. Percy checked it over, or whatever a person did with horses. Knell knew nothing about the animals apart from the evergreen rule that you should never stand directly behind one. The horse shied away from Knell once it saw him. He worried that it might panic and lash out in fear like most animals did when he was too close, but Percy managed to keep it soothed somehow. His voice was a low rumble of persuasion that would convince Knell to settle down from the height of panic and apparently worked just as well on horses.

While Percy was busy horse-whispering, Knell munched on a stolen apple, savoring the sweet-tart taste of it as he peeked into the saddle bags. In an effort to avoid catching the horse's attention, he only took a quick glance at the supplies, and was pleased to spot at least one extra blanket, and promising bundles that must be food. Even a short sword had been secured to the strappings somehow. He slipped the flat stone into one bag and had it neatly shut again by the time Percy charmed the horse into not trampling Knell to death.

Then Percy turned to him and gestured at the saddle. "You first, I'll sit behind you."

Knell let out a startled cough of a noise. Surely Percy didn't intend to have an acolyte known for sending animals into panicked frenzies on top of a beast capable of killing them both. "I think it would be best for me to walk beside the horse. At a distance."

Percy leveled a flat stare at him. "Why the fuck would I get us a horse just to walk? We've got a manor with a dead lord and servants already spreading word across this whole damn village. We need to move as quickly as we can."

"I don't know how to ride a horse," Knell changed tact. He sidled away from the animal, who eyed him warily in return. At least they were in agreement.

"Then today's your lucky day, you're about to learn." Percy knelt and rested his hand palm up on his knee. "I'll boost you up."

When Knell still hesitated, Percy gentled his voice slightly. "Can you trust that I want to get us out of here alive?"

Knell did trust him, it was himself and the horse that were the biggest risks here. But he moved closer to set his foot on Percy's cupped hand anyway. "I would like to say that you have a record of very bad decisions, and I think this is one of them."

The comment earned him a sharp bark of a laugh, but Knell was too busy being heaved upward to fully appreciate it. He scrabbled, panicked, and somehow managed to get his leg slung over the saddle. Much to his surprise, the horse merely waited out his incompetence until he was sitting upright. Percy had to circle the horse to get a proper handhold with his left, but once he did, he swung himself up in a smooth motion and was sitting behind Knell in no time. Knell would feel put out about it if he hadn't been thoroughly distracted by Percy's grin.

"You don't know that half of it."

He could hear the smile in Percy's voice, but something about the way he said it felt ominous, and Knell wondered what he was missing. There was no time to puzzle out an answer before Percy launched right into a quick-fire lesson on horseback riding. Knell fought to keep track of it all in the hope that he wouldn't send them careening off on a spooked horse. By the time he felt confident enough to hold the reins by himself and steer them in a straight line, they were deep in the forest and he'd forgotten the moment of concern altogether.

In truth, Knell suspected the horse was mostly guiding itself and tolerating his existence, which was fine with him. In an effort to distract himself, he fell back on his recent habit of nattering on at Percy.

"I thought poison wasn't an honorable death," Knell said once the manor was a distant shape, nearly lost against the dark of the sky except for the light glowing from its windows. He'd forgotten how to tease someone and was trying to relearn the steps, but he was pretty sure he'd gotten the tone mostly right. He even managed to turn his head enough to glance back without pulling at the reins.

"There wasn't any honor in his death," Percy agreed before his mouth curled up in a mean grin that Knell caught from the corner of his eye. "But it was very fucking satisfying."

His right arm was wrapped around Knell's waist, his left hand resting on his own thigh unless he needed to point Knell back onto the path. How Percy knew where he was going would forever be a source of bafflement to Knell, but he could follow directions easily enough. Aside from the distress of the whole horse situation, he was comfortably warm despite the cool night air and enjoying the rush of knowing Percy planned out a whole rescue just for him.

He chattered on as they traveled, not bothered that the conversation was one-sided. It was Knell thinking aloud with Percy humming here and there in acknowledgment and that was enough.

During the course of their ride, Percy had begun to settle more and more heavily against Knell's back. He'd been trying his best not to notice it too much, but by the time the cave entrance was in view, it had gone from pleasurable closeness and warmth to Percy's weight slowly crushing him into the front of the saddle.

He wasn't just leaning on Knell, it was as if he couldn't hold himself up. Now that Knell thought about it, Percy hadn't responded to his conversation for a while either. He patted Percy's leg and pointed toward the cave, hoping it would rouse him from his slow collapse. Percy didn't move to sit up, but he did tighten his arm around Knell's waist briefly before letting go.

"Do you know how to remove poison from a person's body?" Percy asked, each word laborious and dragging at the pauses between them.

Knell tried to look back at him but couldn't see much more than short cropped hair and the corner of one dark eyebrow. It was for the best that the horse had slowed to a meandering pace because Knell had completely forgotten anything to do with the animal as he considered that very concerning question.

If Percy was ill, if he suspected he was poisoned, why hadn't he said something sooner? He'd told Knell the men hadn't harmed him. And Percy was too smart to make himself ill handling those mushrooms he'd used, wasn't he?

"I've never tried," Knell said, hoping his voice was relatively steady, but his ears were beginning to ring, so it was hard to tell. "Why are you asking, Percy?"

Finally, the horse stopped, lured in by a tasty patch of grass, and Knell was able to turn. He leaned back and shouldered at Percy until he sat upright. The spot where Percy had been resting his face on Knell's shoulder felt cold and strangely damp. Concerns about his tunic were forgotten entirely when Percy lifted his head and Knell saw blood leaking in dark streaks from his eyes, nose, and mouth. Percy's teeth were stained with it when he smiled weakly, his expression dazed, and his voice sounded alarmingly wet.

"Just curious."

# *Chapter 18*

## *Percy*

Knell was yelling, but Percy was too dazed to comprehend the individual words. He'd made it to the ground somehow. Whether Knell had laid him down or simply straightened him out after he fell off the horse was not a problem he felt compelled to solve. Everything hurt and there was a rock somewhere under his kidney that was jabbing annoyingly into his back. Thin hands were patting at his face, then running over his chest and arms. Percy just blinked at the bits of sky he could see between the boughs of trees until Knell's face, pinched expression and all, leaned in to block his view.

"How did you take the poison?" Knell asked, voice tense but no longer cursing him up and down. At least not out loud.

Percy squinted back at him, wheezing through the blood and swallowing it down so he wouldn't choke on it. He could feel warm trails leaking from the sides of his mouth and nose. Considering his vision had gone a blurry pink, he figured he was bleeding from his eyes as well. He managed to croak out a single word. "Wine."

Knell sucked in a sharp breath through clenched teeth, his fingertips tapping out an absent rhythm against Percy's chest. "It's already in your blood, breaking down your organs. I don't know if I can..." His voice had gone from tight frustration to shaky fear.

Percy managed to raise his hand long enough to flop it listlessly on top of Knell's. He smiled, knowing it was probably more gruesome than reassuring. "S'alright."

"It is not!" Knell snarled at him, hands clenching in his shirt. He visibly gathered himself, took a deep breath, then spread his hands out, palms flat and fingers splayed against Percy's chest. He closed his eyes with a frown. "I'm going to fix this because I can't yell at you if you're dead. This will probably feel unpleasant, but you need to hold very still."

That wasn't going to be an issue. Percy could barely feel his limbs, much less move them. His guts, on the other hand, felt like someone had cut him open and poured in hot metal. He grit his teeth and swallowed down more blood with a spasm as it pooled against the back of his throat.

There was a tugging sensation in his chest and his heart stuttered off beat before struggling to resume, the pulse pounding in his temples. Knell was sweating. Percy noticed it when he blinked away the red from his swimming vision. There was a dull thrum where Knell's hands touched him, and that tugging sensation came again. It felt like something was slithering through his veins, blood being pulled in the wrong direction. His heart thudded hard under the strain, and black spots burst in his view. Percy gasped, back arching, and Knell pushed him down with a grunt.

The fight between his blood and his heart finally eased and Percy gasped, lungs seizing as he sucked in blood, but it was choked off as a liquid sensation crawled up his throat. He tried to cough, to do anything, but Knell held him down with surprising strength. Then something thick rose up to coat the inside of Percy's mouth. It tasted of old iron, sickly and sour. Before Percy could attempt to spit it out, a mouth covered his and Knell's tongue slipped against his own.

Percy made a noise halfway between a gurgle and a squawk, unprepared for whatever the fuck was happening. Knell kissed him without an ounce of skill but a good amount of determination, practically mapping out the topography of Percy's teeth before pulling away. Percy heard him spit, then that mouth was back on his and he understood. Knell was pulling the poison out of him.

He let himself go limp and wondered at the strangeness of the situation. Percy was laid out in one of his weakest moments, leaking blood and other fluids from every orifice and feeling about as unattractive as a human could be while a man he had hated and been disgusted by just a few short weeks ago was attacking his mouth like he wanted to take Percy's tonsils as a reward for his hard work. It wasn't a kiss, which was good because it would've been a horrendous one, but it wasn't *not* a kiss either. Percy deliriously contemplated this, then mentally shrugged. He hadn't built his reputation making good decisions after all.

Knell leaned away to spit out more of the poison. When he returned, Percy leaned up into his touch. This time, it was unmistakably a kiss.

Knell made a startled noise directly into his mouth but didn't pull away until most of that sickly iron taste was gone. He spit into the grass nearby then blinked down at Percy, bewildered. "What are you doing?"

Unable to help himself, Percy grinned. The grin he knew made most people want to slap him, and he doubted that the mess of his face was doing him any favors.

"These might be my last moments," he said, managing to hook his right arm around Knell's back. Luckily, he was still leaning hunched over Percy, so it wasn't a far distance to go. "I'm making sure they're good ones."

Percy tugged him back in, and to his delight, Knell went easily. He had just enough time to wonder at the unexpected softness of Knell's lips before he blacked out.

# *CHAPTER 19*

## *Percy*

Percy woke in bits and pieces, surfacing hazily for a moment before sinking again, unable to find his footing. When he dragged himself onto the shore of consciousness at last, he felt oddly refreshed. Rejuvenated, even. It made him immediately suspicious. When he tried to move his body felt too languorous and heavy to budge, which was almost a relief.

With considerable effort, he managed to get his eyes to open and stay that way. Knell was sitting above him, with Percy's head pillowed on his crossed legs. Even disregarding the unflattering angle, he looked like shit. The circles under his eyes were darker than ever, his skin waxy and paler than normal, the hollow of his cheeks sharp and shadowed. When he blinked down at Percy, one eye opened a touch slower than the other. Still, Percy stared and found him lovely.

"Hi," Percy managed, his voice a creaking wreck.

Knell's eyes went glossy with tears and his mouth pressed in a flat line of displeasure. "I'm very angry with you," he said in a watery voice as he folded himself down to rest his forehead against Percy's.

"That's fair." Percy would have pulled him into his arms if he could move. He did his best to look contrite when Knell sat up again, though he wasn't sure how successful he was. It wasn't an expression he wore often. Knell sniffed but managed to blink back his tears before any could fall, looking strained too thin.

Percy squinted at him then clicked his tongue. "Your tears look grey. You took in some of the poison!"

Knell scowled at him, which was a first. That and the yelling. It was nice to see him coming out of his shell. "You don't get to criticize! It's just a lingering effect from pulling the poison out of *you* after that foolish plan! I already took care of it." He looked away to glare at the wall of the cavern with a huff, but it only took a moment before he glanced back down at Percy with a reluctant frown and said, "Thank you for being worried, but I'm fine."

He was being too nice, probably trying to hold back while Percy was unwell, but fuck that. Percy had acted like an idiot, and he deserved to get yelled at. If anyone deserved to do the yelling for once, it was Knell.

"Better than I was?" he prodded.

That pinched frown was back, but this time it wavered as Knell's brows drew down as well. Perfect, he was bottling up too much already, and Percy always knew the shortest route to pissing someone off. "Yes, better than you were! You should have told me what happened as soon as we left, but *no*, you had to wait until the last possible moment!"

Knell was gesturing angrily with his arms but still so careful not to jostle Percy's head in his lap. Percy had to bite back a smile at how considerate he was even while furious. He schooled his expression though, not wanting to undermine Knell's anger here. He was right. There had been a dozen better ways to execute his plan, and Percy had chosen the worst one. Knell's hands trembled against his chest where he clutched fistfuls of Percy's shirt.

"What was I supposed to do?" Knell asked in a whisper, a plea. "What was I supposed to do if I lost you here?"

Percy forced his hand to raise far enough to brush weakly at Knell's sharp cheekbone. "Survive."

Knell glared at him even as he tilted his head into Percy's hand. "You don't get to tell me how to live if you let yourself die."

He had a point there. Easy to tell someone else what to do when you weren't around to deal with the consequences.

"I'm sorry I worried you," Percy said, because it was true. His hand began to fall as his strength waned and Knell caught it in his own, keeping it pressed to his cheek.

Percy brushed his thumb back and forth against the edge of Knell's jaw. Ached for how tired and worn he looked. "What did it cost you?"

Percy thought about the wreckage his innards must have become after consuming the magebane-laced wine. Knell might be immune to most illnesses, but even his chaos-altered humours had to be unbalanced. He was going to hold onto the fact that Knell had pulled the poison into his own mouth to help Percy, not knowing if it might kill him, too. What a matching pair of fools they were.

He'd seen the effects of magebane on a person. It didn't simply kill them, it turned their insides into an unidentifiable mush, a bloated corpse full of rotting liquid. It was a foul thing, and a painful one—something he could now personally attest to. He was grateful that Knell hadn't seemed to take on any of the effects. But how had he healed Percy? Who or what had paid the price for Percy's life so far out in the forest?

Thanks to a series of nervous and somewhat muddled explanations after his confession about being able to steal life without use of a foci or touch, Percy had an inkling of how Knell's powers worked. Plenty of it was still so much mystical horseshit to Percy, but he'd been able to grasp the basics. Knell had the ability to reach for a person's life... energy? He'd started describing it as threads of light, and Percy had gotten a little lost. But apparently, Knell could grab onto that energy and steal it away, into himself or someone else. That was the price of his healing abilities.

As far as Knell knew, he was the only flesh-mage—*acolyte* in his words—that could do so. Which was overwhelming to think about but useful. It was a damn good thing that Knell didn't seem interested in wreaking havoc across the kingdom. He had the kind of power that mages spent centuries chasing after. The kind of power they would do much worse than kill for.

Knell had that wan, starved look about him that came from overusing his powers, and it certainly explained why their bags looked as if they'd been ransacked. He would bet good coin that Knell had eaten what he could to stop the worst of the hunger the effect of his healing caused. Percy hoped he'd found the dried meat that had been stashed in the saddlebags.

*Saddlebags.*

Percy pulled Knell's hand down to his chest and ran his thumb over the ridge of Knell's knuckles, the skin thin and delicate over knobby bone. "The horse?" he asked.

Knell's expression was carved with misery at the question as he hunched in on himself. He stared at Percy's hand touching his like he was hoping to memorize the sight. "Do you really want to know?"

How often had he asked that same question, and how often had Percy let him shoulder the burdens alone?

Percy hummed a sound of acknowledgment and kept up the soothing motion of mapping out Knell's hand, the callused pad of his thumb finding tiny scars as he did.

"Haven't got anything to bury it with," he said, regretful that he couldn't even do that much in thanks for the life he'd stolen. A person out to murder him was one thing, and while he'd still take his life over the horse's, he wanted to treat her sacrifice as respectfully as he could.

Knell's shoulders relaxed a fraction, though his voice was still wary. "That won't be a problem."

Percy paused to tilt his head at Knell, surprised. "You managed to bury her?"

Knell avoided Percy's eyes. "Not quite. I, ah, simply sped up the natural process a bit. The trees here will do well."

That must be a nice way of saying he'd rotted away a whole horse corpse into the forest soil. Percy was honestly more impressed than disgusted. Knell was terrifying and incredible.

Quiet settled over them and though he wanted to know what that strange expression on Knell's face meant, he must have drifted because when he opened his eyes the light had shifted. Not a lot, but enough to know he'd fallen into a doze. Knell was still sitting in the same place, holding his hand and looking like a dog without a home on a cold night.

"Spit it out," Percy said, more of a mumble than a demand. Knell must feel worse between the two of them, and it made him cranky to think Knell wouldn't just lie down and rest. That he hadn't tucked in close to steal Percy's body heat like he usually did.

Knell startled at the words, making Percy wonder if he'd dozed off as well, eyes half open and sitting upright, or if he'd just been lost in thought.

It had to be the kiss. Another thing Percy had fucked up. What else would make Knell hesitate the way he was? Probably trying to be considerate of Percy's feelings. Percy saw his reluctance to answer and was just about to tell him to get it over with when Knell pulled his hand from under Percy's to twist his fingers together nervously, shame written across his features.

"I ate the horse," he admitted, voice as quiet as it was rough.

Not about the kiss then.

"You ate th—" Percy cut himself off, no point in repeating it. Knell looked ready to curl himself up into nothing. But still, he had some questions. "*All* of it?"

Surely, he couldn't have. The man looked like he'd lost weight in the past few hours, not gorged himself.

Knell shook his head. "Just... just enough to stay in control."

Fuck, shit, damn, and hell. This was Percy's fault, every bit of it. He forced his sluggish body to respond, dragging himself up far enough to get his elbows under himself. It was like his limbs were weighed down with boulders. He had to pause for a breather halfway to sitting up. Knell moved from beneath him, and Percy already knew the self-deprecating little shit was probably thinking up some excuse for Percy not wanting to touch him or something equally foolish.

He gestured impatiently with his fingers toward a sloping hunk of rock coated in moss and thankfully Knell caught on despite Percy's struggle to catch his breath. Thin arms hooked under Percy's and heaved him the short distance so he could recline in a sitting position. When Knell tried to skitter away, Percy snagged the hem of his tunic in his fingers and refused to let him get far.

"Sit," was the best he could manage while it felt like he was trying to relearn the basics of breathing, but Knell listened, folding to his knees beside Percy with a worried look.

"Percy," Knell started, but Percy cut off whatever that apologetic tone was preparing for.

"Listen real fucking close, Knell," he managed between pants as his breathing finally began to settle. When Knell nodded, Percy forced himself to take a slow, deep breath and let his lungs know they needed to settle the fuck down.

He looked directly at Knell, those bright eyes burning into his own. "I'm sorry."

Knell tensed, almost flinching with surprise, his eyes wide and mouth fallen open. "What?"

"I'm sorry I put you through that. I'm sorry I made things worse. I'm no good at heroics, that much is goddamn obvious. You keep having to save me instead." Apologies had never come easy to Percy, but this one felt right. "I'm sorry you had to do it alone."

Knell sat with that for a long while, enough for Percy to start feeling slightly more human again. He wiggled his toes as sneakily as possible. Not that Knell would have noticed, he was staring hard down at his own hands or at Percy's face with a level of scrutiny that was uncomfortable. There were no platitudes that would make the situation better, so Percy offered none.

"Why did you come back for me?" Knell finally asked.

"Because leaving you behind, leaving you with *them*, wasn't an option. Not for me." Percy replied simply.

"And the, ah," Knell's tongue darted out to wet his lower lip. He lifted a hand as if to touch his mouth before he dropped it again and flushed a darker grey. "The kiss?"

"Did you not enjoy it?" Percy asked, curious. He doubted that Knell had much opportunity for pleasure in the past several years, and he suspected it hadn't been common before then, but either way his efforts couldn't have ranked very high on the list considering the circumstances. He also hadn't exactly asked first. Knell cared for him, that was clear, but it didn't mean the feeling was a romantic one.

Knell frowned in thought for a long moment, then shrugged with his shoulders and hands, looking lost. "I don't know. I was a little preoccupied at the time trying to keep your organs together."

Percy had to concede to that. "Would you want to try again?"

The offer caught Knell off guard, based on his stunned expression and full-bodied twitch, though Percy wasn't sure why. He didn't make a habit of kissing people he didn't want to, even if he had been dying. He'd also killed quite a few men and a lord, poisoning himself in the process to save Knell. Surely, that was statement enough of his affection. Knell stared at him, brow furrowed as if he was trying to translate the words into another language.

When Percy just watched him in return, raising an eyebrow as the silence grew, Knell swallowed and glanced away, eyes darting from place to place in the cavern nervously. "I... I don't..."

The words came out with stilted effort and Percy held up a hand in placation. To his relief, movement was getting easier, bit by bit.

"You can say no."

It was a simple statement, one Knell must have sensed the truth in because he calmed. His eyes darted over Percy's face so quickly that they flashed blue and green and silver with every movement.

"I don't want to say no," he admitted, holding himself very still.

Percy smiled and, if forced to confess, might not even blame it entirely on the aftereffects of being horribly poisoned. "Alright then."

He would have said more, but Knell darted forward to press their mouths together in an inelegant kiss, bumping noses and licking briefly across Percy's teeth as he caught him mid-smile. He sat up just as fast, his face gone an even darker splotchy grey. Percy was still blinking away his surprise while Knell sprinted through several stages of preemptive rejection, looking far too upset for someone who had done nothing more offensive than give Percy a welcome, if clumsy, bit of affection.

"I'm sorry. I thought that—no, I did it wrong. I should have, I don't know. Asked? Waited? I'll just—" His disjointed rambling cut off with a startled noise as Percy came to his senses and wrapped an arm around Knell's waist before he could move away.

"Knell," he said with weary patience. Knell looked at him, close enough now that he was leaning over Percy more than sitting next to him, crooked teeth biting at the corner of his mouth anxiously.

"Yes?" Knell asked, wringing his hands so hard Percy could hear a knuckle pop.

He recaptured one of those hands in his own, lacing their fingers so Knell wouldn't hurt himself. "You can kiss me, but let's try something a little slower, eh? My mouth tastes like shit, and I know yours probably isn't much better after that rescue."

Knell swallowed again, eyes trained on their locked hands with a dazed expression, his cheeks and ears dark. "Uh."

He didn't say anything else, but the noise seemed positive. So Percy pulled him closer, moving slow to give Knell plenty of time to resist, but he went easily. This time, Percy led by example with a soft press of closed lips. Once, twice, a lingering third that left Knell melted into a bony puddle on top of him, and Percy stopped caring about keeping track.

When they parted, Percy opened his eyes to find Knell staring at him and suppressed the urge to snort. Of course Knell would be the type to leave his eyes open the whole time. He contained his amusement to a little smile that lifted one side of his mouth and Knell stared at that, too. His man was looking a bit poleaxed.

"You alright there, Knell?" he asked, just to be sure.

Knell was still flushed and he floundered now as well, clearly struggling to think in full sentences. "Hm," he managed, probably aiming for contemplative but stumbling right into strained.

Percy grinned so wide his lip ached where the old scar bisected it. Knell pushed himself up, clearing his throat and pointlessly smoothing down his long-ruined clothes with the hand not still held in Percy's.

"Well," he tried again, sounding just as flustered as before.

Percy was enjoying himself immensely. Knell opened his mouth, glanced at Percy's smiling face, then promptly closed it without a word. Cleared his throat again unsteadily and gave up on speaking altogether to stare resolutely toward the far end of the cavern as if he might find some composure buried in the rock there.

They were in no state to keep moving despite the danger. Percy was still adjusting to his newly regrown organs, and Knell's body was a battleground between anxious fear and hunger, neither allowing him a moment's rest.

He'd eaten all that he could from their supplies before he'd resorted to the horse. That he'd killed her as quickly and painlessly as he could before using her to save Percy had been no comfort. The fresh memory of it curdled his appetite but did nothing for the hunger gnawing at him.

And there was something different about Percy. He kept reaching out for Knell, just to touch him. He'd *kissed* him. Several times. It was so much better than he remembered.

Percy *liked* kissing him.

Percy, for some reason, had decided he liked *Knell.*

The emotional ups and downs of the past day were overwhelming to put it mildly. But there would always be plenty of awful experiences to suffer through, he could allow himself to wallow in the good ones for as long as he could.

All the good couldn't keep Percy from testing his patience, though. Knell had given him very clear instructions not to move, but he should have expected that Percy would make a terrible patient. He kept trying to get up, rushing his own already miraculous—if Knell did say so, and as the one who put Percy's organs back together, he very much said so—recovery. He finally agreed to settle down and stay where he was if Knell laid out all the remaining supplies for him to look over before they were packed away again.

"I can tell you what I ate if that's easier," Knell offered, but Percy shook his head.

"The housekeeper packed it. I want to know what she sent us off with."

Knell carried the items over, a little embarrassed at the state he'd left everything in, even if he had a good reason. Reorganizing the supplies he'd torn through hadn't been his top priority at the time. "I thought you scared off all the staff. You made her stay and help?"

Percy scoffed. "I didn't make her do anything. The woman was stubborn as a mule. She sent off the rest of the staff and then looked me right in the eye—as I was poisoning the soup pot, mind you—and told me she didn't want the place in flames or ruins."

"Brave housekeeper," Knell said, impressed.

"A smart one. You know as well as I do that just half the valuables in that manor were worth more than the rest of their ramshackle village combined. She didn't give a damn about the lord or his men, but with them dead, the village would need to turn some sort of profit before the next pissant flounced in."

Everything was laid out in front of Percy, a generous selection even without the fresh food he'd eaten. Two sets of clean, if worn, clothing and matching cloaks—Percy was quick to discard the ragged one he'd been wearing—a patched blanket, a flint and steel striker, a short sword, whetstone, and a small sack of oats. Knell fished out the flat, engraved stone and half a braid of garlic that he'd taken on the way out of the manor. He'd eaten the other half but given it up when his nose and eyes began to burn and run.

"A cooking stone?" Percy moved as if to sit up. Knell clicked his tongue in a chiding manner, not noticing he'd imitated Percy until he saw the amused expression on his face.

"I saw it on the way out. I didn't know what it was, but I had the feeling it was valuable," Knell admitted.

"Damn right they are." Percy held out his hand, and Knell passed the flat circle of stone to him for a closer look. "Meant to be for travelers and adventure-minded types, but the truth is that only the rich can afford them."

He grinned at Knell, who had never felt so compelled to keep stealing kitchen items, but if it kept earning him those delighted expressions, he'd find a way to haul off an entire oven next time.

"This means we can cook without risking a fire," Percy said, running his hand over the surface of the stone.

"There's one more thing," Knell added, because his personal standards weren't exactly high, but he wasn't going to sit there and be jealous of a mildly enchanted rock.

The last item was a palm-sized purse containing a few silver and copper coins. It wasn't something either of them would have expected to be included.

"Payment for the job, I suppose," Percy mused with grim humor. "She must have really hated working for him."

Knell hesitated but was too curious not to ask. "You knew him, didn't you? The lord of the manor. You said you had debts to pay."

Percy's humor faded, and he flipped a coin along his knuckles with a frown, watching it spin rather than looking at Knell. "He used to be an ally, or we thought he was at the time. Stayed with us, with the man we now call King," he added with bitter emphasis. "Long enough to earn our trust and then sell our secrets to the highest bidder."

He dropped the coin back into the purse and let Knell take it, not at all hesitant to hand his money over to a thief. "I suspected something was off, but the golden boy didn't want to hear a word said against his friend. I was stupid enough to drop the matter, and it got my whole crew killed."

Debts indeed. Knell was starting to understand Percy's impulsive behavior. "I'm sorry."

Percy frowned at him. "What for? Not like you were there."

Knell shrugged one shoulder. He had the feeling Percy didn't get many apologies, and likely not from the backstabbing lord before he killed him. "I'm sorry no one listened. That you had to lose the people close to you before they did."

Something flashed across Percy's expression, a brief moment of unchecked pain, before it was gone again. Tamped down with ruthless efficiency. "What's done is done," he said, his voice a touch rough. "The bastard paid his price. That's all the justice I can ask for."

Clearly, he had no interest in continuing the thread of conversation. Knell floundered for a topic that wasn't equally depressing until Percy took pity on him and pointed to their older supplies.

"Still hungry?"

Knell's stomach grumbled before he could say anything and Percy nodded like it was answer enough. "Bring over whatever grains are left, then fill the pot with water. Let's put this stone to work and see if we can get you fed."

As it turned out, Percy was able to cobble together a generous stew from their supplies. He boiled water, scooping away any impurities that rose to the top before adding mashed garlic cloves crushed between two spoons—"My mother would skin me for this, but it's not like we've got a chopping block or proper tools."—a generous handful each of rice and barley, a potato cut into chunks, and pieces of dried squash that expanded as they absorbed the water. Salt and herbs were sprinkled in, then it was left to simmer until the whole thing had gone thick with plump grains, nearly overflowing from the pan.

Armed with a spoons, they dove in. Knell was careful to keep to his side until Percy declared he was full, and then he cleared the rest of the pan to the last grain. He finally sat back, full at last and so grateful he could cry. Percy looked better for eating, if tired, and Knell gathered up the pan and spoons to clean, something that was becoming his habit after a meal.

He was still wiping down the pan when Percy stood, scrubbing the last of the dried blood from the edges of his eyes and nose with his ruined shirt. Then he picked up the sword and walked carefully over to grab the mostly empty pack, ignoring Knell's protests all the while.

"What are you doing? You need to rest!" Knell insisted, stepping into Percy's way.

"I need to get us some more supplies before we move on, and the sooner that gets done, the better."

Knell wanted to yell at this stubborn man. "Then let me do it. I was the one who ate all the food." There, a perfectly practical counter.

"You look ready to keel over." Percy shot back with blunt honesty —the nerve of him!

"You were half dead a few hours ago!" Knell poked him in the chest.

Percy glared at him, unmoved. "And because you saved me, you're half dead *now*. I know this kind of forest, and I remember exactly where to go. I'll be fast." His expression had softened but his tone was implacable as he moved around Knell toward the entrance.

"You'll come back?" Knell asked, unable to keep the question locked behind his teeth.

Percy paused to look at him before answering, his voice gentler. "Yes. I'll be back as soon as I can, a few hours at most."

Satisfied as he could be, though far from pleased, Knell brushed his hands down his own blood-stained clothing and tried not to worry too much. Scrubbing the pan and repacking their supplies would keep him busy for a short while. That would have to be enough.

"Hey."

Knell turned back and then froze as Percy planted a kiss on his forehead. A warm, unmistakable press of lips just below his hairline.

Percy leaned back with a little nod to himself like he was pleased and left without another word. Knell stood there for a long time, head empty of thoughts, staring off after Percy though the man had long since vanished from view.

When he finally managed to get himself to move, vaguely in the direction he was supposed to be going, it took a good while longer to remember what he was meant to be doing. Tasks took twice as long as they should, and the whole time, Knell would swear he could feel that spot of warmth on his forehead, his face going hot if he thought about it. Which he did. Often.

When Percy returned a few hours later, exactly as promised, he kissed the same spot again, and Knell resigned himself to being useless for the immediate future.

# Chapter 20

## *Knell*

"Right now, we're sitting at the base of the largest mountain peak, and we have two options," Percy said, raising two fingers around his rolled bread as he listed their choices. "We either risk getting caught by kingsmen trying to cross through the pass toward the coast or we take our chances with whatever cave bullshit comes our way by attempting to go under the mountain. Given that we've killed several fairly important people on our way here and pissed off the Fate-blessed King himself, I'm pretty sure attempting the pass would be suicide."

They sat on opposite sides of the cooking stone, close enough to warm their folded legs and to trade the bread dough as Knell shaped it for Percy to cook on the pan. He'd shown Knell the trick to folding a crushed mixture of mashed potatoes and the wild garlic that he'd brought back—along with a whole pack of tightly bundled greens and tubers—into the dough. Then the round buns were carefully flattened between his palms so each one had a layer of filling when bitten into. The food was delicious, and it took him a moment to register Percy's words when he was so distracted.

"You'd prefer the tunnels?" That was a surprise. Percy hated traveling through the cave system, that much had been obvious from the start. Knell had expected him to choose fighting for his life above ground over the possibility of being lost in the dark.

Percy hesitated, clearly thinking the same, then narrowed his eyes at Knell thoughtfully. "How confident are you that these wyrm tunnels will reach the other side of the mountain? You said they stayed close to the surface to hunt but had lairs further in."

The fact that Percy remembered the conversation—from a time when he hadn't trusted Knell at all and was determined to part ways—was a little thrill on its own. "So far, they've been just like the tunnels beneath the prison where I and the rest of the acolytes lived. In theory, they should be similar in other ways as well," he explained. "There's no reason a Great Wyrm should stay to one side of a mountain range. It clearly had time to explore, considering how far we've come.

"I think if we find a tunnel leading toward the heart of the mountain, we should be able to cross through its old lair and to the other side. There's no telling how safe the passage is or how long it will take. Wyrm tunnels are fairly direct, but I've never attempted to go further than necessary before."

Percy rolled his bread into a log-like shape that was easy to hold and took a bite. Knell copied it while Percy was distracted, intrigued by the idea. Not distracted enough, apparently, because Percy smirked, though his voice remained level and serious. "The wyrm might be dead, but other things must have taken up residence in its lair since then. We'd have to constantly be on guard, and since I can't see, that'll be difficult."

Knell considered it as he chewed, then gestured at the lichen-covered rock all around them. "The moss. We've seen it in several of the caverns."

Percy nodded. "It glows in the darkness, but last time I tried being clever with light I nearly got eaten by cave crabs."

"Shell spiders," Knell corrected.

"I'm not fucking calling them that," Percy shot back without a pause. "I don't know why it makes them worse, but it does."

Knell snorted a laugh but pulled himself back on task. "We could collect some of the moss. It doesn't draw in as many creatures as a fire would, and you wouldn't be completely in the dark."

"How do you know it won't lure in more things that want to eat me?" Percy shoved the last of his bread into his mouth and raised his eyebrows at Knell. It shouldn't have been charming.

Knell finished his own bread and gave a helpless sort of shrug, which was immediately undermined by his eagerness to take the final bread Percy lifted from the pan. "I don't, not really, but it doesn't hurt my eyes nearly as much as the light from a torch, and I see plenty of small patches of it around. Smaller creatures often hide in it, so it doesn't seem likely that it's a draw for predators."

This was all wild guesswork, but he couldn't think of a safer way to give Percy a chance to see within the caves. "Is the risk of the tunnels so much better than the chance of being caught? For you, I mean. I certainly don't want to run into any of the kingsmen again."

He regretted the words as soon as they left his mouth. He'd given Percy the perfect excuse to part ways again, to escape the dark of the tunnels and leave Knell to finish the journey alone. Percy may have developed some amount of affection for him but Knell knew it wasn't meant to last beyond this journey. There was no cure that he knew of for the changes his body had been put through. He was living on borrowed time at best before he was caught and killed. Percy might be a wanted man but someone as resourceful as he was could evade the King's grasp if given half a chance. Proximity to Knell would only put him in harm's way.

He knew this and was doing his best to accept it, but Knell selfishly wanted to stay beside Percy as long as he could get away with it.

Unaware of Knell's internal struggle, Percy shook his head once slowly, then again with more conviction. "No. Whatever horrible creature might be dwelling in these caves will still be better than having to see that bastard's smug face again." There wasn't a trace of humor or exaggeration in his voice or expression.

"Was the hero you followed so awful?" Knell asked, too curious to let it lie after he'd collected so many little hints over their time together.

"You want to know why I turned traitor?" Percy asked, like he'd been waiting for the question, a bitter smile on his face as he lifted his scarred stump of a wrist.

Knell picked at the last of his bread, tearing it into pieces and eating them slowly. "If it's something you want to share, I'll listen.

You know I like to ask questions. " That earned him a huff, a ghost of a laugh. "But I doubt it'll change what I think of you."

"And what's that?" Percy asked, amused, but his smile was a sharp-edged thing.

Knell met his eyes and held them. "That you are kind."

Percy's smile fell and his gaze shifted just past Knell's shoulder. "Delusional," he muttered, dismissing Knell's words, but his ears had gone flushed.

Percy certainly had the capability for violence, but Knell doubted that he'd cut down an ally out of greed or pettiness. And it sounded as if he'd been a comrade of sorts to the Prophesized Hero. Why had he tried to kill him on the battlefield?

"I hated him," Percy said, his voice quiet. "He had everyone else wrapped around his finger, but I couldn't stand the bastard, even if we were fighting for the same cause."

"How did you meet?" Knell asked.

Percy winced in embarrassment. "I led a crew of bandits near Valmere. I'd made a name for myself there. Really thought I was some kind of important back then. We would wait along the road for merchants passing through with goods from the port towns, headed in the direction of the palace. They always had the best loot, and we were always looking to stick it to anyone in the vicinity of nobles."

He shrugged a shoulder at Knell, one side of his mouth crooked up in a humorless half-smile. "If rich folks were hard to come by, we robbed whoever looked like they might have something decent to steal."

Knell tucked his knees close to his chest and wrapped his new cloak around himself, enjoying the warmth. He'd discovered a handful of dried apricots that had gone unnoticed at the very bottom of the saddlebags and nibbled slowly at his share of them, savoring the sweetness as he nodded at Percy to continue. If Percy was waiting for some sort of condemnation of his past, well, Knell would need to hear something much more damning if he was going to pass any sort of judgment.

"Along comes this perfect target, some naive farm boy, not even bothering to hide away his coin purse. We went about our usual act and this kid had the nerve to try and lecture us. Said he was on some grand quest. We laughed at him, of course, then I decided to have a little fun and let him challenge me."

Percy was getting into the rhythm of his storytelling, his half smile wryly resigned. "Looking back, it's like reading a storybook. Should've known what role I was to play from the start, but that's hindsight, I suppose."

"He won?" Knell guessed.

Percy nodded. "Couldn't fight for shit, but he was clever. Always so fucking clever, that one.  Knew exactly what to say to get me pissed off and distracted, then I was on my ass in a ditch in no time, much to the amusement of my crew. They took a liking to him, asked about this *quest* he kept going on about until we found ourselves roped up in it all somehow. Damn near every day it felt like there was some task to hunt down an ancient item, or pluck a flower that only bloomed once a century, or kill a fucking troll. One after the other, until it unearthed some convoluted scheme about a sorceress and a plague and the old king behind all of it."

Percy was rubbing at his wrist absently as he stared off into his memories, dragging his nail along the edge of his scars in a way that worried Knell.

"He had this charm to him that could convince you of anything. He'd make you feel like a part of something bigger, like you might just change the world. But it always seemed to end badly for everyone but him." His voice had gone softer, flatter than Knell had ever heard it. "When you travel with heroes favored by gods, you eventually realize that you're nothing more than an acceptable sacrifice."

Knell laid a hand over Percy's, stilling his restless scratching before he could break the skin. Percy went still, then sighed and let his hand relax under Knell's. Feeling brave, Knell slotted his fingers between Percy's, hoping it would give him some small bit of comfort.

"What's your name?" he asked, then clarified when Percy shot him a confused look. "Your full name."

Percy's brow smoothed out of its perpetual furrow and he blinked in surprise. Knell wondered if it was so rare for anyone to ask when Percy made it clear he disliked being called Percival. Percy glanced back and forth between his eyes, and Knell realized how close he'd gotten, sitting right beside Percy and leaning into his space. He began to sit back, but a gentle squeeze of Percy's fingers against his kept him right where he was.

Then a smile, small but real, changed Percy's whole expression, and Knell forgot about anything else.

"Persistence," Percy said in a low, warm tone, not a trace of bitterness to be found. "My name is Persistence."

Knell felt like he was filled with bubbles and light. He couldn't have stopped himself from smiling if he'd bothered to try. "It suits you."

Percy huffed in annoyance, but his eyes were amused. "Because I'm a stubborn bastard, I know." He hesitated, then added, "It's a tradition from my mother's people, naming kids after traits you hope they'll grow into. Or not. I don't remember the details, but either way, I'm sure she probably wished she'd picked something different."

"I like that about you." Knell squeezed Percy's hand gently. When he had begun clasping it with both of his own? He really should keep better track of what his body was up to.

"You don't give up. Not on life, or on escaping this... this *shitpile* of a kingdom." That felt good to say. Knell really did hate the place and everything that had been wrought upon him there, even before he'd been chained to a chaos god from another realm. "And you didn't give up on me."

A flush crawled up Percy's neck and across his face despite his scowl, much to Knell's delight. "You're going to be a fucking menace, aren't you?"

Knell just patted his hand and smiled in response.

The rest of the story unfolded in bits and pieces as they traveled, strung together in tales from Percy's journeys. It was as if all the reticence Percy had for speaking openly had fallen away now that he'd decided Knell was to be an object of his affection, the fact of which still left Knell equal parts baffled and elated. The looming threat of their impending separation was something he refused to contemplate, so he encouraged this new willingness to talk by prodding Percy for details of his time before the final battle. He wanted to learn everything he could.

Percy didn't share much about his childhood, but from the small mentions here and there, Knell could tell it hadn't been an easy one. Parents lost to one of the many illnesses that swept across the kingdom in waves. Left to survive on his own and, being large for his age and of dour demeanor, he fell in with thieves and brigands before moving on to form his own band.

Knell wondered how it compared to his own childhood, if he'd taken a similar path to thievery himself. So much of his memory was still lost to him, with no way of knowing if it would ever return in full. He had only scraps of memory, a scent or color that was so vivid he wished he could place it but was left grasping for any thread of context to anchor it with. He tried not to linger on those failures. These days were limited, and too happy to stain with heavy thoughts he'd have plenty of time to indulge in later.

What Percy had no hesitation in sharing were his experiences while traveling with the Prophesized Hero, a man everyone in the kingdom must know of now, the boy-turned-hero-turned-king. Knell asked for his name once, and Percy's expression had darkened so much as he answered that Knell decided never to speak it aloud if it made Percy so viscerally upset. But otherwise, Percy was more than willing to share stories of his adventures, some amusing, most dangerous, and several tragic—for those following the Hero, if not for the man himself.

"I'd been a road bandit for more than a decade. Finding so much as a musical charm or a chest with a locking spell on it was rare enough to earn us a damned good payout. Then as soon as that boy joined up, he was a magnet for cursed daggers and enchanted lockets and whatever else he fucking tripped over that week." Percy gestured animatedly with both arms after Knell had asked if he carried any enchanted weapons—the answer had been a firm and resounding *no*.

Knell had discovered half a dozen new sounds of annoyance Percy made just for these stories, delighting in each and every one. The soft glow of gathered moss, bundled into a packed ball and hung from Percy's belt by a short stretch of rope, lit the space around them just enough for Percy to see where he was stepping. Even so, he didn't protest Knell's hand resting on his back, kept nicely warm between the cloth of Percy's shirt and the weight of his pack. Knell could feel Percy's heart beating, the rise and fall of breathing under his palm, more of a comfort to him than Percy could know.

From what he gathered, Percy had been reduced to little more than a pack mule by the men who had previously trusted his decisions implicitly. They used to look to him when deciding plans, to value his input, but by the end, he considered it a good day if he managed to avoid another argument by miring himself in chores. All the unpleasant but necessary labor no one else wanted to do. The crew—who used to be *his* crew—were quick to pile on more. Any respect they had for him eroded over months of being undermined by, in Percy's words, *a fucking man-child*.

"And don't get me started on prophecies!" Percy had worked himself up to a near shout, grumbling at a lower volume when he realized his voice had begun to echo. Knell hummed a little encouraging noise of acknowledgment and made a mental note to ask about prophecies at the soonest possible opportunity.

When it came time to rest, they made a good team. Percy cooked, preparing enough for their meal and the day ahead, often with some variation of that now familiar and beloved flatbread. Knell had gotten better at shaping the dough for Percy, who experimented with flavors and fillings from their limited supplies. The extra breads were left to cool and then packed away to eat during their travels. Percy made dense meals, more filling than they looked, and Knell found himself with more energy each day than he could recall in recent memory.

Every time Knell complimented his food, which was every time Percy cooked, Percy's mouth crooked up in a satisfied little smile and he'd offer Knell another portion.

Night, or as near to night as they could guess, was its own beast, and one Knell would gladly let consume him. Sleeping back to back under a single blanket in tense silence was a thing of the past. Percy curled bodily around Knell, the two of them bundled in double layers of thick, if now slightly dirty blankets. Full of good food, warm, and feeling strangely safe pinned down by Percy's bulk, Knell was sure he'd never been more comfortable, no matter the circumstances.

By all means, he should have slept better than ever, if not for the way every worry pushed aside during the day circled with fangs bared in the quiet as Percy's breathing went deep and even. Instead, that comfort was his only armor when they clawed and snapped at every weak spot. It kept him from falling into that same hopeless place Percy had found him in once before, kept him from losing control and tapping into his powers in an attempt to separate himself from his body.

During those long nights, he forced his breathing to stay even, guided by Percy's soft snores. Focused on Percy's steady, calm heartbeat and the weight of another body pressed close to his without a care. The warmth of their shared cocoon settled into his bones. It anchored him, and while the worries gnawed away at his mind, they couldn't steal that from him.

If Percy had kept his distance until they parted ways, would it hurt less? Knell doubted it. The loss of Percy's company was something he'd mourn either way. This closeness and affection, no matter how short-lived, was a gift he wouldn't trade for anything.

Two full days, by Percy's best guess, passed without incident. He was caught up in telling stories to Knell and, for once, didn't feel the urge to exaggerate any of his own deeds or importance. He laid out the events less like a story and more like a list of complaints. From disorganization in the camp setups—and who inevitably ended up digging all the shit pits and making sure the water was safe for drinking?—to the baffling eagerness to strike out on every suicidal-sounding quest they stumbled upon. Vented about how his protests had fallen on uninterested ears, and not only due to his general lack of tact or patience for foolishness.

He painted a picture of himself as truthfully as he could. Knell had seen the worst of him already, but he wanted to erase those lingering notions that he was gentle or kind or, gods forbid, heroic in any way. Yet, Knell was hanging on to his every word, and Percy supposed if Knell was determined to like him despite it all, he could let himself bask in the attention.

Knell, a man who'd seen worse horrors than even Percy on his many terrible quests could imagine, let out endearing little noises of astonishment and intrigue at all the right parts of Percy's tales. It would have felt obnoxious if there was any hint that he was pretending for Percy's benefit. But as far as Percy could tell, Knell was deeply invested in the stories, sympathetic without being cloying, and —much to Percy's pleasure—he'd taken to scoffing softly under his breath every time Percy mentioned the Prophesized Hero.

Knell hadn't gotten any less tactile either. One thin hand pressed comfortingly against Percy's side as they walked, helping guide him away from obstacles he hadn't seen yet in his small circle of dim light, warmed to match Percy's own body heat. His thumb brushed back and forth in a soothing motion he doubted Knell even realized he was doing.

And those small reassuring pats. It had taken several of them to recognize the pattern. Knell would absently pat his side or arm when he spoke of fallen comrades. It was a bit of a stilted comfort, but it was so very *Knell* that it sparked a warm glow in the deep well of loss that had been a constant companion for years now. And Knell had the gall to call Percy kind. The little shit.

To go through the things Knell had—those that Percy knew of, and all that he didn't—and then to be stuck with a miserable sot like Percy, only to prove himself more patient and resilient than anyone else Percy had ever met? Knell was the kind one. Percy only hoped, now that he'd taken his head out of his ass and come to his senses regarding the man at his side, that he could repay that with affection a hundred times over. Could cook and care for him, tuck him close at night and keep him warm. Could share the parts of his past that Knell was so curious about.

He should have known better than to let himself get caught up in another story and in telling it, had distracted Knell as well. It wasn't until he took a deep breath between one complaint and the next that the uneasy quiet hit him.

How long had there been an air of anticipation humming through the tunnels?

Percy stopped mid-word, snapping to full alert. Knell stumbled to a halt beside him. His breath hitched before he could ask why as he came to the same realization Percy had. The hilt of Percy's newly acquired short sword was a comfort under his palm. He squinted into the dark beyond the light of the moss lamp, but it was as useless as ever, so he leaned toward Knell and kept his voice low.

"What do you see?"

Knell was looking around, peering into the void stretched in front of and behind them, his luminous eyes darting from place to place, but he shook his head. Nothing. The silence lurked around them and without the echo of their voices or footsteps, their breathing sounded louder than it should.

There was an odd scent as well, different from the smell of still air and damp stone he'd gotten used to. It was almost familiar, and Percy took a deep breath through his nose, trying to place it.

"Smell that?" he asked.

Knell sniffed at the air, a thoughtful frown creasing his brow. "Like a storm," he said after a moment of thought, clearly trying to find the right words.

It *was* like the air before a storm, and the scent-memory of it nagged at him until he heard the low hissing growl and it fell into place. "Ah, fuck," he said, with feeling.

Skyfire lizards nested up in the craggy peaks of mountains, what the hell was one doing down here in the tunnels? He'd only crossed them once before, on another hare-brained quest. It had been a time-sensitive hunt to find the Goddess' Tears, which turned out to be gems that—un-fucking-surprisingly—had been embedded in ice giants, bringing them to life. But on their way up the mountain, they'd disturbed these ornery beasts.

To be fair, they were simply animals guarding their nests. If Percy had the ability to breathe lightning, he would have been just as eager to blast the Hero off the face of the mountain. He could relate to being a short-tempered, territorial bastard who bit back, but even climbing up an ice-blasted mountainside had left him with more options than the tunnel they were currently in. A straight line with nowhere to dodge, they were the perfect targets.

That storm scent grew stronger, and the hairs on Percy's arms stood on end as a spot of crackling white light appeared and began to grow in size further down the tunnel. It was too far for Percy to get to the lizard before it let loose, and he'd seen how powerful those lightning strikes were; it could blast a crater into solid rock after carving through several men. He was, to his own disgust, useless as he always seemed to be when it came to these goddamned caves.

"Knell, can you—"

Knell was already doing his thing. His eyes had gone unfocused and brighter than ever, one hand raised toward the distant light. "I can stop the breath, but not the lizard. It's gathering energy too quickly," Knell gasped.

Percy launched into motion, sword drawn and thankful he could do something of use for once. "Focus on the breath! I'll handle the rest."

Trusting Knell to do his part, he sprinted toward the light. Nothing more than a fanged snout was visible beyond the bright, crackling light, and every hair on his body stood upright as he drew closer. He was running in blind and relying on memories from a fight that happened while he was half-frozen, exhausted, and caught in a snow flurry. His chances were terrible.

Percy grinned and felt a wild laugh bubble up in his chest. Finally, a decent fucking *fight*.

The first stray finger of electricity caught his blade as he swung low, throwing his full weight and momentum behind the strike, which was good because he felt every muscle in his body seize up like a clenched fist. The sword struck true—thank fuck this cave lizard seemed to have the same weak spot as its mountain peak cousins— and sank deep enough to hit bone. Lukewarm blood slicked over Percy's hand, but he managed to keep hold of his sword as the lizard reared back. It shrieked as its leg buckled under it, turning its head toward Percy, who could see nothing but a mouth full of lightning. There was a noise like a fizzle and a pop, then a burst of white light.

The lizard screeched again, and Percy didn't have time to contemplate the lack of pain as jaws snapped shut a hairsbreadth from his face. The lightning breath was gone, dispersed somehow into nothing. Around the edges of the bright lingering spot that had been burned into his vision, the shape of the lizard was barely visible in the glow of his moss lantern. Just enough to see it rear for another strike, toothy maw open and ready to take his head. Moving on practiced reflex, Percy braced himself and stabbed upward as hard as he could into the soft underside of the lizard's jaw.

More blood sprayed him as he struggled not to lose his grip on the sword. The lizard was seized in death throes as the blade was driven through the roof of its mouth and into its brain, its tail slamming against the wall of the tunnel with such force that Percy felt it under his boots.

He was close enough to feel its last breath wheeze out in a fetid rush against his face, to see the reflective gleam of one large red-hued eye glaring at him as it died. The sword slipped from his blood-slick hand and Percy let it, rolling away from the weight of the lizard as it went limp and hit the ground. He caught his breath and got to his feet, wiping his unpleasantly sticky hand against his pants. Once the worst of the blood had been cleaned from his palm, he held up his battered moss lamp to look over the beast.

It was about the size he remembered from the mountain top—too damned big. The head would be nearly on level his own when standing, the length of the body about three times his height. And it definitely looked dead. It also looked wrong. Its eyes were bulged and its proportions looked off balance, strange dark veins crawling across its scaled body. Percy shuddered and leaned away from it. Kill confirmed, he wondered at the oddly peaceful feeling he had before it registered that there was no clever one-liner or snide remark. Blissful silence.

Shit, *silence.*

"Knell!" Percy called. He turned back toward the direction he'd left Knell and spotted him staggering into the very edge of Percy's field of light. Cursing, he moved to help, but Knell threw up his hands, tiny sparks of white lightning dancing between his spread fingers.

"Don't touch!" Knell's voice crackled with power, his eyes were miniature aquamarine suns. Percy stopped where he was, hand still outstretched but not making contact. His chest went tight at the look of pain on Knell's face, the stiff stagger of his walk, like it hurt to move.

"What do you need?" he asked, his voice dropping to the soothing tone he normally saved for spooked horses—and now, he supposed, spooked former cultists.

"Too much," Knell said, his voice crackling as much as the lightning. "Can't hold it all, I need s-somewhere to..."

Percy pointed at the dead lizard. "Put it back."

Knell paused, blinked at him as the reply sank in slowly, then followed the line of Percy's hand and let out a static-laced, "Ah."

Percy watched, holding himself back from reaching for Knell's arm as he wavered but managed to stay on his feet. Knell pressed his hands to the lizard's flank and took a deep breath. His whole body seemed to glow, humming with power. Little arcs of lightning danced where his hands touched the lizard and the smell of cooking meat rose in the tunnel.

The carcass twitched once, its claws moving as if to grasp some invisible prey. Then it exploded.

# Chapter 21

*Knell*

The tunnel, Knell, and Percy were all coated in a layer of vaporized, steaming, half-cooked meat with an undertone of rot. No one could blame Percy for heaving up his last meal a moment later.

After scraping off as much as they could and two more dry heaving fits from Percy, they were once more on their way—if in more battered spirits than before. Knell felt half cooked and half dead but had enough coordination left in him to fetch Percy's sword from where it had been thrown by the blast. Percy wiped it off as well as he could with the somewhat clean inner lining of his cloak, which had then been abandoned in the tunnel with the rest of the gore as a lost cause.

"What do you think it was doing all the way down here?" Knell asked. He'd been gathering any information Percy knew of the skyfire lizards in an attempt to keep them both as distracted from themselves as possible. The stench had only grown worse as the flesh warmed and begun to dry on their bodies. Percy looked ill anytime he glanced down at himself. It was also a good way for Knell to keep himself awake as they staggered along the tunnel, his ears ringing and his skin tingling painfully. He was hungry again, that inescapable gnawing, and he was so tired of it.

He caught Percy watching him worriedly and did his best to dredge up a reassuring smile. Percy hardly looked convinced, but he didn't push it, instead answering Knell's questions as best he could.

"No idea. Far as I knew, skyfire lizards stuck to mountain peaks, but I'm no beast master. Maybe they hibernate within the mountain."

"Do you think we'll run into more?" Knell hadn't spotted any signs of another, but then he hadn't seen the first one coming until too late anyway.

Percy licked over his teeth and spat with a grimace. "I fucking hope not." He scowled into the darkness ahead of them and hummed low in his throat the way he did when he was parsing through old memories. "They're territorial, I remember that. If this one was nesting nearby, maybe we can avoid running into any of its kin."

That sparked another thought and Percy snapped his fingers, though they mostly squelched. "A beast that size might be able to find food down here, but water is scarce. If it has a den nearby, then there must be a water source."

Knell brightened up at his words. "We could get clean!" He'd spent the last few years of his life treading in filth, but now that he'd gotten a new taste of cleanliness, he was loathe to give it up again. He liked when he smelled nice and his skin didn't itch, he felt lighter for it. And if his hair wasn't washed, then how would he get Percy to spend long minutes petting it at night? Unacceptable.

"If we find it. And if there aren't more of the bastards lurking about, ready to eat us," Percy groused, then let out a huff of a laugh as Knell's stomach grumbled at the mention. "I don't know how you can be hungry with this stench in your nose."

Knell tried to shrug it off casually but ended up swaying hard and stumbling instead. Percy caught him, wrapping his right arm around Knell's waist to help him stay upright.

"That little trick took a lot out of you, did it?" Percy asked, that worried line carved between his brows.

"Sorry," Knell said as he sorted himself out, unable to meet Percy's eyes and wishing he'd done better in the fight. "That lightning breath—I couldn't contain it. I couldn't control it when I returned it to the body, either. I think it took some of my energy with it." He winced and gestured between their gore-coated selves. "Maybe if I knew how to handle my powers better..."

Percy snorted. "It's been maybe a fortnight."

It didn't sound like he was mad about the fight. Knell made a questioning noise and stumbled as he turned to look at Percy, who clicked his tongue at him in mild rebuke even as he helped haul Knell upright once more.

"You spent years with a god in your head bellowing orders and puppeting you around, right?" Percy started, clearly working himself up to something. "Then suddenly it's gone. But you've still got these— no offense—freakish powers you barely know the rules of, get stuck on the run in a cave with some rude asshole," Knell tried to interject, but Percy simply talked over him, "and you managed to not only control your powers but use them in ways I've never fucking heard of. You just stopped a skyfire lizard's lightning breath, Knell. Not even the fucking god-touched Prophesized Hero managed that."

He grinned at Knell, who tried to think of a single response and failed. His face felt hot and his heart was beating too fast. How could Percy sound so *reverent*?

They'd slowed to a stop, and Percy bodily turned Knell so he could look him in the eyes. "You *healed* me. More than once. You tore down a homunculus and pulled poison out of my *blood*."

Percy brushed aside a lock of flesh-crusted hair and kissed his forehead, just at the hairline above his right eye. Probably the cleanest spot he could find, Knell thought distantly just before his mind went blank in order to focus completely on the soft brush of chapped lips.

"So stop putting yourself down. You make me sound like jack shit in comparison."

Oh.

Huh. That was... that was something. Thoughts were a bit of a struggle at the moment, but Knell was sure he'd think of a good response soon. Percy watched him with a smug look until he tried to cross his arms, then quickly abandoned the attempt as everything squished wetly.

Knell was laughing before he could stop himself, too many feelings bubbling up all at once to culminate on this ridiculous man and his dramatic grimace of disgust. It was a rough and cracking sound, but Percy stared at him like he'd seen the first bloom of spring after a long winter. He was smiling back by the time Knell got a hold of himself, though he rolled his eyes and pretended to grouse.

"C'mon then, let's try and find somewhere to wash this shit off."

Knell grinned, still tired and aching, near cramping from hunger and half nauseous from the stench of it all, but unable to stop.

"Yeah," he agreed, voice so much warmer than he'd intended.

Percy blinked at him, swallowed, and abruptly turned on his heel to march on with determination. Knell couldn't tell through the gore, but he would bet with confidence that Percy's ears had gone dark.

It wasn't long after that they found the lizard's nest. A wide stretch of natural cavern with a low ceiling that had them weaving between mineral pillars in swirling shades. The air was humid, if not entirely warm, and glowing lichen lined the crevices everywhere, lending light across the expanse of the cavern. Knell wondered what color they were, but Percy had outpaced him at the sight of several circular pools of water, pausing here and there to scan for threats. Knell followed at a more sedate pace, also wary of other lizards, but saw no sign of another nearby.

Water spilled down along several flat, tiered pools that rose toward the ceiling like stairs, the slow trickle only filling about half of them. The stone itself was slightly warmer than the rest of the cavern and Knell peered into them curiously. Nestled into one of the dry bowl-like hollows was a clutch of eggs.

There were five eggs in the clutch, each the length of Percy's hand and shaped like those of a snake, with unpleasantly soft shells. Percy was just about to ask how they should be dealt with when Knell's stomach growled nearly loud enough to echo in the chamber. Knell looked sheepish, but not so much so that he wasn't also eyeing the eggs with a look of curious hunger.

Percy sighed. "I don't care, but we're both washing before we touch any food whatsoever. We are fucking disgusting."

The water was warm compared to the cool of the chamber. Which meant it was merely lukewarm, but that was better than the icy cold he'd been expecting, and Percy would take every win he could get.

He hesitated to foul the water with the filth they were covered in, and thankfully, there were separate pools that captured overflow from the main spring. Percy chose the largest of them to use. This place was made up of bowl-like dips and smoothed rock and mineral deposits so the whole cavern looked as if it were made from melted wax. Perhaps not the most aesthetically pleasing, but a definite improvement over trying to scour himself while standing trapped between endless needles of stone teeth above and below.

It was a relief to strip down and unceremoniously dump the pile of meat-crusted clothing into a second pool for soaking. Those were a problem for later. Knell followed at a less frantic pace. By the time he stepped into the water, Percy was kneeling, the water up to his hips at the deepest part of the pool, and scraping the worst of the mess off his skin. Knell passed him one of their much-abused squares of cloth to use as a rag—he must have taken the time to dig it out of their bags— and Percy took it with a murmur of thanks before scrubbing at himself with fervor.

Knell helped him wash his left arm after Percy's third or fourth hiss of frustration at trying to scrub with his right wrist and the cloth. He returned the favor by helping Knell wash and untangle his hair, grateful the head housekeeper had thought to tuck in a comb among their supplies. If Percy took a bit of extra time just to enjoy the sensation of soft strands under his fingers once Knell's hair was clean, then who was to say? After the day they'd had, he couldn't be begrudged a moment or two of small pleasures.

There was no sensuality to the bath. Knell was too exhausted to focus on anything more than getting clean and Percy was too aware of how much they'd fouled up the water, which had a soggy layer of rehydrated flesh pulp floating across the surface like pond scum.

With effort—and a second dip in an uncontaminated pool—they were finally washed and dressed in fresh clothes. The outfits were too rich for Percy's taste, and didn't fit either of them quite right, but they were clean and that mattered more than anything else at the moment. Knell emptied the packs so the bags could be washed while Percy took to scraping the worst of the mess from their soaked clothes before scrubbing them. Working together, they managed in good time and laid everything out to dry as best they could. Knell was flagging, though he never complained, and Percy was glad for an excuse to escape the meat-scum water to focus on cooking, making sure they both scrubbed themselves up to the elbows in clean water first.

There were vents above them in the ceiling of the cavern, shadowed and perfect for crawling beasties to hide in. Percy had kept a wary eye on them and made sure to nudge Knell to a flat space that wasn't directly beneath one. "Think we can cook in here without luring out any unwanted guests?"

Knell followed his gaze upward and made a thoughtful noise. "If these lizards are as territorial as the ones you've run into before, there's a good chance anything nearby will avoid this den for a while. Besides, there's a feast sitting down the tunnel, and most animals prefer an easy meal."

Percy scowled to himself at the reminder, his skin itching even after he'd scoured himself clean. "I suppose you're right. Grab that cooking stone. Do you know how to complete the rune on it?"

Before he'd finished the question, Knell was already scuttling into motion to grab the stone from the pile of cooking supplies. He looked at Percy, eyes bright in the dim, and swallowed hard enough for Percy to hear it. "I've seen you do it, I can manage. Will you be making more of your bread?" he asked hopefully. Hungrily.

Percy very firmly reminded his libido that it was not allowed to wake back up when he'd been absolutely befouled with lizard guts not an hour ago and shook his head. "You need more than that. I won't cook those horrible fucking eggs you've been eyeing, but I'll tell you how to do it if you swear to properly scrub the pan after."

"Really?" Knell asked, though he was already halfway to the nest. He didn't wait for an answer before he was carrying the eggs back in his arms, their soft shells slumping together and looking fit to burst over Knell's clean outfit. But they made it across the way intact and Knell set them down in a lumpy pile, contained within a shallow dip in the floor near the rest of their supplies.

Knell used a small pale rock to carefully finish the rune etched onto the stone's surface, which began to change color as it heated up. Meanwhile, Percy sifted through their small collection of seasonings, selecting the salt and a few herbs. "You'll have to cook them two at a time. It'll be basic fare but should be as filling as any meat."

With their pan set on the cooking stone, Percy dropped in a pinch of fat, watching it melt as the pan warmed up. Once it was liquid and shimmering, he nodded at Knell, who had to pierce the egg with a knife in lieu of cracking it. Thick, yellowish egg with a dark orange yolk spilled into the pan where it began to sizzle and turn solid.

"Add the next one quickly and stir with a fork. Don't stop until I say." Settling down next to Knell, Percy crossed his arms to keep from reaching out to help. Knell was perfectly capable of cooking a meal, or at least he would be by the time this was done.

A second egg was poured into the pan, and Knell quickly stirred it all into a wet mess with their shared fork. Percy sprinkled in the salt and herbs, eyeing the amounts and hoping they worked on these as well as they did with chicken eggs. Knell could tell him, because Percy wasn't about to try it. Eggs were perfectly fine in small portions, but he had the suspicion these would do him more harm than good. That dark veining of the Chaos Bringer's lingering effect had touched them and Knell might be immune, but Percy sure as hell was not.

They weren't the prettiest eggs ever made, but to Percy's surprise, they weren't the worst either. They smelled alright and had formed a soft, fluffy mass thanks to Knell stirring as they cooked.

Percy watched as Knell blew on a hot forkful and took a bite, then another, with one of those indecently pleased noises he liked to make while eating. Thankfully, Percy's libido had been thoroughly compartmentalized, but he suspected the combination of Knell and his little noises of appreciation would be a danger to him in the near future. It would take a while for regular meals to fill Knell out, and Percy looked forward to the challenge. He would make sure those meals were damned good ones too, once they were out of here.

He ate his own dinner, the last of his foraged greens rolled into the leftover onion-filled flatbreads he'd made the night before. They still had dry grains and ingredients to make a decent stew, but it would be the last of his fresh supply until they either made it out or died in here. He savored the taste as he continued instructing Knell.

The first pan was gone in moments, as Percy had suspected, and the last three eggs were cooked in a similar fashion. This time, Knell was able to eat at a pace that didn't give Percy indigestion just from watching. He took each bite with obvious relish, and Percy made a mental note to learn more egg-based recipes if such a simple food made Knell so happy.

Knell glanced sidelong at him once he could focus on something other than immediate hunger, working up the nerve to attempt something approaching a sly look. Maybe he'd been aiming for coy, but that ever-present suspicious air of his dampened the effect.

"I could kiss you for all this generosity," he said, though his voice wavered the slightest bit, breaking the illusion of confidence.

Percy brushed his hand against his pants and grinned at him daringly. "Then you should."

He'd never really understood the appeal of flirting, it felt like a waste of time when people should be straightforward about what they wanted, but he had to admit that if it earned him a flustered ex-cultist, he was coming around to the concept. He took his time finishing his own meal as Knell faltered, went dark in the face, then failed to start a coherent sentence several times in a row before he lurched sideways to plant a kiss that felt more like an ineffective attack against Percy's cheek.

Knell pulled away just as fast, shoving a forkful of eggs into his mouth as if it would convince Percy the kiss hadn't happened, but Percy was grinning, then laughing at how endearingly terrible Knell was at this. Knell paused at the sound like a startled rabbit, eyes wide and cheeks bulging with food. It made Percy laugh hard enough to snort, after which he coughed and quickly regained his composure, but Knell's eyes were shining with delighted amusement as he chewed. Percy looked away, clearing his throat.

"Eat your horrible fucking eggs," he bit out, focusing back on his own food with determination as Knell finished chewing to let out a familiar, wheezing laugh beside him.

After the night's rest, they packed and set off again. The clothing they'd washed and laid out was nearly dry but had taken on a powerful stench of rot, and the choice to leave them behind was unanimous. Percy grumbled about losing the last of his own clothing, but the spares fit well enough to get by.

Knell looked more affected by the loss, lingering near the clothes and running his fingers over the frayed threads of embroidered flowers and vines. It had been his first outfit other than his robes in who knew how long. Percy supposed he could understand why he'd be upset to leave them, and he'd been fond of the embroidery. Surely, that was a skill a person could learn to do one-handed.

At the edge of the lichen's dim glow, Percy waited for Knell to finish while he secured his newly built moss lamp to his belt. When

Knell was ready, he lingered near Percy with a sideways glance, expecting a comment, but Percy just gestured for him to take the lead.

Carrying the lantern meant Percy had some visibility, if only a pace or two around himself, and the sheer relief at being able to see the floor under his feet had surprised him. It no longer felt as if he were standing alone in a void, and had the added benefit of allowing him to watch Knell as they walked. He wasn't half as absentminded as he seemed, scanning the tunnel ahead of them and occasionally behind. Percy didn't hear anything, but it had been made very clear several times over that more lurked out of sight than he knew. Percy himself glanced up every few steps, unable to forget the sensation of an insect the length of his arm dropping down onto him.

Dangers aside, the walks were mostly long and tedious, and it was nice to have something to look at. He lingered on Knell's features, curious how they could look so different to him, though very little about them had changed, just Percy's perception of him. The proud arch of his nose, the curve of his brows like bold ink strokes against his skin, the dark circles ringing grey eyes, offset by the bright aquamarine glow of his irises. Percy drank him in and smirked each time Knell glanced his way and caught him staring.

The skyfire lizard had been a lesson in not letting himself get too distracted, so when Knell asked him for more stories of his past, he answered as best he could without getting lost in the memories. In turn—and bracing himself for the worst—he asked questions of Knell's past, from before his time under the control of the Chaos Bringer.

"Oh," Knell said with a look of surprise at the first question, which was when he'd taken up thieving. "My memory isn't very clear, I'm afraid. I mostly get glimpses, but I know I began when I was fairly young. I can't seem to help myself sometimes. I'm sure it's gotten me in all sorts of trouble."

"Five prisons worth, apparently," Percy teased, then wondered if it was a sore spot. He'd never been good about knowing where the line was until he'd long since crossed it.

To his relief, Knell let out a raspy little chuckle. "And that was only when I wasn't able to outsmart the guards." He bit at the corner of his lip, wringing his hands, and Percy wondered if he'd fucked up the conversation after all. "I really do have a bad habit of taking things without even realizing I've done it."

Percy steered him away from a dip in the floor that would've tripped Knell in his distraction. "And?"

Knell reached into his cloak and pulled out a sheathed dagger—Percy's dagger—with a contrite expression. "I'm sorry."

Percy stared at it, then at his own belt where he had attached the short sword and makeshift lantern. When the hell had Knell stolen it, and why the fuck hadn't Percy noticed it was gone?

He took the dagger with a huff of a laugh, impressed. "You're damn good."

Knell stared at him. "You're not mad?"

"Can't fault a man for such a finely honed skill," he said, cheerfully lying. If it had been anyone other than Knell he'd be pissed, but it wasn't, so what did he care? "My own fault for being careless enough not to notice it was missing."

That left Knell off-kilter, with no response but a soft, "Oh."

Percy continued to pepper him with occasional questions, trading tidbits of themselves back and forth. They both knew how to read, though Knell could recall pieces of far more stories. He must have had access to books, and a lot of them, at some point in his life.

Knell had a mysterious, deep-seated hatred of radishes with no memory of why. Percy admitted that he had a sweet tooth few people knew about, which prompted Knell to gasp and near shout, "Honey cakes!" in delight when the words dredged up a memory.

As the hours passed, the tunnels grew warmer, then drier, leaving Percy's throat feeling parched. They were carefully navigating another of several paths that led further into the mountain, often at slight declines—Knell keeping a careful eye ahead of them while Percy used the glow from his lichen lamp to make sure their footing was solid—when he first saw the light.

Percy pointed it out to Knell, who nodded. "Another moss patch?"

"I don't think so. We haven't passed any of them since the temperature started rising, and it's the wrong color. That looks like light from a fire."

"What color is the light from the moss?" Knell asked.

Percy was briefly puzzled by the question before he remembered Knell's inability to see color, then had to actually consider how to explain it. "It's hard to describe, but a sort of blue? A bit like your eyes, actually."

A complicated expression crossed Knell's face and he jerked to a stop hard enough that Percy ended up several steps ahead of him. He had to backtrack to see him in the limited light of the moss lamp. Knell looked like he'd been given a good knock to the head. "My eyes are blue?"

"You didn't know?" The possibility hadn't occurred to Percy, but who would Knell have asked?

Knell shook his head. "I knew they were different. I used to have dark eyes. But by the time the changes took hold, well..." He touched a fingertip near the corner of one eye.

"None of you could see color." Percy finished for him. Knell gave a little half shrug and nod, shoulders curling further into his hunch than usual. That wouldn't do at all.

Percy brushed his knuckles against Knell's cheek, then cupped his jaw when Knell leaned into it. "They're not just blue."

"What?" Knell asked, distracted. He was starved for touch, that had been obvious from the start, and Percy would give him as much as he wanted, but this was also important. Percy might be useless at reassurance and comfort, but he could be insistent and immovable, which would have to be close enough.

"Your eyes. They're brighter than the moss in here, and they're more green than blue. Like a gem lit from the inside. Or the color of a mage flame when it burns too hot."

Knell's face went warm under his palm and he'd wrapped his own hand around Percy's wrist. He didn't attempt to push him away but simply held on, brushing his thumb back and forth against the thin skin of Percy's inner wrist. Imitating the motion of Percy's own thumb along the edge of the dark circle under Knell's eye.

"Unnatural, then," Knell tried to joke weakly.

Percy hummed in thought, not about to let Knell disregard himself. "Captivating," he argued, and a thrill of smug glee went through him when Knell's jaw went slack.

"What color are yours?" Knell blurted out, clearly desperate to take some attention off himself.

Percy hadn't noticed how close he'd leaned in until he stood back, flustered. "Just brown. Like soil."

Knell smiled, pleased with himself at turning the tables, "That's a good color."

Not ready for the fluttering in his stomach that Knell's compliments caused, Percy tilted his head in the direction of the mystery glow. "We need to keep moving."

Despite his words, he lingered for another moment before he stepped back with reluctance, dropping his hand from Knell's face. If they were somewhere less filled with endless horrible creatures ready to kill and eat them, Percy would have leaned in for a kiss. From the way Knell's eyes lingered on his lips, he was thinking the same thing. "Better to find out what that is before something else finds us, with our shit luck."

"Right, yes." Knell agreed, nodding too long. Then he stood there until Percy raised his eyebrows and Knell remembered he had to lead the way. He cleared his throat and began heading in the direction of the light, limbs moving stiffly as he tried and failed to act casual.

Then they rounded the curve of the tunnel, and every other thought was forgotten. It looked like a portal to hell, a jagged entrance four times Percy's height carved in sharp contrast to the dark of the caves. Everything beyond it was fire and crackling heat.

# *Chapter 22*

## *Knell*

The cavern was immense, so large Knell didn't have a scale to compare it to. Even the biggest of the underground caverns he and his brethren had claimed paled in comparison. It was as if the center of the mountain had been hollowed out by some great hand. The ceiling vanished into shadows somewhere high above them, and streams of molten lava flowed sluggishly along far below.

He winced against the brightness of it—was it red like hot metal from a forge or the yellow-orange of fire? Heat buffeted against Knell's skin, making it feel tight and dry in mere moments. Stretched ahead of them was one of several pathways, strange bridge-like structures of stone worn smooth over time, held up by natural arched pillars carved from millennia of lava flow. It was wide enough that they could've driven an ox cart down the center with room to spare on either side, but the footing was uneven and deceptively slick, like it had all been coated in glass. They'd have to walk carefully.

Near the center of the immense space, connected to the path of a lower bridge running parallel to theirs, was a plateau with a strange mound at the center. Knell couldn't make out much more than that, between the distance, the searingly bright light, and the haze of shimmering heat that blurred large swathes of air.

Percy's hand caught his elbow, and Knell turned to see him blinking in an attempt to adjust his vision. His grimace of discomfort left his teeth bared and his brows furrowed low over his eyes. It was cute, Knell thought as he squinted through the light himself.

When Percy was able to open his eyes more than a sliver, he looked to Knell, who had resigned himself to keeping his eyes as close to shut as possible, already feeling an ache behind them. "I'll take the lead. You're liable to walk right off the fucking edge."

Knell was quick to agree. Between the oppressive heat, the haze in the air, and Knell's sensitive vision, he'd misstep in no time at all.

Just a short time ago, the thought of ending it all had been a comfort, but death had become less appealing the longer he spent with Percy. Even if things hadn't changed, he'd much rather not have the meat cooked from his bones in the process. He doubted he'd get those soft forehead kisses that set his heart thudding in the afterlife, so he'd have to make sure he collected them as greedily as he could beforehand.

Instead of sharing any of this—there was a time and place, and hovering above a lava pit was not it, he was proud of himself for recognizing that—he nodded and patted Percy's comfortingly sturdy arm. Percy shifted his grip to the back of Knell's tunic, gathering a fistful of fabric. Knell imagined Percy lifting him bodily by the scruff to be carried the whole way and decided that the heat was definitely getting to him. Probably best for Percy to keep hold of him in a way that would mitigate the risk of Knell dragging him off balance if he slipped.

Percy pushed him in front, a gentle parody of their first day in the caves together. Only this time, Knell was the one who couldn't see, following Percy's guidance. That gruff voice gave the occasional warning of, "rough patch, watch your feet" or "move to the left, I'm not diving after you if you fall."

They were nearly halfway through the cavern before they were close enough for Knell to finally make out what the strange shape atop the plateau was. His eyes went wide enough to water, though the tears evaporated just as quickly in the heat and all he earned himself was an afterimage seared onto his sight.

"Is that... a dragon?" he asked, desperately blinking in an attempt to clear his vision as he stumbled to a sudden stop. Percy walked into him, then had to keep them both upright because Knell was too distracted to get a handle on his own limbs.

It *was* a dragon, the most coveted of the Great Wyrms. At least, the remains of one. A massive, petrified corpse took center stage on the platform like a morbid statue. The platform itself was roughly the size of a palace ballroom. The creature had to be at least four times the height of an average man and much longer. A serpentine tail was coiled defensively around itself, tipped with a wicked barb that looked like it could slice a warrior in two. It was frozen in an exhausted slump, curled around itself, clawed forelimbs draped over a portion of its tail, the large head lolled listlessly to the side. Glinting fangs framed the jagged line of its mouth, and there were hollow sockets where its eyes had been.

The dragon's body was studded heavily with swords and spears that had managed to pierce its thick, armored hide, more broken shafts peeking from the tender spaces between the edges of scales. And that was only what Knell could see from this distance, desperately squinting for more details.

It was likely this was the very same wyrm that had created the tunnels they were traveling through. This must have been its lair, something very few humans had ever seen, much less survived to speak about, and even those souls had long departed the mortal realm from sheer age. Dragons had been extinct for centuries now. Only lesser wyrms, the smaller cliff-dwelling cousins of true dragons, still lived, and their numbers dwindled every year due to hunting. For their eggs, for their scales, for any part of them that men could dream up false medicinal remedies to sell, squeezing every bit of coin out of a dying race.

Percy tried to keep Knell moving, but he braced his feet, blinking hard to see as much as he could despite the brightness of the room. "Wait, wait! Percy, it's a *dragon*!"

The hand guiding him finally stopped trying to push him along as Percy listened. Both of them were panting from the heat and their brief struggle, but Percy held him steady so Knell could take in as many details of the sight as he could, feeling more awed by this than he ever had under the thumb of the god he'd served. Though dead, clearly brought down by humans, there was something majestic about this creature. Something undeniably fierce.

The platform around the dragon was pale, a contrast to the rest of the room, and it took some teary-eyed squinting to recognize that it was because the entire space was littered with bones and armor from warriors who had met their end here. Knell couldn't help but root for such a vicious denial of humanity's imagined superiority.

"It's beautiful," Knell whispered in awe. He felt Percy startle, the fist clenched in the back of his robes jerking the tiniest bit.

He expected to be rebuked for stalling their progress in such a dangerous place, but Percy only breathed out a small sigh before speaking. "Yeah. I guess it is."

Knell grinned and glanced back at Percy, whose eyes darted away from Knell as if he hadn't been looking at the dragon at all.

They'd have to finish crossing soon, the heat was making him lightheaded, but he took one last look at the dragon anyway. Now that he'd adjusted a bit to the room and his eyes were more open than shut, he caught the glimmer of something protruding from the very top of the dragon's form.

It was a spear, light reflecting from the shaft and what small part of the blade wasn't buried in the dragon's back. Unlike the other weapons, this one seemed untouched by the ravages of time, gleaming as if it had been polished that morning. Knell patted Percy's side with quick little taps as if Percy might have forgotten he was right there, too excited to keep himself under control.

"Look, Percy, there! A spear, and a magic one at that," Knell said, pointing at it and feeling the oddest sensation that this was meant to be. He could almost imagine an impossible beam of sunlight somehow filtering all the way down to the heart of the mountain just to shine on the weapon, an almost chorus-like hum whispering at the edges of his senses. He hadn't realized he'd begun moving toward the branch of walkway that led closer to the platform until Percy's grip tugged him back and he was shaken by the scruff.

The siren call of a hum faded from his senses, and Knell shuddered as he came back to himself. Percy's expression was dark with real annoyance, though it wasn't aimed at Knell. He was glaring toward the dragon, or more accurately, toward the spear.

"That," he started with a growl, "is a goddamn *trap*. Fucking magic weapons stuck in ancient monsters. That shit's for goddamn heroes. You think all those skeletons were there when the beast died?" He'd all but lifted Knell to his toes to get his attention and glared as he set him back on his heels.

Knell shook his head, glad to have Percy to focus on. The pull of magic couldn't compare. Percy's scarred lip drew up into a sharp snarl but his eyes were dark with concern as much as anger.

"No, those poor fucks all thought they were destined to wield some dragon-slaying weapon and paid the price. I've been on too many bullshit quests to fall for that." He took Knell by the shoulders and turned him to face the path straight on. "Keep moving, and don't look at it."

They doubled their pace under Percy's guidance, Knell only too happy to follow his lead. Sick dread knotted up his insides in place of that honeyed lure, and he kept his eyes focused on the path ahead. "Did you also feel—"

"Yes. Ignore it," Percy cut him off sourly, but Knell could see right through it now. Percy had kissed him, and kept doing so, starting each day with a press of lips to his forehead. Percy could have abandoned him a dozen times over by now, could have left Knell in the hands of a greedy lord and his men. Could have let Knell wander right into death's embrace under the influence of a probably cursed weapon. But he always chose to steer Knell to safety, to draw him back on the path and keep him centered.

Even if Percy chose to part ways for good the moment they finally escaped this mountain, Knell would treasure this journey they'd taken together. It didn't matter that Percy likely had no idea the value these memories would hold for Knell. Acknowledgment wasn't necessary for him to tuck them close to his heart for as long as it continued to beat. Percy had changed everything for him, and he liked to think that he might leave a lasting impression on Percy as well.

The thought kept him focused, overpowering any chorus call that might want to pull him away. What would he do with a magic spear anyway? Knell was the villain heroes were meant to slay. If he could even pick the thing up, it'd be a nice bit of wall decor at best. They crossed the rest of the cavern in steady, even steps and contemplative silence, drowned out by the roar and hiss of lava roiling below.

Stepping back into the tunnels was a relief but they continued on without pausing to relish it. At one point, a small swarm of shell spiders rushed their way, drawn in by the light and heat. Percy looked ready for a rematch, sword in hand, but the creatures merely swept past them, skittering up the wall and around their feet, single-minded in their focus. Knell knew the feeling all too well.

The air and stone around them cooled gradually as they moved further from the heart of the mountain at a steady incline. Knell pushed on until his limited stamina flagged too far to keep going, and they stopped for a rest in a small alcove. Here the air was less like standing in front of a baker's hearth but still warm. He was glad Percy had taken his cloak before Knell could overheat, swinging it over his own shoulders rather than slowing them down to pack it away. Sweat had dried on their skin, along with a thin layer of gritty, smoky dust. If only the lingering unease of being compelled into action under the power of that spear's lure could be washed away as easily as the grime, but even hours later, it made Knell itch more than any amount of dirt or sweat could.

Knell rested his forehead against the wall of the tunnel, blessedly cool against his overheated body. His head ached and his skin still felt stretched too tight from the heat. A few days of freedom from the Great one's thrall wasn't nearly long enough, and the sensation of something taking control of his body haunted him. Memories circled close around his desperately hoarded shelter of calm, ready to drag him into the dark once more. A ringing started up in his ears, growing louder by the moment. The scars across his chest felt tighter than usual and burned with the ghost-sensation of old pain.

He hadn't realized that his breathing had gone choppy and ragged until Percy's hand tucked into his, where it hung limply at his side. Calloused fingers slipped between his own slack ones, squeezing gently to catch his attention.

"Knell, look at me." Percy's voice was calm but serious, and Knell turned his head to do as he asked, keeping his cheek pressed to the cool stone. He felt foolish, bodily tucked against the wall, cowering away from some unseen enemy while Percy stood next to him perfectly at ease, but he couldn't work up the courage to move. Percy didn't try to pull him away, he simply held his hand, anchoring Knell in his body rather than his drifting mind. "We made it through."

"It won't lure me back there, will it?" Knell asked quietly.

Percy stepped closer, nearly pressed along Knell's side. Their combined body heat was uncomfortable after a day of trudging through sweltering tunnels, but Knell found the nearness too comforting to care.

"I don't think so. I stopped feeling the pull once we left the cavern. Has it still got a hold on you? Any ominous whispering in your mind telling you to go back?"

"No, just the usual ones," Knell joked weakly.

Percy leaned his shoulder against the wall, tilting his head to rest his cheek on it as well, his perpetual scowl softened to a concerned frown. Knell wanted to stare at him for hours. It was easier than trying to face the seething pit of everything he was feeling at the moment.

"Can I hold you?" Percy asked. "I can't do anything about the magic shit, but if it helps..."

The only compulsion was his own eagerness as Knell pressed to Percy's front without a moment's hesitation. Wrapped his arms tightly around Percy's waist and buried his face against his shoulder before he'd finished the offer. Percy's arms tucked around him in return, bodily shifting them until he was leaning his weight onto Knell, sandwiching him between his own warm bulk and the wall.

Along with the pressure came a feeling of calm that suffused Knell, sinking into his bones and stealing away his tension. Even the pull on his scarred chest as his shoulders were pressed into the wall under Percy's weight was nothing more than an afterthought. With a small, absent effort, he drew on the tiniest bit of his power to loosen the muscles and skin slightly, allowing him to take a deeper breath and ease his shoulders out of their hunch for a few minutes. It wouldn't last, just like this comforting hold couldn't go on forever, but for now it was perfect. Panic receded, back to lurking in the corners rather than clamping down on his heels.

*Nevermind*, he corrected as Percy planted a soft, lingering kiss against his forehead. *Now it's perfect*. Knell had been oh-so casually dragging a hand through his hair to keep it brushed back from his face, hoping Percy would take the hint without having to actually attempt to write 'kiss here' on his forehead without a reflection, and felt a sliver of smugness that it had worked.

The first was followed by a second and then a third kiss next to his eye. Then another along the curve of his cheek and Knell all but melted at the tenderness. He curled his fingers into Percy's shirt, clutching handfuls of the cloth, and tilted his head to catch Percy's mouth with his own.

Time turned slow and syrupy. Knell felt simultaneously light as air and perfectly anchored as they traded kisses, close-mouthed and more comforting than passionate, until Knell's head was empty of anything other than the two of them.

Some amount of time later that, quite frankly, Knell couldn't care less about calculating, Percy pulled away with a soft nip at the corner of Knell's mouth. "We should drink some water."

Feeling as relaxed and shapeless as a freshly cracked egg, Knell wanted nothing more than to sink back against Percy and ignore the world for a little longer, but now that Percy mentioned water, his throat felt drier than ever. He dragged his tongue against the roof of his mouth and reluctantly agreed that Percy was right.

He parted from Percy with reluctance and took the water skin when it was handed to him. Drank in carefully conserved sips until Percy stopped looking at him like he might shatter. That line of concern was etched between Percy's brows again, not likely to fade anytime soon, but he was a man of action rather than words. He'd only push if Knell made it clear he wanted to talk, and Knell wasn't ready to lose the fragile bubble of peace they'd just built.

Once Percy was satisfied Knell felt steady enough to proceed, they continued on until they found themselves a suitable nook to tuck themselves away in. Percy, more perceptive than he would admit, offered to sleep in shifts to keep watch in case Knell felt the pull of magic while defenseless. He wanted to keep his hand free to reach for his weapon in the case of danger, so they sat together against the wall and Knell cradled Percy's scarred wrist between his hands. Sleep, when it came that night, was deep and dark and left no memories in its wake.

<h1 style="text-align:center">CHAPTER 23</h1>

## Knell

It was late the next day—their travel impeded by the slow death of Percy's moss lamp, which had withered in the heat of the felled dragon's lair and never recovered—when they found the exit.

There was a breeze carrying a sharp, briny scent, then the first traces of light. A low crashing roar became apparent soon after. When they emerged, shuffling sideways through a cleave in the rock wall twice their height, it was onto a shallow shelf of stone above an alarming drop and a view that stole Knell's breath from his chest.

Water stretched out toward the horizon in every direction, crashing against the rocks below them in waves large enough to fill the air with misty spray. Far across the water, there were other mountains, hazy with distance. The sun was setting out of view behind the mountain at their backs, but the late afternoon light reflected off the surface of the water in pools and streaks of dazzling brightness that hurt Knell's eyes. He kept them open anyway, too eager to take it all in.

"The ocean," Percy said from beside him, his voice full of as much awe as Knell felt. "I've never seen it before."

The clearest memory Knell could compare it to was a lake large enough to require a ferry from one side to the other, and even then a person could spot a friend on the far shore if they had a decent vantage. The sheer scale of this was beyond anything he'd imagined. No story of sailing to the end of the earth could have prepared him for the sight.

"To think there was so much water in all the world," he wondered aloud as he reached out to grasp Percy's arm, overwhelmed by all that he'd seen in a few short days. From the fall of a god to a cavern of fire and liquid rock that housed a legendary Great Wyrm's tomb, and now an ocean that stretched on forever, parting briefly for lands unknown to him.

Thankfully, Percy had enough sense to grip a handhold along the entrance to the tunnel, keeping both of them steady as Knell wavered beside him. While Knell was busy gawking at the view, Percy had leaned forward a bit to look down the length of the cliff and pulled Knell from his existential crisis with a little noise of surprise, just barely heard over the crash of water below.

"There's a port," Percy said, craning his neck as far as he safely could and squinting. Knell followed the line of his gaze, thankful there was less reflected sunlight in the shadow of the mountain, and spotted the cluster of sails half hidden by the natural curve of the rock face.

Percy turned to Knell with a boyish grin, shifting the ocean down to second place in Knell's eyes. "We made it, Knell! I think I might even know where we are. If I'm right, then this piss-awful journey is almost over."

Knell smiled back as best he could, dread settling into his gut. Knowing he was on borrowed time with Percy didn't make the thought of their approaching separation any easier. Percy had been clear from the start that they would part ways at the end of their journey. No matter what affection Percy might feel for him now, Knell knew he was little more than a walking death sentence. It was written on his skin, reflected in his eyes, it was his very blood.

If Percy made it far enough, he could blend in, even with his distinctive scars and lost hand. There were plenty of people who'd crossed paths with beasts or lost limbs in battle. But Knell had never heard of grey-stained features like his own in anyone other than his fellow acolytes. His existence put Percy in danger, no matter his own feelings.

Knell wished—not for the first time, nor the most fervently, but with more wistfulness than ever before—that things could be different. Losing Percy would break him in ways even a god of chaos hadn't managed.

For the first time in a damn long while, Percy was feeling good about the future. He was still the most wanted man in the kingdom, which was objectively terrible on all counts, and just about every moment spent in these nightmare caves had been equally shitty, but he'd also met Knell. A man he would have killed without a thought if he'd been in good enough condition to give it a go. And in the reverse, Knell had endless opportunities to rid himself of Percy but chose not to for reasons he genuinely couldn't fathom. Percy had enough self-awareness to recognize that he was a short-tempered, violent bastard with few kind thoughts and fewer kind words.

They'd been traveling together for what had to be more than a fortnight, and Percy felt like a new man—less reborn, more like he'd aged a few decades and lost more than a hand on the way—but his opinion of Knell had been a rare shift for the better.

Knell had changed too, and his journey would be a much harder one than Percy's. He might have to adjust to the loss of his hand along with his freedom within the kingdom, but Knell was haunted by things he couldn't train away or outrun. It was the price paid for regaining his personality and awareness of the world, but Percy suspected Knell would pay it again given the choice, for every moment of wonder he'd seen cross Knell's face.

Percy didn't have the imagination to guess the breadth of horrors Knell had seen, trapped under a different mountain and the control of the Chaos Bringer, surrounded by fanatics and unable to do more than survive. It was the only way his standards could be low enough to consider Percy, asshole extraordinaire, as kind. Knell, who for all his frailties, was one of the strongest people Percy had ever met. Who had been nothing to him but some wretch of a cultist and become someone Percy didn't want to live without. Precious in a way Percy couldn't remember feeling for anyone before, so deeply it was almost frightening. He'd turn around and traverse the tunnels again if that's what it took to keep Knell close.

He'd throw a fucking fit about it, but he'd go.

To Percy's good fortune, Knell's terrible judgment continued in the form of returning his affection to some degree. He certainly didn't mind kissing, that much was obvious, and Percy couldn't help but feel smug that a simple kiss from him was all it took to render Knell useless with stunned surprise. Maybe Knell had simply been so starved of attention and touch that he would gravitate toward anyone halfway decent, but Percy had never been the generous type. So unless Knell said otherwise, Percy was damned well keeping this unpolished gem of a man to himself. For the rest of their lives—however long or short that may be—if he had anything to say about it.

If they made it out of this mess, he hoped to spend the next few decades smothering Knell in actual kindness, as much as Percy was able, until he was spoiled with it. Absolutely ruin him with affection, provide him with good food, watch him fill out to a healthier weight, and show him every small and large wonder in the world just so he could hoard all those awed expressions. Percy was greedy for him, and he'd always been a hedonist at heart.

He'd been plenty motivated to find a way out of the kingdom since he woke up in that damned stinking ditch, but now he was making, discarding, and upgrading plans for two to escape with as little notice as possible. He wouldn't leave Knell in this shitpile of a kingdom, as Knell had so perfectly described it. How far had word of the Chaos Bringer spread in neighboring lands? The cultists were a lesser known evil, but Knell's features weren't something they could hide forever. They just needed enough time to fabricate a less damning explanation.

Below them, he could see that the shape of the cliff face was made of a strangely geometric rock, pillars rising in layers to create a gargantuan and terrifying stepping stone path toward the sandier shore for anyone unafraid of dying or recklessly desperate. If they made one wrong move... Well, it would be a painful but hopefully quick death battered against the rocks.

They'd discovered the cave exit at high tide, and Percy wasn't about to risk slipping to his grisly demise on wet rock or swept away with a wave just because he'd spotted the port city and been overly eager. It would still be there tomorrow. Percy and Knell would either see it then or die in the attempt.

Dinner was stew, made from the remainder of supplies and bulked with the last of their grains. Knell ate quietly, more withdrawn than usual. Percy wondered if lingering worry from the day before was to blame. The draw of the spear had been uncomfortable, but he knew enough about various blessed or cursed items to recognize the feeling of it. The lure must have stirred up far worse associations for Knell.

His assurance that they'd be out of the caves by mid-morning didn't seem to help much. Knell only relaxed when Percy sat close enough to warm him from knee to shoulder as the evening air turned cold, sharing the cloak between them. It was nice knowing that Knell was reassured by his touch. Finding the right words had always been a struggle for him, unless the goal was to stir up trouble. Percy's strength lay in facing threats head on, weapon in hand and unflinching in the face of danger.

Well, it used to be, he thought ruefully, staring at his stump of a wrist before forcibly shaking the thought away. There was nothing to fight here. In this moment, what he needed to do was provide warmth and comfort, and he was perfectly capable of gently crushing Knell's unease out of him as they slept.

# CHAPTER 24

## *Percy*

Percy had one hand and a man who might be carried off by a strong enough breeze. The less said about their trip down the cliff face, the better.

They ended up wading through hip deep water in the last stretch between the crumbling edge of the cliff and the rocky beach. Knell hung from Percy's arm like a limpet, weighed down by his wet clothes and bodily swaying as each wave tried to drag him away. They arrived soaked and twice as ragged as they'd been before the water. Finally having dragged themselves to shore, Knell had all the charm of a wet rat, slumped and miserable and shivering. Only his nose could be seen past his curtain of wet hair, and Percy couldn't help but laugh at the sight.

Knell perked up at the sound, scraping his hair back messily and smiling crookedly back at him, teeth chattering. Percy grinned and waved his hand between them. "We are a sorry sight, aren't we?"

Knell huffed a little sound of amusement, and Percy decided that was his good influence. He shrugged off his pack, grateful it hadn't taken too much of a soaking and more grateful still that he'd had the forethought to consolidate all of their supplies. Knell would likely have drowned trying to balance himself as well as the weight of their belongings without a day's worth of swimming skill that he could remember.

He retrieved Knell's cloak and handed it over, watching as Knell shrugged it on. The deep hood was pulled low over his face and the front held closed over his shivering form, hiding the grey of his fingers within folds of cloth. With Knell's hunch exaggerated and his head hung low, hair dripping in ragged locks, he almost looked worse than the day Percy met him, lurking in his bulky robes. This cloak was a sensible brown, and Knell mostly resembled a sickly vagrant, which is exactly what Percy had been aiming for.

Percy's own cloak was long gone, abandoned with the remains of the unfortunate skyfire lizard, but that was fine. He was relying on his gut instinct that this was the port town he hoped, and that it hadn't been receiving regular news from the rest of the kingdom for years now. They might have informants, but even then, crossing under the mountain had gone faster than any route through the pass above. Chances of his wanted status, much less his likeness on paper, making it this far were slim. Not impossible, with magic at the King's disposal, but Percy didn't exactly have a lot of options or time to second guess.

His job would be to distract from Knell's general... everything, and if there was one thing Percy was confident he could draw from his younger years, it was how to make himself the center of attention.

The port was a cramped place, buildings clustered closer together than Percy was used to outside of much larger cities, but it made sense if he was right. One easy way to check; he led Knell along the street sandwiched between the docks and the first line of haphazard storefronts, down to the largest street in the port. It was paved with cobblestones and wide enough for carts to pass on either side, though the street itself was crowded with merchant stalls and the noise of sellers trying to out-shout one another. Percy knew Knell caught on when he heard the gasp from beside him.

"Is that the pass?" Knell asked, his voice rougher than usual. Whether it was an act or the cold and water making him sound that way, he wasn't sure. Whatever the cause, Percy decided to find a room and a hot bath as quickly as possible. The mere thought of getting clean and having a bed to sleep on was enough to make him near giddy.

"It *was* the pass," he replied, feeling equal parts smug and relieved that his guess had been correct.

A towering wall of rocks filled the place where the pass had been, the surrounding mountainsides crumbled in obvious evidence of where they'd originated. It wasn't easy to guess the scale of it from where they were standing, but the buildings either bravely or foolishly situated near the base at the end of the road looked toy-like in comparison.

"From what I know, a few generations ago this mountain came alive with a fury. Spewing fire and rock and smoke, shaking the earth in its rage," Percy said. "A massive landslide filled the pass and no one's managed to properly breach it. Every time the kingdom sent crews to clear the way, it would cause another slide. Plenty of people think it's cursed. Won't even go near it even under orders, and the job was abandoned."

Percy was close enough to see the gleam of Knell's eyes from behind the fall of his hair as he stared at the wall of stone.

"It doesn't *feel* cursed." He paused, then added carefully, "At least not from this distance." Percy could tell Knell had no intention of exploring closer to see if that changed. "Why was the mountain so angry?"

Percy glared at anyone watching them too closely as he cast back into his memory. The tale was old, one he'd heard as a child when news reached his home of the abandoned efforts to open the pass. His mother had been upset, he recalled, cut off from the route to her ancestral homeland.

"A local god," he started, then shook his head. That wasn't quite right. "No, not a god. A spirit. Some fool on a quest killed a local guardian spirit and the mountains were displeased."

The realization hit them both and they shared a look.

"The Great Wyrm," Knell whispered, eyes wide behind his hair. Percy nodded, seeing the shape of it now. There hadn't been any treasure in that lair, none that would have survived the heat anyhow, but the creature had been hunted all the same.

Percy hoped whatever self-claimed hero who'd done the deed had died in the effort.

"C'mon," he said, tilting his head in the direction they'd originally been headed along the path of the docks. "One thing a port city's guaranteed to have is rooms for rent. I want a hot bath and a warm bed, in that order."

Knell hesitated, and Percy took a guess. "You can join me or have your own room. Your choice, but I won't say no to the company."

"Oh," Knell replied, and that one word carried such pleased surprise that Percy didn't care which option Knell chose if it made him that happy. "I'll... stay with you, if you don't mind."

If Percy happened to strut a little more proudly than he meant to when pretending he was traveling with a sickly friend, well, he dared anyone to make it their business to say something about it.

The locals stared at them, but Percy sensed it had more to do with being spotted as ragged strangers wading in from the water rather than anyone sizing them up for a hefty reward. Anytime someone wandered too close, Knell let out a wheezing, hacking cough that kept even the nosiest locals at a safe distance. The place was populated by sailors and fisherfolk, none of whom wanted to risk bringing an illness on board a ship.

They found themselves at a decently sized inn, speaking with the innkeeper, a person of indeterminate gender with dark skin as weathered as any decent fisherfolk's. The moment they confirmed the inn would haul up a bath and hot water for a price, Percy dug out a few coins, printed with the old king's head but still perfectly good bits of silver. They vanished under the innkeeper's hand and were replaced with an iron key.

"Third door down the hall. When d'ya want the bath?" they asked in a voice that managed to be both bored and suspicious.

"Once I get back," Percy replied. Desperate as he was to demand it now, he had errands to run while the day was still young, and he wasn't about to leave Knell alone with strangers, not even bathwater haulers.

The innkeeper eyed Knell, who looked barely more than a bundle of damp-spotted cloth and tangled hair, but to Percy's relief, they said nothing. They hadn't lingered over Percy's scars either—his most distinctive feature mentioned in the bounty aside from the newly missing hand—but simply glanced over him with the assessing gaze of a sharp business owner.

"I'll pay for a meal to take up now," he added, placing a few copper pieces on the counter. They vanished as smoothly as the previous coins. The innkeeper tilted their head toward the large room beyond the bar, clustered with tables mostly empty thanks to the hour. Livelihoods built around the sea meant boats were out before dawn and wouldn't return until evening.

"Anchor'll get you some stew." The innkeeper must have been referring to the spotty teen boy weaving between tables, carrying food and drink. He glanced up at the mention of his name and nodded. Circling back through the kitchen doors to hand Percy and Knell a couple of bowls filled to the brim. Percy's stomach growled, though one look at the stew and he knew he wouldn't be eating it. Beside him, Knell's stomach growled louder in response, like it had been challenged. Percy hurried them along past the innkeeper's judgmental look, passing his bowl to Knell so his hand was free as he led the way.

The room was as cramped and worn as the rest of the town, but it was clean enough and the door locked properly. Percy stared at the bed, with its thin mattress and visible holes worn into the edges of the blanket. It was barely big enough for Knell, much less adding a man of Percy's size. He wanted to drop onto it facedown and sleep for a week.

*Or*, he let the thought of something more strenuous but just as tempting settle in as he glanced over at Knell. It had been a long time since he'd burned through weeks of tension with bed sport and even longer since he'd felt so drawn to do so, but he couldn't deny that it was a damned nice thought.

Then he carefully set the thought aside as Knell pulled back his hood, looking around with blatant curiosity. He was hungry, that much was obvious, but the shadows beneath his eyes were deeper as well, and his shoulders were slumped in more than pretense. He really did look worn to the bone. Finding some decent food, along with leads on travel anywhere far from here, slotted themselves neatly into Percy's top priorities.

He'd have plenty of time to ask Knell if he'd like to fuck Percy through the mattress later, when he didn't look likely to keel over just from the suggestion.

"Lock the door behind me," he said, dropping the key into Knell's hand.

"You'll come back?" Knell asked as it hit his palm.

At Percy's scowl, he rephrased his question. "When will you be back?"

While Percy thought it over, for all of a second or two, Knell helpfully ran his hand through his drying hair, pushing it away from his forehead in a complete failure of casual pretense. Percy pressed a kiss there anyway. "I should be back in a few hours. By sunset at the latest." His voice turned serious. "Don't open that door for anyone but me. If someone tries to break in, use this on them."

Percy set Knell's own knife in his hand, surprising him. The dagger had been sheathed at his hip as usual, and the kiss had been a perfect distraction for a little sleight of hand. Percy felt smug as can be when Knell smiled, charmed by the trick. It must have been a long time since someone had managed to steal something off of him.

"I promise," Knell said, closing his hand around the dagger and brushing Percy's fingertips with his own.

Satisfied, Percy left, a growing list spooling out in his mind. First, necessities, and then a way out of this kingdom once and for all.

A few lucky fishing boats were making their way back to shore with the early catches, and the market had begun to liven up with the lunch crowd.

Percy was nearing the opposite edge of the market when one of the many scents permeating the merchant's square caught him off guard. A sense memory that threw him back to his childhood so suddenly he stumbled to a halt, looking around for the source of it. He spotted a tidy little booth selling all sorts of wares clearly brought in from other kingdoms. On the counter—near the elbow of an old woman who looked to be in the middle of a serious negotiation over fancily patterned cloth—was a cluster of little red clay jars.

Percy's chest went tight at the sight of them. The squat round shape was unmistakable, and he'd never seen another kind with that exact shade of earthy, black-speckled red. The clay was only found along rivers in his mother's homeland. As he drew closer to the stall the scent grew stronger, and he knew without a doubt these were the real deal.

The stall owner had wrapped up her latest sale, and by the look on her face, she'd gotten the better bargain out of it. She turned to him with a welcoming smile and an assessing gaze. "Something catch your eye, my good sir?"

Percy, who disliked the game of niceties and negotiations that was bartering but knew enough not to let himself get fleeced, let his attention wander over the various wares with his habitual frown before gesturing toward the jars with a lift of his chin. "What's in those? I can smell it clear across the square."

There. A test, and from the way the woman narrowed her eyes at him briefly, even as her smile widened, she knew it. Sly old crone. She waved a hand over the jars like a prize. "These are a miracle like you've never seen. Plenty of liars out here hawking perfumed tallow, but this is the real deal. I couldn't lie about it even if I wanted to."

She winked and stuck out her tongue, showing off the black sigil of truth inked on the surface, crisp as if it had been tattooed yesterday. It was an old custom and rarely practiced anymore unless as punishment. A curse for liars and an outdated method of seeking truth from suspected criminals. A lifetime without even the kindest of lies able to pass their tongues, those who were innocent had no recourse. There was no way to reverse it that Percy knew of.

But it could also be faked. If it was a ruse, it was both a damned bold and clever one. Percy had to admire the audacity either way. "Tell me more," he said, not needing to play up his curiosity. He knew exactly what it was and he would be leaving with one in hand. The question was how much coin he'd part with to do so.

The merchant's eyes gleamed and Percy mentally sighed. He was going to return with a lighter purse than he'd hoped. But when he remembered the effectiveness of the salve his mother had rationed carefully through his childhood, he knew it would be worth it.

He left the exchange feeling ragged but had managed to save some coin through sheer stubbornness. His prize sat reassuringly heavy in his bag, which he carried across his front rather than over his shoulder, sneering at anyone who wandered too close. He hadn't gone far when he spotted the ship.

It stood out among its fellows, the shape of the prow so different from the others. Shallower on the water and with sails twice as wide, dyed in vivid shades of blue. Percy could have sold the cloth of a single sail and lived like royalty for months, yet the crew looked like any other on the docks, if a bit better washed and groomed in comparison. But it was their features that drew him in. They reminded him of his mother, of the glimpses he saw in Ruth or his own reflection.

It explained the salve, and it opened up an opportunity Percy hadn't seriously let himself consider until that moment. He mentally weighed what he had left in his purse, laid out his argument in his head, and started toward the ship.

# CHAPTER 25

## *Knell*

So this was the end.

Alone in the room, Knell sat on the edge of the bed and tried not to scream. A roil of anger clawed at the cage of his ribs, the likes of which he hadn't felt in years. A desperate, naive fury at the unfairness of the world that he was honestly surprised hadn't been burned out of him years ago. Then again, when was the last time he had wanted to cling so tightly to something other than his freedom? Always plotting an escape until he'd been trapped in the inescapable, and now all he wanted was to be held as tightly as possible by one man.

He wanted to have all the time in the world to know everything about Percy. To point at every plant he saw just to hear the man launch into explanations with that look of concentrated animation. To drown himself in Percy's attention, gorge himself on kisses, and if those occasional heated looks meant Percy wanted more, then Knell wanted to devour him whole. Drive out thoughts of anything but Knell. Wanted to bring him pleasure, in bed and out, and bask in knowing he'd been the reason, like a feast of his own making.

But that wasn't all. He wanted to hoard Percy's smiles, his scowls, his loud bark of surprised laughter, every beautifully arrogant smirk and endearingly smug grin. He wanted them to be his. He'd gone so long without this feeling, or anything close to it, that he wanted to dig his nails in and drag it close, tuck it inside his bones where the hollow pit sat, and keep taking as long as Percy allowed.

Greedy.

He felt so *greedy* for Percy. Covetous and possessive, making him hold back from reaching out because if he did, he'd never let go. Even if Percy would be amenable to such a thing, he doubted he'd want it from Knell of all people.

He knew his form was unsightly, but the lingering look Percy had given him before leaving made him wonder. So he allowed himself to consider a few of the possibilities he'd locked away at the back of his mind since that first visit to the underground spring. Knell had hardly been in any state for more than getting clean—and even that had to be done for him—but his eyes worked just fine. Percy in any state of dress, or lack thereof, was a lovely sight.

Shaking that last thought away—something to revisit later—Knell paced restlessly around the room, antsy enough to leave. The impulse was just barely outweighed by common sense and Percy's request that he stay here, as safe as he could be and away from prying eyes. Getting caught would endanger more than himself. Instead, he gave in to the rumbling ache of his stomach and sat in front of the two bowls of stew Percy had bought and left with him. For a moment, he felt the urge to find Percy and make him eat as well until he noticed the stew was laden with chunks of meat. The scent wafted up, tempting enough to make his mouth water.

Both bowls had been meant for him from the start. He wanted to cherish the man who gave and gave and tried to pretend he was just some thoughtless lout. Was this love? This ceaseless, near-painful joy crushed in the grips of yearning? It didn't warm so much as it burned like fire, one Knell would gladly stoke into an inferno and step into the flames.

The food was delicious, chunks of pale fish and vegetables in some sort of rich dark broth with puddles of oil shimmering across the surface. It was spicy enough to make his eyes water and burned all the way down. Knell savored every bite, delighted by the lingering tingle left from licking his lips. He'd eaten creatures with similar effects thanks to their venom, but this tasted much better and without the risk of paralysis.

When the stew was gone—even eating as slowly as he could, it didn't last long—Knell had nothing to do but worry and wait. He picked at his nails until the cuticles began to bleed, then forced himself to stop. Wandered to the window and eased the shutter open a crack to peek out at the street below. It was early afternoon and the sun was bright, thin bars of warmth falling through the slats of the shutter. Knell dragged over the chair to sit and leaned his crossed arms on the ledge to feel those little touches of warmth.

He squinted out across the expanse of ocean, to those far off mountains in one direction, and an endless stretch of water in the other. Sparkling waves and smooth sky flung out toward the horizon until they met in the middle. Were they the same bright blue he remembered, or was the ocean a different color than lakes? He'd have to ask Percy.

It was easier on his eyes to watch the people below, where there was less for the light to reflect from. Figures moved about from buildings to stalls, from ships to dockyards, people on errands and one or two skulking about with an air of trouble. Most were sailors, which made sense so close to the docks. It smelled like brine and fish, tar and hemp rope and sweat. Not exactly pleasant, but so alive that Knell relished it. He tapped a little rhythm to himself, fingertips against the dry wood of the windowsill, and watched a hundred little plays of mundane life laid out before him, more compelling than any tale of fame and glory.

He hadn't even noticed it had grown dark aside from spotting a figure trundling down the street with a rickety cart, lighting lamps along the way. The knock at the door startled him out of his trance, and he jumped with a quiet exhale, nearly falling from his chair.

"It's me," Percy's voice came from the other side of the door and Knell rushed over to unlock it. Percy stepped inside, shutting the door behind himself with a kick of his heel, arms full of whatever he'd bought. He glanced at the two empty bowls on the table as he dropped his bundled purchases onto the bed and gave Knell a satisfied nod. "Good, you ate. I brought back some dinner if you're still hungry. We can eat once the bath is filled."

Knowing that meant strangers arriving with the tub and water, Knell took up his cloak and pulled it on. He was reaching for the hood when Percy's hand cupped his jaw. Knell froze, arms awkwardly raised in the air, staring at Percy who had gotten very close. They stood in that frozen tableau for a moment until Percy raised his eyebrows the slightest bit in question, not bothering to hide his amusement, and Knell realized he was waiting for *permission.*

He threw himself against Percy, forgetting his hood. Who gave a shit about anything other than kissing? He sure didn't. He managed not to smash their mouths together too roughly, eager for a taste of Percy's laughter. Feeling brave with the end of their time looming, he swiped his tongue against Percy's smiling mouth, thrilled by the sharp breath it earned him and even more so when Percy's hand slid into his hair to cup the back of his skull for a deeper kiss.

When the polite knock and muffled "Bathwater for the room?" interrupted them, Knell was pressed full-bodied onto Percy, who had allowed himself to be pinned against the wall. He had one hand at the side of Percy's neck, pulse racing under his palm. His other hand had snuck its way up inside Percy's shirt to press against his side, feeling his ribs expand with every breath as they broke apart.

Percy licked his lips and grinned like a wolf at whatever he saw on Knell's face, then gently untangled his hand from Knell's hair and tugged his hood up and over, hiding his face from view before answering the door. Knell, dazed and hot all over, stared at the wall until he could think in full sentences again. Then he staggered over to sit on the edge of the bed, well out of reach from the door, and watched the proceedings through the fall of his hair.

The boy from downstairs dragged in a battered tin tub, a luxury even with rust creeping along the outer seams. It looked big enough for either of them to comfortably sit in, which said more for Percy than Knell. They might be of similar heights, but Percy certainly had more bulk to him. Hot water was hauled in by the double bucketfuls until the tub was half full and steaming, and when the last one had been poured, Percy tossed the boy a coin.

He gave a grateful nod, didn't look anywhere near Knell, and was out the door almost as fast as the coin vanished into his pocket. Percy locked it behind him and turned to Knell.

"You want to go first?" he asked.

Knell pushed his hood back and shook his head. "I can wait." He'd warmed up and dried off while waiting in the room. As inviting as the water was, he knew Percy had been craving a proper hot bath for longer than he'd known him. He wouldn't deny him the pleasure.

Percy shrugged and began to undress, smirking when Knell didn't even pretend not to watch. He sank into the tub with a groan of pleasure that made Knell's face go hot, then relaxed all at once, loose-limbed with sheer pleasure. He basked in the hot water for a long moment before he began to clean himself.

Knell didn't bother trying to occupy himself with anything other than watching Percy, tucking his knees up and resting his cheek on his crossed arms. It was a familiar position, curling up tight to conserve heat and hide away in small spaces, but now he felt at ease, full of stew, breathing in the herbal scent of soap, and listening to the soft splash of water. Happy to let his mind drift in the small noises of the room, his eyes following Percy's hand as he scrubbed himself down with a sudsy cloth.

Percy was brisk and efficient in this as he was in most things. Knell almost asked him to slow down and enjoy the moment more, but that seemed a strange thing to tell a man who presumably knew perfectly well how to bathe himself. And given Knell's history, he had more practice at it than Knell did in recent years by a long stretch.

Still, when Percy grunted in annoyance, trying to reach his back, Knell slipped off the bed and settled on his knees behind him, tapping the back of Percy's hand with his fingertips before taking the rag.

"Let me help?" he asked.

Percy looked at him over his shoulder, probably weighing his stubborn need to constantly prove himself against Knell's offer, but eventually nodded. His shoulders eased as Knell scrubbed his back and then his right arm, dark eyes watching him and his face relaxed in a rare look of contentment. Knell maybe got a bit ahead of himself washing Percy's chest, but before he could decide if he was brave enough to try any lower, Percy caught his hand and kissed the inside of his wrist, snuffing out any coherent thoughts in an instant.

"I picked up a few things you might like at the market. I also have good news," Percy said, still holding Knell's wrist in a gentle grip. Knell was tempted to climb in with him, wet clothes be damned. "I found a ship willing to trade work for passage."

Knell's body went cold, every bit of playful ardor sapped out of him in a rush so sudden he would have stumbled had he been on his feet. "A ship?"

Percy nodded, looking pleased with himself. "And better yet, a ship from the north, my mother's homeland. They have no ties beyond some minor trade in this kingdom, so there would be no reason for word from the King to reach that far. Or for them to care if it did." Percy leaned back in the tub, his eyes closed and his thumb tucked into the crease of Knell's palm as he cradled his limp hand.

"Is it far?" Knell asked softly.

Percy opened his eyes halfway, looking more relaxed than Knell had ever seen him. He squeezed Knell's hand a little as the side of his mouth crooked up into a smile. "A few weeks sailing. Far enough to never see this shit stain of a kingdom ever again."

"Oh," Knell said, and he knew as soon as Percy's brows drew down in concern that his voice had come out as small as he'd feared. But he couldn't think of anything to add. No reassurances would form over the ringing in his ears.

Percy sat up, eyes intent on Knell's face. He let go of his hand to brush his fingertips over the sharp curve of Knell's cheek. "I know it's sudden, but this is good news. A fresh start to a new life."

Knell had no interest in any sort of start, fresh or rotten, without Percy. But Percy had been clear from the beginning, it wasn't his fault Knell had developed outsized notions and grown attached. If nothing else, he would make himself be glad for Percy's sake. For the knowledge that Percy would be safe.

He covered Percy's hand with his own, pressing it flush to his cheek, and tried to smile. It felt more like a grimace, ill-fitting on his face. "You're right. It *is* good news. How..." He swallowed down the bitterness of asking and tried again. "How long before the ship departs?"

"Tomorrow morning."

It was a good thing Percy had looked away to fish out the washing rag from the water because there was no way Knell could have hidden the panic on his face in that moment. He managed to school his expression somewhat by the time Percy looked up again.

Caught up in his plans, Percy was distracted enough not to make note of Knell withdrawing. He continued scrubbing himself down, only dropping the cloth to point in the direction of the pile he'd left on the bed. "Look over there. I picked up some things for you."

Following Percy's instructions, Knell found a set of clothing, a pair of boots—used but in good condition with thick soles—and a squat red clay jar with a sealed lid that had a strong medicinal scent to it. "This is all for me?"

"I certainly can't fit those clothes," Percy said, standing up from the bath to dry off. Knell watched water slide down his back before he made himself turn away, desire wrestling with misery until he felt nearly sick with it.

The clothing was cut in a similar style to what he'd seen the local sailors wearing. Thick, sturdily woven handiwork that would keep him warm and hold up over time. They had high collars and little peg shaped buttons and loops rather than ties. The pants were cropped above the ankles, and the boots would tie up to mid-calf. Each piece was plainly practical but comfortable looking, and though he couldn't tell the colors, none of them were black.

Percy's hand reached past him for the other set of clothes, in a similar style but a larger size, and he heard Percy dressing somewhere behind him. "The bath is all yours."

Knell turned toward him, not surprised to see that the clothing suited Percy well. His shirt was sleeveless, and Knell mentally thanked whatever tailor had made the choice. He clutched his own new outfit to his chest, overwhelmed with emotions too knotted up to pick apart. That familiar line of concern formed between Percy's brows as he took in Knell's posture.

"I can leave if you want," Percy said with a gesture to the door.

It was kind of him to offer and the perfect excuse for Knell's discomfort, but he didn't want Percy to go. "It's fine, you can stay."

Percy scanned his face carefully now, but Knell remained as placid as he could until Percy nodded.

"Alright, then." A kiss was pressed to his temple, and Knell could weep. "Wash up and I'll show you the best purchase I made once you're done."

Equal parts miserable, curious, and reluctantly charmed, Knell began to undress. He felt Percy's eyes on him and did his best not to hide from that gaze. The previous times they'd bathed together, he'd been in the comforting shroud of darkness or under the muffling influence of the Great One. Here in the late afternoon light he was uncomfortably visible and all too aware of it. Percy would look away if he asked, he had no doubt about that, but he wanted this. Wanted Percy to look at this body of his and see something other than a threat, a warning, a reminder of every horrible moment Knell had lived through since his initiation. To find something desirable and worthy of affection in the skin and scars he could barely look at himself.

It was exhilarating and terrifying, and he nearly slipped when he stepped into the tub too quickly, sitting faster than he'd intended and splashing water to the floor. He heard a chuckle, but when he looked over, Percy was studiously organizing his supplies and eating what looked like layers of roasted vegetables stacked on a skewer. Face warm, but unable to stop a little smile from briefly curling the corner of his mouth, Knell set to scrubbing himself down.

The levity didn't last long. Tension hung in the room as thickly as the humid heat of the bath, even after Knell had finished washing and Percy pushed open the shutters for fresh air. He knew it was his own sour attitude in response to Percy's enthusiasm, but he had no idea how to fix it.

When he'd dried off and managed to get his pants sorted—those little buttons were trickier than they looked—Percy stopped him from pulling on the shirt.

"Hold on a moment. This will be easier to do before you finish dressing," he said, gesturing toward the little clay jar Knell had noticed before. Knell eyed it, putting together all the clues he'd been given, and flushed hotly. Percy followed his line of sight and grinned but shook his head.

"It's not pleasure oil."

Knell wasn't sure if he was more relieved or disappointed by that. In the end, curiosity won out. He stepped closer and resisted the urge to cross his arms over himself, taking a single steadying breath as he let Percy look over his scarred, crooked, emaciated form.

Percy's expression didn't change. He just tugged a damp curl of Knell's hair teasingly and let him be, turning to pick up his dagger from the table. He ran the edge of the blade along the seal of the pot to open it, releasing a stronger wave of that stringent herbal scent. Inside was a pale, waxy cream with a green tint to it. He held it out to Knell and gestured at the jar with his wrist.

"Take some on your fingers and massage it onto your chest. It's good for easing the tightness of scars."

Oh, this man. This ridiculous, generous, kind-hearted bastard. Knell wanted to cry. It must have shown on his face because Percy looked alarmed.

"Oh fuck, was that wrong? I thought it might help. Sometimes you roll your shoulders or rub at your chest like it hurts and I just..." He was standing there, looking so painfully unsure that it knocked Knell back on course.

He dipped his fingers into the pot, scooped up a small mound of the thick salve, and began smoothing it across the worst of his scars. It warmed quickly against his skin, spreading easily and tingling in the places he still had sensation. Heat bloomed where he rubbed the salve, followed by a cool prickle. When he'd covered the entirety of his chest, he was surprised to find he could take a deeper breath than usual. His shoulders lifted back a bit more than they normally could without straining. While he still had to hunch, he could feel the difference, minuscule as it seemed.

Percy was still hovering nearby, jar in hand, watching Knell like a concerned hawk. Knell tried to think of something to say and ended up throwing himself at Percy instead. He clung with arms and legs as tightly as he could in a full-bodied hug while Percy staggered and cursed as he tried not to drop the jar.

"Thank you," Knell said, repeating it several times over. Even if the salve had been useless, he would have loved it. Percy was leaving, but he had taken time and money to try and make Knell more comfortable before he went.

The jar clattered as it was set roughly on the table and Percy's arms finally wrapped around him in return. "I take it the salve worked?"

Knell gave him one last squeeze, then eased back to his feet. "Where did you even find this?" he asked, picking up the jar to inspect it. The smell was intense but not unpleasant, sharp and almost spicy, though Knell couldn't identify any of the ingredients.

"My mother used the same kind when I was a child. She had old scars that ached and used this when I got scraped up. Haven't seen any in years, but I'd know that scent anywhere."

What could he do other than tell Percy how much he meant? It didn't matter if Percy never looked back after they parted ways, he deserved to know that he was never second best. Not to Knell.

"You," he started, throat already closing up when Percy met his gaze but he refused to falter there, "are everything."

Percy opened his mouth, ready to dismiss Knell's words like he always did, and that was unacceptable.

"No, I want you to listen to me." Knell's voice was firm this time. He planted himself and refused to back down, something he learned from Percy. "You are *everything*. You are a walking contradiction, so determined to insist you're all gruff and spite, but every action you take is one of generosity." Knell gestured at his own body, all the things he despised about himself on display. "You hated me when we met, and still you treated me the way no one else would have."

"I treated you like shit," Percy argued, scowling.

"You treated me like I was human!" Knell's voice rose sharply and he took a breath. "Even when you were scared, when you refused to use my name, you at least *looked* at me. You never laughed at my pain or hurt me just to see how I would react. When I was cold or lonely, you said you didn't care and then reached out anyway."

His eyes had gone blurry again, but Percy was standing there stunned and Knell wasn't going to waste the opportunity to lay this all out before Percy could throw up his prickly defenses again. "You've seen me at my most monstrous. You know exactly what I'm capable of, and yet when I got lost in myself, you held me."

He placed a hand on Percy's chest, palm flat to feel his heartbeat thundering away. "You are a fool and a hothead. You rush forward into danger without thinking, and you kill without regret." Percy flinched back and Knell closed his hand into a fist, grasping a tight handful of his shirt to keep him in place.

"That's nothing compared to the things I am. I don't know what you see when you look at me, how you could find anything in me worth wanting, but I'll take it. Because you are so much more than your faults. You are *kind*. Kind, and beautiful, and with more humanity than anyone I've ever met."

Knell let go of Percy's shirt, crossing his arms over his bare chest and swallowing hard. How could he put it in words, the level of devotion he'd be willing to give? Certainly more than Percy would ever ask for. "If I could crack open my chest to keep your heart near mine, or offer my own to you, I would. Because you keep giving and I've always been a greedy, selfish creature. I want to take it all and beg for more. For that, I'm sorry."

Percy was fucking furious. Also incredibly turned on, but mostly furious.

"This isn't some act of charity. The fact that I didn't slit your throat just to watch you bleed out is a low fucking bar. You're better than I'll ever be, no matter what some fuckoff god of chaos made you do. *You outlasted it*." Percy bit out. Knell was staring like he didn't believe him, so Percy cut to the quick of it, not wanting any misunderstandings.

"I like you," he said bluntly, looking Knell dead in the eyes and watching him go completely still. "You've more than proven yourself capable. You're damned brave and twice as reckless, but who the hell am I to criticize? I trust you, and I can still count the number of people who fit that criteria on my hand."

Percy held up his one hand and waggled his fingers in demonstration, then gestured toward Knell, whose cheeks and ears had gone a dark, splotchy grey. "I also find you very attractive, so stop putting yourself down. You should know by now that I don't bother with flattery. If I tell you I like your looks, then you can damn well know it's true. I just so happen to be an ornery asshole with excellent taste, and I don't like anyone insulting the person I'm fond of."

That flush went right up to Knell's hairline and Percy grinned, smugly pleased and not at all subtle as he eyed Knell from head to foot. He felt the grin turn predatory as he watched that flush spread down Knell's chest. Then he scowled, because that defeated tone in Knell's words at the end of his confession sounded too much like he was giving Percy an excuse to end things.

"Think you can scare me off with all this talk about taking?" he scoffed, not about to let Knell's lightning-bright eyes look at anything but him. "I dare you to try. I'd give you *everything*."

The air practically crackled between them, and Percy let Knell choose where this would go. He couldn't figure out why Knell looked so heartbroken at times when he thought Percy wasn't paying attention. The man had a lot to work through, but if he thought Percy would take a coward's route out of this, then he was about to learn just how committed Percy could be when his mind was set. If Knell wanted to part ways, then that was his choice and he could damn well say so rather than waiting for Percy to run scared. But that was hardly fair to expect from a man who'd had every choice stolen from him for half a decade, wasn't it?

In the end, Knell looked away, still glassy-eyed and with that expression Percy couldn't parse, like he was yearning desperately but still afraid to reach for what he wanted. Considering Knell's past, and Percy's own temperament, he couldn't blame him. There had to be a hundred more eloquent and reassuring ways to say how he felt. Too bad Percy didn't know any of them. He gave up on words, and opened his arms instead, hoping he hadn't screwed things up too badly.

Knell latched onto him like a lamprey, and Percy curled his arms around him in return.

"If this is too much, then tell me, but don't think you can scare me off. All this horseshit about being greedy and selfish, from the man who's done nothing but save my life at every turn."

Knell's arms tightened, face buried in the curve of Percy's neck and shoulder. "I do want this," he said in a watery voice, so softly Percy almost missed it. Then again, louder. "I want this."

Percy leaned his cheek against Knell's curls, counting rabbit-quick heartbeats against his own. "Good."

They held each other long enough that Knell had to hunt down the candles in the dark once they parted.

The last hours before bed were spent giving their clothes a good scrub and spreading them out to dry near the newly-lit fire, then repacking their bags. Knell lingered over that task the longest, holding each and every item—asking Percy if he was sure Knell could have it— before tucking it away neatly. Percy figured if he'd gone as long as

Knell had without anything of his own to his name, he might be a little weird about his belongings too.

The night was mild, but after weeks spent in cave tunnels, Percy had no intention of sleeping at any temperature other than toasty warm. He piled their blankets on top of the inn's before climbing in and let out a blissful sigh. It didn't matter that the bed was thin enough to feel each support slat underneath and poky with straw, it was perfect. To be clean and warm, with a full stomach and tucked into a real bed with a man who'd earned his closely guarded affection? Felt pretty damn good.

Percy's priorities had certainly shifted, there was no denying that. He used to dream of glory, power, riches beyond imagining, and the loyalty of those who followed him. He waited for the usual bitterness to rear its head, but it never did. His old self would hardly recognize him now. *Good riddance*, he thought ruefully. There were still a thousand ways things could go wrong by morning, but as he lay there with Knell half draped over him, bath-warm, all sharp elbows and knobby knees, he felt nothing but content.

This was, of course, the moment Knell decided to open his mouth.

"What could you possibly find attractive about me?" Knell asked, his tone baffled. Percy wondered at how dense the man's skull must be to ask that when they were laying pressed tightly to one another, legs tangled and Percy's arm thrown over Knell to hold him close.

But there was a thread of that yearning in his voice, and Percy wondered how long it had been since Knell felt wanted. He ran his palm up the curve of Knell's spine as he considered his answer.

"Sometimes, when you're out hunting, you might encounter a beast you weren't meant to. A wolf with pups, a bear out from winter's hibernation, things you aren't prepared to face. And just looking at them, you can only pray that they're not interested in you because if they wanted to hunt you down, then you wouldn't stand a chance."

Knell shifted, careful not to roll right off the edge, and planted his elbow on the bed, resting his chin in his palm so he could look down at Percy's face. His brow was crinkled in confusion, but he was listening intently, pinning Percy in place with those eyes of his. Percy lifted his hand to cup Knell's cheek, running his thumb along the curve of one sharp cheekbone and tracing the dark hollow under his eye.

"When you stare at me like that, with so much intent, it feels the same way. Like I've caught the attention of a predator I can't win against."

Knell blinked, looking surprised. "I'm..." He floundered, not sure what to say in response. "Sorry?"

Percy huffed, equal parts amused and annoyed. "It wasn't a complaint."

He smirked when he felt the skin under his palm heat as blood rushed to Knell's face, and it spread into a grin at the strangled "Ah," Knell managed. Someday, these simple admissions wouldn't knock him so off-kilter, but until then, Percy would relish every time it happened.

"Now go the fuck to sleep. If you're half as exhausted as I am, we'll both need as much rest as we can get," Percy grumbled, nudging Knell back into position. "Save any other ridiculous questions until morning."

Knell's gaze lingered on his face, and that strange, hungry, longing expression was back. Before Percy could ask about it, Knell kissed him, deeply enough for Percy to consider changing his mind about resting. Then he pulled away and settled against Percy, hot face tucked against his neck.

"Damn, good night to me, then." Percy managed.

He buried a smile into soft, clean curls as Knell let out a wheezy little snicker, finally relaxing. Tangled up in warm, close comfort it wasn't long before sleep lulled Percy under, and he went, unresisting.

# CHAPTER 26

## *Knell*

Knell did not sleep. His thin veil of humor and calm unraveled as Percy's breathing went even and deep with slumber. Ugly thoughts crept in, not just his own fears and anxieties but ideas of delaying Percy's departure. If he missed the ship, they'd have more time together. The temptation of it lurked at the front of his mind for most of the night and well into dawn. He watched the sun rise, broken into hairpin slivers by the closed shutters, and didn't wake Percy. There were no crows nearby to call the dawn, he noticed.

*I'll give you everything.* Knell wanted it to be true.

He kept his ear pressed to Percy's chest, listening to that slow, steady heartbeat, his own thudding double time with every second he delayed until the knot in his stomach was too painful to ignore. What was he doing? Ruining Percy's plans just for a few more days together? Days that would be tainted by his selfish manipulations. He was a terrible liar. Percy would know exactly what he'd done and hate him for it.

Knell shook Percy awake, feeling even worse when he was greeted with a sleepy look of affection that vanished when Percy saw the light in the room. He sat up with a curse and threw off the covers, nearly rolling Knell off the narrow bed in the process.

"Shit, shit, we're late." Percy was hissing to himself, tugging on his outer layers and swearing under his breath as he fought with the peg buttons on his coat one-handed. "Damn fucking unnecessarily complicated horseshit."

Knell helped gather their dry clothing, folding Percy's neatly and pilfering the inn's cake of soap to tuck into Percy's bag. Percy was shoving Knell's folded clothes into his bag with less care and more speed. He grabbed the straps for both packs in his hand and gestured to Knell's cloak with his wrist.

"Let's get moving. There's just enough time for some food if we're quick," Percy said, looking distracted.

Knell slung his cloak on, dragging his feet. He'd never been so unhappy to share a meal with Percy, but the reality of losing him was crushing in from all sides, too fast for Knell to pretend he was fine.

When he made it down to the nearly empty sitting area, Percy had already purchased plates of breakfast, a bowl of something porridge-like that he was shoveling down and eggs for Knell. He stared at the plate, feeling numb while Percy rattled off some sort of list, worried about the time. His voice sounded distant, and Knell realized he was pulling away from himself, the way he did when he was expecting pain.

Next thing he knew, Percy was standing, gesturing at him to get up and settling Knell's pack into his arms as he said something about the room key. Knell watched him go and wished he could make himself say something. Do something. Ask Percy to stay. But he couldn't. He held his pack in one arm and picked up his plate of eggs, not sure why and feeling lost.

"Knell?" Percy's voice cut through the muffled cotton of his mind and Knell began to settle back into himself, upset that he'd wasted so much precious time.

Percy had returned, sack slung over his shoulder and frowning at Knell. "Why are you still standing there? It took near all my coin and two hours of proving myself competent at deck work to earn our passage. We're not missing this ship. Take the eggs with you if you want. The plates are all fit to be thrown out, they won't miss them."

Knell stared at him, wondering if he'd misheard, for long enough that Percy's frown went from annoyed to worried. "We can grab something else on the way if you don't want the eggs, but we're not wasting any food. I'll eat them."

Unable to think of a single response, Knell numbly held out the plate. Percy plucked up the fork, stabbed both stiffly fried eggs, and shoved it all in his mouth to chew. Then he turned to go, clearly expecting to be followed. He was halfway to the door when Knell found his voice.

"We're leaving together?" Knell finally managed. It came out more brittle than he'd meant, ready to shatter at the slightest pressure, heart in his throat and desperately hoping he'd been wrong this whole time.

Percy stilled, shoulders tense, then turned slowly. He stalked towards Knell, who held his pack to his chest and instinctively stepped back until he hit the wall, knees weak. Not because he was nervous, despite Percy's threatening glower, but because he wasn't sure what else to do with this unexpected, foreign burst of hope lighting up his insides. Hugging the bag close meant he kept his hands occupied and out of trouble because Percy was obviously upset and looked like he needed to let go of some steam without Knell interrupting.

Percy crowded into his space, leaning his hand and forearm against the wall above Knell, caging him in. He loomed, teeth bared in a snarl.

"Did you think I was getting on that ship *alone*?" Percy asked in a low, foreboding voice. Knell shivered with a jolt of something that definitely wasn't fear and shook his head, eyes wide.

"You're stuck with me," Percy continued, his gaze boring into Knell's with an iron certainty that took his breath away. "As far as I'm concerned, there's nowhere in this world you could skulk off to that I won't follow. You wanted my attention, and you have it, from now until you make it *very* clear that you've changed your mind."

Knell's face was hot—the whole room was hot. He was sure his hands would be shaking if they weren't clutching so tightly at his pack, and blood was rushing in his ears. None of that could keep him from grasping at every word from Percy, his heart racing at what it meant.

Percy's nose was nearly touching his own, and his voice was low, biting out words in a growled whisper. "So unless I've got this wrong," his eyes narrowed and it was clear he knew he hadn't, "then you can forget any goddamn foolish ideas about parting ways and get on that fucking ship."

Knell felt like he'd caught a skyfire lizard's lightning breath, all that power crackling along his nerves, only this time he didn't want to let it go. Knell licked his lips, took a deep breath, and began to smile. A shy, bright joy had filled his chest, suffusing his whole body in a white-hot giddiness he wasn't sure what to do with. There was no stopping the grin that left his face aching with the force of it. Percy wanted to *keep him.*

"Alright," he whispered into the sliver of space between them.

Percy scowled down at him for a moment longer, but the crinkles at the edges of his eyes had deepened, and Knell could tell he was pleased. He stared at Knell's smile, then shoved himself back with a huff, settling his own bag more securely on his shoulder. "C'mon then. We've got a ship to catch."

Knell nearly vibrated in place, trying to contain himself. His emotions tapped into his powers until he felt ready to burst at the seams. But not here. He couldn't forget about the risk of being seen, much less climb Percy like a tree and cling with all the tenaciousness of a shell spider. Knowing Percy might just let him didn't help. Then he remembered they were leaving *together.* He had a whole ship's journey worth of opportunities to steal.

And hopefully, enough time to convince Percy to keep him forever.

He forced his power to settle even as it strained against his control and hurried to follow. Stepping into the space at Percy's side, he pulled his hood lower to hide the grin he couldn't contain.

Percy grumbled as they walked, annoyed complaints of, "*I can't believe you fucking thought,*" and "*As if I wasn't goddamn clear as crystal,*" but he'd slipped his arm around Knell's waist like he was worried he'd wander off if he didn't have a good grip, so Knell didn't pay the words any mind. Percy could curse him up and down for a fool the rest of their lives as long as Knell was there to hear it.

The fucking *nerve* of this rat, Percy fumed, indignant as he held Knell close against his side. He was as furious with himself as he was with Knell for such a ridiculous miscommunication. Had he not made himself very fucking clear? Apparently fucking not.

Righteous as it was, his anger was being outweighed by the warm flutter in his chest at the way Knell's face had lit up incandescently when he realized Percy hadn't intended to leave him behind, as he'd somehow deluded himself into thinking.

The walk was short, mostly spent by Percy wrestling his emotions into order. Under his arm, Knell was trembling like he was cold, though when Percy looked at him, all he saw was the curve of a smile half hidden in the shadow of his hood, so he didn't ask. He could find out later once they were both on the ship and finally, *finally* leaving this thrice-damned cursed kingdom.

Indigo and robin's egg sails looked like mended patches of sky as they approached the ship, wary sailors eyeing them, especially Knell, apprehensively. Looking the part of a sickly pauper helped in town, but no one wanted to risk a ship plague. Percy ignored them, it was the captain he needed to convince. He'd negotiated pay for their passage, now he just had to make sure they didn't get left ashore.

The captain was a stout woman with strong arms, a heavyset middle, and laugh lines that belied her no-nonsense expression. Her hair was black and straight, with scattered strands of grey, shaved on one side and plaited back neatly from her round, weathered face. She summoned Percy over with a jerk of her chin and eyed Knell as they approached.

"You never mentioned he was sickly," she said in his mother's tongue. He was rusty at it, but she wasn't a woman of fast speech, so he managed to parse through.

"He's not. Just had a hard couple years. Troll blood in the family line showed up strong in him," he replied solemnly in the common trade language, not looking to offend but also not wanting to risk a misunderstanding. He made sure to use the northern word for troll, hoping he'd pronounced it properly. It was the best lie he could come up with and one he'd thought of while out the day before.

Trolls from the north, the far north, were creatures of snow and rock, and they bled a dark blue that tinted their pale skin. Their eyes were solid white, if he remembered correctly. He'd never seen one of their rare mixed offspring, and he hoped the captain hadn't either. There was nothing other than perhaps a blood curse that Percy could conceivably use to excuse Knell's looks. He wouldn't be able to hide himself in such close quarters for long, and it would be better to set the record now than to let rumors simmer.

The captain eyed him hard, but Percy was as stubborn as they come and held her stare before politely glancing aside. She turned her stare on Knell next. "Let me see, then," she said to him in accented but smooth tradespeak.

Knell glanced at Percy, who nodded, and he slowly reached grey hands out from his cloak to push back his hood, meeting her eyes with his own. Percy shifted his footing into a better stance, ready to fight his way back off this boat if needed. The captain's eyes widened, but there was no immediate recognition, no fear or disgust.

"You're not sick?" she asked Knell bluntly.

Knell shook his head. "No, just in need of a few good meals," he tried to joke, but his tone was too flat to be anything other than stilted. He'd spoken in perfectly smooth tradespeak. Interestingly, he had an accent more common to the western edge of the kingdom.

"Your husband doesn't provide for you?" The captain used a northern term for a masculine head of household. Percy felt himself scowling at the suggestion that he was lacking but held his tongue. He wasn't the one she was asking and it would only look worse if he cut in to answer. He did find himself deeply pleased at being referred to as Knell's husband in his mother's language. It was a good cover, and meant he and Knell were guaranteed a shared space. And it couldn't hurt to get used to the term a little early.

Knell didn't know the word, but the captain's gesture between them implied something intimate. His face flushed, but he looked far from bothered. The captain seemed fascinated by the color he turned, a splotchy array of grey tones.

Thankfully, Knell wasn't thrown off by the implication and he reached out without looking to pat Percy's side, as had become his habit. "Oh! No, he does. He's very good at it, actually!"

At the captain's flatly dubious look, Knell shrank in on himself, touching his hand to his own sunken cheek with a grimace. Percy's patience was thinning, but before he could say anything, Knell squared his shoulders as best he could and met the captain's eye with determination. "He is very good to me. Better than anyone I've met before," he said, voice steely with quiet certainty. Percy's face heated, both pleased and guilty because he hadn't even begun to truly spoil this man.

"He helped me when life left me with nothing, and I might not look it, but I'm happier than I have been in years." Knell faltered a bit there, eyes darting away and hands wringing together as the moment of defiance passed with a more hesitant "Ah, if you'll pardon my tone, Captain."

Percy was so damned proud of him.

He smirked at the captain, knowing it was the face he'd been told a dozen times over was his most punchable expression, but he couldn't help it. The captain rolled her eyes, apparently convinced Percy wasn't stealing away troll kin and starving them under her watch.

"Fine. You get the same rations as everyone else, you'll work for your passage, and I won't have any trouble on my ship, or you're off it." She leveled them both with a hard look. "Whether that's on land or over the side depends on your behavior."

Knell nodded quickly, and Percy tilted his head down in acknowledgment as well. "Understood."

"One of the boys will show you your cabin. Don't expect luxury. Now, out of my sight, I have more important things to deal with."

They were quick to obey, giddy with relief as they waited for whoever was meant to guide them to their quarters for the voyage and let the captain return to her duties, which mainly entailed barking orders at everyone. Percy saw Knell reach for his hood as a pair of crew passed close by, looking at him with startled surprise but not fear. Watched as Knell's hands paused and slowly dropped, leaving his face bared to the world.

Percy let him have the moment, pride blooming in his chest as he stared out across the water toward the north. Knell pressed closer to his side, fingers catching at his own and followed his gaze out toward the horizon.

"A fresh start?" Knell asked, voice soft but eyes bright as he looked at Percy, gleaming silver in the sunlight. He ran his other hand through his hair in that not-even-slightly subtle way of his, pushing it away from his forehead with a hopeful look. Percy grinned, then leaned over to plant a kiss against the pale grey skin, wondering how it would look after some time in the sun.

"Fuck this shit-awful kingdom," Percy said with feeling. Another kiss, this time to Knell's cheek, curved from the width of his smile. The corner of his mouth after that, and then Knell met him halfway for a real kiss, brief but perfect. "A fresh start. We'll fucking steal it if we have to."

# *Acknowledgements*

This book started with an offhand joke about my desire to see a romantic fantasy featuring two of the least likable archetypes in the fantasy genre. From there, I spent the next year possessed by that idea as I wrote this book. But it wouldn't have happened under my power alone, and this story wouldn't be nearly as good as it is without the help of some amazing people.

As always, thank you to my mom, who has supported every one of my dreams no matter how far-fetched, and might never read this book but will buy it anyway just to have it on her shelf. Thank you to my siblings and family as well, who believe in me when I struggle to believe in myself.

Thank you to Alex, for your enthusiasm and support on all of my projects but particularly this one. You went above and beyond.

Thank you to Ariana, Percy and Knell's official godmother, the ultimate writing cheerleader, and the reason this book is a thousand times better than it would have been if I hadn't had her to brainstorm with.

Thank you to Rowan and Amy, the incredible artists working on this book's illustrations and cover art. It was an honor and a pleasure to work with you both.

Thank you to Charlie, Michael, and Anker, for all of your helpful feedback and editorial work. If there are any typos remaining, I am entirely to blame.

And I certainly can't forget all of the amazing Kickstarter backers who made the first edition of the exclusive Bonedust Press print run possible. Thank you all so much for believing in this small press's debut title, with special thanks to Ariana Maher and JJ Mack!

**Jasmine Walls** is an award-winning writer, editor, artist, and hot chocolate enthusiast based in California. She loves stories that are unique, inclusive, and fun. She is also the founder and operator of Bonedust Press.

**Rowan MacColl** is a New York comic artist and illustrator who has done book covers, ttrpg illustrations, and graphic novels. She loves dark fantasy, romance, elaborate historical costumes, and her cats. Her fingers are nibs and her blood is ink.

**Amy Phillips** dwells deep in the eternal corn maze of Indiana, offering ttrpg characters and game designs from between the stalks. Occasionally, she makes time for a book cover, like this one.

**Charlie Knight** is a professional editor, book coach, and queer SFF romance author.

**BONEDUSTPRESS.COM**